Thomas E. Lightburn served twenty-two years in the medical branch of the Royal Navy, reaching the rank of Chief Petty Officer. He left the service in 1974 and obtained a Bachelors (Hons) degree at Liverpool University. After teaching for sixteen years, he volunteered for early retirement. He then began writing for *The Wirral Journal* and *The Sea Breezes*, a worldwide nautical magazine. He interviewed the late Ian Fraser, VC, ex-Lieutenant RN, and wrote an account of how he and his crew crippled the Japanese cruiser, *Takao*, in Singapore.

Tom is a widower and lives locally pursuing his favourite hobbies of soccer, naval and military history, the theatre, art and travel.

Published work

The Gates of Stonehouse
(Vanguard Press 2005)
ISBN: 978 184386 203 4

Uncommon Valour
(Vanguard Press 2006)
ISBN: 978 184386 301 4

The Shield and The Shark
(Vanguard Press 2006)
ISBN: 978 184386 350 2

The Dark Edge of The Sea
(Vanguard Press 2007)
ISBN: 978 184386 400 4

The Ship That Would Not Die
(Vanguard Press 2008)
ISBN: 978 184386 436 9

The Summer of '39
(Vanguard Press 2009)
ISBN: 978 184386 561 2

A Noble Chance
(Vanguard Press 2010)
ISBN: 978 184386 647 3

Beyond the Call of Duty
(Vanguard Press 2011)
ISBN: 978 184386 714 2

The Russian Run
(Vanguard Press 2012)
ISBN: 978 184386 840 8

DEADLY INFERNO

To Keith.

Thomas E. Lightburn

DEADLY INFERNO

Best Wishes

[signature]

Vanguard Press

A CIP catalogue record for this title is
available from the British Library.

ISBN 978 1 84386 736 4

*Vanguard Press is an imprint of
Pegasus Elliot MacKenzie Publishers Ltd.*
www.pegasuspublishers.com

First Published in 2013

**Vanguard Press
Sheraton House Castle Park
Cambridge England**

Printed & Bound in Great Britain

Dedication

This book is dedicated to the men, women and children who lost their lives during the German air raid on Bari on 2 December 1943.

Acknowledgements

I wish to express my gratitude to the staff of Greenwich Library and the Imperial War Museum, London for their valuable assistance.

My thanks also to David Ord of Seacombe Library, Wallasey for his computer expertise.

I am also indebted to Dr. S. K. Mukherjee, MBE for correcting the medical details in the manuscript.

My thanks to Liverpool Maritime Library for furnishing me with details of convoys leaving Liverpool between 1940 and 1943.

I am also grateful to Lieutenant Commander George Storey R.N (Retd) for providing me with a valuable history of Haslar Hospital, Gosport.

Last but not least, I wish to thank Mr George Southern for the use of his excellent book, *Poisonous Inferno*, which I have drawn upon in preparing this book.

PART ONE
THE COMMANDER

CHAPTER ONE

Commander Jeremy Pendleton picked up his blue Parker fountain pen and with a feeling of excited anticipation, sat back in his chair and pondered the future. The time was 0900, the date Saturday 15 August 1943. In two days he and his ship would undertake a mission known only to himself, the Prime Minister and their Lords of the Admiralty.

The morning sun penetrated the thickness of the glass porthole above his desk warming the back of his head. Lying next to several coloured folders was a stack of forms awaiting his signature. He paused, pen in hand and listened to the all too familiar thud of footsteps moving about outside his cabin and on the upper deck. To these, was added the constant soporific sound of the ship's generator and the sharp smell of diesel oil. As he signed his name to a request for a supply of 20mm ammunition, he felt a sense of elation run through him; at last he was going back to sea.

Pendleton finished signing the paper, stood up yawned and walked across the linoleum-covered deck to the small stainless steel washbasin. He felt tired and was tired about to turn on the cold-water tap when he caught sight of himself in the shaving mirror. A pair of pale blue eyes under which lay dark pouches stared back at him. His thick, wavy dark brown hair was streaked with grey and the lines either side of his straight, aquiline nose, had, over the past six months become deeper, glaring evidence of his recent brush with death.

'My God,' he muttered, staring at his once heavily tanned face, 'you look more like forty-six than thirty-six.' With a weary sigh he stepped back from the mirror and lighted a cigarette; so much has happened since he was discharged from hospital.

Pendleton breathed out a steady stream of smoke and allowed his thoughts to go back two months ago to a warm morning in early July…

As Pendleton left his bachelor's quarters close to the War Office, he felt a shiver run down his spine, it was as if nature was giving him a warning that something unusual was about to happen.

Pendleton entered his office and removed his cap. He then hung up his gas mask and steel helmet and sat down. He hardly noticed the criss-cross patterns on his desk made by the pale sunlight rays filtering through the heavily taped French windows; the same boring desk he had occupied for the past six months. In each corner rested a wooden IN and OUT tray. Both were empty. Lying on a green, leather bound, unstained blotting pad was a folded copy of *The Times*. In front of this was a silver inkstand complete with a black, service issue fountain pen. Close by a shiny brass ashtray lay empty awaiting the first dog-end of the day. Next to this was a small stack of yellow folders alongside a black telephone, its lead disappearing off the end of the desk. In clear view of any visitor, a varnished wooden nameplate stated his title, "Commander Pendleton. Assistant Planning Officer".

Almost unconsciously he lit a cigarette and allowed a thin trail of smoke to trickle from each nostril as he glanced around the room. In the far corner was a bulky green filing cabinet. Attached to the centre of a high, white, stuccoed ceiling, the bright light from a double strip of neon highlighted the sheen on the four oak panelled walls. On each of these hung the framed yellowing photographs of famous elderly admirals and battleships. The only redeeming features in the room were its two brown leather armchairs, a small folding-down drinks cabinet and a thick blue carpet studded with tiny gold anchors.

Pendleton stood up, stubbed out his half smoked cigarette and turned around. Thrusting his hands into his trouser pockets he peered through the French windows. Below stretched Horse Guards Parade with its grey gravel shining in the morning sunlight. He watched as soldiers, breathing heavily as they elevated and lowered the gun barrels of the several anti-aircraft batteries dotted around the wide square. In the distance the trees of St James's Park lay like a miniature forest surrounded by more ack-ack gun emplacements and high above, grey-skinned barrage balloons shimmered in the warm air. From a tall flagpole on the roof of Buckingham Palace fluttered the golden banner of the Royal Sovereign. Despite having had their famous building bombed during the Blitz, the monarchs remained in the city, defiant against the might of Goering's Luftwaffe.

Pendleton withdrew a hand from his pocket band unconsciously ran a finger along the small scar above his left ear. With hunched shoulders he leaned both hands on his desk and closed his eyes. For a fleeting second he was back on the bridge of HMS *Landbury,* the destroyer he had commanded during a convoy to Murmansk. He vaguely remembered being engulfed by a blinding, yellow flash, feeling a searing pain in his head then, oblivion.

A week later he woke up in a semi-darkened room. His head was heavily bandaged. There was a dull throbbing pain in his head and his mouth felt like sandpaper. At first, when he opened his eyes all he saw was a blurred outline of people. Gradually, faces he didn't recognise came into focus. One of these belonged to a tall, stocky man with pale blue, penetrating Slavic eyes.

'My name is Doctor Vladimir Serensky,' he said in good, clear English, and for a fleeting second Pendleton thought he was in England.

'Where...where am I?' Pendleton asked anxiously.

'You are in a hospital in Murmansk,' replied the doctor, smiling while reaching down and checking Pendleton's pulse. 'You were hit by a shell splinter and suffered a fracture to a bone on the side of your head. You've also sustained a bad concussion. If the splinter had penetrated your brain, well, who knows?' he added, slowly shaking his head.'

For the next week Pendleton remained in bed. Doctor Serensky examined him daily, shining a small torch into both his eyes and checking his blood pressure. After ten days the bandages were removed.

Two days later, Pendleton was taken by ambulance to the cruiser *Belfast.*

Upon returning to Portsmouth Pendleton was admitted to the Royal Naval Hospital, at Haslar, Gosport. Two weeks later, after a series of X-rays and tests he was sent to Osbourne House, a convalescent home on the Isle of Wight once owned by Queen Victoria. While recuperating, the Commanding Officer, a crusty, retired admiral, informed him he had been awarded the DSO.

Pendleton had no dependants. His parents were dead and Martha, his wife and two-year-old son Harold, had been killed in the Blitz. David, his younger brother was lost when his merchant ship was torpedoed en route for Murmansk. Sadly, their photographs that should have been resting on his desk were now at the bottom of the Barents Sea.

Christmas 1942 and New Year, spent in the Officers' Club, Mayfair, had been a boring affair. Afterwards, he was glad to be back in the navy, albeit behind a desk at the Admiralty signing and countersigning orders then passing them to a higher authority.

As each day passed Pendleton became restless. He was a natural born sailor and despite the traumas of the past he longed to feel the deck of a ship under his feet.

With mounting frustration he was forced to sit and read about Operation Husky, the invasion of Sicily, wishing he was there doing the job he was trained for. He knew Stalin was pushing Winston to start a second front. Like many senior officers he also knew the most likely area where this would occur was the Mediterranean. This would require a massive amount of sea power to support the land forces. Who knows, he said to himself, maybe

I'll get back to sea. But much to his chagrin, when the Allies mounted a massive invasion of Sicily, Pendleton remained desk bound.

Pendleton sat down and with a frustrated sigh lit another cigarette. The bold headlines in *The Times,* read, *American forces under General Patton capture Palermo. Monty's Eighth Army occupies Catania. German Forces escape across the Straits of Messina to Italy* did little to improve his demeanour.

At first the meeting with Admiral, Sir Harper-Smyth, KCB DSO and Captain Roger Boyle, DSO RN, appeared to be routine. The date was Wednesday 20 July, the time 0900. The admiral was a burly, fleshy-faced, fifty-year-old whose white hair matched his bushy eyebrows. Now, in his sixtieth year he was considered too old for a sea appointment, a fact that continually rankled with him.

Captain Boyle was a tall, middle-aged, crusty, officer with piercing dark eyes, who had been called out of retirement in 1940. He was head of Tactical Planning, organising convoy routes and allocating escorts. Both officers opened their briefcases and took out documents and placed them on a wide oak desk.

The room was typical of those used throughout the Admiralty – wall to wall leather bound books, high ceilings with a small but elegant crystal chandelier and heavily taped bay windows. Water carafes and writing material lay on the desk complete with leather bound chairs. An attractive, dark-haired Third Officer Wren sat in a corner discreetly taking down the minutes.

These meetings were convened on a weekly basis. Afterwards, the admiral would report their findings to Prime Minister Winston Churchill and the War Cabinet.

Glancing furtively over his thick, horn-rimmed glasses, the admiral's dark brown rheumy eyes looked at Captain Boyle then at Pendleton. What followed next was more of lecture that an exchange of views.

'Secret intelligence reports from Ultra at Bletchley Park tell us that Doenitz has moved many of his U-boats from the Atlantic into the Mediterranean to attack convoys sending men and material to Sicily. Hopefully this will reduce our merchant shipping losses in the Atlantic which, during the first six months since Christmas have been over 500,000 tons.' He spoke in a deep resonant voice that seemed to echo around the room. 'As you know,' he went on, 'due to the Germans changing their code system, Ultra have been unable to intercept and decipher coded messages sent by U-boats to the Wolf Packs, thus enabling the convoys to take evasive action.' With a furtive smile he glanced over his spectacles and added, 'Thank goodness that has now changed. Bletchley have now cracked the German's code. Even so, I'm confident our use of RADAR and Asdic will give Doenitz a run for his money. Do you have any questions?'

Pendleton uncrossed his legs and trying not to sound too bored, replied, 'No, sir, not from me.'

Captain Boyle who was staring out the window, turned and said, 'Err...no, thank you, sir.'

The admiral removed his glasses and wiped them with a handkerchief then lit a cigarette. Exhaling a stream of smoke he went on to state that the Japanese advance in the Pacific had been halted at Guadalcanal. In Europe, the German 6th Army lay at the gates of Stalingrad, but had failed to capture the oil fields in the Caucasus.

'Like Napoleon a hundred years ago,' he said then stubbing his cigarette out in a shiny round, brass ashtray. 'They may become victims of Russian resistance and the ferocious winter.' He ended by saying, 'As you know, apart from Tunisia, the Allies control the whole of North Africa from the Atlantic to the Nile. However, the Luftwaffe occupying Italy and Sardinia are still attacking our convoys to Sicily. The route through the Straits of Gibraltar must be kept clear at all cost.' The admiral stood up and replaced his spectacles, indicating that the meeting was over. 'Thank you, gentlemen,' he said shaking their hands. Then, smiling at the Wren officer he added, 'Type up the minutes and I'll sign them later.'

Captain Boyle and Pendleton placed the documents in their briefcases, stood up and made their way to the door.

'Before you go, Commander Pendleton,' said the admiral, lighting another cigarette, 'could I have a private word?'

Pendleton opened the door allowing the captain and the Wren officer to leave.

'Of course, sir,' replied Pendleton, somewhat bemused at the admiral's request.

Pendleton closed the door and approached the admiral, who was standing behind his desk wafting away a cloud of tobacco smoke. He indicated Pendleton to sit down. He then took another drag of his cigarette and staring keenly at Pendleton, said, 'How do feel about going back to sea again?'

CHAPTER TWO

For a few seconds Pendleton was too surprised to speak.

'I take it you have fully recovered from your injury?' the admiral said, an expression of concern etched in his round, fleshy face.

'Yes, sir,' Pendleton managed to reply, half expecting to be questioned about some operative error. 'I saw the specialists in the naval hospital at Portsmouth two months ago and they gave me a clean bill of health.'

The expression on the admiral's face immediately changed. 'Splendid, splendid,' he replied with a smile. 'Then, I take it you wouldn't mind going back to sea?'

'Of course not, sir,' blustered Pendleton. 'Anything's better than sitting behind a desk.'

The admiral stubbed out his cigarette, sat back in his chair and interlaced his fingers across his chest. 'Tell me,' he said, giving Pendleton a curious stare. 'How much do you know about mustard gas?'

'Not a great deal, sir,' Pendleton replied, somewhat taken aback by the question. 'Except it was used in the last war by the Germans.'

'And in this war, also,' said the admiral, untwining his fingers and sitting forward. 'Mustard gas shells were fired at the 1st South Lancashire Regiment when the BEF was in France in 1940.'

With a puzzled expression, Pendleton said, 'Forgive me, sir, but I fail to see the connection between me going to sea and mustard gas.'

'I'm coming to that,' replied the admiral, pursing his lips and frowning. 'Now, what I'm about to tell you is top secret. Understand?'

'Of course, sir,' answered Pendleton, sitting back in his chair and folding his arms.

'Intelligence informs us the Germans have stocks of mustard gas. If the enemy use it again we might be forced to retaliate, but at the moment we don't have the facilities to manufacture the stuff in bulk. Only the Americans have the capacity to produce the gas on a large scale. The problem is they lack the expertise to do so. The Americans want to produce some for purely retaliatory purposes, should the Germans use it on our troops or civilians and Winston agrees.'

'But surely, sir,' said Pendleton, feeling slightly agitated, 'the use of gas was outlawed by the Geneva Convention after the First World War?'

The admiral gave a quick nonchalant shrug of his shoulders. 'Tell that to Winston. He witnessed the use of gas in the last war and agrees with the Americans. We should be prepared in case it is needed.'

'I agree, sir,' replied Pendleton, still somewhat puzzled, 'but I still can't see the connection between that and myself going to sea.'

'Have you ever heard of Professor Henri Goldberg?' asked the admiral.

'No, sir,' Pendleton replied, shaking his head slightly, 'I can't say I have.'

'This professor is one of the world leading experts on mustard gas,' said the admiral. 'He and his daughter escaped from Nazi occupied France in 1940 and came to England. She is a nurse and joined the navy and at present is stationed at Haslar. Apparently, the professor has discovered a new formula that has increased the toxicity of the gas. Winston wants Professor Goldberg to be taken to Nova Scotia. Here, he will be transferred to the Americans and taken by sea to Edgewood Scientific Centre in Maryland where, with the professor's expertise and knowledge, mustard gas is going to be produced. And that, my dear chap,' the admiral went on, staring keen-eyed at Pendleton, 'is where you come in.'

'How do you mean, sir?' Pendleton asked, raising his eyebrows.

'You are to take command of HMS *Zimba*,' the admiral replied, 'and transport the professor to Nova Scotia.'

'*Zimba!*' exclaimed Pendleton, his eyes lighting up. 'Isn't she one of those fast Tribal class destroyers?'

'That's right, my boy,' the admiral replied, opening a packet of Players and handing one to Pendleton. He took one himself and lit them both with a small, silver lighter. 'As you know, the other Tribals, *Matebele, Sikh, Zulu* have been sunk. Only *Ashanti, Eskimo, Tartar, Nubian* and *Zimba* are left.'

'But why can't this professor simply send the new formula to the Americans and let them get on with it?' Pendleton asked.

The admiral smiled and gave a short laugh, 'Oh that we could,' he replied. 'Unfortunately, or fortunately, depending on the way you look at it, the professor refuses to write the formula down in case it's stolen. It's firmly stuck in his head, hence the reason for him having to be sent personally to the Americans.'

'But why me, sir?' Pendleton added taking a deep drag of his cigarette and exhaling a steady stream of smoke. 'Surely there are more senior officers than me who are capable of the job?'

'Indeed there are,' replied the admiral. 'But experienced commanding officers like you are in short supply. Unfortunately,' the admiral continued, '*Zimba*'s present captain, Commander Peter Okey has developed pneumonia and is now a patient in the Royal Naval Hospital at Haslar, Portsmouth.'

'Peter Okey,' replied Pendleton, leaning forward and flicking ash into a large brass ashtray, 'I know him well. We did a gunnery course together at Whale Island a few years ago.'

'Right,' retorted the admiral. 'How soon can you join *Zimba*?'

'Whenever you like, sir,' Pendleton confidently replied.

'Good,' answered the admiral. With a satisfied smile he sat back in his chair, and went on. 'I'd like you take command of her on Monday the 1st August, that's in ten days, I hope that'll give you enough time to hand over to your relief.'

'Oh, I'll manage that all right, sir,' Pendleton replied enthusiastically, 'but tell me sir, will his daughter be coming also?'

'No,' replied the admiral. 'She'll accompany him to the ship, then leave.' Placing both hands down on his desk, he looked sternly at Pendleton, and continued, 'Now, to business; *Zimba* is in Portsmouth. She's just had a boiler clean. To all intents and purposes the crew think she's going on convoy duty.' Raising his bushy eyebrows, he gave a wry smile and added, 'I know it's a bit of a pier head jump, but I'm sure you'll manage. Now for the details,' the admiral said firmly. 'The professor will come aboard at midnight on Monday 7 August. You will sail straight away for Reykjavik where you will refuel and continue to Nova Scotia. You are to avoid contact with the enemy and on no account are you to engage any U-boats. Your job is to get the professor to Halifax safe and sound. Is that understood?'

The admiral's words made Pendleton inwardly flinch. After all, it wasn't every day he was ordered to avoid action with an enemy. 'But, what if we're attacked, sir?' he asked, frowning slightly while breathing out a stream of tobacco smoke.

'Then, of course you must defend yourself,' replied the admiral, narrowing his eyes, 'but take evasive action whenever possible.'

The admiral stopped talking as a pretty, fair-haired Wren came in carrying a silver tray with a matching coffee set.

'Thank you, Miss Duncan,' said the admiral, smiling as she set the tray down on the desk, 'that'll be all.'

The admiral stubbed out his cigarette then reached across and poured out two cups of coffee and passed one to Pendleton. 'Sugar?' he adding with a smile, 'what little there is of it.'

'Thank you, sir,' said Pendleton, picking up a teaspoon and stirring his drink. With a quizzical expression, he went on, 'May I ask a question, sir?'

'Of course,' said the admiral, sipping his tea.

'It all seems a bit cloak and dagger,' replied Pendleton, reaching across and stubbing his cigarette out in the ashtray. 'Why can't this chap be transported by plane, or even in a submarine?'

'Apparently he suffers from Ménière's disease,' said the admiral, taking another sip of tea. 'Altitude or depth in a sub affects his balance.' Placing a spoonful of sugar in his tea, he went on, 'And there is something else?'

'Yes,' Pendleton replied quizzically. 'And what is that, sir?'

'The professor had a heart attack last year, and from what I can gather, his health isn't too good.'

'*Great Scott*!' exclaimed Pendleton, sitting forward and spilling some tea into his saucer. 'What happens if the old boy dies en transit?'

'It's up to you to make sure he doesn't,' said the admiral, looking up while slowly stirring the contents of his cup.

'I see,' Pendleton warily replied. 'Looks like the surgeon lieutenant onboard will have his work cut out.'

'Quite so,' the admiral answered flatly. He finished his tea, placed the cup and saucer on the tray, then went on, 'Now, after you have transferred the professor to the Canadians, you are to leave Nova Scotia, join up with a convoy en route to England, leave in mid ocean at a pre-arranged venue and proceed to Reykjavik, refuel and return to Portsmouth.'

'Are there any problems onboard *Zimba* that I should know about, sir?' Pendleton asked finishing his drink.

The admiral shook his head and replied, 'The usual things, tiredness through being at sea too long, leave breaking and a spot of drunkenness. John Carter, the First Lieutenant has recently joined the ship. Before the war he was an Olympic yachtsman and I do believe he's engaged to a Wren officer stationed in Plymouth. As

28

you would expect he is a damn good seaman but he's just settling in.'

'What happened to his predecessor?'

'Lieutenant Commander Joslin had a heart attack four months ago,' replied the admiral, shaking his head. 'Just as well the ship was in Malta. Poor chap was admitted to the naval hospital at Bighi.'

'Good Lord, sir,' replied Pendleton giving the admiral a dubious look. 'That sounds rather ominous. Anything else?'

The admiral raised his bushy eyebrows and shook his head. 'Not really, Lieutenant Commander Paddy O'Malley, your engineer is a good man. He's a bachelor and at forty he's the oldest man onboard. Like you, he was in the merchant service before the war. The other officers and many of the crew are HOs.' (Hostilities Only.)

With a tired smile Pendleton replied, 'Sounds somewhat familiar, sir.'

The admiral pushed his bulky five feet plus up from his chair. 'Right,' he said firmly, 'that's settled. *Zimba* is alongside Fountain Lake Jetty. She's fully ammunitioned and ready for sea. I'll circulate the necessary signals and have a railway warrant sent to you. Your orders are all in here,' he went on, handing Pendleton a sealed, buff-coloured envelope. 'I suggest you take *Zimba* to sea for a few days to see how she handles. Needless to say, until you sail for Reykjavik this is all top secret. I suggest you take the Chief Engineer into your confidence and discuss the fuel situation, and put the doctor in the picture. Good luck, my boy,' he added as they shook hands, 'and thank you for being so co-operative.'

Upon leaving the room Pendleton felt his heart pounding like an express train. Going back to sea again was just what he had hoped for. Walking down the corridor to his office he was only too aware that what lay ahead was no ordinary mission.

CHAPTER THREE

On Monday, 1 August, a private car picked Pendleton up outside the War Office building at 0630 and took him to Waterloo Station. With the help of a tired-looking RTO (Railway Transport Officer) petty officer he arranged for transport to meet him upon arrival at Portsmouth. Three hours later, after passing fields and towns glistening with early morning dew, the train arrived at Portsmouth Harbour Station.

The dull greyness of the day matched the dreary Victorian buildings lining The Hard, a stretch of busy road close to the station. From over the nearby dockyard wall the yardarms of HMS *Victory,* Nelson's flagship at Trafalgar, and the stately, red-bricked Semaphore Towers, could clearly be seen. A stiff, chilly breeze blew down the Solent, fluttering the flags on the many warships anchored in the Sound.

Outside the station, a tilly (nickname for a Utililicon, a standard blue van used throughout the navy) was waiting for Pendleton. After returning the salute of the driver, a three-badge able seaman with a greying beard, he climbed inside. In a matter of minutes they drove past the gates guarded by two stout policemen and entered the century's old cobbled-stoned dockyard road. Gantries, dozing like lazy storks towered in the dull August sky. Masts and yardarms belonging to a host of warships dominated the skyline. The seasoned smell of diesel oil and dust hung in the air. Wooden boxes containing a myriad of stores, coils of wire, pipes and anchor cables littered the wharfs waiting to be carried onboard by muscular arms.

All this brought back familiar memories to Pendleton. The tilly stopped at the bottom of a gangway leading up to HMS *Zimba,* her pennant number, G55 painted in black barely visible over the ship's grey and green camouflage.

As every sailor knows, the first sight of the ship he is about to join is usually exciting, and in time of war, very apprehensive. Pendleton's reaction was no exception. As he watched the white ensign hanging lazily from her stern, he felt a strong sense of pride run through him. He allowed his eyes to take in the superbly flared fo'c'sle and a sharp clipper bow, giving the immediate impression of speed. Further along, looking squat and formidable rested her two 4.7 gun mountings their twin gun barrels shining in the early morning sunlight. The open bridge brought back memories of his previous ship. For a fleeting moment Pendleton could almost feel the Atlantic spray whipping against his face. Then came her tall, lattice mainmast, yardarm and halliards moving idly in the morning breeze. Behind the two rakish funnels was the heavy secondary armament consisting of two-pounder pom-poms, 20mm Oerlikons and a Vickers machine gun. Further along lay the quadruple tubes of the 21inch torpedoes. Mounted over the after deck house he could clearly see the twin barrels of X turrets guns. And finally on the quarterdeck rested the rack of two depth charge throwers.

'My God,' Pendleton muttered to himself as walked up the gangway. 'These Tribals look as if they would frighten any enemy.'

The time was just 1015. As Pendleton stepped over the brow (the top of the gangway), he heard *Stand Easy* being piped. To his surprise, the only two figures who greeted him with a salute were the duty quartermaster, a timid looking ordinary seaman, and a tall, fresh-faced midshipman.

'Where is the Officer of the Day?' Pendleton retorted, returning their salutes. Glaring angrily at the young officer, he added. 'He and the duty PO should be here.'

'Petty Officer Jenkins is at Stand Easy, sir,' the midshipman nervously replied, 'and the Officer of the Day is, err…'

At that moment a tall, fair-haired, officer arrived, hastily buttoning his doeskin jacket. After ensuring his cap was on straight he stood to attention and saluted. 'Sorry I wasn't here to meet you, sir,' he said in a thick, plummy voice, 'I'm the Officer of the Day. I was err…called away, Lieutenant Frank Reed, sir, Electrical Officer.'

'Busy in the wardroom having coffee, no doubt,' snapped Pendleton sarcastically, 'and where is the duty PO and the First Lieutenant?'

Lieutenant Reed felt his cheeks burning. He was a twenty-three year old Cambridge graduate engaged to Daphne, a Third Officer WAAF stationed in Plymouth. Before the war he had been a junior stockbroker in the City. Reed had volunteered for the navy in 1942 and *Zimba* was his first ship. Nervously blinking his dark blue eyes, he turned to the quartermaster and said, 'Go and fetch Petty Officer Jenkins…'

'Never mind about that,' Pendleton snapped. 'Show me to my cabin and tell the First Lieutenant to report to me immediately. That is, if he can tear himself away from his coffee.'

Pendleton's day cabin was situated in the for'd section of the ship. Following Lieutenant Reed through the open hatchway, Pendleton was welcomed by the familiar smell of diesel oil, paint, tobacco and mansion polish. He took a deep breath, licked his lips and immediately felt at home.

With Lieutenant Reed leading the way they went down a flight of steel ladders and along a passageway. On the way they attracted the attention of several ratings lined up outside the NAAFI. A few were dressed in half blues while some merely wore overalls tied around their waists. One or two stood to attention; others simply ignored the OOD and their new captain and carried on smoking and talking. Pendleton noticed this and wasn't impressed. Clearly, the discipline onboard left a lot to be desired.

Pendleton's day cabin was bigger than he expected. From a low-slung deck head hung two strips of neon lighting along with cables and wires attached to metal frames. A highly polished oak door opened into a small pantry, and next to this, another door led into a small bathroom. Snug against the port bulkhead was a desk on which rested a stack of folders, a signal book, a heavy looking brass ashtray and an angle-poised lamp. Above this, next to a framed photograph of King George VI and Queen Elizabeth, was a wooden plaque on which was a Red Indian holding a bow and arrow. Underneath, written in scrolled gold Latin was the ship's motto, which translated meant, *Speed, Wins The Day.*

A green metal filing cabinet, screwed to the deck occupied another corner. And lying against the starboard bulkhead was an oaken wardrobe. Next to this, resting on a two sets of wooden drawers was a bunk with a blue coverlet embroidered with an anchor. A well-polished, thick wooden support, eight inches in height was fitted in a groove situated along the outer side of the bunk. This was so placed to prevent its occupant rolling out in rough weather. Over a pillow were an overhead bed light and a voice pipe connected to the bridge. The deck was covered in brown, shiny linoleum and a heavy iron cream-coloured deadlight, suspended from the bulkhead by a chain, attached itself above an open porthole.

'Out pipes, hands turn to,' came the strident voice of the duty QM, heralding the end of Stand Easy.

'No doubt the First Lieutenant will grace me with his presence in due course,' Pendleton grunted sarcastically. He then placed his briefcase on his desk, took off his gas mask and Burberry then, and with a tired sigh, sat down.

'You may carry on, Reed,' said Pendleton, adding ominously, 'I'll speak to you again later.'

Avoiding his captain's accusing gaze, Reed muttered, 'Very good, sir,' turned and left the cabin.

Using a silver knife Pendleton quickly slit the admiral's letter open. Its contents confirmed the arrival of the professor and his daughter, adding, "details of the mission can be disclosed to your officers immediately after sailing for Reykjavik. All shore leave is to be cancelled on the night prior to sailing".

Pendleton read the letter again then leaned back in his chair and lit a cigarette. As he did so, a knock came at the door. A broad-shouldered officer came in and removed his cap, revealing a well-groomed mass of dark hair parted neatly on the left side. He appeared to be in his mid twenties and his handsome, weather-beaten face looked to have a permanent blue shadow. The two and a half wavy navy gold rings on each sleeve showed he was an RNVR, (Royal Naval Volunteer Reserve) Lieutenant Commander. Behind him, looking slightly pale and nervous stood Lieutenant Reed. Like most of the other officers, he was Hostilities Only. (HO)

'Sorry I wasn't on deck to meet you, sir, John Carter, First Lieutenant,' said the officer. He spoke with a slight southern accent and his slate grey eyes showed no sign of an apology. 'The signal said you would arrive later today.'

Pendleton gave Lieutenant Reed a flinty stare and said, 'Please carry on.'

As soon as Reed had gone Pendleton sat back and looked accusingly at his First Lieutenant.

'Signal or no signal, Number One,' snapped Pendleton. 'The Officer of the Day together with the duty PO should be on the brow at all times. This was your responsibility and you neglected it.'

'Excuse me, sir,' Carter replied indignantly. 'You weren't expected until the afternoon and I was merely having a coffee.'

'Indeed,' Pendleton replied, still fulminating. 'You ought to thank your lucky stars I wasn't the port admiral. If it had of been you would be in charge of barge on the Thames. Furthermore,' he added, angrily, 'I wasn't too impressed with the crew. Some of them were out of the rig of the day and showed a lack of respect as I came onboard. This is intolerable. Do I make myself clear?'

Pendleton's words bit into Carter and he felt his cheeks burn. He quickly realised that to argue with his new captain would only make matters worse.

'Yes, sir,' he simply replied. Avoiding his captain's gaze he gave a slight shrug of his shoulders, and said, 'You're quite right, sir, it won't happen again.'

'I certainly hope not,' snapped Pendleton. 'As you know, the First Lieutenant is responsible to me for the discipline onboard a ship. So far, I've seen precious little evidence of this. Now,' he went on, 'I take it everyone is onboard?' It was more of a statement than a question.

'Yes, sir,' said Carter, 'all except two ratings who are sick on shore. Every senior rating and officer are onboard except Surgeon Lieutenant Fulford who is in Haslar visiting Commander Okey.'

'Right,' replied Pendleton, taking another drag of his cigarette before angrily stubbing it out. For a fleeting second he contemplated telling Carter about the professor and the mission, but decided it wasn't appropriate to do so. Instead he said, 'I will see all officers in the wardroom at 1200. We shall put to sea at 0800 on Wednesday.' He paused and gave Carter a searching look. 'I intend to see how efficient you handle the ship. Meanwhile carry on and ask the engineer officer to come to and see me.'

'Very good, sir,' answered Carter, 'and sir, I…'

'Just carry on, Number One,' Pendleton replied impatiently waving a hand.

Feeling like a reprimanded schoolboy Carter left the cabin and closed the door. Outside stood Leading Steward Gale, a tall, pasty-faced lad from Yorkshire. His light brown hair was plastered down with Brylcreem and he wore a short white coat. Using one hand he carried a small tray containing a silver coffee set.

'I thought the new skipper would like a drink,' Gale said. With a look of curiosity in his dark blue eyes, he added, 'What's he like, sir.'

'You'll soon find out,' Carter replied warily. 'Just make sure you put plenty of sugar in his coffee, I think he needs sweetening up.'

"Windy" as Gale was nicknamed, knocked on the door and entered.

'Coffee, sir,' he said, placing the tray on Pendleton's desk.

'Who are you?' Pendleton grunted while opening his briefcase.

'Gale, sir, I'm your leading steward, how many sugars?' as he poured coffee into a small silver cup.'

'I don't take any,' Pendleton replied gruffly, 'and in future, bring me coffee or any other drink in a decent sized mug. There's not enough coffee there to satisfy a mouse.'

'No sir, I mean very good, sir,' spluttered Gale, blinking nervously. Almost as an afterthought he added, 'By the way, sir, your trunk arrived yesterday. I've taken the liberty of unpacking your gear and stowing it away.'

'Thank you, now you can take this away,' said Pendleton quickly finishing his coffee. 'And by the way,' he added frowning at his steward, 'try not to use so much of that hair cream, you smell like a lady's boudoir.'

Feeling somewhat insulted Gale picked up the tray and cup and left the cabin.

Just then, the pipe, *Up Spirits*, echoed from the tannoy. Pendleton glanced at his watch. The time was 1130.

A few minutes later another knock came at the door and in walked a heavily built man wearing a set of pristine white overalls. Pendleton judged him to be roughly the same age as himself. A thin line of sweat trickled down each side of a face that was well lined and deeply tanned. He quickly removed a battered cap that had seen better days. In doing so he revealed a mess of untidy ginger hair that looked as if it had never been combed.

'I believe you sent for me, sir,' he said in a soft, mellifluous Irish accent. 'Lieutenant Commander O'Malley, Chief Engineer.'

As he spoke he displayed a row of uneven white teeth and the corners of his dark green eyes creased into a grin.

The sight of this big man smiling down at him suddenly changed Pendleton's mood.

'Oh, yes,' replied Pendleton standing up and offering his hand, 'Paddy, I believe you are called. Do come in and sit down.'

Pendleton offered the engineer a cigarette, took one himself and lit them both. 'Tell me, Paddy,' said Pendleton, sitting back in his chair. 'Just how fast can this ship go?'

Pendleton's question caught O'Malley by surprise as he expected the captain to be aware of such details.

'Roughly 36 knots, sir,' O'Malley answered cagily, 'but her two 22,000 Pearson geared turbine engines could, if pushed, do 38.'

'Good,' Pendleton replied thoughtfully. 'Where we're going we might we'll need all the speed you can give us.'

'How do you mean, sir?' O'Malley asked, taking a deep puff of his cigarette. 'More racing around the Atlantic after stragglers?'

'Not exactly,' Pendleton replied, evasively, 'something slightly different.' He then told O'Malley the details of transporting Professor Goldberg to Nova Scotia, adding, 'It seems this boffin is a leading expert on mustard gas. I want to ensure we are ready to sail anytime after midnight on the 7th. We will be taking on extra fuel when we reach Reykjavik. Of course, this is top secret, the crew will be informed after we have sailed.' Pendleton paused and for a few seconds studied O'Malley's deeply lined features. O'Malley was an older man who had probably been at sea longer than himself. Pendleton therefore felt he could confide in him. 'Tell me, Chief,' he said extinguishing his cigarette, 'what do you make of the First Lieutenant?'

O'Malley sat back in his chair and pursed his lips. 'To be sure, sir,' he replied, 'this is only Peter's second ship. His first was a minesweeper. He's a keen lad and handles the ship well. However, he's inclined to be a slack discipline wise.'

'Hmm, yes,' muttered Pendleton, 'I've already found that out.' Pendleton placed both hands on his desk and stood up. 'Now, I take it your department is ready for sea?'

'That it is, sir,' O'Malley replied with a toothy grin. 'Ready to take you anywhere.'

'I'm glad to hear it,' replied Pendleton. 'We'll be sailing on Wednesday. I want to see how she handles. And by the way,' he added with a grin, 'when we're alone, drop the "sir", my name's Jeremy.'

Paddy's face broke into a wide grin. 'I think you'll find she'll handle like a woman,' he said, 'unpredictable at times, but given a wee bit of coaxing, she responds well. Now, will there be anything else, err…Jeremy?'

'Yes, you can show me where the wardroom is,' replied Pendleton reaching for his cap.

CHAPTER FOUR

The wardroom was situated in the after section of the ship, below decks next to the turbo generator room. Leading off a small passageway was the First Lieutenant's cabin and officers' quarters. Nearby was the Ship's Office and further along a hatchway led into the depth charge compartment.

The atmosphere in the wardroom was a mixture of anxiety and curiosity. Except for the occasional outburst of nervous laughter, the conversation was muted.

'You've met the new captain, Number One, what is he like? I believe he's got the DSO.' The speaker was Lieutenant David Foster. He was a slightly built twenty-three-year-old with straight black hair and pale blue eyes. His girlfriend, Mary worked for an estate agent and lived with her parents in Emsworth, a leafy village outside Portsmouth. Before the war Foster had been an assistant bank manager. Now, he was the ship's navigating officer. His small caboose with all his charts was situated in the after section of the bridge above the captain's sea cabin.

'You're quite right, David,' replied Carter, glancing furtively at Foster over his cup of coffee. 'And he lost his last ship on an Arctic convoy. As to what he's like,' he added, lowering his cup and looking warily around at the others, 'you'd better ask Frank, here,' he said looking at Lieutenant Reed.

'He seems like man who likes to do things by the book,' said Reed. 'He gave the First Lieutenant a rocket for not meeting him when he came onboard.'

'You make him sound like Captain Bligh, sir,' remarked Sub Lieutenant John Hailey. Hailey, who had gained a First in Oxford in Medieval and Modern History, was the Supply Officer. He was in his mid twenties, a bachelor, small, and fresh-faced with black, well-groomed hair, and dark, intelligent eyes.

'You know what they say,' interjected Lieutenant Sam Small, sipping a cup of coffee. 'A new broom always sweeps clean. If you ask me, a bit of discipline wouldn't hurt anyone.' Sam was the ship's gunnery officer. He was twenty-four, a bachelor with broad shoulders, a firm, angular face and the lantern jaw of a boxer. Before the war he played wing three quarter for Harlequins. He had dark, brooding blue eyes and stood a little over six feet with thick wavy fair hair. Sam was a strict disciplinarian who expected a high standard of gunnery from his men and invariably attained it.

'It's all very well for you Whale Island wallers,' laughed Sub Lieutenant Colin Coburn, a tall, dark-haired twenty-four-year-old bachelor with matinee idol looks. Colin was the ship's Radar and Asdic officer and as such was invariably cooped up in a small compartment under the bridge. 'All you do is bellow at your men and they jump like rabbits. Think of us poor fellows going half blind looking at screens and hearing nothing but pinging all day and night.'

'You poor bugger,' interrupted Lieutenant Jim MacIntyre, shooting Colin a sympathetic glance. 'You ought to come out on the quarterdeck when we're firing those bloody depth charges, my 'andsome.' "Mac", as he was affectionately called, was a blunt speaking West Countryman. After joining the navy as an able seaman, he worked his way through the ranks and was commissioned in 1941. He was thirty-six, married to Mavis, had two teenage daughters and lived in Helston. 'Then you'd have something to moan about,' he added finishing his coffee.

In the far corner of the room, well away from the others sat two nervous looking young men. A year ago both had been at Grammar School. After a three months course at King Alfred College, they were now midshipmen, colloquially called "snotties", junior officers with little or no time served at sea.

'They certainly do go on, don't they Harry?' said Percy Stockforth-Johnson, the broader of the two, whose dark rugged features and beady brown eyes contrasted sharply with the fresh complexion, blond hair and blue eyes of his colleague, Harold Porter.

'I'll say,' replied Harry, glancing furtively at his more senior colleagues. 'From what I can gather, the new captain is a bit of a tartar.'

At that moment the door opened and all eyes turned, expecting to see their new captain. Instead, in came Surgeon Lieutenant Henry Fulford, a slightly built man who, as he removed his cap, displayed a small bald crown surrounded by a cluster of light brown hair, neatly parted on the left side. Fulford was twenty-nine, a bachelor with a pleasant personality and bedside manner. He qualified as a doctor in 1939 then enlisted on an HO basis in 1942. *Zimba* was his first seagoing appointment.

'My goodness', the doctor said, looking enquiringly around the room. 'Why all the worried looks?' As he spoke his pale blue eyes creased into a smile. 'And before anyone asks, Commander Okey is still unwell, but sends his regards to one and all. Now, will someone tell me what's happening?'

Just then Paddy O'Malley came in, followed by Pendleton. As they entered the room, "secure, cooks to the galley. Hands to dinner", was piped over the tannoy.

'Good afternoon, gentlemen,' said Pendleton, quickly looking around. 'Please carry on smoking and I'd be grateful if someone could muster me a cup of something.'

A few minutes later the small, sallow-faced figure of Knocker White, the wardroom PO Steward appeared and handed Pendleton a mug of steaming hot coffee. The PO then disappeared into the wardroom pantry and on the order of the First Lieutenant, pulled down the shutter.

Looking at the faces of his fellow officers, Pendleton realised that they would soon become familiar to him as his own. Glancing at his surroundings he felt a slight twinge of nostalgia. Covered in pale yellow chintz, the leather chairs and benches around the cream coloured bulkhead brought back memories of his last ship.

Boxed in cables and wires and four strips of neon fitted snugly into a low-slung deck head painted white. In the centre, resting on a dark blue, thickly piled carpet, a highly polished oak table made the room look larger than it was. On the starboard side three open portholes allowed in the anaemic afternoon light. Next to the door on the port side was a sideboard housing a small library and lattice mail rack. Close by was an open hatchway leading to the officers' galley and a small bar above which hung a framed photograph of the King GeorgeV1 and Queen Elizabeth.

Pendleton finished his drink and placed the mug on a nearby table. He then looked up and studied the anxious expressions in the officers' eyes.

'In case you haven't already heard,' said Pendleton with a slight punctilious air. 'I'm Commander Jeremy Pendleton and so far I've not been impressed by what I've seen.' He paused for a few seconds allowing his vitriolic words to sink in then continued. 'The discipline onboard seems lax and the few crew members I have met appear to have forgotten to stand to attention when their captain passes them, or are too damn lazy to do so.' As he spoke he noticed one or two officers shuffling nervously while giving each other quick, nervous glances. 'I expect a high standard from all departments and to that end we will sail on Wednesday morning for evolutionary exercises. In the meantime, my predecessor's Standing Orders will remain. I will also be addressing the ship's company on Monday morning at 0900. Now,' he added, taking a deep breath, 'does anyone have any questions?'

Sub Lieutenant Coburn made a slight gesture with his hand and introduced himself.

'Yes, what is it?' Pendleton asked staring directly at the officer.

'Will our next trip be convoy duty again, sir?'

'All will be revealed in due course,' Pendleton replied, allowing a sly smile to play around his lips.

Lieutenant Small was next to ask a question. He also introduced himself then said, 'Rumour has it we'll be going to the Mediterranean, any truth in it, sir?'

'Wait and see,' Pendleton answered flatly. 'But I'll be interested to see how efficient your guns crews are.'

'We managed to hit a few Stukas on the last convoy, sir,' Sam replied confidently, 'so I can vouch for their efficiency.'

'I'm glad to hear it,' answered Pendleton with a wry smile. He then glanced quickly around and added, 'I will be speaking privately to each of you in due course. Now, if there's nothing else, please carry on.'

After Pendleton had left, Foster turned, grinned at Lieutenant Reed and said, 'What was that you said about Captain Bligh, Frank?'

News of their new commanding officer spread around the ship like an electric current. Petty Officer Steward "Knocker" White, listening in the wardroom pantry made sure of that. Next to him stood his assistant, Officer's Steward, Jock Thompson, a tall, thin-faced young lad with acne. At rum issue he told the cooks and stewards and other members of the Supply and Secretariat branch to expect the worst.

'Knocker says he's a right bastard,' said Jock, sipping his tot.

'Well he can't be worse than Okey,' retorted Mick Channon, a slightly built, fair-haired young Sick Berth Attendant from Plymouth. 'The bugger once gave me rocket for being ten minutes adrift, so 'e did.' He gave a short laugh, downed his tot in one straight gulp, then with a mischievous smirk, added, 'But I got me own back when I used a blunt needle to give him a tetanus jab.'

These remarks were overheard in the after seamen's mess who in turn told their opposite numbers up for'd. By the time the "buzz" reached the stokers' mess deck, Pendleton's reputation was a cross between Long John Silver and Captain Kidd.

Bob Jenkins, the Seaman Petty Officer, who should have been on duty when Pendleton came onboard, was in the Senior Rates mess having his tot. He was a well-built, grey haired three-badge man who had seen service in almost every part of the world.

'From what the duty QM told me,' he said standing next to the tall, imperious figure of Digger Barnes, the Chief GI (Gunnery Instructor), 'the new skipper seems a bit of a tartar. He certainly gave the First Lieutenant what for.'

'Serves him right,' retorted Digger Barnes, taking more than a generous sip of his rum. 'The Jimmy should 'ave been there. No bloody excuses.'

Senior ratings were issued with neat rum. Junior rates had theirs diluted two in one with water. Like most of the senior ratings, Digger joined before the outbreak of the war and was regular navy. He was a no-nonsense, tough talking Yorkshireman, with thin, greying dark hair.

'Aye,' interrupted Bill Conyon, the Chief Bosun's Mate. Above the breast pocket of his threadbare jacket was a row of fading World War One medals. His snow-white, bushy eyebrows matched his mop of untidy hair and his face, tanned by the sun of a dozen oceans, resembled a baked walnut. Whenever he spoke his watery pale blue eyes wrinkled into an infectious grin. In 1939 Bill had been due for his pension and had hoped to settle down with his wife Hilda on a small farm outside West Kirby in Cheshire. However, much to his disgust he was forced to sign on for the duration. 'And don't let the captain hear you call him, "skipper",' Bill grunted, displaying a row of tobacco-stained teeth. 'That's what they call a captain in the merchant navy.'

'Well I hope he's a better seaman than old Okey was,' added "Pony" Moore, the Chief Cook, a large, portly bald-headed man with the pallid, fleshy features. Mopping his sweaty brow with an off colour handkerchief he continued, 'If you remember he almost rammed that tanker when we came into Guzz last year.'

'Don't I bleedin' well know it.' The speaker was Chief Coxswain, Jack Tolby, a tall, rangy man with red hair from Toxteth, a suburb of Liverpool. Narrowing his dark brown eyes he shook his head and said, 'The bugger gave me a sudden order to turn to port and if I 'adn't managed it in time we'd 'ave been a gonner.'

Just as Tolby had finished speaking the door opened and in came two men. The taller of the two was Bill Grundy, the Chief ERA. Bill liked his booze, but due to constant threats of divorce from Ida, his long-suffering wife, he had recently become temperate. His ruddy complexion was streaked with sweat and the dark bags under his blue eyes were a legacy of working long hours during the recent boiler clean. His battered cap had seen better days and he wore a set of overalls that had once been dark blue, but were now scrubbed pale grey.

Behind Grundy was PO Writer Harry Potter, a small young man who before the war was a bank clerk. Upon entering his dark brown eyes blinking behind thick, horn-rimmed glasses settled on an aluminium jug resting on a table next to a brown Bakelite beaker.

'I hope you rum rats have left some for me,' he said, adding sarcastically, 'some of us have to work.'

'Pack it in, Pansy,' replied Bill Grundy in a deep North Country accent. 'You young uns drink far too much if yer ask me.'

'Bollocks!' snapped PO Potter, 'and *don't* call me Pansy!'

The others looked at one another and burst out laughing.

CHAPTER FIVE

After addressing his officers Pendleton spent the next few hours in his cabin examining the ship's books. Reading the doctor's medical report on the health of the ship's company reminded him of Professor Goldberg's heart condition. He unhooked the telephone receiver from its attachment on the bulkhead and dialled the sick bay number.

The clear, well-modulated voice of Doctor Fulford answered, 'Surgeon Lieutenant speaking.'

'Captain, here,' replied Pendleton. 'Sorry to bother you Doc, but could you come and see me right away?'

'No bother at all, sir,' replied the doctor, looking at SBA Channon while raising his eyebrows. 'I'll be up right away,' said Fulford, standing up and giving Channon a guarded look. 'That was the captain. He wants to see me chop-chop.'

'Bugger me, sur,' said Channon, his West Country burr suddenly becoming more pronounced than usual. 'Don't tell me he's sick already?'

The sick bay was situated on the starboard side of the after deckhouse. With two cots, a black leather examination couch, desk, medicine cabinets, it was fairly small. Two neon strips provided adequate lighting and brown linoleum covered the deck. Resting on top of a small fridge was an old Imperial typewriter, purloined by Channon from the pay office. Almost directly above the sick bay was X gun, which, when fired made everything shake like a miniature earthquake.

The doctor picked up his cap and put it on. 'Somehow,' he replied, taking a quick sip of his tea, 'I doubt it,' and left the sick bay.

Pendleton was sitting at his desk reading a signal concerning the medical condition of Commander Okey. A knock came on the door and in came the ship's doctor.

'Please come in, Doc,' said Pendleton, standing up and offering his hand, 'nice to meet you privately. Do sit down.'

'Thank you, sir,' replied Fulford, removing his cap as they shook hands, 'I do hope this isn't a professional call.'

Pendleton gave a half-hearted laugh. 'In a way it is,' said the captain, sitting down behind his desk and offering the doctor a cigarette.

'No thank you, sir,' Fulford replied raising a hand, 'I don't use them.' He gave Pendleton an inquiring look and added, 'So tell me, sir, what exactly is the problem?'

'Don't worry,' Pendleton replied with smile, 'I'm not sick or anything.'

He called into the pantry and told Gale to bring in two coffees. He then sat back in his chair took a deep drag of his cigarette and breathed out a cloud of smoke. 'For the moment, Doc,' he said, craning forward and flicking ash into an ashtray. 'What I have to tell you is strictly secret.'

Gale appeared carrying a mug for the captain and a cup and saucer for the doctor. He set them down on the desk.

'Thank you, Gale,' said Pendleton. 'Now, I'd like you to leave us.'

Sensing something suspicious was afoot, Gale nodded then said, 'Very good, sir,' and left the cabin. Outside he met PO Steward White.

'There's summat funny going on, Knocker,' he said giving the PO a suspicious glance, 'I can feel it in me water. The captain and the Doc are havin' quite a conflab.'

A wide grin spread over Knocker's sallow features. 'Maybe the old man's caught the boat up,' he replied and disappeared down a steel ladder.

Fulford crossed his legs and listened intently as Pendleton explained the nature of *Zimba*'s mission. 'It seems the professor is an expert on mustard gas,' said Pendleton. 'And the Americans are anxious to use his knowledge to manufacture some themselves. As a precautionary measure, so I'm told.'

'Mustard gas, eh?' mused Fulford. 'I did some work on gases at Oxford. As I recall it has a distinctive, garlicky smell and is yellow. It can also be lethal if used extensively.'

'Quite so,' Pendleton replied warily. 'As you can appreciate it is imperative that the professor arrives in Canada safe and sound, do you have any questions?'

'Just one, sir,' replied Fulford, taking a good gulp of coffee. 'Whereabouts onboard will this professor be staying?'

'In my day cabin,' answered Pendleton. 'Naturally, when we're at sea I'll be using my sea cabin.'

'Would it be prudent if I gave him a quick examination when he comes onboard?' Fulford asked, pursing his lips, 'just in case…'

'Let's wait and see what state the old boy's in, shall we, Doc,' Pendleton replied cautiously. 'And don't hesitate to tell me if you need anything. Now, please carry on I'm sure you've plenty to do.'

On his way back to the sick bay Fulford realised the responsibility concerning the professor was a grave one. A long journey across an ocean strewn with every danger from U-boats to heavy, rough seas would not be ideal for an elderly man suffering from a cardiac condition.

In the sick bay, SBA Mick Channon was sitting at his desk making notations in the M177A, the dangerous drugs section of the Store Account. The door opened and the doctor came in.

'What's the matter, sur,' said Channon, noticing Fulford's furrowed brow, 'you look worried. Anything wrong?'

The doctor shook his head and with a weary sigh, sat down on the spare chair and said, 'Do we have a plentiful supply of morphine?'

The doctor's question gave Channon a start. 'Funny you should ask that, sur,' he said, 'I'm just checking that now. We've got a hundred ampoules.'

'Mmm ...' muttered the doctor, nervously biting his lip, 'that should be enough, but better order a few dozen more, just in case.'

'Just in case of what, sur?' Channon enquired anxiously, 'surely we have enough...' He paused and gave Fulford a searching look. 'Excuse me, sur,' he went on, 'is there summat 'appening like. Is there summat I should know?'

Feeling guilty at not being able to confide in his assistant, Fulford guardedly replied, 'There is, but I can't tell you at the moment, so just order the morphine, there's a good chap.' He then picked up his cap and left, leaving Channon with a distinct feeling that something serious was in the wind.

That evening Pendleton sat in his cabin, reading the ship's log. *Zimba* was the latest of her class to be built. She had a complement of 190 officers and men. Since her commissioning on 21 December 1941, the ship had been almost continually at sea, either on convoy duty or patrolling the English Channel. He lit a cigarette and sat back in his chair, deep in thought. Clearly, he had inherited a crew that were tired. No doubt, this accounted for the apparent laxness he had so far encountered. Allowing thin trails of smoke to emanate from each nostril, he wondered if he had judged them too harshly. He knew only too well the effect being at sea for weeks on end could do to a person. Nevertheless, discipline onboard a warship was the bedrock of success and must be maintained.

The duty QM's voice over the tannoy announcing, "Men under punishment muster outside the regulating office. Clean up mess decks and flats for rounds", interrupted his thoughts. The time was 1900.

The daily routine for HM Ships in harbour was the same. Hands fell in at 0630. After breakfast, the ritual of "Colours" was performed when the white ensign was hoisted on the quarterdeck at 0800. At 1030, morning *Stand Easy* was piped. Then came Up-Spirits, the daily issue of rum at 1130. Secure from work was at 1600, when liberty men went ashore. The Officer-of-the-Day's rounds every evening consisted of a tour through the mess-decks and along the upper deck to check the mooring-wires and to ensure the ship was properly darkened. Secure and Pipe Down at 2200 followed this.

Pendleton sat back in his chair and contemplated accompanying the OOD on his night rounds, then quickly dismissed the idea. At that moment, the pantry door opened and in came Leading Steward Gale.

'Bubble and squeak for supper…err dinner, sir,' he said, hoping at last to evict a pleasant response from his captain. 'Is that all right, sir?'

'If that's what everyone else is having,' said Pendleton, nodding approvingly while stubbing out his cigarette, 'then I'll have the same.'

Two hours later Pendleton was still sat at his desk going over more reports, when exactly at 2000, "Colours. Attention on the upper deck. Face aft and salute" came over the tannoy.

An hour later night rounds was preceded by the intermittent piercing noise of the boson's pipe and the clump of footsteps gradually fading away as the OOD, duty PO and QM, worked their way around the ship inspecting each mess. A series of pips by the bosun's pipe over the tannoy at 2200 signified Pipe Down. Pendleton sat back in his chair, rubbed his tired eyes and yawned. Half an hour later, after taking a quick shower he was lying in his bunk. It had been a long day and as he lay in the dark listening to the gentle hub of the generator, he closed his eyes and thought of his late wife. 'Back at sea again, Martha dear,' he murmured to himself, 'here's hoping it ends better than the last time,' and fell asleep.

CHAPTER SIX

The next day dawned clear with a biting northerly wind. Shortly after 0800 Lieutenant Commander Carter knocked on Pendleton's cabin door, removed his cap and came. In one hand he held a small, green hard backed signal log. .

'Good morning, sir,' he said, handing the log to Pendleton. 'The recent batch of signals have arrived.' With an air of confidence, he added, 'Except for the wind, it looks like being a decent day for a change.'

'Thank you, Number One,' replied Pendleton, flicking through the signals. 'Anything important to report?'

'Not really, sir,' Carter replied, 'just routine stuff.'

Pendleton closed the log and stood up. 'Right,' he said firmly. 'As we didn't have divisions yesterday, let's take a walk around the ship.'

Carter had expected this and had warned Sub Lieutenant John Hailey, the OOD, to make sure the duty watch had washed down the upper deck and stowed away any loose gear. 'And John,' added Carter, looking at the ship's bell, 'get someone to give this a quick rub and make certain the brass work on the bridge is up to scratch.'

Hailey's round, fleshy countenance broke into a mild smirk. 'Bloody hell, Number One, doesn't he realise it's Monday. Most of those onboard have got hangovers from last night's run ashore.'

'Hangovers or no hangovers,' replied Carter dismissively. 'He's got eyes like a hawk and will miss nothing.'

An hour after Carter's conversation with Hailey, they left the captain's cabin. Closing the door, Pendleton glanced at Carter and said, 'Let's start with the bridge, shall we, Number One?'

With Carter in the lead, the two officers made their way up a flight of steel steps and passed the wheel-house and chart room then up another similar stepway onto the bridge. In sharp contrast to the warmth below decks, they were met by a gust of bitterly cold wind. With a satisfied smile, Carter noticed a young sailor clutching a wad of cotton waste was busy polishing one of several brass voice pipes leading to various parts of the ship.

'Open to the elements as usual,' remarked Pendleton, glancing up at the dark, cirrostratus clouds racing across the sky.

'Not quite, sir,' said Carter. 'When we're at sea canvas covers can be attached to that tubular steel framework you see fixed to the sides of the bridge. At least it gives us some protection.'

Pendleton pursed his lips, then replied sardonically, 'That's if it isn't ripped away in the wind.' He then looked at the sailor busily polishing a voice pipe. 'What's your name, lad?' he asked, 'and what part of ship are you?'

'Ordinary Seaman Cross, sir,' replied the sailor, standing stiffly to attention and saluting, 'fo'c'sle party sir.'

'I see,' answered Pendleton, returning the sailor's salute. Casting a critical eye over the nearby compass and brass binnacle, he added, 'I suggest you give these two a going over as well. Carry on.'

'Yes, sir, right away, sir,' stuttered the sailor, who immediately set about the task as ordered.

Pendleton stepped up onto the well-scrubbed wooden grating that lined the for'd part of the bridge and eased himself into the tall oak chair. The panoramic view showed the environs of Portsmouth. In the distance, hidden behind the chalky mass of Portsdown Hill lay Southwick House, the home of SHAEF (Supreme Headquarters Allied Expeditionary Forces). It was here in June 1944, that General Dwight D Eisenhower would take the historic decision to invade Europe. Further along the crenulated walls and towers of Porchester Castle, built around 1086 came into view. The irony of its position was probably lost on the local inhabitants. For it was from here during medieval times that armies embarked for an earlier invasions of France

Pendleton took a deep breath and took in the exhilarating sight of warships either anchored in mid harbour or berthed alongside wharfs and jetties. The rooftops of Whale Island, with its parade ground, evoked memories of a gunnery course undertaken over a year ago. Across the harbour he could see the houses of Gosport and the arc of Pneumonia Bridge leading to the naval hospital at Haslar. Close by lay HMS *Hornet,* the navy's MTB base, while opposite Southsea the black, cigar-shapes of submarines lay alongside the jetties of HMS *Dolphin.* The sight, steeped in naval strength and tradition sent a tingle of pride running down Pendleton's spine. My God, he thought as he turned away, it feels wonderful to be back again.

With a slight effort Pendleton slid off his chair. 'Could do with a cushion, Number One,' he said, running a hand over the top of the wooden seat. 'I expect I'll be spending most of my time here.'

'I'll speak to the wardroom PO, sir,' replied Carter with a grin, 'can't have you getting bum sores.'

Ignoring his First Lieutenant's feeble attempt at a joke, Pendleton allowed his eyes to take in the steel wave breaker on the fo'c'sle, and white ensign fluttering from the metal jackstay.

'The anchor chains and capstans could do with a lick of paint, Number One,' remarked Pendleton, glancing sideways at Carter. 'But I'm pleased to say the two sets of 4.7s look smart. I only hope they fire as accurately as they look and you can tell Guns I said so.'

My God, thought Carter, he's human after all. With a wry smile, he replied, 'I'm sure Lieutenant Small will be glad to hear it, sir.'

The two officers made their way down into the citadel (the main part of the ship). From the regulating office situated on the port side came the unmistakable Scouse accent of Chief Coxswain Jack Tolby.

'If I catch you two buggers smokin' when youse are supposed to be washing down the upper deck,' he ranted, 'I'll 'ave yer scubbin' out every heads in the ship, d'yer 'ear me now?'

'Yes, Chief,' muttered two voices in unison.

The office door was half open. Pendleton looked inside and saw Tolby's dark brown eyes peering up from his desk at two able seamen. The chief's jacket was undone and he was smoking a cigarette. The tallest of the seamen was Dinga Bell, a ginger-headed, thin-faced lad from Hull. His mate, Yorky Woods, was small and stocky with untidy black hair and a round, chubby face. Wearing faded blue overalls over dark blue jerseys, they stood with their hands by their side, inclining their head and trying, unsuccessfully, not to smile.

'And you can take that supercilious grin off your faces,' snapped the chief, impatiently stubbing out his cigarette. 'This is not the first time you two 'ave been caught skylarking when you should 'ave been working. If it 'appends again, you'll both be fer the high jump. Savvy?'

'Yes, Swain,' muttered the two ratings, nodding their heads.

'Now fuck off the two of yer,' growled the chief, 'and mind what I said.'

'Ahem,' coughed Pendleton as the two ratings turned and wearing expressions of contempt, made their way along the corridor. The chief looked up, and hurriedly buttoning his jacket, stood up.

'Everything all right, Chief?' asked Pendleton.

'Yes, sir,' replied the chief. 'I've just been reading the riot act to those two loafers. Chief Tolby, Coxswain.'

After shaking hands Pendleton nodded and asked, 'Any news of the ratings who are sick on shore?'

'Not as yet, sir,' replied Tolby, shaking his head. 'I'll expect they're swingin' the lead, like those two were.'

'Right,' replied Pendleton with a sly grin. 'Carry on, Chief, I'm sure we'll be seeing a lot of each other in the future.'

Onboard a destroyer the Chief Coxswain was responsible for discipline. He also took the ship's wheel during action stations and when the ship entered or left harbour.

Stopping outside the NAAFI, several ratings saw Pendleton and promptly stood to attention. Clearly, his comments regarding discipline were making an impression. A tall, stout, narrow-faced man with untidy dark brown hair, stood behind the counter serving nutty, (sailors' term for sweets and chocolate) and cigarettes.

'Carry on, please,' Pendleton said looking at the line of sailors. Then, smiling at the stout man, said, 'I take it you're the NAAFI manager?'

'Yes, sir,' he replied in rich Yorkshire accent. 'Harry Bates. Is there anything I can get you, sir?'

'Not at the moment, Mr Bates, thank you,' said Pendleton.

Doing their best to avoid the hot air shooting up from the open hatchways leading into the boiler and engine rooms, they continued along the passageway. Passing the main galley they reached the exit hatchway. As they did so, Pendleton smiled to himself as he overheard a sailor shout, 'Come on *Master Bates,* hurry up with me tickler.' (Tickler, sold in tins, is tobacco used by sailors who rolled their own cigarettes.)

The upper deck was a hive of activity. Under the steady gaze of petty officers, working parties were busy washing, cleaning and polishing. The guns' crews on the two-pound pom-poms and 20mm Oerlikons stopped and looked at their new captain. What they saw must have made an instant impression on them. Standing over six feet tall and wearing his gold leaf encrusted peak cap at a rakish angle, Pendleton looked the epitome of a destroyer captain. Giving the men a cursive nod of his head, he and Carter passed the twin sets of torpedoes on the well deck. Nearby the ship's whaler lay outboard, suspended from two davits by a series of ropes and cleats. Onboard were six ratings sitting on the cross boards and the coxswain holding the tiller. Watching them was the stooped, white haired figure of the Buffer. In one hand he held an old wrinkled cap. The other hand was busy scratching his head. In doing so strands of hair caught the breeze making them wave wildly, as if he'd been given an electric shock.

'Yer were too slow gettin' into the fuckin' boat,' the Buffer yelled at the seamen. 'If someone had fallen overboard, the poor bugger would 'ave drowned afore you got to 'im.'

'Good afternoon, Chief,' said Pendleton, studying the Buffer's weather-beaten features. 'I don't believe we've met.'

'No sir,' replied the Buffer, quickly putting on his cap. 'Chief Bosun's Mate Conyon, sir,' he replied, giving Pendleton a quick salute.

Noticing the row of faded medal ribbons on the Buffer's jacket and his wrinkled countenance, Pendleton asked, 'I notice you've seen quite a lot of service, Chief.'

'Yes, sir,' grunted the Buffer, 'I was a boy seaman onboard the old *Queen Lizzy* at Jutland.'

'Were you, by Jove?' Pendleton replied, suitably impressed. 'Are there any problems I can help you with?'

'Not at the moment, sir,' said the Buffer, stroking his chin. 'But the buzz is we're going to sea on Wednesday. Is that right, sir?'

'News travels fast onboard this ship, doesn't it Number One?' came Pendleton's laconic reply.

Carter smiled weakly, nodded and replied, 'So it would seem, sir.'

The two officers continued towards well deck. When Pendleton was sure they were out of earshot of the Buffer, he looked at Carter with a quizzical expression and said, 'Just how old *is* the Buffer?'

Giving his shoulders a nonchalant shrug, Carter replied, 'Nobody's quite sure, sir. It seems the date of birth on his service documents are so faint it's hard to tell.'

The two officers entered the after deckhouse. After passing the sick bay they arrived outside X Gun barbette, (the round section of the gun's base). Suddenly, they heard a loud, rasping voice barking,

'*Check, check, check.*' The sharp clanging and grating sound of X gun's mechanism followed this as the gunners went through their drill.

'By gum,' cried the voice in a thick Yorkshire accent. 'You're as slow as a cartload of monkeys, let's do it again.' A few minutes later, a tall, imperious figure ducked out from the entrance of X gun into the passageway. Beads of sweat ran down the sides of his leathery complexion. His black shoes gleamed like glass and the creases in his trousers were knife-edged. Upon seeing Pendleton he snapped to attention and gave a parade ground salute and said, 'Chief GI Barnes, sir.'

'Good afternoon, Chief,' replied Pendleton, returning the salute and offering his hand. 'I'm glad to see you and your team are hard at it.'

'Practice makes perfect, sir,' the chief replied as they shook hands. 'Can't 'ave too much o' that, can we, sir?'

'Quite right, Chief,' Pendleton answered nodding his head approvingly. 'Do carry on.'

Pendleton followed Carter around the base of the gun turret through a hatchway onto the quarterdeck. A rating was busy polishing the ship's bell, and nearby Lieutenant Jim MacIntyre, was talking to Taffy Hughes, a tall, dark three-badge petty officer.

'I expect we'll be off to sea in a few days,' Pendleton overheard MacIntyre say to the PO, 'so make sure everything's secure.' Upon seeing the captain his heavily tanned face broke into a smile and he saluted. 'Good mornin' sir,' he said in his inimitable gravely Cornish accent. ''Avin a quick walk around, I see.'

'Yes, indeed,' Pendleton replied. 'But tell me, Mac, how do you know we are going to sea so soon?'

An all-knowing expression spread across his weather-beaten features. 'If yer don't mind me saying so, sir,' he said with a sly smile, 'it's all round the ship, so it is.'

The rating who was polishing the ship's bell stopped what he was doing and said, 'Oh eight 'undred on Wednesday ain't it sir?'

'Pipe down, Boyo,' rasped Petty Officer Hughes. 'Or you can carry on doin' that at tot time.'

'It never ceases to amaze me, Number One,' said Pendleton, shaking his head in disbelief, 'how the buzz gets around when something is supposed to be secret.'

'Lower deck tom-toms, I suppose,' joked Carter, as they walked onto the quarterdeck.

Under the eagle eyes of a stocky built Seaman Petty Officer with hawk-like features, several ratings were busy cleaning the twin sets of depth charge rollers. Among the group Pendleton recognised the two men the coxswain had given a dressing down earlier. Both appeared to be laughing and joking while using a small wire brush to clear away bits of debris from a roller.

'Pack it in you two,' cried the petty officer, 'or to be sure, you'll both be seeing the coxswain again.'

The PO's warning and the sight of the First Lieutenant and Pendleton immediately took effect. They glanced furtively at one another, stopped laughing and carried on working.

'You are?' Pendleton enquired, noticing the PO's jacket was undone.

'Petty Officer Munroe, sir,' replied the PO, saluting.

With a look of concern Pendleton stared at a line of drum-like objects secured to the port guardrail. 'And how often do you check to see the depth charges are secure?'

'At every watch, sir,' replied the PO, 'especially at sea.'

'Make sure you do,' said Pendleton. 'And the next time you address me make sure you're properly dressed.'

No sooner had Pendleton and Carter left than the PO hurriedly buttoned up his jacket, muttering, 'Miserable bugger, maybe he thinks he's on a bleedin' battleship, instead of a destroyer.'

.

CHAPTER SEVEN

At precisely 0700 on Wednesday 3 August, "Hands fall in for leaving harbour. Special sea duty men to your stations", was piped around the ship. A stiff northerly wind sent dark clouds scudding across a leaden sky as squawking seagulls circled in the air swooping on gash (naval term for rubbish etc.) thrown overboard after breakfast. Near the harbour entrance, the choppy waters of the Solent lapped against the walls of Fort Blockhouse, built a century ago to protect against the French, now in use to deter another more deadly foe; and in the distance, shrouded in the early morning mist, lay the verdant hills of the Isle of Wight.

Zimba was berthed ports side to, facing the Solent. Both lookouts were closed up and the protective canvas screen had been rigged around the bridge.

'Coxswain on the wheel, Able Seaman Roberts also closed up also, sir,' shouted Jack Tolby from wheelhouse. Above his head, the bridge voice-pipe curved in front of him. Near him stood "Big Geordie" Roberts, a thickset three-badge telegraphman from Newcastle. Resting his tobacco-stained fingers on the brass handle of the revolution indicator, he pensively awaited orders that would be transmitted to the engine room and bring *Zimba* to life.

'Thank you, Chief,' replied Pendleton who was sat on his chair quietly smoking his third cigarette of the day. 'Ring on main engines, and stand by.'

Nearby, Lieutenant David Foster and the First Lieutenant along with Petty Officer Yeoman Bob Jeffries, a tall, red-faced Scotsman, trained their binoculars on the centre window of the third floor of Semaphore Towers. Each wore light brown duffel coats. Some, like

Pendleton had scarves wrapped around their necks and wore woollen gloves.

'Signal flashing from shore, sir,' cried PO Jeffries, 'slip and proceed when ready.'

'Thank you, Yeoman,' Pendleton replied. Raising his voice slightly he added, 'Please acknowledge.' He then turned to Carter and with a cautious smile, said, 'She's all yours Number One, let's see how you handle her.'

'Very good, sir,' Carter responded confidently. 'I'll use the headspring.'

Zimba was moored to the quayside by four separate ropes (called springs), two leading aft, one leading forward, and one, a short one, going out at right angles to the ship's side. Carter walked to the port wing and using as loud-hailer, shouted to Midshipman Porter who, along with the Buffer and his team, was on the fo'c'sle awaiting orders.

'Single up to the stern wire!' he yelled. 'Take off the fore and aft breast-ropes.' Porter nodded to the Buffer who, in turn passed the order to two ratings. They heaved the ropes over the bollards and let them slide into the water. A member of the shore party hauled them in. 'Remove the fore and aft ropes,' called Carter.

Only the head rope and headspring remained. Carter ordered the head rope to be released.

'White flags showing on the quarterdeck, sir!' yelled the starboard lookout.

'Very good,' shouted Carter, 'fenders in.'

In order to show the bridge that everything was clear aft, flags called *screw flags* were used (red for foul, white for clear).

'Slow ahead,' Carter shouted, praying the ship's side wouldn't scrape against the jetty.

Almost straight away everyone felt the faint vibrations of the engines. This was the trickiest and dangerous part of the manoeuvre as it was now that accidents could occur. With a slight twanging sound the headspring became taut allowing the ship's stern to swing out. It then slackened off enabling the ship to roll slightly.

'Release headspring,' Carter shouted to those on the fo'c'sle. No sooner was this done then Carter bent to the voice pipe, and in a calm voice, ordered, 'Engines half ahead.'

Immediately, the flurried, foamy noise of the screws churning the water could be felt as the ship moved imperceptibly away from the jetty.

Carter turned, his handsome features glistening with perspiration. With an expression of intense satisfaction, he looked at Pendleton and said, 'What course shall I set, sir?'

Pendleton grinned, allowing a flurry of ash to fall from his cigarette.

'That was very well done, Number One,' Pendleton replied. 'I can see now why you were an Olympic yachtsman before the war, but I'll take her from here.'

"Attention on the upper deck, face the starboard" was piped as *Zimba* increased speed and nosed her way through the harbour. The order to the ship's company to face either the starboard or port was given as a salute to other warships.

By 0930 *Zimba* had nosed her way into the Solent. In doing so, the ship was met by a stiff northwesterly wind churning the sea into a mass of angry white horses.

'Starboard twenty,' ordered Pendleton, leaving his chair and taking hold of the voice pipe.

'Starboard twenty,' repeated Chief Coxswain Tolby. 'Twenty 'o starboard wheel on, sir.'

Pendleton waited for the ship to move, but to his surprise, nothing happened. He then felt the ship slowly heel slightly over and change course. Feeling the deck cant slightly, Pendleton smiled to himself; Paddy O'Malley was right, given time and patience she will respond well.

Away to starboard, the leafy coast of Lee-on-Solent soon faded away in the morning mist.

Pendleton resumed his seat. A feeling of exhilaration ran through him as he felt deck vibrate as *Zimba* cut through the sea.

'Steer starboard, twenty. Full speed. Revolutions two zero, Number One,' ordered Pendleton. 'Let's see how Paddy's turbine engines shape up. We'll remain a few miles off the Hampshire coast. I want to keep as far away as possible from those U-boat bases in France.' He bent forward, unhooked the ship's intercom.

'This is the captain speaking,' he announced in a quiet but authoritative voice. 'In ten minutes we will increase speed. Make sure everything is secure. That is all.'

In the boiler room, Danny Wilson, the Chief Stoker stood on the shiny steel grating, his hands clasped behind his back, a patient attitude he had developed over the past fifteen years. The temperature was 20 degrees Fahrenheit and rising. Beads of warm perspiration trickled down his pale, florid features. Danny was a tall man with tired-looking brown eyes. Under his well-worn cap his sparse dark hair, heavily tinged with grey was a sweaty mess. Next to him stood Paddy O'Malley, his Engineer Officer. Unlike Paddy whose overalls were spotless white, those worn by Danny were a faded blue, unbuttoned to show a chest full of small, curly grey hairs.

'Here we go again, sir,' Danny said giving Paddy a searching look, 'more bloody speed trials. When we did this last year my false teeth rattled so much I almost choked, so I did.'

Paddy took off his cap and wiped his brow with the back of his hand. 'To be sure you'd best take them out then, Chief,' he replied with a grin. 'I've got a feeling the captain's going to push the old girl to the limit.'

In the seamen's and stokers' mess decks the duty cooks made sure all crockery was stowed away and hammocks properly secured.

'Why is it Knocker,' said an rating to a stoker across in the opposite mess, 'that every time I'm cook of the grot and this bloody ship pisses through the sea, water always seems to find its way into the mess. I beats me so it does.'

'Maybe the rivets need tightening,' replied the stoker, grinning while using a soggy dishcloth to wipe the mess deck table. 'If I were you, Nobby, I'd wear a lifejacket.'

In the sick bay, Mick Channon was busy stowing away kidney dishes and surgical instruments, when Doctor Fulford came in.

'Good morning, Channon,' he said, taking off his cap and sitting down at his desk. 'Anything for me today?'

'Not really,' replied the SBA, pouring water into a small, aluminium kettle, 'just the usual loafers trying to dodge duty. Tea, sur?'

'Please,' said the doctor. Staring inquisitively at his empty desktop, he added, 'Was it necessary to clear everything away?'

Channon's fresh-faced features broke into a sly grin. 'You wait till the ship really gets goin' sur,' he warned, switching on the kettle. 'Anything that's not secured or stowed away leaps into the air. It's just like an earthquake, so it is.'

'Indeed,' muttered Fulford, carefully rubbing his smoothly shaven chin. 'Perhaps I should adjourn to my cabin, then.'

'Best place for yer, sur,' replied Channon, nodding approvingly as he poured the boiling water into the kettle. 'I'll bring yer down a mug of tea when it's brewed.'

On the bridge the sound of the wind whipping against the canvas awning sounded like the crack of a rifle. Arcs of white water cascaded over the ship's bows as she shuddered in and out of the undulating, dark green sea. In the distance, black low-lying altocumulus clouds shrouded the coastline, threatening rain.

'Two British warships approaching, sir, green four zero,' yelled Able Seaman Bungy Williams high up in the crow's nest. After repeating what he saw down the bridge voice pipe he added ominously, 'And closing fast.'

'Thank you,' answered Pendleton. Picking up the engine-room intercom he said, 'Increase revolutions two, oh, full ahead.'

'Very good, Jeremy,' came engineer's good humoured reply, 'I only hope the boiler doesn't explode!'

'Don't worry, Paddy,' Pendleton replied confidently. 'I'll take full responsibility.'

Lieutenant Foster bent down and looked across the Pelorus and took a compass bearing. 'Ships now bearing green, three zero zero, sir,' he cried out, 'roughly three miles away. At this speed they will pass us a mile or so to starboard.'

Like a racehorse suddenly let loose, *Zimba* bounded forward, her bows bouncing up and down as she cut through the heaving sea. Voluptuous clouds of spray cascaded onto the fo'c'sle, swirling and swishing before being carried away on the wind. The white ensign on the quarterdeck threatened to tear itself away from the jack: halyards and rigging rattled wildly, vibrations running up through the deck sent tingling sensations up legs and spines, while the violent dipping and diving motion of the ship forced everyone to grasp anything at hand.

In the mess decks, men off duty clung onto stanchions, tables or any fixture to steady them. Men in the boiler and engine rooms weren't so lucky. One stoker slipped over and bruised his back. Another sprained his ankle while a young stoker, experiencing sea duty for the first time, vomited all over his oppo. Others stared wildly at dials and pressure gauges waiting for one or the other to crack.

'Jesus Christ, sir!' CERA Bill Grundy shouted to Paddy O'Malley, his blue eyes wild with a mixture of excitement and fear. 'What's the old man trying to do, kill us all?' The jangle of the voice pipe interrupted him.

'Engine room, Engineer speaking,' said Paddy, unhooking the voice pile.

'What's our speed?' asked Pendleton in a calm, steady voice.

Paddy glanced disconcertingly at the speed gauge, then clearing his throat, replied nervously, 'To be sure, Jeremy, we're doing almost thirty-seven knots.'

'Thank you,' Pendleton answered calmly. 'Reduce revolution two zero.'

'Praise be to God,' gasped Paddy, 'the lads down here are all shaking like jellies, so they are.'

Just as *Zimba* bounded passed the two warships, one of them flashed a signal.

Yeoman PO Bob Jeffries's ruddy features wrinkled into a wet grin. 'Message reads, sir, "Where's the fire, or are you on a promise?"'

Pendleton tossed his head back and gave a short, throaty laugh. 'Reply, "Catch us if you can and I'll tell you".'

In the sick bay, Mick Channon was lying on one of the cots, clinging tightly onto the side rails. As the ship slowed down the door opened and in came Doctor Fulford.

'Sweet Jesus, sur,' cried Channon, climbing out of the cot. 'You look as white as a sheet. Are you all right?'

'I…I think so,' gasped the doctor, sweat running down the sides of his face while leaning against the fridge. 'You were right. It did sound like an earthquake. I thought we would damn well capsize. Have we had any casualties?'

'Just a few bumps and bruises,' replied Channon, 'nowt serious.'

The ship gradually reduced speed to a mere twenty knots leaving a trail of fizzy white foam in her wake.

'Well done the engine room and boiler room,' Pendleton said down the voice pipe. 'The ship handled well,' with a sly grin, he added, 'I hope you were not too shaken up.'

In the engine room CERA Bill Grundy stood holding the top set of his false teeth. 'Not too shaken up, he says,' cried the chief, wiping his sweaty brow with a piece of cotton waste. 'One of me fuckin' teeth is broken, so they are.'

'Never mind, Chief,' cried Paddy, 'maybe the doc can glue them together.'

On the bridge Pendleton turned to Carter, who was scanning the area with his binoculars, and said, 'Now that we've got that out of the way, Number One, let's see what else we can conjure up to amuse the crew.' He unhooked the voice pipe and cried, 'Unidentified aircraft approaching on the port bow. Hands to action stations!' He then leaned forward and pressed the alarm bell.

One by one each department closed up for action. All the ship's guns trained to port: engine and boiler rooms, operations room, lookouts were doubled. The Chief Coxswain took the wheel and the first aid parties reported their readiness. Meanwhile, Pendleton sat on his chair, patiently smoking while studying his wristwatch. Shortly afterwards, he leaned forward and unhooked the ship's voice pipe.

'This is the captain speaking,' he said sternly. 'That was a drill and it took far too long. Be prepared for the alarm bell to sound at any time night and day.'

During the morning walls of fine rain came sweeping in from the west. Angry bow waves curled high over the fo'c'sle as the ship dipped, rolled and careered through the heavy seas. Every so often the ship shuddered and performed an unbalancing corkscrew motion making the strongest stomachs feel queasy.

Despite this, various damage control evolutions were carried out. "Leaky" bulkheads in the boiler room were shored up. Fire in the main galley and engine rooms was tackled. Using Neil Robertson stretchers, first aid teams evacuated "casualties" from various parts of the ship to the sick bay.

Shortly after 1315, the pipe, "asdic contact made. Action stations. Depth charge parties close up", echoed around the ship. Once again, the sound of men running to their stations could be heard everywhere.

'Much better, Number One,' said Pendleton, studying his wristwatch. 'That only took six…the ringing of the bridge telephone interrupted him. Midshipman Stockforth-Johnson immediately unhooked the receiver. A look of horror suddenly came over his face, '*My God, sir,*' he yelled. '*Man overboard from the quarterdeck!*'

CHAPTER EIGHT

The events that followed seemed to take ages, but in fact passed in minutes.

A rating arrived onto the bridge, his face covered in perspiration. 'Man overboard, port side, sir,' he gasped, wide-eyed and breathless, 'it's Able Seaman Woods, sir. He fell off the quarterdeck.'

Pendleton was the first officer to react. Quick as a flash he picked up the engine-room voice pipe and shouted, 'Stop engines, slow astern.'

Without waiting to be told, Carter ordered, 'Away sea boat's crew, man overboard. This is not a drill!'

He needn't have bothered. The words *"man overboard"* flew around the ship like wildfire. The whaler's six-man crew immediately galvanised themselves into action. Whoever was in the water was one of theirs: a shipmate whose life was in their hands. They also knew that without a lifejacket and exposed to bitterly cold waters and strong currents of the English Channel, the chances of anyone surviving were slim. Speed was therefore imperative.

'Look lively, now,' yelled the Buffer, who was overseeing men turning the winch that would lower the lifeboat into the sea. Near them stood Jack Tolby, the Chief Coxswain and Chief GI Digger Barnes. Like everyone else they had anxious expressions etched on their faces.

Each man scrambled onboard the whaler, sat down on the thwarts and grabbed hold of the lifeline suspended above from a rope span between the davits. On the orders of the Buffer the falls were lowered. Suspended a few feet above the waves, the disengaging gear was released and the whaler flopped into the sea. Waves immediately bounced against the small vessel causing it to rock violently. The boat-rope attached from stern of the ship stretched as the whaler moved away. Tug Wilson, the whaler's coxswain, a burly two badge Leading Seaman, quickly released the rope. '*Out oars,*' he yelled. '*Stand by to pull together.*'

By this time *Zimba* was barely moving.

'I only hope there's no bloody U-boats in the area,' Yeoman PO Jeffries remarked cautiously to one of the lookouts, 'if there is we'll be a sitting duck.'

Pendleton also was aware of the danger. Nevertheless, his conscience wouldn't allow him to let a man drown.

'Keep the speed at five knots,' shouted Pendleton down the engine-room voice pipe. 'Wherever the poor blighter is I don't want him being sucked under by the propellers.'

All hands were on the port side of the upper deck. Each man strained his eyes, hoping to see a head bobbing about among the rolling waves. This included the crow's nest lookout, Leading Seaman Jumper Collins, a tall, wiry lad from Doncaster. With his binoculars firmly clamped to his eyes, he eagerly searched every wave and trough on the ship's port side.

On the quarterdeck the guardrails and gash shoot had been removed. In their place were two depth charge traps. One of the nine men depth charge team was Able Seaman Dinga Bell. Standing close by was Seaman Petty Officer Joe Jenkins, Lieutenant MacIntyre and Midshipman Porter. The black oilskins they wore glistened with spray. Everyone stared anxiously out to sea while steadying themselves against the swaying of the ship.

The First Lieutenant arrived, his face red and sweaty.

'What happened, Jim?' he asked Lieutenant MacIntyre.

'Able Seaman Woods and him were at it again,' replied the officer, glaring angrily at Able Seaman Bell.

'No, sir,' cried Bell, rainwater running down the sides of his flushed face. 'The ship rolled like. One minute I 'ad 'old of

'Slinger, then the ship rolled an' I 'ad to let go of 'im. The next thing I 'eard wuz a yell as 'e fell over. It wuz an accident, sir, I swear it, an accident…'

'A likely story,' replied Carter, glaring scornfully at the sailor.

In the crow's nest Able Seaman Jumper Collins peered though his binoculars anxiously scanning the sea. Feeling the rims of the binoculars pressing hard against his eyes, he carefully moved his head in an arc, first one way, and then another. For a few seconds, the pale afternoon sun shining on the sea distorted his view. Suddenly, he saw what looked like a black dot about a mile away. At first he thought it was a piece of debris. Then, as each wave subsided he noticed what was obviously a hand attempting to wave.

'*Man in the water a mile away on the port bow!*' he yelled excitedly down the voice pipe. (A nautical mile is 2,000 yards.)

Straight away, everyone on the bridge focussed his binoculars away to the left.

'*I see him, sir!*' shouted Midshipman Porter, straining his young eyes. '*I think he's trying to wave.*'

After a few seconds, Pendleton, Lieutenant Foster and the others also saw what appeared to be someone's head bobbing in and out of the waves.

'Half ahead, revolutions two oh, hard a port,' cried Pendleton down the voice-pipe. Glancing first at Lieutenant Foster, then at Midshipman Foster, he yelled, 'Grab a loud-hailer and give the coxswain of the whaler directions. Pilot, then phone the quarterdeck and tell Number One we've sighted someone in the water, and you'd better inform the Doc in case he's needed.'

The news that Woods had been sighted spread like an electric current around the ship. Everyone, including the cooks, who should have been in the galley preparing supper, was now on the upper deck. As *Zimba* slowly heeled to port tension was running high. All eyes were concentrated on the stretch of dark green, choppy sea directly ahead of the ship. After what seemed like an eternity, everyone onboard cheered as Woods was spotted, occasionally disappearing under the sea while trying frantically to wave a hand.

Zimba was now about two hundred yards away from where Woods was floundering. Pendleton ordered all engines to be stopped. The ship was then caught in a heavy swell and began to roll awkwardly. Dark clouds hovered high above but thankfully the rain had stopped and visibility was relatively clear.

Meanwhile, Tug Wilson was steering the whaler towards Woods' waving hand. '*Pull hard together!*' he yelled craning forward, '*and put yer backs into it!*'

His five-man crew didn't need any encouragement. Knowing what was at stake they rowed like they had never done before. The whaler was about fifty yards away from Woods, when suddenly he was engulfed by a huge wave. When it had settled there was no sign of him.

'He's gone under*!*' cried one of the oarsmen, 'the bugger's disappeared!'

At that moment one of the whaler's crew, a small stocky lad, let go of his oar, took off his inflated life belt and dived overboard.

'You mad bastard, Spider!' yelled Tug Wilson, watching anxiously as the sailor swam towards the spot where Woods was last sighted. 'You're gonna get yersel drowned!'

'He'll be OK, Tug,' shouted one of the crew, 'Webb used ter swim fer the navy.'

Ignoring the sailor's remark, Tug cried, 'Come on, haul away to port. And stand by with a lifebelt.'

Onboard *Zimba* everyone on the upper deck watched anxiously as Able Seaman Webb reached the spot where Woods was last seen and dived under the waters.

At that precise moment, a cry came from Leading Seaman Buck Taylor in the *Zimba*'s radar compartment. 'Surface contact, bearing red four oh, oh, roughly five miles away, sir.'

By 1943, most warships had been fitted with radar. This was the one weapon that the Atlantic war badly needed. It was a means making a contact day or night or in thick, foggy weather, and show the course and speed. Together, with much improved Asdic sets, they were a formidable weapon against the U-boat menace.

'Jesus Christ!' cried Pendleton. 'That's all we need. Sound action stations.'

With a hint of panic in his voice, Carter replied, 'What are you going to do, sir, you can't just leave…'

Pendleton shot Carter a dagger-like glance. 'Don't tell me what I can or can't do, Number One,' he snapped, 'just carry out my order.'

'Aye, aye, sir,' replied Carter. Feeling his face redden, he turned away.

Over the jangling noise of the alarm bell came the voice of Midshipman Porter.

'The diver's rescued the man, sir,' yelled Foster, 'he's being pulled into the whaler.'

Pendleton's mind was racing. Above everything the safety of his ship and its crew was paramount. If he left the men in the whaler they could possibly be picked up later, either by *Zimba* or another ship.

'How far away is the contact, Number One?' Pendleton asked, feeling the blood pounding in his head.

'Three miles and closing, sir,' Carter replied, 'We're well within range of her torpedoes.'

'I'm well aware of that,' Pendleton replied impatiently. 'Switch the Asdic on over the tannoy.

A few seconds later the intermittent, sharp "pinging" of the Asdic echoed around the ship. Pendleton listened anxiously as the time between every cycle of sound increased, indicating the nearness of the submarine.

'Full ahead,' cried Pendleton. 'Tell the depth charge party to stand by. I'm going to attack the bastard.'

Meanwhile, Able Seaman Woods was lying in the whaler, gasping for air and vomiting streams of salty seawater. In between

71

retching, he gazed up, glassy eyed up at the soggy figure of Able Seaman Webb.

'Th…th…thank you, Spider,' he spluttered, 'I wuz a gonner fer sure.'

'You can thank me at tot time, Woodsy,' replied Spider, dragging a piece of slimy seaweed from his hair. 'Now pipe down and…'

The voice of Tug Wilson yelling above the wind suddenly interrupted him.

'The bloody ship's pulling away,' cried Wilson. 'What the fuck's the captain doing?'

A few of the crew let go of their oars, stood up and began shouting and waving frantically. The whaler immediately became unsteady as waves splashed over the sides. With a look of bewilderment they watched as *Zimba* increased speed and gradually moved away.

'For fuck's-sake, sit down in the boat afore we capsize,' yelled Tug Wilson, 'summat must be up. They'll be back for us, just you see.'

Onboard *Zimba*'s upper deck men watched forlornly at their shipmates in the whaler waving at them.

'Indeed to goodness, boyo,' cried Able Seam Jones, a small, stocky lad from Swansea. 'They probably think we're pissing off and leaving 'em.'

'Bollocks, Taffy,' replied Leading Seaman Chats Harris. 'Tug Wilson will know there's a damn good reason for the ship leaving, so pipe down and keep yer eyes skinned.'

Tension on the bridge mounted as the sharp sound of pinging gradually became louder.

'Contact two miles away, sir, on the starboard bow,' came the report from below, 'and I think she's surfacing!'

CHAPTER NINE

After exchanging anxious glances with Carter, Pendleton said, 'Inform Guns, Number One. Tell him what's happening and to stand by to open fire.' Pendleton then unhooked the tannoy voice pipe. 'This is the captain speaking,' he said, trying his best to sound calm. 'A submarine is surfacing away to starboard. If it's a U-boat I intend to engage her.'

In the crow's nest, Jumper Collins swung his binoculars away to the right. At first all he saw were choppy white horses. Then, like a sea monster rising from the deep, the unmistakable shape of a submarine broke the surface, walls of water pouring from its rounded bows. Seeing the pennant on the side of her black, squat conning tower, Collins yelled down the voice pipe. 'She's the EJ16, one of ours, sir.'

'Thank goodness for that,' said Pendleton giving Carter a sigh of relief. 'Flash her a signal, "Glad to see you, have you had any luck with Jerry?"'

From the flickering Aldis lamp on the submarine's conning tower came the caustic reply, "Not lately, but we had you well in our sights!"

Pendleton's weather beaten features broke into a wide grin. 'Let's go back and get the whaler, Number One. If Woods is fit enough, I'll see him and Bell at defaulters tomorrow. Secure from action stations,' he paused and with a wry smile, added, 'I don't think we need to practise man overboard, Number One, the whaler got away in record time. Tell the boat's crew well done and make sure they get an extra tot of rum.'

Promptly at 0900 the next day Coxswain Jack Tolby, marched Woods before Pendleton, who was standing behind a highly polished wooden table with a slanting top. Looking pale and contrite, Woods stood stiffly to attention.

'Off caps,' snapped Tolby. 'Able Seaman Woods is charged with leaving the ship without permission, and in doing so endangering the life of the ship and the ship's company.'

'Do you plead guilty or not guilty?' Pendleton asked leaning forward on the top of his desk.

'Not guilty, sir,' Woods replied, blinking nervously. 'It weren't my fault, I wuz pushed, sir, Able Seaman Bell did it, sir…'

'Mmm…I see,' muttered Pendleton. Glancing enquiringly at Carter, he went on, 'You are this man's divisional officer have you anything to say in mitigation?'

Carter cleared his throat and saluted. 'Woods is a capable seaman sir, but spoils himself by his poor behaviour.'

'Miserable bugger,' Woods said to himself, glaring defiantly at Carter. 'A fine defensive officer you turned out to be.'

'I believe you had been warned before by the coxswain about skylarking while on duty,' said Pendleton, staring steely-eyed at the defendant. 'Do you understand the severity of the charge?'

'Err…I think so, sir,' replied Woods, 'but as fer leavin' the ship without permission, sir, I wuz pushed…'

Pendleton furrowed his brow, straightened up and said, 'Dismissed the ship and seven days' stoppage of leave and pay.'

'But sir…' pleaded Woods.

'Pipe down,' bellowed Tolby. 'On caps, about turn, quick march.'

A few minutes later, Tolby marched in the tall, ginger-headed figure of Able Seaman Bell. The charge of assisting a man to leave the ship without permission was read out. Despite denying the charge, Bell was given the same sentence as his friend.

The previous evening Pendleton had sent for Carter. He was alone in his cabin explained the nature of *Zimba*'s forthcoming mission, including the professor's heart problem.

'Sorry I couldn't put you in the picture earlier, Number One,' said Pendleton, offering his First Lieutenant a cigarette and lighting it, 'but secrecy is paramount. You do understand?'

'Of course, sir,' replied Carter, who, after taking a deep drag of his cigarette, asked, 'who else knows, sir?'

'The engineering officer and the doctor,' answered Pendleton. 'I will address the officers in the wardroom on Monday at 0900, and the ship's company after night rounds the same day.'

'What about leave, sir?'

'Weekend leave to three out of four watches to expire at 0800 on Sunday,' replied Pendleton.

Standing outside Pendleton's cabin, pretending to be polishing the door, Gale overheard almost everything. In the mess later that evening he could hardly contain his excitement.

'We're taking some professor to Canada,' he cried, staring around at his messmates. With a salacious grin he added, 'He's got summat wrong with his ticker, and there's woman, his daughter, coming onboard.'

'So that's why the MO was checking to see if we had enough morphia,' Channon muttered, blowing across the top of his mug of tea. 'An old man with a dodgy heart and a woman to look after him, eh.'

'I wonder where she'll sleep?' chimed in one of the stewards.

'With me, I hope,' grinned Channon, taking a deep gulp of his drink.

Later in the sick bay Channon had asked Fulford to confirm what Gale had told him.

'Yes, I'm afraid Gale is right,' Fulford had replied, expressing at the same time the need for secrecy.

'Fat chance of that onboard here, sur,' Channon had replied with a grin.

CHAPTER TEN

Monday 17 August dawned clear with a bitterly cold westerly wind sweeping down the Solent. On the same day, some two thousand miles away, American, British and Commonwealth forces met up at Messina, thus securing Sicily. The scene was now set for Operation Baytown, the invasion of Italy.

Meanwhile, *Zimba*'s crew had returned from weekend leave. Pendleton addressed them shortly after 2100, explaining the nature of the mission.

In the senior rates' mess, the Buffer turned to Chief GI Digger Barnes. 'No good'll come of 'avin a woman onboard, mark my words,' he said, filling the blackened drum of his old meerschaum pipe with tobacco, 'it's bad luck, I tell yer.'

'You daft bold bugger,' retorted the Chief GI. 'The captain didn't say the professor's daughter would be sailing with us.'

'Personally, I 'ope she is,' interrupted Jack Tolby, placing a friendly arm around the Buffer. 'A bit of skirt would make a change from seeing your ugly mugs. And if she plays her cards right...' he added with a salacious grin...

'I don't know,' interrupted PO Writer Harry Potter. 'Are all you Scousers sex maniacs?'

'Only those who support Liverpool, Pansy,' replied Jack Tolby, letting go of the Buffer's shoulders and picking up a mug of tea.

'And *don't* call me Pansy,' retorted Potter, glaring angrily at Tolby.

Thanks to Gale, most of the ratings in the other messes already knew what was happening. Nevertheless, they received the news with mixed feelings.

'It'll be a bloody rough crossing,' commented Telegraphman Geordie Roberts, 'I've done quite a few trips to Iceland afore the war and it's enough to freeze yer bollocks off.'

'Well, it mighn't be so bad,' remarked Leading Seaman Dusty Miller. 'At least we'll be away from the soddin' U-boats.'

'I wouldn't count on it, if I were you,' yelled a stoker from the opposite mess. 'Last week HMS *Gurney* was torpedoed off the southern coast of Iceland. A mate 'o mine went down with her, nice feller, he owed me a tot.'

Earlier in the wardroom the officers greeted the news with equanimity.

'It'll be quite pleasant, really,' said Sub-Lieutenant Coburn, grinning accusingly at Lieutenant MacIntyre. 'Maybe we'll have a bit of intelligent conversation for a change.'

'Cheeky, whippersnapper,' scowled MacIntyre, 'I were sailing in the North Seas when you were in nappies. You'll be grinning with then other side of yer face when we hit them heavy seas.'

'Well, then,' interrupted Lieutenant Reed. 'You'll be able to regale the old boy with some rousing sea stories, won't you, Mac?'

'I shouldn't if I were you, Mac,' added Doctor Fulford, who paused slightly before continuing. 'That reminds me. I hope Channon has ordered plenty of Hyoscine Hydrobromide tablets.'

'What are they for, Doc?' enquired Midshipman Porter.

'The dreaded mal de mer,' replied Fulford, pulling a face, 'seasickness my boy. This is my first trip and if what Mac says is true I'll probably need them.'

The time was a little before 2345 and the ship was darkened. Pendleton left his cabin and made his way along the main passageway dimly lit by eerie blue lighting. The somnolent atmosphere was punctuated by the sharp sound of the turbine engines and the dull throb of the generators, clear signs that the ship was ready for sea.

Parting the black canvas curtains that covered the hatchway Pendleton undid the clips and stepped out onto the upper deck. The greatcoat he wore under his best doeskin uniform failed to protect him from a blast of cold August air cutting right through him. After blinking a few times to accustom his eyes to the dark, he saw the tall, broad shouldered outline of OOD, Lieutenant Sam Small. Behind him stood Surgeon Lieutenant Fulford, Joe Jenkins, the duty PO and Quartermaster Able Seaman Dolly Gray. A group of sailors wearing duffel coats stood on the far side of the deck, blowing into their hands and stamping their feet.

'Good evening, gentlemen,' Pendleton said, returning their salute. 'No sign of our guests, then?'

'No sir,' Lieutenant Small replied curtly. 'Special sea duty men are closed up ready to leave harbour, sir.'

'Thank you, Guns,' Pendleton said staring down the gangway. 'We'll be leaving as soon as the professor is safely onboard and his daughter has left.'

As they spoke streams of vaporised breath issued from their mouths. High above an anaemic moon moved imperceptibly between dark clouds, cloaking the dockyard in pools of pale yellow light. Masts and yardarms of warships lying in dry docks and wharfs were barely visible, and across the harbour the roofs of Gosport lay shrouded in darkness.

The heavy-set figure of Paddy O'Malley appeared through the hatchway. His normally pristine white overalls were spotted with small, irregular patches of black oil. He gave Pendleton a confident smile, took off his cap and mopping his sweaty brow, said, 'As you can hear, sir, we're all ready for sea.'

Pendleton realised there was no need for his engineering officer to report this, and grinned. 'So I gather, Paddy. I take it you're here to see what our guests are like?'

'Who me?' Paddy cried with mock laughter, 'to be sure I'm just doin' me duty, so I am.'

The sound of a car engine suddenly drew everyone's attention.

'This must be them,' muttered Pendleton, staring expectantly down the wharf.

'I certainly hope so, sir,' said Carter, blowing into his hands. 'It's getting a might chilly standing around.'

The dipped headlights of tilly came into view and stopped near the foot of the gangway. The driver drew back the door and stepped outside. The woman he helped to climb out wore a red headscarf, a black Burberry and shoulder bag. She reached in and withdrew a suitcase and placed it on the ground. She then took the arm of a man wearing a grey homburg and dark overcoat and helped him to climb out the vehicle. The man was quite small and appeared to have a slight stoop.

'Petty Officer Jenkins, look lively and go down and help the lady with her luggage,' ordered Carter.

Jenkins immediately hurried down the gangway.

'Evenin' miss,' he said, feeling rather self-conscious. 'Please let me take yer case, and err...follow me onboard and mind 'ow yer go, it's bit slippy like.'

'Thank you,' replied woman, giving Jenkins a grateful smile. 'This way Papa,' she added, glancing first up the gangway then at her father, 'as you can see, they are expecting us.' Her English, spoken with a soft, mellifluent French accent was clear and concise. The woman took hold of her father's elbow, and with PO Jenkins leading, they walked carefully up the gangway.

Upon reaching the top of the gangway Pendleton stepped forward and reaching out he took hold of the woman's arm and helped father and daughter onto the deck.

'I am Commander Pendleton, the captain,' said Pendleton, saluting. 'Welcome onboard.' He then introduced the three officers.

'Good evening, gentlemen,' the woman replied smiling as they shook hands. 'I'm Nadine Le Brun, and this is my father, Professor

Henri Goldberg.' Unlike her father, a small middle-aged man, barely five feet four, she was in her early thirties and almost as tall as Pendleton. However, Pendleton wondered why her surname differed from her fathers.

The dim blue light from the QM's desk didn't allow Pendleton to see the faces of his guests clearly.

'A pleasure to meet you, sir,' said Pendleton. Unlike the woman's warm, gloved hand, the professor's limp handshake was ice cold. He wore a pair of metal-framed spectacles and from the end of his bony nose a small pear-shaped dewdrop quivered precariously.

'It's very kind of you,' the professor throatily replied. 'I do hope I'm not too much trouble.' Like his daughter, he spoke with a distinct, clear French accent.

'I trust your journey wasn't too tiring,' Pendleton added, glancing warily at the professor's drawn features.

'My father is very tired,' interrupted Nadine. 'He's been travelling most of the day.'

'Then I suggest you both follow me,' replied Pendleton, indicating a hand. 'It's far too cold to be standing around talking.' He glanced at Fulford and said, 'Perhaps you would like to come with us, Doc.' Looking dismissively first at Carter then at Lieutenant Small and Paddy, he went on, 'I think you three should carry on as I expect we'll be getting under way soon.'

With Pendleton leading, the group disappeared down a set of steel ladders. When they were safely out of sight, Dolly Gray turned to Petty Officer Jenkins. 'She's a bit of all right, ain't she, PO?' he said with a lecherous grin. 'I only 'ope she's sailing wiv us.'

'Pipe down, Gray,' rasped Lieutenant Small. 'And see if you can rustle the PO and myself a mug of kye.'

Walking along the dimly lit passageway Pendleton turned to the professor and said, 'You may find your quarters a little cramped, but we'll try to make you as comfortable as possible.'

They finally arrived at Pendleton's day cabin. Leading Steward Gale, his tall, lanky frame resplendent in a pristine white jacket opened the door and they went inside.

Under a clearer light, Pendleton was able to study his guests more closely.

Nadine stood a little over five feet six with high cheekbones, wide sensuous lips and a straight nose the end of which tilted slightly. The red silk headscarf she wore under her Burberry served to highlight her clear, porcelain features. But it was the stunning beauty of her violet eyes, framed under dark eyelashes that held Pendleton's attention. She was the most beautiful woman he had ever seen and when she looked at him he felt an unaccustomed sense of excitement run down his spine.

In stark contrast, the professor wore a thick overcoat and a woollen muffler. Under this was an ill fitting dark blue pinstriped suit, white shirt and tie. His black shoes, although highly polished were slightly scuffed. He removed his homburg thus revealing a full head of snowy white hair and a high forehead. By this time the offending dewdrop had disappeared from the professor's nose. His pale face was heavily lined, and under thick greying eyebrows, two intelligent, dark eyes peered inquisitively over a set of yellow, horn-rimmed spectacles.

'My goodness, Captain!' Nadine exclaimed, looking around approvingly. 'The room, err…cabin,' she added quickly correcting herself, 'is bigger than I thought. I take it these were your quarters? Where will you sleep?'

As she spoke she let go of her father's hand and removed her headscarf. She then shook her head allowing a cluster of chestnut coloured hair to quickly unfurl around the nape of her neck. Her oval shaped face, devoid of make-up was clear and smooth and when she spoke, Pendleton noticed how her captivating violet eyes, framed by curved black eyelashes, creased into a warm smile.

'This is my day cabin,' Pendleton replied. 'When we're at sea I'll be using another one up fo'rd.

'You are very kind,' she answered graciously. 'I'm sure my father will be comfortable here.'

As Nadine spoke she studied the tall, broad shouldered man that would be responsible for the safety of her father. Pendleton's heavily tanned handsome features and air of confidence immediately made her feel the professor was in good hands. However, staring into his clear, pale blue eyes she detected a slight expression of sadness. It wasn't permanent, but appeared only when he smiled. She remembered seeing a similar reaction in the eyes of people in France as they awaited the arrival of the Germans in 1940.

'I do hope you haven't been too inconvenienced, Captain,' she said, staring up at Pendleton while nervously toying with her handkerchief.

Returning her gaze, Pendleton replied, 'Not at all, it is a pleasure.'

Standing nearby, Fulford gave a short cough and glanced enquiringly at Pendleton. Pendleton immediately turned to the professor and said, 'Allow me to present Surgeon Lieutenant Fulford, the ship's doctor.'

'A pleasure to meet you, Doctor,' said the professor shaking Fulford's hand. 'I suppose you know about the heart attack I had last year?'

'Yes, sir,' replied Fulford, noticing a faint smile playing around the professor's thin lips. 'I believe you still have a slight heart murmur. May I ask if you are receiving any follow-up treatment?'

'My father carries Digitoxin tablets, Doctor,' interrupted Nadine as she helped her father off with his overcoat. Placing a comforting hand on the professor's arm, she smiled and went on, 'The specialist in Harley Street was pleased with his progress, so I hope he won't need them.'

'I'm sure he won't,' replied Fulford, giving her a reassuring smile. Then looking at the professor, he continued, 'But if you feel the need to do so please call me any time day or night, I am completely at your disposal.'

'Thank you, Doctor,' the professor replied with a slight nod of his head, 'you are very kind.'

Pendleton noticed Gale standing in front of the pantry door. He beckoned him over and introduced him to the professor. 'Gale will be looking after you. If you need anything special in the way of food, please don't hesitate to ask him.'

'A pleasure to meet you,' replied the professor, shaking Gale's hand. 'I eat anything except pork,' he added with a tired smile. 'But I'm particularly fond of fish and chips.'

'Beggin' yer pardon, sir,' replied Gale as he took the professor's overcoat from Nadine and folded it neatly over his arm. 'You've come ter the right place. If we 'ad our way, we'd live on 'em, day and night, so to speak.'

'Ahem,' interrupted Pendleton, 'thank you, Gale, that'll be all for now.'

Pendleton glanced quickly at his wristwatch and was about to speak when Nadine cut in.

'I think it is time I left,' she said glancing apprehensively at her father then at Pendleton. 'From what I've been told you are waiting to sail, are you not, Captain?'

'Yes,' Pendleton replied. He looked and suddenly felt as if there was nobody else in the cabin except Nadine and himself. She also experienced an odd, but compelling sensation and for a few seconds they held each other in a hypnotic gaze.

Quickly regaining his composure, Pendleton gave a nervous cough, and said, 'We are due to sail as soon as you have left.'

'Then, Papa,' said Nadine, placing a tender arm around her father's shoulders, 'I'm afraid I must leave.'

Clearly moved at the prospect of saying goodbye to his daughter, the professor replied, 'Yes, Cheri, I suppose you must.'

Tears suddenly welled up in Nadine's eyes. 'Don't come up on deck Papa,' she said, kissing his cheek and hugging him. 'It's too cold and you've taken off your coat.'

'As you wish,' the professor answered hoarsely. Reaching up and gently touching her cheek, he added, 'You'd better go now. We mustn't keep the navy waiting.'

'Oh Papa,' sobbed Nadine, 'I'll be worried sick until I hear from you.' Glancing apprehensively at Fulford, she added, 'You will take good care of him, won't you. Mother died last year from pneumonia and he's all I have in the world.'

Fulford gave her a reassuring smile, and said, 'Don't worry, Sister, he's in good hands.'

Nadine gave her father a final hug and kiss and with tears streaming down her face said, 'Au revoir, Papa, and God bless you.'

The professor's eyes moistened. For a few seconds they held each other in a tight embrace. 'Au revoir, Nadine, Cheri,' he muttered, 'now you must go.'

Without bothering to put on her headscarf, Nadine turned quickly, and followed by Pendleton, left the cabin. After negotiating the ladders she stopped, took a small pink handkerchief from her shoulder bag and dabbed her eyes.

'I'm sorry,' she said, glancing apologetically at Pendleton. 'It's just…'

'No need to apologise,' Pendleton replied, raising a hand. 'I understand.' He then escorted her along the passageway. Outside on the quarterdeck the cold night air blew strongly against their faces. Nadine shivered and hurriedly donned her headscarf, knotting it tightly under her chin. Overhead a full moon darted between heavy grey clouds, engulfing the quarterdeck with an occasional flood of pale light. Lieutenant Small and PO Jenkins stood close by, two dimly lit figures silhouetted against the darkness.

'The lady's transport's waiting on the jetty, sir,' said Lieutenant Small.

'Thank you, Sam,' answered Pendleton. 'Draw up the gangway and order special sea duty men as soon as Sister Le Brun has left the ship.'

Sensing Pendleton and the woman wanted a few seconds of privacy he and PO Jenkins discretely stepped aside, leaving them alone at the top of the gangway.

'Thank you for everything, Commander,' said Nadine, offering her gloved hand. In doing so her eyes momentarily caught the moonlight. The effect of her gaze was like an electric current running through Pendleton. Her hand in his felt soft and warm.

'Not at all,' he managed to say. 'And please try not to worry. Your father will be fine. I assure you.'

For a few seconds longer than was needed they shook hands. Perhaps it was his imagination, but he was sure she gave his hand a slight squeeze before releasing it. With a quick movement she unzipped her handbag and took out a small diary and fountain pen. She unscrewed the top and hurriedly wrote something.

'Incidentally,' she said, tearing a page from her diary. 'Your predecessor, Commander Okey is a patient on the ward where I work in the naval hospital.'

'Oh really,' replied Pendleton staring down at her. 'Please give him my regards and wish him a speedy recovery.'

'I'll do that,' Nadine said handing him the small sheet of paper. 'I have written the telephone number of my ward and the sisters' quarters on the paper. When you return, please contact me and let me know how my father is. I know he will write, but his letter could take ages to reach me.' She paused, and with pleading expression in her moist eyes, went on, 'Will you do that? I shall miss him very much.'

'I understand perfectly,' Pendleton solemnly replied. 'The ones we love are always near and dear to our hearts, especially when they are no longer with us.'

'Au revoir, Captain, and God's Speed, to you and your ship,' said Nadine. She quickly turned and with PO Jenkins in close attendance, made her way down the gangway and climbed into the tilly.

Feeling his heart pounding against his ribs, Pendleton watched as the car disappeared into the darkness, wondering when, or if, they would meet again.

PART TWO
THE WOMAN

CHAPTER ELEVEN

Sister Nadine Le Brun didn't need an alarm clock to wake her up. Years of early rising had trained her system to come alive at precisely 0630. The wind rattled against her window and the blackout curtains were drawn. With a sleepy yawn she reached across and switched on her bedside light. Fumbling with an open packet of Players she lit her first cigarette of the day.

Nadine's living quarters were spacious and comfortable. Her single bed, covered with a pink eiderdown fitted snugly into one corner. Close by rested a dressing table and mirror. Then came a small settee and two brown leather armchairs and a highly polished oaken wardrobe. The floor was fitted with a soft brown carpet and from the ceiling, painted in pale cream, hung an electric light surrounded by a pink lampshade. A few watercolours broke the monotony of walls covered with floral patterned wallpaper and in a far corner a door led into a bathroom neatly tiled in white.

Nadine knuckled her eyes, hoping they were not too bloodshot. Seven hours ago she had said a tearful goodbye to her father and she hadn't slept well. By now he would be somewhere at sea. For the umpteenth time she told herself he was in good hands. This would be the first time since they came to England that neither she or her father could pick up the telephone and speak to each other, discussing personal problems or simply enjoying the comforting sound of one another's voices.

She lay back in bed remembering those dark days in Paris a month before the fall of France in June 1940. On 10 May, the Germans attacked Belgium and Holland. Their forces emerged from the forests in the Ardennes near Sedan, and by 13 May had reached the River Meuse. The advance of the Wehrmacht was relentless. A week later the Germans had enveloped the port of Dunkirk.

Nadine closed her eyes, recalling the night her father visited her in her apartment. The professor wore an old raincoat over his usual blue suit, and under his grey homburg his face was pale and drawn. In the distance the dull rumble of gunfire told of the imminent approach of the enemy.

As the professor entered the room the worried expression in his watery, dark brown eyes, told Nadine something was wrong. His stoop seemed more pronounced and he was sweating profusely.

'What's the matter, Papa?' she cried, taking his arm and ushering him inside. 'You look terrible.'

'What's the matter, you ask?' the professor reiterated. His voice sounded high-pitched and almost hysterical. 'Can't you hear,' he added, taking off his spectacles and wiping them with a handkerchief. 'The cursed Boche is almost on out doorstep.'

'Oh Papa, please sit down,' Nadine said, helping him into an armchair, 'and I'll get you some brandy.'

'It's no use, Nadine,' gasped the professor, wringing his hands in despair. 'We are both Jews, and if the Germans arrive you know what will happen to us? We'll be deported like those in Holland, Belgium and Poland.'

'But you're an eminent chemist and I'm a nurse,' Nadine said, picking up a small bottle and pouring a good measure of brandy into a glass. 'Surely they won't harm us.' As he accepted the glass she noticed his hand was trembling.

'Oh yes they will,' replied the professor warily. 'Nadine Cheri,' he went on after taking a sip of his drink. 'There is something I haven't told you.'

'And what is that, Papa?' she asked tentatively.

The professor took another sip, ran his tongue across his lips and placed the glass on a nearby table. 'For some tine now I have been working on a process that would improve the strength of mustard gas,' he said, peering nervously over his spectacles. 'A few months ago, I discovered a new formula that would do precisely that. The formula is safely locked in my head and will stay there until I can put it to some use, preferably against the Boche. If the Germans arrest me, they're sure to torture me to get any information they think I have.' He stopped speaking and with a faraway look in his eyes, sighed, 'Nadine, my dear, I'm only glad your dear mama is not here to see all this, God knows what she would say.'

'The same as my Pierre would have said,' Nadine replied with a nostalgic sigh. 'Do what you think is right and trust in God.'

With venom in his voice, the professor continued, 'The Nazi swines have raped and pillaged every town and city they've conquered.' He paused and finished his drink then went on, 'I'm sorry, Cheri,' he added despairingly, 'but the time has come for both of us to leave France.'

'*Leave France, Papa!*' Nadine exclaimed. '*That's impossible!*' The thought of leaving the city where she grew up and went to college and learned English then later studied medicine, filled Nadine with dismay. '*But Papa!*' she cried frantically. '*Where would we go?*'

'To England, my dear,' the professor replied. 'They would welcome us with open arms.'

Nadine stepped back, a worried look in her eyes. 'But, how would we get there? The Germans have almost reached the coast, so we couldn't go by boat.'

'No, Cheri,' answered the professor. 'My contacts at the Sorbonne have arranged for us to travel by train to Spain. I have submitted my resignation and transferred my money to Lloyds bank in London. I suggest you do the same. As you know, Spain is neutral, so from there, hopefully we can catch a boat to England.' He paused, reached up and gave Nadine's arm a confident squeeze. 'Now, Cheri, don't look so worried and give me another brandy.'

Three days later, with what little jewellery she possessed tucked in her handbag and carrying a suitcase full of clothes, Nadine and her father boarded a train at Gare du Nord. The railway station was crowded with people fleeing from the approaching Germans. Babies were crying, children, clinging to their parents looked bewildered as families crowded into each compartment. Luckily Nadine and her father managed to find two seats. Six hours later after a bumpy, tiring journey they arrived at Santander. From here they managed to catch a boat to Plymouth and took a train to London. Feeling exhausted, they booked two rooms at Paddington Station Hotel. The next day the professor arranged an interview with senior officials at the War Office. The professor's earlier prophecy proved correct.

After presenting his credentials he was offered a position at London University's research laboratory. Nadine and her father moved into a flat in Chelsea, and instead of sitting in an air raid shelter listening to bombs devastate the city she decided she must do something for the war effort. Remembering Pierre's love for the sea, she volunteered for nursing duties with the Royal Navy. After being interviewed by a board of stern-faced matrons and doctors, she was accepted as a junior nursing sister. Two weeks later, after passing a medical examination and being measured for her uniforms she underwent a seven-day lecture on naval discipline and routine. She now held the honorary rank of lieutenant and after a tearful goodbye to her father, travelled to the Royal Naval Hospital at Haslar, Portsmouth. The time was a little after midday.

A tilly was waiting for her outside Portsmouth Harbour Station. The driver, a small, elderly man wearing a blue suit and an old flat cap, greeted her.

'Sister Le Brun?' he asked with a warm smile. 'Welcome to Portsmouth.' He spoke in a soft Hampshire dialect and his friendly attitude immediately relaxed Nadine.

'Yes,' she replied, feeling slightly self-conscious. 'Are you going to take me to the hospital?'

'Yes, ma'am.' As he spoke his pale blue eyes wrinkled into a ready smile. He took hold of her luggage, slid open the door and placed it in the back of the vehicle and helped her inside.

The journey around the environs of the Hampshire countryside took half an hour. After passing through the leafy towns of Fareham and Stubbington, they arrived outside the tall, iron gates of Haslar, shortly before 1300.

Nadine's first sight of the Royal Naval Hospital, Haslar, impressed her. At the end of a wide, gravelled path, flanked on both sides by elm and maple trees was a large, brown-stoned, three-storey building. Its intricately designed pediment embossed with the Royal Coat of Arms dominated the dull grey skyline. This imposing frontal façade consisted of three floors, the first two floors having three windows. The top ones were much smaller than those below. These were slightly arched and much longer. All the windows were criss-crossed with white tape to prevent the spread of bomb splinters. On the ground floor sandbags covered the much smaller windows of offices. Near the main entrance were rows of blue, naval ambulances and a few private vehicles.

'That large archway at the bottom of the building you can see leads into an arcade,' said the driver, pointing with a finger. 'In Nelson's time, that's where patients were brought up in wooden carts from the jetty close to HMS *Hornet*. That's the MTB Base we passed as we came in. The iron rails in the cobble-stoned floor in the arcade can still be seen. Needless to say they're not used today but patients from the ships are still landed at the jetty and brought up to the hospital by ambulance.'

Gazing through the dimly lit arcade Nadine caught a glimpse of the rest of the hospital stretching either side of the main front. '*Mon Dieu!*' she exclaimed, 'it's much bigger than I expected.'

'As you've probably noticed,' the driver went on. 'It's shaped like a square with one end missing. When it was finished, it was the biggest brick building in Europe.'

'I can well believe it,' replied Nadine gazing around wide-eyed.

The tilly drove passed a row of ambulances outside the main entrance and turned left.

'Those blocks on your left are A and F wards,' said the driver. He then pointed out a small, but imposing red-bricked church. 'That's St Luke's,' he said. 'It's as old as the hospital itself. You can even get married there if yer want,' he added throwing back his head and laughing.

'Thank you,' Nadine replied, smiling, 'I'll try and remember that.'

They continued around a wide road and stopped at the end of a gravelled pathway leading to an old, three storey Victorian building. On either side of the path was a well-kept lawn and flowerbeds in full bloom. At the end of the path two sets of steps led up to a highly polished oak door flanked on either side by a pair of grey-stoned, Doric columns.

'Well, here we are, ma'am,' said the driver as the tilly came to halt. 'This is the sisters' quarters, or, to give it its correct title, Eliza MacKenzie House, built in 1890.'

'Eliza MacKenzie,' Nadine repeated, as she drew back the tilly door and looked up at the building. 'Who was she?'

'In 1854, she and Florence Nightingale took six nurses to the Crimea. The work they did was so good that in 1884, the naval nursing service was formed, so they named the sisters' mess after her. OK?'

'Thank you,' Nadine said giving the driver a friendly smile as she stepped out of the tilly, 'you certainly know your history.'

'I ought to, ma'am,' he replied as he reached behind and lifted her suitcase out onto the ground. 'My name is Len Lloyd, I'm an ex sick berth chief petty officer. After spending twenty-two years in the navy, I ought to know a thing or two about the place.'

Carrying Nadine's suitcase, he escorted her to the front door.

'This is where I leave you, ma'am,' said the driver as he touched his cap. 'Good luck, to yer,' he added, touching the rim of his cap, 'I'm sure you'll settle down all right.'

Nadine thanked him and accepted her suitcase. Feeling very nervous she pushed open the door. Inside, the distinct smell of mansion polish and the faintest touch of perfumed powder filled the warm atmosphere. An elderly, sallow-faced man wearing a short white coat and blue trousers sat behind a small oak desk.

'Good afternoon, ma'am,' he said glancing down at an open book on his desk. 'You must be Sister Le Brun.' He then reached across and removed a key from a board. 'My name is Hopkins; I'm the hall porter. The matron warned me to expect you. Now, you're in room 20 on the second floor. The senior sisters are on the ground floor.' Walking around his desk he picked up Nadine's suitcase. Directly ahead of them was a long corridor. Nodding towards it, he continued, 'The dining room is down there on the right, next to the matron's office. She left a message asking you to report to her at 0900 tomorrow. Now, if you follow me I'll take you to your quarters. Dinner at 1900, breakfast between 0730 and 0800.'

When they arrived outside Nadine's door Hopkins opened it and handed her the key.

'If you need anything, ma'am,' he said with a smile, 'you know where I am.'

'Thank you,' replied Nadine and went inside.

After unpacking Nadine lay down on her bed and despite feeling excited at her new surroundings, soon fell asleep. It was just after 1800 when she woke up. She took a shower and changed into a long-sleeved white blouse, pleated grey skirt and black matching flat-soled shoes, then made her way downstairs. In doing so the distinctive smell of cooking filtered around her nostrils. She felt too nervous to eat but thought it best to make an effort to meet some of her colleagues.

The wallpaper of the dining room was brightly decorated in pale yellow and green. The room was quite spacious and well lit by

95

a glittering crystal chandelier. Two bay windows with their blackout curtains drawn, overlooked the lawn. Highly polished brown linoleum and a dark green carpet covered the floor. A long table with a pristine white tablecloth lay in the middle of the room. In the centre of the table rested a shiny silver candelabrum.

A group of nursing sisters were sat down on either side of the table. Some were eating while a team of Officers' Wren stewards, wearing white aprons, served others with their food.

My goodness, thought Nadine, staring around, compared with the sparseness of Paris General, this looks more like a banqueting hall. One or two nurses looked up, nodded and gave her a pleasant smile. A blonde girl, waving a piece of bread, beckoned Nadine to a chair next to her.

'Come and sit down, love,' she said in a pleasant northern accent. 'You look as if you could do with a nice cup of tea.'

An attractive brunette sitting next to the blonde grinned and added, 'Be careful, dear, she'll be after your chocolate ration.'

The attitude and welcome banter immediately made Nadine feel relaxed. With a nervous smile, she sat down.

'Anne Patterson,' said the blonde, as they shook hands. With an inquisitive expression in her dark green eyes, she went on, 'You sound foreign, if you don't mind me asking, love, where are you from?'

'France,' Nadine replied. 'I worked in Paris before I came here.'

Giving Nadine a sympathetic glance, Anne said, 'I'm from Doncaster, you're a long way from home, aren't you? Do you have any relatives over here?'

'Only my father,' answered Nadine, glancing nervously down at the table. 'He's in London working for the War Office.'

Giving Nadine a sympathetic look, Anne replied, 'I see…if you need anything, all you have to do is ask.'

'That's very kind of you,' Nadine graciously replied.

A fresh-faced nurse with sparkling blue eyes and short brown hair overheard Nadine and introduced herself. 'My name is Leila Hansen, I'm from Copenhagen,' she said nodding her head and smiling, 'welcome to Haslar.'

Removing a crumb from the corner of her mouth with a finger, Anne began to giggle and muttered, 'This place is beginning to resemble the League of Nations.'

Nadine smiled but didn't reply. A Wren steward appeared and politely asked her what she wanted for dinner.

'Err…just soup, please,' Nadine replied, carefully unfolding a napkin and placing it on her lap. She still felt very tired, so when the soup arrived she took a few sips and after thanking the nurses for their kindness, excused herself and returned to her room. She quickly undressed and although excited by her new surroundings, quickly fell asleep.

Nadine opened her eyes, blinked a few times and stretched out her arms. The blackout curtains on her window were drawn. The time by her wristwatch was 0700. Suddenly, she remembered her appointment with the matron. She quickly reached up and switched on her bedside light. She then lit a cigarette, and after a few quick drags, stubbed it out in an ashtray. With a feeling of excited apprehension, she flung back the bedclothes and leapt out of bed.

Fifteen minutes later she emerged from the bathroom and began to dress. After slipping into a set of dark blue cami-knickers and matching brassier, she sat down and brushed her hair. She then pinned it into a bun and applied a faint touch of lipstick and face powder. Extending each leg in turn she drew on a pair of thick, black service-issue stockings. The rough material of her suspender belt rubbed against her thighs, so she changed it for a smaller one trimmed with lace; after all, she thought with a faint smile, nobody will ever know the difference. Standing in front of the mirror she climbed into a pale blue, long sleeved shift with a white collar that hung limply against her full figure. Over this she put on a long white crisply starched apron that reached the hem of her previous garment. A wide black belt with a silver buckle firmly applied around her waist gave her figure the appearance of efficient femininity. She picked up a small blue shoulder cape trimmed with a thin red line and placed it around her shoulders. Her heart bounded with pride as she gently touched the gold anchor and Red Cross on the oblong-shaped insignia pinned to the right side. This indicated her honouree rank of lieutenant. She smiled as she carefully placed her white cap over her head and slipped on a pair of white cuffs around each wrist. She then turned and checked to ensure the seams in her stockings were straight and that her black, flat-soled rubber shoes were polished. 'Yes,' she muttered, admiring herself in the mirror. 'If Papa and Pierre were here, they would be proud of me.'

CHAPTER TWELVE

After a few brief good mornings to Leila and her colleagues, Nadine had breakfast then left the mess. By the time she arrived outside the matron's office, the time was 0855. She nervously swallowed and ran her hand down the front of her uniform and made sure her cap was straight. She then knocked gently on the door and entered.

A heavy-set woman wearing a white cap and a dark blue uniform sat behind a large oak desk. In her right she held a black fountain pen and was writing into a book. A few strands of grey hair barely visible under her cap curled loosely down the sides of her round, fleshy face. She stopped writing and looked up as Nadine came in.

'Come in, my dear and welcome to Haslar,' said the matron, putting down her pen. She stood up, displaying a stout girth and five feet stature. The deep brogue in her voice was straight from the "Emerald Isle" and the steel-rimmed glasses perched on the end of her nose exaggerated the sharpness of her small, dark brown eyes.

'My name is Matron O'Hara,' she said as they shook hands. 'To be sure,' she added with a wide smile while indicating a brown leather armchair, 'please sit down. You must be Sister Le Brun.'

Nadine thanked her and as she drew up a chair glanced around the room.

The office was quite large. On the oak panelled walls hung framed photographs of medical staff past and present. Behind the desk, cluttered with papers was a framed photograph of King George V1 and Queen Elizabeth. From a high, stuccoed ceiling neon lighting bathed the room in a clear, yellow light. A navy blue carpet embossed with tiny gold anchors covered the floor. Two armchairs, a small settee, rested under a bay window criss-crossed with white tape. A bulky green metal filing cabinet occupied one side of the room close to a hat stand from which hung a blue Burberry and gas mask.

The matron resumed her seat. Sitting forward and clasping both hands, she looked solemnly at Nadine, and said, 'I see you and your father are French. You poor thing, you must be worried sick about the fate of your country and your people.'

'Yes, I am,' Nadine quietly replied as she sat down.

Peering over her glasses the matron gave Nadine a reassuring smile. 'I am sure our country and those like yourself who have been forced to leave Europe will do all they can to help them. Now,' she said, releasing her hands and sitting back in her chair, 'how are you are settling in? Are your quarters comfortable?'

'Yes, thank you, Matron,' Nadine nervously replied. 'My room is very comfortable indeed.'

Having earlier studied Nadine's documents, the matron gave Nadine a confident smile and said, 'You seem to be eminently qualified, my dear, and we're very glad to have you.' Just then a tall, dark-haired nurse came in carrying a tray of coffee. 'Thank you, just place it here, dear,' the matron said, pushing a few papers aside from her desk. The nurse placed the tray down then turned and left the room.

'Would you care for some tea, Sister?' the matron asked, reaching across and picking up a small brown teapot.

'Merci, err…thank you, Matron,' Nadine replied, realising how dry her mouth was. 'That would be fine.'

'Splendid,' replied the matron, pouring out the drinks. 'Then we can discuss your immediate future. Do you have any particular wards you like to work on?'

'Not really, Matron,' Nadine replied, accepting a cup and saucer. 'I don't mind where I work.'

'Good,' said the matron. 'Even though it's rationed do help yourself to sugar. Now,' she added flatly, 'the sister of B1 ward has gone sick, so I think you'd better start there. Have you done much orthopaedic nursing?'

'Yes, Matron,' Nadine confidently replied, 'quite a lot.'

'Then I suggest you report there as soon as you can, dear,' replied the matron, smiling pleasantly. 'And don't hesitate to come and see me if need be.'

Nadine finished her tea, thanked the matron and left the room.

Like all the wards in Haslar, B1 was long and rectangular. Tall windows, criss-crossed with white tape allowed plenty of light. Blackout curtains lay in folds at each end waiting to be drawn before air raids. A row of twenty beds stretched on either side on a highly polished wooden floor. Heating was provided by an underground system of water piping and the walls were painted in a pleasant pastel green. Extra warmth was obtained from an ugly looking marble topped fire grate, which when fed with coal was inclined to emit fumes of foul smelling smoke, making the atmosphere, especially at night, warm and muggy. At one end of the room was a table on which rested a stainless steel steriliser. Close by was a glass cabinet containing shelves full of kidney dishes, metal syringes and an assortment of medical instruments. Next to this a door led into the sister's office. Outside the ward was a galley complete with a gas cooker, helpful for allowing night staff to make a meal. The wards were well organised and efficiently run by both ward sister and the leading hand.

Nadine quickly learned the ward routine. Unlike Paris General where civilians were employed to do the cleaning, in Haslar, the medical staff diligently carried out these duties every morning. Beds and lockers were drawn out and the floor behind cleaned and polished. The beds were then returned and aligned in neat order. Using a long-handled bumper the centre section of the ward was worked on until the oak panelled floor shone like burnished bronze.

Lockers were cleaned, water carafes changed. The sister and the leading hand would then ensure everything was "spic and span" ready for the ward doctor's daily rounds at approximately 1000.

Nadine remained on B1 ward for the next eighteen months, nursing cases suffering everything from fractured spines to amputations of lower limbs. Some of these cases were civilians injured during the bombing of Gosport.

In late 1942, after a spell of night duty, she was transferred to the Sick Officer's Block, where she was put in charge of the medical ward. On a cold November morning the matron called her into her office.

'Do sit down,' said the matron, indicating a chair. She sat forward and clasped her hands together. 'I'm sorry to tell you your father was admitted to Guy's Hospital yesterday,' she said sympathetically. 'The ward sister telephoned me half an hour ago,' she paused and with a reassuring expression on her face, added, 'and from what she said, I gather he is very comfortable. Now, I suggest you take a few days' compassionate leave and go and see him.'

Sick with worry, Nadine threw a few clothes into a canvas grip and wearing her Burberry over her uniform, caught the first train to Waterloo. From here she took a taxi to Guy's Hospital.

A tall, elderly grey-haired sister showed her to a small private ward where her father lay in bed asleep. Close to the bed was a bulky oxygen cylinder attached to which was a length of red rubber tubing and celluloid mask. Close to his bed was a white, metal table on which rested his glasses, a water carafe and a tumbler.

The sister stood near the door watching as Nadine hurried to his bedside. With a sinking heart, Nadine stared down at the professor's pale face barely visible over the bedclothes.

Sensing someone was in the room, the professor slowly opened his eyes. Even without his glasses he immediately recognised his daughter and smiled.

'*Oh Papa, jai ete si inquiet de vous, comment vous sentez-vous?*' cried Nadine. (Oh Papa, I was so worried about you, how are you feeling?)

'*Je suis beaucoup mieux et il est merveilleux de vous masi s'il vous plait laissez-nous parler anglais.*' (I am much better and it is wonderful to see you, but please, let us speak English), he muttered weakly. Removing an arm from under the bedding he reached out and grasped Nadine's hand and said, 'Do not worry I am all right. Am I not Sister?'

'Indeed you are, Professor,' replied the sister, giving him and Nadine a reassuring smile. 'The heart specialist says you'll be out of bed in a few days.'

'Oh Papa,' said Nadine bending down and kissing him on the forehead. 'Tell me what happened?'

'Oh, it was nothing,' the professor replied, trying his best to make light of his plight. 'I was in the lab and felt a slight pain in my chest. Nothing much. However one of the lab technicians saw me and called an ambulance.' While he spoke tears welled up in his daughter's eyes. 'There, there, now,' the professor went on, giving Nadine's hand a slight squeeze. 'You heard what the good sister said, I'll be up and about very soon.'

After a tearful, "au revoir", Nadine kissed her father on both cheeks. She then thanked the sister and left the room. She found a small hotel close to the hospital and for the next two days visited her father twice daily. On her final visit the professor, clad in an old green woollen dressing gown, was able to walk with her to the end of the corridor and say goodbye.

The following morning, tired but grateful that her father's health was improving she left London. A week later the professor was discharged from the hospital and although the heart specialist was still monitoring his condition, he was able to resume work at the university.

All this happened almost four months ago.

At 1100 on the morning of Monday 4 July, Nadine was summoned to the matron's office. Dreading the thought that her father might have had another heart attack, she knocked on the door and entered. To her surprise and relief, she saw two dark suited gentlemen sitting in the armchairs, quietly sipping coffee. Still holding their cups both men stood up when Nadine entered the room.

One of the men was tall, straight-backed with thick well-groomed grey hair, and a narrow, tanned face. The gold and green striped tie he wore with a white shirt suggested either a military connection or club membership. The other man was small and stout with a pale, fleshy face whose shiny bald head ringed with the remnants of fair hair, gave him a monk-like appearance. His dark red tie and cream coloured shirt matched a maroon waistcoat that failed to hide a more than ample waistline. Looking incongruous against the matron's dark blue cape and gas mask, two black overcoats, umbrellas and a pair of shiny bowler hats, hung from a corner hat stand.

'Good morning, Sister,' said the matron, rising from behind her desk. 'Sorry to drag you away from your duties only these two gentlemen have come to see you. They're from the, err...the government.'

'*Mon Dieu!*' exclaimed Nadine staring anxiously at the two men. 'What is wrong? Has something happened to my father?'

'No, no,' interrupted the taller of the two raising a hand. He like his colleague had placed their cups and saucers on a nearby table. 'Your father is quite well. Please allow me to introduce us. I am Sir Reginald Templeton.' He spoke in a clipped manner typical of an army officer or civil servant. 'This gentleman here,' he added, nodding towards the smaller man, 'is Archibald Crossley. He and myself work for British Intelligence.'

The words, "British Intelligence" immediately startled Nadine. A feeling of foreboding slowly crept over her. As they shook hands she felt her heart pound like an express train against her ribs.

Displaying a row of small, uneven white teeth, Crossley smiled and in a deep, plumy voice, said, 'Please don't look so disturbed, Sister, we've not come here to lock you up in the Tower.'

'Then, why *are* you here?' Nadine demanded, staring inquisitively at both men.

At that moment the sound of matron giving a slight cough while pushing back her chair, drew their attention.

'Perhaps,' she said, walking around her desk, 'I think it would be wise if I left and let you discuss things in private.' She made her way across the room and opening the door, turned, looked at Nadine and added, 'I'll be with the mess cook discussing the weekly menu if needed.' She smiled benignly at the two men then left the room.

'Perhaps we should all sit down,' said Sir Reginald looking pensively at Nadine. Both men used the armchairs while Nadine sat on the settee.

'Sister Le Brun,' said Sir Reginald Templeton, opening a small silver cigarette case and offering one to Nadine. 'Has your father ever discussed his work with you?'

'Err...yes he has,' replied Nadine, looking up while accepting a light from Templeton. 'I believe he was working on a new form of mustard gas.'

Both men glanced alarmingly at each other.

'Indeed,' Crossley replied furtively. 'And did he go into details?'

'Not really,' Nadine slowly replied. 'Only to say it was more deadly than that used in the last war.'

Furrowing his brow, Templeton took over the conversation. Flicking ash into a brass ashtray, he looked at Nadine, and in a stern voice, said, 'What we're about to tell you is top secret. Do you understand?'

'Yes, I do,' Nadine replied glancing suspiciously at both men. 'But what has all this to do with myself and my father?'

For the next twenty minutes Nadine listened intently as first Templeton then Crossley, informed her about plans to send the professor to America via Canada.

'The professor's knowledge of mustard gas is badly needed by the Americans,' said Templeton. 'And *Zimba* is one of our most modern warships. I can assure you, he'll be well looked after on the journey.'

'But *why* is my father badly needed?' Nadine asked, frowning as she nervously stubbed out her cigarette. 'Surely the Americans have their own scientists capable of doing his work. Why not inform them by letter or even a secret telegram?'

'Can't take the risk,' cautioned Templeton. 'Either might be intercepted by the enemy, and besides, the Americans don't possess anyone with your father's expertise.'

'The Prime Minister is adamant that the professor must be sent to them. And that my dear,' added Crossley sitting back in his chair and raising both hands, 'I'm afraid is final.'

'What has my father to say about all of this?' asked Nadine, accepting another cigarette from Templeton.

'At first he was reluctant to go,' replied Templeton. 'But after we explained the importance of the mission he finally agreed.' After a slight pause, he added, 'The professor's train arrives at Portsmouth Harbour Station at 2345 on Monday 17 August, platform 2. Transport will pick you up outside your mess at 2245. You will meet your father and be taken into the dockyard to HMS *Zimba*. Is that clear?'

'Yes, perfectly clear,' muttered Nadine, biting her lip. 'Poor Papa, all he wanted to do was to come over to England and continue his work in peace.'

'Maybe his work will help to bring about the very peace we're all seeking,' replied Crossley, smiling confidently at Nadine.

CHAPTER THIRTEEN

The morning after her meeting with Templeton and Crossley, Nadine decided to telephone her father as soon as possible. Before doing so she took a shower. Wearing her hair bunched up beneath a rubber cap she felt the warm water invigorate her body. Turning off the shower she rubbed her body down with a large white towel. She then removed her cap and shook her glossy, chestnut brown hair allowing it to fall in small curls around the nape of her neck. Finally, feeling refreshed she caught sight of herself in the mirror and let the towel drop in an untidy heap on the floor. For a few seconds she surveyed her body, which at thirty was still neat and trim. She closed her eyes and using both hands gently squeezed her firm breasts, remembering how Pierre used to caress and kiss her nipples when they made love. Allowing a hand to run over her firm stomach onto the damp triangular mound of fine hair, she was half tempted to touch the spot Pierre used to probe and press with such tenderness. The thought momentarily made her head spin. Suddenly, the sound of someone knocking on the door broke her reveries.

'I take it you're up and about, Nadine,' came the cheerful voice of Anne Patterson. Anne occupied the room next door and had taken Nadine under her wing.

'Yes, thank you, Anne,' Nadine shouted. 'I'll be with you shortly.'

After breakfast Nadine was tempted to use the private telephone in a small cubicle at the end of the corridor to contact her father. However, a glance at her wristwatch showed she was already late for work.

Outside the mess the sky was dark and dismal and sun almost non-existent. Gathering her ankle length, blue cloak around her to protect against the cold, blustery, wind, Nadine felt her rubber-soled shoes crunch into the gravelled pathway that led past St Luke's Church to the Sick Officers' Block. This was an old two storey Victorian building on the far side of the hospital. All officers had separate cabins leading off a long corridor stretching the length of each section. Those patients requiring surgery were dealt with on the ground floor, while medical cases occupied the floor above. Surrounding the entrance was a gravelled pathway wide enough to accommodate an ambulance.

Nadine wiped her feet on a rubber mat, turned the brass handle of the highly polished oaken door, and went inside. The warmth and familiar smell of antiseptic and mansion polish had an immediate cathartic effect.

Passing the open door of the office belonging to the Sister Iris Jasper, who was in charge of Officers' Surgical, Nadine jokingly enquired, 'Good morning, Iris, all quiet on the Western Front?'

Iris was an attractive ash blonde whose boyfriend was a lieutenant in the Royal Navy. Her office was similar to the matron's except in one corner was a glass-topped trolley. The top shelf contained X-rays, a stack of buff-coloured patients' bed tickets, while on the bottom shelf rested kidney dishes and an assortment of surgical instruments.

'Good morning, Nadine,' replied Iris, looking up from behind her desk and smiling. 'No fresh cases during the night, the night duty sister's report is on your desk. Coffee in half an hour.'

'Thank you, Iris,' replied Nadine, sitting down on a chair. 'Any news of your sailor?'

'I'm hoping Larry will be back soon,' answered Iris. With a mischievous smile she lowered her voice and went on, 'With a bit of luck, we'll be able to snatch a weekend at that hotel just outside Gosport. The one I told you about.'

'You mean "The Wild Stag"?' replied Nadine, shaking her head and grinning.

'Yes, that's the place,' said Iris, who with a saucy glint in her eyes, added, 'it's at the top of the High Street. The rooms are lovely and the food's quite good. Not that Larry and I spent much time eating'.

'You shameful hussy,' laughed Nadine. 'I only hope the matron doesn't hear about it.'

'I don't care if she does,' said Iris dismissively. 'We should take what happiness we can. God knows how long this war will last.'

'Mmm...perhaps you're right,' Nadine replied, giving her friend an understanding nod of her head.

At the bottom of a winding stairway, carpeted in the ubiquitous dark blue, was a lift with two wrought-iron grill gates big enough to fit a trolley and stretcher. Near the top of the stairs a tall, fair-haired nurse carrying a tray, greeted Nadine.

'Just going to do the admiral's pressure points and make his bed, Sister.' The admiral in question was an eighty-year-old gentleman suffering from chronic gout. With a teasing expression on her face, the nurse added, 'He's a randy old devil and I'll probably have to douse his privates with a drop of camphor oil, that'll dampen his ardour.'

Nadine smiled and walked into her office which was a replica of the one downstairs except her window gave an unimpeded view of the hospital. On her desk, next to a black telephone was a small pile of patients' bed tickets and the night sister report book. As Sister Jasper had mentioned, the report didn't contain anything startling. A few minutes later a knock on the door ushered in the day staff. This consisted of a small, stout staffs nurse, a male leading hand, two sick berth attendants and two nurses. This was a daily routine during which patients' progress and treatments were discussed, prior to doctor's rounds at 1030.

After the morning briefing the staff left. Nadine stood up and closed the office door. She then sat down and picked up the telephone, waited for the dialling tone then told the operator who she was and asked to be connected to London University. Shortly afterwards a female voice came on the line and asked her what department she wanted.

'The main laboratory, please,' replied Nadine, knowing at this time of day her father would be there. A few seconds later, a male voice came on the line.

'Laboratory, who is speaking please?'

'My name is Nadine Le Brun. I am professor Goldberg's daughter,' she replied tersely, 'could I possibly speak to him?'

'Of course,' the voice said. 'Just a second, I'll get him for you.'

Nadine overheard a voice telling her father Nadine was on the line.

'Oh, tres bien!' she heard the professor cry. His tone became stronger as he picked up the receiver and said, 'Nadine, Cheri, what a lovely surprise, how are you?'

'I'm fine, Papa,' she replied. 'But yesterday I had two very important visitors about your forthcoming visit.'

The professor quickly interrupted her. 'Please Nadine,' he said, almost in a whisper. 'Be careful what you say, someone may be listening.'

'I understand, Papa,' replied Nadine, her voice full of concern. 'But are you sure you're doing the right thing, especially after your heart attack?'

'I am perfectly all right,' the professor answered calmly. 'The specialist says my heart suffered no damage, so you're not to worry. I take it you have been told about the arrangements?'

'Yes, Papa,' Nadine replied, adding anxiously, 'and remember to pack plenty of warm clothes.'

'Yes I will,' laughed the professor. 'Now I must go. I'll see you soon. I love you, Cheri, au revoir.'

Feeling tears welling up in her eyes, Nadine muttered, 'Au revoir, Papa, I love you too,' and put the receiver down.

During the next month, Nadine threw herself into her work. Two weeks before she was due to meet the professor an ambulance pulled up outside the block and Commander Peter Okey was brought in on trolley. Nadine greeted him as he was wheeled out of the lift into the corridor.

'Good morning, Commander,' said Nadine. 'How are you feeling?'

'Not to good, I'm afraid, Sister,' he grimaced. 'It's this damn chest of mine.'

'Well, don't worry,' Nadine said, giving Okey a reassuring smile. 'The duty medical officer will see you shortly, meanwhile we'll get you safely tucked up in bed.'

The diagnosis inside his bed ticket said he was suffering from left lobar pneumonia. The commander was a thirty-two, six feet plus, stocky man with dark brown hair greying at the sides. His weather-beaten features were swiftly fading as the dark smudges under his blue eyes exaggerated the paleness of his face.

With Nadine in close attendance, two nurses took Okey to a cabin and helped him off with his uniform. From his suitcase a nurse took out a pair of red silk pyjamas.

'Very fetching, I must say,' remarked one of the nurses as she helped the commander into them. 'You'll have all the nurses after you in these, sir,' she added chuckling slightly as she tucked several pillows behind him. .

'Make sure there's an oxygen bottle and mask placed at his bedside,' said Nadine as she opened Okey's medical folder and read the details on his history sheet.

Suddenly she felt her stomach contract. The man lying in bed before her was none other than the captain of HMS *Zimba,* the ship that was to take her father across the Atlantic. My God, she thought, pneumonia is a serious illness. He could be hospitalised for some considerable time. How, she wondered, will this affect the arrangements organised by Templeton and his colleague? Would another officer take command of the ship, and if so, how would this affect her father's mission?

CHAPTER FOURTEEN

'I see your ship is now minus her captain,' remarked Nadine, doing her best to sound calm.

'Yes, Sister,' Okey gasped while trying to catch his breath. 'But I expect someone else will be appointed, but goodness knows who that'll be.'

The commander's forthright reply failed to pacify Nadine. For the next few days she waited on tenterhooks to hear that the mission was either cancelled or postponed. She rang her father and told him about Okey being admitted to hospital.

'Please don't worry, Cheri,' he had said, reassuringly. 'The Royal Navy will manage, you'll see.'

Shortly after 2245 on Monday 17 August, wearing a Burberry over a thick, tweed skirt and jacket and carrying her gas mask, Nadine left the mess. Hoping the sound of the gravel crunching under her feet wouldn't be heard by anyone, she made her way down the path. As she did so, a bitterly cold wind threatened to tear off her headscarf. High above a full moon, flitting between clusters of dark clouds, bathed the hospital buildings in a pale, yellow light. Nobody was around and the eerie silence added to her apprehension.

A black staff car was parked on the road near the end of the pathway. Upon seeing Nadine approaching, the driver, who was leaning against the bonnet, stubbed his cigarette out and opened the rear passenger door.

'Evening, ma'am,' he said taking Nadine's elbow and helping her inside, 'a bit chilly but thank gawd it isn't raining.'

Nadine was surprised to see the same driver who had met her when she arrived over a year ago.

'Thank you,' she said. 'Mr Lloyd, isn't it?'

'Yes, ma'am,' he replied, touching the peak of his cap, 'and you'd be Sister Le Brun. I recognised you as soon as I saw you.'

'I see we're travelling in style, this time,' Nadine remarked as she climbed into the plush leathered back seat. 'What kind of car is this?'

'A Bentley,' replied Lloyd. 'Nowt but the best fer yer this time.'

There was very little traffic about so the journey around the harbour only took half an hour. By the time they arrived outside Portsmouth Harbour Station the time was 2240. The masts, yardarms and superstructure of various warships could be seen silhouetted against the dark grey sky.

A weary-looking ticket inspector told Nadine which platform the train from London was expected. Ten minutes later, out of the gloom she heard the sound of the train approaching. Shortly afterwards, bellowing clouds of vaporous steam, the train arrived. With a steady grind of the wheels the train gradually shunted to a standstill. A few seconds later compartment doors opened and several passengers stepped onto the platform. Among them was a group of noisy sailors returning from the fleshpots of London. Behind them, wearing an overcoat and a grey homburg stood the professor. He was carrying a suitcase and looked slightly lost. Upon seeing him Nadine's face broke into a broad smile.

'*Papa! Papa!*' she cried, waving a hand while running along the platform. Ignoring a chorus of wolf whistles from the sailors, she threw her arms around the professor and kissed him on the cheek.

'*Bonjour, Papa*,' she cried, catching her breath, 'merveilleux de vous revoir allait. Comment c'est passé votre voyage?' ('Hello, Papa, wonderful to see you again. How was your journey?')

114

'Long et fatiguant, moi suis huereux de vous voir, comment allez vous?' (Long and tiresome, but I'm glad to see you. How are you?') replied the professor, giving her a hug.

Taking hold of his suitcase, she replied, 'Je suis bon et j'espere que vous etes aussi.' (I am well and I hope you are too.)

Outside the station Mr Lloyd was standing by the Bentley smoking a cigarette. Seeing Nadine and her father he opened the passenger door allowing them to enter.

'Let me have that, sir,' said Lloyd, taking hold of the professor's suitcase. After stubbing his cigarette out, he opened the boot and placed the suitcase inside. He then climbed into the car. 'I'm to take you to HMS *Zimba,*' he said over his shoulder. 'She's at Fountain Lake Jetty, sir, ain't that right?'

'Yes,' replied the professor, staring at the driver's reflection in his rear-view mirror. 'Do you know where it is?'

'Oh yes, I do sir,' replied Lloyd. 'When I was in the navy I joined quite a few ships there, so I did.'

After showing their individual identity cards to a policeman Lloyd drove the car into the dockyard. Passing wharfs and the dark shapes of several warships in dry docks the car stopped at the foot of a gangway leading up to a destroyer.

'This is it, sir,' Lloyd said with a touch of pride. 'HMS *Zimba,* one o' the navy's fastest ships.'

Silhouetted against the dark grey sky, the twin funnels and superstructure seemed to tower over the wharf.

'*Mon Dieu*! muttered the professor staring out of the car window. 'It's much bigger than I thought.'

With the exception of a blue light at the top of the gangway, the ship was in complete darkness. The driver climbed out and opened the passenger door allowing Nadine and her father to step out onto the cobbled surface. Just then, a petty officer appeared and took hold of the professor's suitcase. 'This way, please,' he said, glancing first at Nadine then at the professor. 'And be careful, the gangway's a bit slippery.'

115

'Thank you,' replied Nadine. Turning to Mr Lloyd she asked, 'You will wait for me, won't you?'

'Of course, ma'am,' he replied, 'and take yer time. I'm in no hurry.'

Lloyd watched as the three figures walked up the gangway and were met by two officers. He assumed the taller of the two, who wore three gold bars on each shoulder of his overcoat, was the captain. After shaking hands and exchanging a few words Nadine and her father were led away through a hatchway.

The driver climbed back into the car, lit a cigarette and waited. Half an hour later Nadine and the captain returned. Lloyd watched as they stood facing one another. They shook hands and seemed to take quite a long time to say goodbye. Before leaving, he saw Nadine open her handbag, write something on a piece of paper and give it to the officer. She then turned away and was helped down the gangway by the same petty officer that met them earlier on. As the car drove away, Lloyd glanced in his rear-view mirror and saw Nadine look back at the ship. She then turned away, opened her handbag and brought out a lace handkerchief and dabbed her eyes.

'Are you all right, ma'am?' Lloyd enquired, giving Nadine a quick glance.

Nadine didn't answer. Instead she nodded and with a sigh, stared out of the window. Although it was some consolation to have seen that her father would travel with a doctor in close attendance, she was still worried. Luckily, the ship's captain seemed to share her concern.

Gradually, the heavy atmosphere inside the car produced a soporific effect. Nadine's eyes slowly became heavy; the last thing she remembered before falling asleep was seeing the worried expression on her father's face and the warmth in Pendleton's eyes as they said goodbye.

The next morning, shortly after nine o'clock Nadine was sat down at her desk. Standing next to her was a leading sick berth attendant and staff nurse. They were going through the night sister's report.

'By the way, Sister,' said the leading hand, 'Commander Okey's kit has arrived from his ship.'

'Thank you,' replied Nadine. 'Just leave it in the corridor and I'll have it sent to him.'

Earlier, during breakfast, Nadine had racked her mind thinking of a way to ask Commander Okey about Pendleton without seeming over inquisitive. She couldn't very well tell him she had been aboard *Zimba* and met Pendleton. He would be bound to ask her about the details behind her visit.

Sitting in her office, she suddenly had an idea. After the staff nurse and LSBA had left, Nadine went to see the commander. He was sitting up in bed with his head and shoulders half hidden under a copy of *The Times*. Upon hearing the door open he put down his newspaper, displaying the top of a newly laundered set of green silk pyjamas. The dark lines under his eyes had disappeared but his face remained milky white.

'Good morning, Sister,' he said cheerfully. With a wicked grin he added, 'You look more beautiful every time I see you. I do hope you've come to do my pressure areas, the hands of your LSBA are so rough.'

'Sorry to disappoint you, sir,' she said, tucking in some loose bedding. 'I've just come to tell you the rest of your kit has been sent from barracks. It arrived this morning,' she paused momentarily and doing her best to sound casual, went on, 'By the way, has a new captain been appointed to your ship?'

'Oh yes,' replied the commander. 'His name is Jeremy Pendleton, a splendid chap.'

'I take it you, err…know him, then?' she asked tentatively.

'Yes I do,' said the commander, raising his eyebrows and smiling. 'We did a gunnery course at Whale Island a few years ago. However, I must say, I was very surprised when I heard about his appointment.'

'Oh yes,' answered Nadine. 'Why was that, if it's not too personal a question?'

'Not at all,' replied the commander, pushing himself higher in the bed. 'You see, the poor chap has had a pretty rough time. First he lost his wife and son in the Blitz, then his brother, David, went down with his ship. To make matters worse Jeremy was badly injured when his ship was sunk on her way to Murmansk. When he recovered, he was sent home and given a quiet job in the Admiralty.' He stopped talking and broke into a bout of coughing. Reaching across to his bedside table he took hold of a small stainless steel mug, flipped open the lid and spat out a frothy green amount of phlegm. 'That's better,' he said wearily. After replacing the mug he flopped back into his pillows, his face covered in perspiration. 'Now where was I?' he asked, pulling out a spotless white handkerchief from his top pocket and dabbing his brow. 'Oh yes, dear Jeremy. Quite frankly, after what he'd been through I thought it unwise of the powers that be to give him another seagoing job, but there you are,' he added with a weary sigh, 'these things happen, don't they?'

'Yes,' Nadine quietly replied, 'I suppose they do.'

Now she knew the explanation for the painful, far away look in Pendleton's eyes and the meaning of his words as they said goodbye; it was the same feeling she had experienced when Pierre was killed. Suddenly she felt as if an emotional bond had sprung up between herself and *Zimba*'s new captain.

PART THREE
THE MISSION

CHAPTER FIFTEEN

Shortly after 0200 on 17 August, *Zimba* slowly nosed her way out of Portsmouth harbour. Away to starboard, Gosport and the submarine base at HMS *Dolphin* lay bathed in pale moonlight and high above, ugly grey clouds scudded across the dark sky. Dead ahead, the low, undulating hills of the Isle of Wight stood out in the darkness as the ship altered course to starboard and entered the choppy waters of the Solent.

On the bridge Pendleton turned to Carter and said, 'Increase revolutions one third, Number One, I don't intend to zigzag as I want to get clear of the Channel as soon as possible. And tell the Doc I want to see him.'

Despite the lateness of the hour, Surgeon Lieutenant Fulford was with the professor in the captain's day cabin. Much to Fulford's surprise, the warm atmosphere was tinged with the slight smell of rum. The professor was sitting in one of the two leather armchairs sipping a drink. Under a dark green woollen dressing gown he wore a set of blue and white-striped pyjamas and a pair of well-worn slippers.

'Are you sure I can't give you something to help you sleep, sir?' asked Fulford, fingering a small packet of seasick tablets in his jacket packet. 'We'll be entering the English Channel soon, and I'm informed it can get pretty rough.'

The professor blew across the top of his mug, smiled weakly and in a throaty voice, said, 'That's very kind of you Doctor, but the steward, Gale isn't it, told me that this drink called kye, would do the trick,' he paused, took another sip and licked his lips, 'and I must say, it tastes excellent. Besides, I used to do a lot of sailing in my youth, but thank you all the same.'

Fulford gave a quiet sniff and smiled realising Gale had "spiked" the professor's kye with rum.

'Then I'll wish you a goodnight, sir,' replied Fulford. He placed a piece of paper on a nearby desk and went on, 'I've written the telephone number of my cabin and the sick bay, don't hesitate to call me if you need anything.'

A knock came at the door and in came the lanky figure of Leading Steward Gale. 'Everythin' OK, sir?' he asked, looking expectantly first at the professor then at Fulford.

'Yes, thank you,' replied Fulford, giving Gale an all-knowing smile. 'The professor's just enjoying his drink before turning in.'

Fulford said goodnight to the professor and left. Blinking several times to accustom his eyes to the dark and steadying himself against the roll of the ship, he made his way to the bridge. The canvas awning offered scant protection from the bitterly cold westerly wind. Silhouetted against the dark, grey sky, the pointed hoods of the duffel coats worn by those on duty gave them the appearance of Trappist monks.

'Our guest is safely tucked in, sir,' Fulford said to Pendleton.

'Thank you, Doc,' replied Pendleton, smiling ruefully. 'Best to keep him wrapped in cotton wool until we reach Canada, eh?'

By 0300, *Zimba* entered the English Channel. Pendleton remained on the bridge, one hand resting on the arm of his chair, feeling the steady roll of the ship and listening to the monotonous beat of the engines. Close by stood Lieutenant Small making a notation in the deck-log about the state of the ship. An hourly task carried out by the OOW. Next to him Lieutenant Foster stared into the darkness unaware that the faint glow from the binnacle exaggerated the blueness of his eyes.

'What's our speed and course, Pilot?' asked Pendleton, adjusting his woollen scarf around his neck.

'Course green One, One, Oh, speed twenty-two knots, sir,' replied Lieutenant Foster.

'Alter course to red two, zero, zero, and increase speed to twenty-five knots. I want to keep well away from the French coast. The U-boat bases at Lorient and Brest are too close for comfort, and ensure the clocks go back every hour when we enter the different time zones.'

Pendleton breathed in the evocative, salty smell of the sea, a welcome change from being cooped up alongside the wharf. High above the metallic skeins of dark clouds raced across the sky. Pale rays of moonshine dappled the sea in a blanket of silver light. The hiss of the sea and the steady dip and roll of the ship was almost hypnotic. Pendleton tapped his fingers on the side of his chair wondering how long this peaceful scene would last.

'I'm going down to my sea cabin, Guns,' Pendleton said glancing sideways at Lieutenant Small. 'Call me if anything untoward happens.'

'Aye, aye, sir,' replied Lieutenant Small. At last, with only PO Jenkins and the two lookouts for company, he could relax. At 0400 Lieutenant MacIntyre and Midshipman Porter would relieve them for the morning watch. He squeezed his bulky frame into the captain's chair and placed a cigarette in his mouth. Cupping his hand against the stiff wind he managed to light it. Looking dead ahead, the sharp outline of the fo'c'sle was barely visible. As the bows sliced through the sea a line of iridescent foam coursed down either side of the ship only to disappear into the darkness. A glance behind showed the mast rolling through a slow, gentle arc against a dark sky. Astern, the ship's wake fanned out in a white, foamy mass that stood out against the inky blackness of the sea.

The bridge messenger, Ordinary Seaman Pony Moore, a spotty-faced young lad from Balham, appeared carrying a tray containing four mugs of kye. Steadying himself against the gentle roll of the ship, he passed them around.

'And about time as well,' cried PO Jenkins, allowing Lieutenant Small to accept one before grabbing a mug for himself. 'I thought you'd got lost.'

'I don't suppose you've got a digestive biscuit, ter go with this, 'ave yer, Pony?' shouted one of the lookouts.

'Bollocks,' Pony sarcastically replied, and turned away.

Lieutenant Small grinned and took a sip. 'Pay no attention, Moore,' he said, 'I can assure you the kye is more than welcome.'

Except for steady hub of the engines and gentle roll of the ship, everything was calm and peaceful.

Lieutenant Small took a drag of his cigarette, exhaled and watched as the smoke quickly dispersed in the wind.

Feeling in a philosophical mood, he turned to PO Jenkins, and said, 'Odd, isn't it, PO?'

With an inquisitive expression, PO Jenkins replied, 'What's odd, sir?'

The officer sat back in his chair. 'Here we are in a metal box,' he said pensively, 'containing almost two hundred men, cramped together like sardines, whose sole purpose is to kill people.'

'That's putting it a bit strong, ain't it, sir,' Jenkins answered, shaking his head. 'Wot about the Jerries, they'd just as soon kill us.'

'Yes, I know,' the lieutenant sighed wistfully. 'But somehow it all seems so unnatural.'

'I won't be so if we're hit by a bloody torpedo,' Jenkins replied, laughing. 'If yer ask me, Pony must 'ave put summat in yer kye, sir.'

'Mm…' Small muttered thoughtfully. 'Maybe he should have.'

The time was 0340. Dawn was slowly coming alive. A bitterly cold wind continued to whistle and rattle the cables hanging from the yardarm. Far away on the eastern horizon, a line of pale blue changed imperceptibly into a blur of white as night gradually faded away. Then, in a blink of an eye, the sun rose; daylight cascaded from the heavens bathing the sky and sea in a pale, anaemic light.

The bellies of black clouds scraped the surface of the grey, undulating waters and a new day was born.

At 0345 Lieutenant MacIntyre arrived on the bridge closely followed by Midshipman Foster. Yeoman PO Bob Jeffries came behind. Two seamen relieved the lookouts and another ordinary seaman took over the duties of bridge messenger.

'All quiet, Sam?' said MacIntyre, who despite the wind, managed to light his meerschaum pipe.

'As the grave, if you'll forgive the pun,' replied Lieutenant Small. 'Wind, direction 220, force 2-4, weather and visibility 7 and the sea swell, 21. Barometric pressure 1004 millibars, all in all, a quiet night, Mac.'

'Bloody queer, if yer ask me,' replied MacIntyre, taking a few deep puffs of his pipe. 'I've never known the English Channel to be so calm.'

'Just as well for our guest below,' answered Small. 'At least he'll get a good night's sleep, lucky...'

From the Radar room, the tired voice of Leading Seaman Buck Taylor, interrupted him. 'Large group of surface ships approaching green 120, roughly ten miles away, sir,' he cried in a rich, cockney accent.

'Thank you, Taylor,' replied MacIntyre. He then grabbed the captain's voice pipe and pressed the buzzer.

'Yes,' came Pendleton's muffled reply.

MacIntyre quickly reported the approaching vessels.

'Probably a convoy,' said Pendleton, who was already reaching for his sea boots, 'I'll be up immediately.'

Wresting with the toggles of his duffel coat, Pendleton arrived on the bridge. Using his binoculars he quickly scanned the horizon directly ahead.

'Mastheads, green four oh, sir,' cried one of the lookouts, 'looks like a convoy.'

By this time the sun was up and the sky, a low-lying ceiling of grey, cirrostratus clouds.

'Looks like a fairly small one, sir,' remarked Lieutenant Small who had remained on the bridge

'They're probably coming from the Med,' muttered Pendleton, peering through his binoculars.

'I've counted more than twenty ships and an escort of four destroyers, sir,' shouted the starboard lookout. 'And they're closing fast.'

Buck Taylor abruptly interrupted the lookout. 'Aircraft approaching, red two oh, sir, roughly 6,000 feet,' he yelled, 'about a dozen of 'em. They look like Stukas.'

'*Bugger!*' exploded Pendleton. 'This is just what we didn't want. Sound action stations. Increase revolutions one third.'

The reaction to the alarm bell was automatic and instantaneous. Men, sleeping in hammocks, tables or the deck, woke up, grabbed their gear and hurried to their action stations. In a few minutes all departments were manned.

'D'yer hear there,' said Pendleton over the tannoy. 'This is the captain speaking. A convoy has been sighted on our starboard bow and enemy planes are approaching. I intend to increase speed and pass the convoy as quickly as possible. However, all guns stand by to fire in case we are attacked.'

While listening to Pendleton's address, Fulford grabbed his medical valise and dashed from his cabin. By the time he reached the sick bay the first aid party were closed up. This consisted of PO Steward Knocker White, Officers' Steward Jock Thompson and PO Writer Harry Potts. All three were sitting on the deck, smoking. SBA Channon was sitting at the doctor's desk. Everyone looked at the doctor as he entered the sickbay.

'I've reported the medical party to the bridge, sur,' said Channon, rising from his chair.

'Good,' snapped Fulford. 'I'll be with the professor if you need me.'

The doctor left the sick bay and entered the after deckhouse passageway. Steadying himself, he managed to undo the clips of the hatchway and step outside. Blinking against the early morning glare, he made his way along the upper deck. After opening the citadel hatchway, he made his way down a steel ladder, along a passageway to the captain's day cabin. He knocked and went inside.

Professor Goldberg was sat in his armchair wearing his usual green woollen dressing gown and pyjamas. One hand gripped the side of his chair, and the other held a mug of kye. His white hair was an untidy mess and his spectacles, normally perched on the end of his nose rested on a nearby table. His face was ashen and his eyes, tired and anxious. He looked up as Fulford entered.

'How are you feeling, sir?' Fulford asked.

'A little fatigued,' replied the professor licking his lips and smiling. 'But Gale is looking after me very well.'

Leading Steward Gale, wearing a lifebelt, stood close by.

'Everything's under control, sir,' he said. 'The professor here is just 'avin a night cap, so ter speak.'

'Thank you, Gale,' replied Fulford. Looking at the professor, he went on, 'I just thought I'd come and see if you needed anything, sir.'

Suddenly, the ship lurched forward, dipping and diving as it bounded through the sea. Gale and Fulford clutched hold of a table. The professor leaned forward and grabbed his mug with both hands but failed to prevent spilling some of it onto his dressing gown.

'I'm afraid we might be in for a rough night, sir,' said Fulford apologetically. 'We may even be attacked so I suggest,' he went on shooting a quick glance at Gale, 'that you get dressed and put on a life jacket. Just in case, you understand…'

'Of course,' replied the professor, accepting a cloth from Gale. 'I'll do whatever you say, and thank you for your concern.'

The buzzing of a telephone on the bulkhead interrupted him. Fulford walked across and unhooked it. Before he had time to speak, Pendleton's voice barked, 'Captain speaking, who is that?'

'Surgeon Lieutenant Fulford, sir,' answered the doctor. 'I'm with the professor. Gale is also with him. He seems to be bearing up quite well.'

'Splendid, I thought I'd check to see how he is,' Pendleton replied, his voiced now more calm. 'Give him my regards and keep me informed.' He then hung up.

'That was the captain, sir,' said Fulford, once again steadying himself. 'He sends his regards and hopes you're not too uncomfortable.'

The professor nodded his head, allowing a few strands of white hair to fall over his furrowed brow. 'Thank you, Doctor, but I expect this is going to be a long voyage. Tell the captain not to worry so much about me, and I'm sure you have other responsibilities to attend to.' He paused and gave Gale a grateful smile. 'As you can see, the steward here is looking after me very well.'

'I'm sure he is,' Fulford replied, cautiously sniffing the air.

By this time the convoy was several miles away on the port beam. The early morning sun had disappeared behind low-lying clouds. The wind had increased churning the dark green waters into a mass of white-topped, angry waves. *Zimba* continued to approach the convoy.

All eyes on *Zimba*'s bridge focussed on the V formation of black dots visible in the grey sky.

Suddenly, the guns from the escorts and ships in the convoy opened fire. Red and green tracer bullets arced into the sky. Instantly, the sky became a patchwork of black puffs of smoke as shells exploded around the attackers.

'They're peeling off and diving on the convoy, sir,' shouted one of the lookouts.

Like gigantic black spiders, the gull-winged bombers angled down onto the convoy. Each plane appeared to select a ship. In doing so an ear splitting, banshee wail filled the air. (This sound, nicknamed the *Trumpets of Jericho* was emitted from the sirens attached to their landing gear.)

'That sound the bastards make,' yelled Yeoman PO Jeffries, grimacing while clutching his steel helmet, 'reminds me of when I was on the *Kelly* at Crete when the buggers sunk us.'

As the bombers pulled up from their dive they released a stick of bombs, each containing 4,000 lbs (250kg) of TNT. The missiles wavered then straightened up as they hurtled downwards.

The first attack missed their targets resulting in jets of white water erupting around the ships. The aircraft were now flying low over the centre of the convoy, pursued and harried by gunfire from the ships. Like rows of coloured beads, the tracer bullets followed the planes as they swooped down. The noise was deafening as each plane sought a target.

Pendleton and the others on the bridge watched as the ships, including the escorts, attempted to zigzag in an effort to avoid the hail of bombs. Fountains of water erupted all around as the bombs exploded. After each miss, a wall of watery mist hung in the air like a white shroud, before gradually settling down into a fizzy white whirlpool.

'Shall we open fire, sir?' Lieutenant Small asked eagerly. 'The convoy looks like they could do with all the help they can get.'

Pendleton was only too aware that everyone else on the bridge overheard Small's request.

'I'm well aware of that, Guns,' Pendleton flatly replied. Lowering his binoculars he reached for the engine room voice pipe. The gruff voice of Chief ERA Grundy answered. 'Tell the engineer officer I want full speed,' shouted Pendleton. 'And say I will accept responsibility for any damage to the engines.' He narrowed his eyes and with a look of determination, glanced at Lieutenant Small, then at the First Lieutenant. 'There's your answer, gentlemen,' he replied warily. 'Much as I would like to engage the enemy, as you know, I have my orders.'

'Why aren't we stoppin' ter help them?' shouted one of the men.

'Search me, matey,' replied his oppo' shaking his head in disbelief. 'Gawd only knows what the lads in the convoy will think of us.'

Midshipman Porter echoed the gun's crew's sentiments. Turning to the captain, he nervously said. 'Are we going to slow down and pick up the survivors, sir?'

'You heard my orders, Mid,' Pendleton retorted. 'Now carry on with your duties.'

Midshipman Porter gave the First Lieutenant and Gunnery officer an embarrassed glance and moved away.

At that moment, another Stuka was hit. Pieces of wings and fuselage flew into the air as it plunged into the sea. Suddenly, without regrouping, the enemy aircraft turned away and in a matter of seconds disappeared in the direction of the French coast.

Men on *Zimba*'s upper deck men watched helplessly as black smoke billowing from several of the stricken merchantmen curled high into the air.

'Surely we could have done summat,' muttered one of the Oerlikon gun's crew.

Nobody replied. Instead they stood in silence, confused and feeling slightly ashamed.

'Do you mind if I smoke?' Pendleton politely asked, taking a packet of cigarettes from his pocket and offering one to the professor.

'Not for me,' said the professor with a tired smile. 'But I hope you won't mind if I remain in my bed. It somehow feels safer.' As he spoke the ship lurched sharply to port, before slowly righting itself.

'Yes, of course,' replied Pendleton, holding on to his chair. Lighting his cigarette he went on, 'Is Gale looking after you? Is there anything you want?'

The professor shook his head and with a satisfactory smile said, 'Everything is fine thank you Captain.'

'Are you warm enough?' Pendleton enquired. 'It's very cold outside and I expect when we reach Iceland the barometer will drop below freezing point.'

The professor smiled benignly. Placing a hand inside his dressing gown, he said, 'Nadine reminded me to pack my long johns and a few sweaters, so I'm quite all right, thank you.'

Since leaving Portsmouth, Pendleton had been too preoccupied with events to think about the professor's daughter. Suddenly, the mention of her name brought back the memory of the desperate expression in her eyes as they said goodbye. The note she gave him was still safely tucked in the inside pocket of his jacket. For a fleeting moment, he was tempted to put his hand inside his duffel coat and reassuringly touch it. Instead, he settled back in his armchair and took a deep drag of his cigarette.

'How long has your daughter been married?' he said, trying his best not to sound too interested. 'I noticed she was wearing a wedding ring.'

The professor pursed his thin lips, then in a quiet voice, replied, 'Nadine is a widow. Pierre Le Brun, her husband was a Lieutenant in the French Navy.' He paused and sighed wearily. 'They met in January 1939. She was a nurse at Paris General Hospital. Three months later they were married. Alas, soon afterwards his ship hit a mine in the English Channel and he was killed. They had no children…' His voice trailed away.

Pendleton received the news of Nadine's widowhood with a mixture of relief and sorrow. After all, he knew only too well what it was like to lose a loved one.

'I'm sorry,' Pendleton answered, feeling slightly embarrassed. 'I didn't mean to pry. She, err… speaks English very well,' he added, trying to change the subject.

'Yes,' replied the professor, 'Catrina, her mother was educated in England. She taught Nadine the language. But what about yourself, are you married?'

Pendleton slowly shook his head and briefly told the professor about losing his family and brother.

Raising both hands in a gesture of despair, the professor cried, 'Je suis navre, I am terribly sorry, Captain. This war has given us all crosses to bear, has it not, my friend?'

'Yes, indeed,' Pendleton solemnly replied. 'It certainly has.' He cleared his throat, sat back in his chair and went on, 'As you probably know I have been briefed about your mission to America. But tell me professor, I thought mustard gas was outlawed by the Geneva Protocol in 1925.'

The professor smiled weakly and shook his head. 'So it was Captain, so it was,' he replied. 'But like the Hun has done on many occasions, Germany ignored such rulings. As you may know Hitler used mustard gas against the British at Dunkirk.'

'Yes, I do,' answered Pendleton. Reaching across to a nearby table he flicked ash into a heavy brass ashtray. 'And I'm told it can be lethal if large amounts are contacted.'

'Yes, Captain,' the professor ruefully replied. 'It is also a very powerful carcinogenic agent. The name is derived from the mustard plant, hence the pungent odour it emits. The yellowish gas can penetrate all clothing causing a multitude of burns involving massive yellow pustules on the body, hands and genitals. Anyone receiving fifty percent or more burns usually dies.'

'Great Scott!' exclaimed Pendleton, leaning forward, 'if the Germans used it again it could decimate a whole army. How long have we known about it?'

'Two German scientists Lommel and Steinkopf first developed it on a large scale in 1916 for use by the army,' answered the professor coldly. 'They used it at Ypres. The British retaliated by using it at Cambrai in 1917, then again in 1918 against the Hindenburg Line,' he paused, shrugged his shoulders, and raising both hands in supplication, added, 'so you see, Captain, both countries have been equally guilty.'

'I see,' replied Pendleton, stubbing out his cigarette. 'But tell me sir, what is the treatment, if any?'

'Applications of mild washing up liquid warm soapy water,' replied the professor. 'But, like all types of burns, sepsis is the main danger. The other problems are the development of chronic chest, eye infections and of course, cancer.'

'And now the Americans want your help to produce it in bulk in case it is used against us again,' said Pendleton, 'am I right, sir?'

Peering keenly over his glasses, the professor slowly nodded his head and replied, 'Yes, you're quite right, Captain. But let us pray to God it's never used again.'

Stand Easy, blaring over the tannoy interrupted their conversation. This was followed by a knock on the door and Gale came in holding a large mug.

'Excuse me, sir,' he said, looking at Pendleton. 'But I thought the professor would like a drink.'

'I'm sure he would,' he replied. 'I was just about to leave.' Smiling at the professor, he added, 'If you need anything, sir, just let me know.'

After the comparative warmth of his day cabin, the bitterly cold wind as Pendleton arrived on the bridge felt like a sheet of ice.

'What's our course and speed, Pilot?' he asked, tightening his woollen muffler.

'Three-twenty south, sir, twenty-five knots,' replied Lieutenant Foster. Glancing ominously at the black clouds racing across the sky, he added, 'The barometer's dropping and it looks like we're in for a bit of a storm.'

As if to confirm this a sudden gust of bitterly cold wind sent pellets of icy spray hurtling over the bridge.

'Rig emergency lifelines, Number One,' Pendleton shouted, at Carter, 'and pipe hands keep clear of the upper deck.'

'Aye, aye, sir,' answered the First Lieutenant, nodding towards the duty quartermaster to carry out the captain's order. 'By the way, sir how's our guest?'

With a faint smile, Pendleton replied, 'He'll be quite all right. Gale appears to be doing a splendid job.'

'I must say,' Carter said, using the back of his gloved hand to wipe away water from his face, 'I didn't get a very good look at his daughter, but what I saw impressed me.'

'Really,' answered Pendleton, raising his eyebrows. 'You do surprise me. I thought you were engaged to that Wren in Plymouth.'

'I'm not married yet, sir,' Carter replied with a grin. 'But for someone like her, who knows…'

Glancing pensively at Carter, Pendleton said, 'I'm going to my cabin for a while. Call me if you need me.'

Despite the dull glow from the three bars of the electric fire attached to the bulkhead, Pendleton's cabin felt cold and damp. He took off his wet duffel coat, hung it up and sat down. Feeling inside his jacket pocket he took out a small piece of paper folded neatly in two. On it was written, *"Sister Nadine Le Brun. Officers' Medical Ward, or Sisters' Staff quarters, RNH Haslar extension 44"*.

For a few minutes Pendleton stared at the note. Even though it had been written quickly, the handwriting was small and neat. Still staring at the paper, he sat back in his chair and took a deep breath. Since the death of Martha and Harold, not only had his

136

interest in sex disappeared, he had hardly given women a second glance. Now, here he was, looking at a message from a comparative stranger, who, despite the brevity of their meeting, had stirred feelings inside him that had long since laid dormant. Would it be wise to see her again, he asked himself. If he chose, the message could be the catalyst that might bring them together. However, deep down he couldn't help sensing he was betraying the memory of his wife. Reaching inside his pocket for his cigarette, he gave a deep sigh, hoping she would understand.

CHAPTER SEVENTEEN

Throughout the next forty-eight hours the wind increased, howling eerily through the masts and rigging. Day and night merged into one. Jagged fingers of fork lightning lit up the horizon and angry waves hammered the ship as she corkscrewed through the heaving sea.

'Much more of this and I'll transfer to the army,' groaned Midshipman Stockford-Johnson.

He and Sub Lieutenant Coburn were sharing the middle watch. (Midnight to 0400.) The heavy roll of the ship, the cold blackness of the night and the roar of the wind all contributed to the young midshipman's dismal mood. Their oilskins and those of Joe Jenkins, the duty PO and two lookouts glistened with spray. Faint traces of a pale yellow moon peeked from above as black angry clouds raced across the sky. Lines of foam, barely visible in the dark, streaked down the sides of the ship. Waves, rising above the lee side, curled high onto the fo'c'sle before sweeping along the deck like an uncontrollable tide race.

'Oh do stop moaning, Mid,' replied Coburn, shielding his face from yet another flurry of icy spray. 'We'll soon be in Reykjavik. At least this weather is keeping the U-boats at bay and preventing any of those damn Focke-Wulf Condors from spotting us. So count your blessings.'

Despite feeling the effects of mal de mer, Fulford decided to visit the professor. The time was 0900. Five minutes later after splashing his face with cold water, he entered the captain's cabin. The professor was lying on his bunk. Under his dressing gown he wore his pyjamas and slippers.

'Good morning, sir,' said Fulford. 'Perhaps you'll allow me to examine you once this atrocious weather calms down?'

'Of course,' replied the professor, pushing himself up with his elbows. 'And don't be so concerned, I'm feeling quite well.'

Shortly before 0700 on Saturday 20 August, *Zimba* approached Reykjavik, a massive, natural anchorage situated on the southwest coast of Iceland. In 1940, the British Army had occupied the town. A year later the American Forces took over and built a formidable refuelling base for the many convoys conveying precious cargos to hard-pressed Russia. Evidence of this was the presence of many merchant ships and their escorts, who, having been refuelled awaited orders to sail.

The rooftops of Reykjavik stretching away from the harbour were barely visible in the early morning mist. Dark clouds hid a pale orange sun, and in the distance a snow capped mountainous range dominated the dull skyline. A strong westerly wind whipped up the waters as the ship sailed into Faxa Bay.

'Hands to harbour stations, Number One,' snapped Pendleton. 'Reduce revolutions two third, port five, slow ahead.' His orders were shouted below to Chief Coxswain Jack Tolby in the wheelhouse, who repeated the instructions.

'It looks like the Americans are expecting us, sir,' commented Carter, peering through his binoculars at two naval officers waiting on the jetty. 'How long do you think we'll be here for?'

'We'll be off as soon as we're fully refuelled,' Pendleton replied. 'With a bit of luck we'll be well into the Atlantic by this evening.'

Twenty minutes late *Zimba* was secured alongside the jetty, the gangway was lowered and the American officers came aboard. The taller of the two, a swarthy, well-built commander, led the way. Behind him was a small, fresh-faced lieutenant who, as he walked up the gangway glanced inquisitively at the ship he knew was on a secret mission. Over their uniforms they wore grey greatcoats with silver epaulets donating their rank. As was customary in the

139

American navy, both officers first saluted the flag on the quarterdeck and then the officers waiting to receive them. Pendleton and Carter returned their salutes shook hands and introduced themselves.

'Commander Harry Perrelli,' replied the taller of the two Americans whose southern drawl reminded Pendleton of John Wayne. 'I'm in charge of the port and this officer,' he added glancing at his companion, 'is my Exec, Lieutenant Josh Perkins.' Lowering his voice slightly, he went on, 'We're well aware of your mission, Commander. It's all very hush-hush, as you Brits say. But I thought we'd pay you a visit to tell you I've ordered your ship to be oiled and re-fuelled straight away, and to see if you need anything else.'

'Splendid,' retorted Pendleton, obviously pleased with the efficiency of his American cousins. 'There isn't anything we need, but perhaps I offer you both a spot of tea?'

Glancing craftily at his smaller counterpart the commander grinned and said, 'Only if you add some of that rum I've heard so much about, we're told it keeps your sailors warm in this weather. Isn't that so, Josh?'

'It sure is, sir,' enthused the lieutenant, blowing into his hands and stamping his feet as if to emphasize the commander's request.

Pendleton threw back his head and laughed. 'Of course,' he replied. 'And I know just the man who'll accommodate you. Now,' said Pendleton indicating with his hand, 'perhaps you'd like to meet our honoured guest? I've asked him to remain below just in case somebody ashore notices him. I realise the chances of him being recognised are slim, but I don't want to risk it.'

'Sure, I understand perfectly, Commander,' replied the American, ducking his head as he followed Pendleton through a hatchway. Several ratings stood aside as the three officers made their way along the stuffy main passageway. Outside the NAAFI shop Pendleton noticed the lanky figure of Leading Steward Gale.

'Ah, just the man,' said Pendleton. 'How is the professor?'

'He's sound asleep, sir,' replied Gale, using a hand to smooth his heavily Brylcreemed hair. 'The old boy 'asn't 'add much kip during the past few days cos of that drop of roughers we'ad and 'e's very tired.'

'Thank you, Gale,' said Pendleton. 'When he wakes up, let me know how he is, and keep the medical officer informed.' Almost as an afterthought he gave a rueful smile and went on, 'Oh and bring two cups of coffee to my sea cabin for our two guests, the same brew the professor enjoys so much. Understand?'

Gale grinned and nodded his head. 'Yes, sir, I think I know what yer mean.'

While Pendleton entertained the Americans in his sea cabin, Paddy O'Malley and CERA Bill Grundy were kept busy keeping check on the fuel intake. By 1100 all four of *Zimba*'s fuel tanks were full. O'Malley reported this to Pendleton.

After their second cup of coffee Pendleton escorted the two American officers to the brow.

'Holy smoke,' remarked Commander Perrelli, feeling a warm glow slowly penetrate his insides, 'that was the finest coffee I've ever tasted, wasn't it Josh?'

'It sure was, sir,' replied Lieutenant Perkins, his eyes slightly glazed. 'They don't have anything like that back home in Tulsa.' With a loud guffaw, he smiled at the commander and jokingly added, 'Maybe we've joined the wrong navy, eh, sir!'

No sooner had the two Americans departed than hands fell in for leaving harbour. Fifteen minutes later *Zimba* was heading into the stormy waters of the Atlantic Ocean.

'Set a course, two fifty degrees south, Pilot,' said Pendleton, 'and increase revolutions two third. I want to be about two hundred miles off the coast of Greenland within the next forty-eight hours. And tell the Doc I want to see him.'

'Very good, sir,' answered Lieutenant Foster. He immediately telephoned the sick bay and spoke to Fulford. He then retreated to his maps laid out on a small table in a recess behind the bridge, and worked out the ship's course and speed.

A few minutes late Fulford came onto the bridge shivering against the harsh wind, wishing he had worn his duffel coat.

'You sent for me, sir,' he said, slightly out of breath.

'Yes, Doc,' replied Pendleton, 'How's our guest after that drop of rough weather we had yesterday?'

'He appears to be very well, sir,' replied Fulford. 'I'll be seeing him again this morning.'

'Good,' answered Pendleton. Glancing cautiously at Fulford, he went on, 'We won't be reaching Halifax for another four days. It's important he is well when we arrive there.'

'I understand, sir,' Fulford replied, realising the safe arrival of the professor to Canada was vital to the mission.

Half an hour later Fulford was standing in the captain's cabin. The professor wearing his usual dressing gown over a yellow woollen sweater and grey trousers was sat in an armchair sipping a cup of tea.

'Now that the weather is calmer, I thought I'd come and see how you are,' said Fulford. 'I'm sorry I didn't stay longer yesterday,' the doctor added apologetically. 'But I regret to say I'm not the best of sailors. How are you feeling?'

'Please don't apologise,' replied the professor raising a hand, 'I'm perfectly all right. Gale is still looking after me very well.'

'Err…would you mind terribly if I examined your chest?' said Fulford, quickly adding, 'just routine you understand.'

The professor took a sip of his tea and placed the cup on a table.

'Of course not,' replied the professor giving Fulford a pleasant smile.

The professor stood up, removed his dressing gown and slipped his sweater over his head revealing a painfully thin body, and a chest covered in curly white hairs.

'I take it you want to listen to my heart?' said the professor, smiling while placing dressing gown and sweater across his chair. 'Shall I sit down?'

'Yes please,' replied Fulford. He then opened his medical valise and took out a stethoscope and a narrow rectangular box containing a sphygmomanometer. This was an apparatus used for taking a patient's blood pressure. It consisted of an inflatable cuff and a mercury unit called a manometer to which rubber tubing with a valve was attached. The doctor placed the stethoscope head at the brachial artery situated at the bend of the elbow. Listening with the stethoscope, the cuff was inflated until the sound of the blood was occluded. The valve was slowly released until the blood was heard returning to normal. This is called the *Systolic pressure* and is read off the manometer. In a healthy heart is usually 120 mm of mercury. When the pitch of the blood disappears, this is called the *Diastolic pressure* and is normally 80mm.

The professor sat quietly as Fulford fastened a rubber cuff around his bicep. The silver metal end of the stethoscope head felt cold on the professor's skin. The doctor inflated the cuff while listening to the sound of the professor's heartbeat. With a frown, he noted that both *Systolic* and *Diastolic* pressures were slightly raised.

Fulford removed the stethoscope's earpieces and using his hands, tapped the professor's chest, listening and feeling for any abnormality. Replacing the earpieces, he listened to the professor's lungs and found them clear. He then concentrated on the professor's heartbeat. At first it was steady and regular. Then, suddenly, the "rub-dub" rhythm became slightly louder and irregular. This sudden alteration of the professor's heart rate alarmed Fulford. He then listened to other areas of the professor's heart. Once again, the beat was interrupted by a slight pause, before continuing normally. Wearing a slight frown, he slowly stood back and removed the stethoscope, allowing it to hang loosely around his neck.

'You look worried,' remarked the professor. 'Is there anything wrong?'

'You have an irregular heartbeat,' Fulford replied. 'Did the specialist you saw before we sailed ever mention it?'

'Yes, he did,' said the professor, salvaging his cup of tea before it toppled over. 'He called it sinus arrhythmia. He said it sometimes occurred normally and was nothing to worry about.'

'The specialist was quite right,' replied Fulford. 'But when it happens do you suffer from chest pain or difficulty in breathing?'

The professor shook his head and laughingly replied, 'Not really, but at my age I sometimes get out of breath when I do anything too strenuous.'

'Well,' said Fulford, placing his instruments inside his valise. 'We'll just have to keep a careful eye on things, but I'm sure it's nothing to worry about.'

'Thank you, Doctor,' replied the professor putting his empty teacup on the table and reaching for his sweater. 'That's very re-assuring.'

Fulford hoped his words had sounded convincing, but on his way back to the sick bay he knew that given the professor's medical history, he could suffer a cardiac arrest at any moment.

The time was 1145. "Up Spirits, Hands to Dinner", had just been piped. SBA Channon was sitting at the desk reading a dog-eared copy of *Tit Bits*. He looked up as his boss entered. 'How is the old codger, sur?' Channon asked, laying down his paper and vacating his seat. 'Still in one piece, I 'ope?'

'Not really,' Fulford replied, frowning wearily as he sat down. He then explained in detail what he had discovered. 'I think you'd better take the Dicarbox apparatus to the professor's cabin, just in case. And visit the professor every few hours. Play it down a bit. Just say they're routine calls. Meanwhile, I think I'd better have a talk with the captain.'

The Dicarbox apparatus was a resuscitation unit complete with two 15cu ft of oxygen and CO2 cylinders.

Pendleton was in his cabin busily writing up the ship's log.

'Sorry to bother you, sir,' said Fulford after knocking and stepping inside, 'but there is something you ought to know.'

'Come in, Doc,' said Pendleton, putting down his fountain pen. 'Nothing serious, I hope.'

Trying not to sound too alarmist, Fulford told Pendleton about the Professor's irregular heart beat. When he had finished a serious expression spread across Pendleton's face. He sat back in his chair and in a concerned voice, said, 'Are you telling me our man is going to have a heart attack?'

Feeling his mouth suddenly become dry, Fulford replied, 'He might, sir. Channon and myself will be keeping a close watch on him. However, the professor is a very intelligent man and I don't wish to worry him unduly.'

'Yes, I see your point,' Pendleton muttered uneasily. After pursing his lips, he went on, 'I don't care if you have to move in with him as long as we get him safely into the hands of the Americans. Is that understood?'

'Yes, sir,' replied Fulford, swallowing nervously, 'I understand.'

'Good,' Pendleton answered firmly. 'If anything were to happen to the professor, the repercussions would be serious.'

CHAPTER EIGHTEEN

On the evening of 21 August, the weather worsened. Once again, flashes of lightning lit up the horizon, warning of a storm in progress. A biting northerly wind sent the masses of grey clouds racing across the darkening sky and high above, the pale yellow rays of the moon made the black, undulating sea shine like silver.

'Make sure those life lines are secure,' the Chief Bosun's Mate yelled to a group of ratings on the well deck. Clutching his sou'wester, his harsh voice was barely audible over the sound of the screaming wind.

'Maybe the silly old bugger will fall over and give the sharks a treat,' shouted Big Geordie Roberts to his oppo, Bogey Knight. Both ratings were fighting the elements while checking the soaking wet lifelines strung along the upper deck.

'The fuckin' sharks wouldn't touch 'im bellowed Bogey, wiping his face with his gloved hand. 'The silly old sod's too tough to eat.'

'What was that you said?' bellowed the Chief, glaring accusingly at Bogey.

'Nowt, Buffer,' Bogey cried. 'I just said these knots are tight and neat.'

The Buffer's obscene reply was lost in the wind.

On the bridge, both lookouts were closed up. For the umpteenth time, OOW Sub Lieutenant Coburn felt his face being attacked by blasts of bitterly cold wind. Close by stood PO Yeoman Jeffries and Midshipman Stockforth-Johnson. Huddled in a corner, trying in vain to hide from the weather was the duty messenger, Able Seaman Jumper Collins. As usual, their black oilskins were streaked with water as each dip of the ship's bow enveloped them in a cloud of icy spray.

Suddenly, the sound of the radar room intercom, barely audible over the howling wind, echoed around the bridge.

'Surface contact bearing green two zero, roughly five miles away,' said radar operator, Leading Seaman Buck Taylor.

'What do you make of it, Taylor?' asked Sub Lieutenant Coburn who was Radar and Asdic Officer.

'Could be a sub, sir,' Taylor dubiously replied, 'I'm not sure.'

'I'll come down and take a look,' said Coburn. 'Whatever you do, don't lose the blighter.'

'Shall I inform the captain, sir?' asked Midshipman Stockforth-Johnson, reaching for the intercom.

'Curb your enthusiasm, Mid,' Coburn replied dismissively. 'At least until I've taken a look. It could be a shoal of fish or even a bloody whale.'

In a matter of seconds Lieutenant Coburn descended a steel ladder, pulled back the thick, protective curtain and entered what was nothing more than a small alcove. The atmosphere was warm and claustrophobic. The stark yellow lights flickering from the asdic set and radar screens stood out against the dim, blueness of the neon. Coburn's eyes, already accustomed to the darkness, easily made out the burly figure of Taylor hunched over the radar set. Close by Asdic operator, Paddy Doyle, a thick set Leading Seaman from Londonderry, sat at a desk, earphones clamped to his head. The soporific "pinging" of the asdic could be heard echoing around the compartment.

(The sound waves of an object in the sea were picked up by a large, round dome attached under the for'd section of the hull and was transmitted to the asdic operator.)

Coburn bent down behind Taylor and studied the small black image flickering on the radar's fluorescent screen.

'Good job we received these new 10-centimetre sets, sir,' remarked Taylor without moving his head. 'They can detect a sub on the surface four or five miles away.'

Lieutenant Coburn was about to reply, when the pinging from the asdic apparatus suddenly became louder. 'I think it's turning around and heading towards us,' yelled Paddy Doyle. At the same moment Coburn noticed a sudden increase in the wavy motions on the radar screen.

Coburn felt beads of sweat trickle down the sides of his face. 'I think it is a sub,' he muttered. 'Both of you keep a good watch. I'd better inform the captain.'

As Coburn arrived on the bridge he unhooked the captain's intercom.

'Yes, what is it?' came the calm voice at the other end.

Coburn told Pendleton what was happening. 'Shall I sound action stations, sir?'

'No,' replied Pendleton, who, fully dressed had heaved himself off his bunk. 'I'll go to the ops room and see for myself.'

Both operators glanced up as Pendleton came in. The intervals between each "ping," seemed to have increased. 'How far away is it?' he yelled at Taylor.

'About four miles, sir,' replied Taylor, removing one earphone. 'But it seems to have slowed down.'

'Maybe the blighter's going to dive,' murmured Pendleton, stroking the bristles on his chin. 'What do you think, Doyle?' he added, glancing guardedly at the asdic operator.

'I agree, sir,' replied Doyle. 'The ripples and arcs are flattening.'

Pendleton knew immediately what action he must take. He took a deep breath, turned and hurried onto the bridge.

Making his voice heard above the howling wind, he shouted to Sub Lieutenant Coburn, 'Alter course to red one two five, Colin, and increase revolutions two thirds. Tell engines I want everything he can give me.'

'That'll take us way off our course, sir,' cried Coburn. 'The sub could be one of ours. If it is a U-boat her captain would have a devil of a job firing accurately at us in this weather.'

Adjusting his muffler, Pendleton tersely replied. 'I'm aware of that, but I'm not taking any chances.'

Everyone on the bridge overhead everything Pendleton said. The port lookout, his red face dripping water, bent closely to the duty PO and muttered, 'Don't tell me we're running away again. I know we've got some important geezer onboard, but that don't mean we can't try and sink a bloody U-boat.'

'Pipe down,' growled the PO. 'The old man knows what he's doing.'

'You could 'ave fooled me, mate,' the lookout muttered as the ship heeled over port and increased speed.

Just as the First Lieutenant took over the watch at 0400, the pinging gradually disappeared.

'Contact has faded sir,' came Taylor's voice from below, 'and Doyle says it's gone off his radar screen.'

By Stand Easy those who knew what had happened were discussing the incident. In the senior rates' mess, PO Writer Potter glanced over his mug of tea at PO Yeoman Jeffries, and remarked, 'Surely if the captain had thought it was a U-boat he would have attacked her. Are you sure you heard right?'

'Of course I 'eard right, you dozey pen pusher,' snorted Jeffries, taking a sip of his drink. 'I may 'ave three badges on me arm but me 'earing's OK. I was standing next to the old man when he ordered the ship to alter course away from the sub.'

'Y'mean we ran away again,' muttered Pony Moore, the portly Chief Cook. 'It's gettin' to be a habit, ain't it 'Swain?' he added, shaking his head while glancing suspiciously at Jack Tolby.

'Search me, mate,' replied Tolby. 'As far as I know, we 'ave ter get this professor to Halifax all in one piece.'

149

At that moment Chief Bosun's Mate Bill Conyon came into the mess. His duffel coat was soaked and his walnut features streaked with rainwater.

'Just the man,' retorted Pony Moore. 'I hear we've sighted a bloody U-boat and the old man turned the ship away. Is that right, Buffer?'

'That's right,' the Buffer replied, rubbing his hands together. 'And remember this. We're on our own, and if we get a tin fish up our arses there'll be no bugger around to help us, so it's just as well we're well away from the bastard. Now, I 'opes you lot 'ave left me some 'o that tea, I'm freezin' me bollocks off.'

Most of the men below in the mess decks weren't even aware of the danger posed by the nearness of the U-boat. Those off duty were either in their hammocks or trying to prevent their mugs of tea from sliding off the tables as the ship corkscrewed her way through the heavy Atlantic swell.

Meanwhile, the professor's blood pressure and pulse remained higher than normal.

'I take it everything is in order?' the professor asked Channon.

'Nowt to worry about, sur,' replied Channon, clinging to the end of a table as a wave bounced against the bulkhead. 'Just you lie back and take it easy.'

At that moment Gale entered the cabin carrying a mug of kye.

Channon sniffed the air and his eyes lit up. 'Is that fer me,' he said, reaching out a hand.

'Bugger off to the sick bay and make yer own,' replied Gale, grinning while handing the drink to the professor. 'This is fer our honoured guest.'

Early next morning a faint glimmer of dawn suddenly appeared on the horizon. In what seemed like seconds, a pale blue haze rose into the sky turning the darkness of the night into dull grey. The bitter northern wind had subsided and the sea, normally wild with heavy rolling waves, was now relatively calm. However, the calmness was to prove deceptive.

On 23 August, just after 0700, the voice of Able Seaman Jumper Collins, the port lookout, yelled, 'Fog bank about five miles ahead, sir.'

Using his binoculars, OOW, Lieutenant Commander Carter, saw a massive bank of dense, bluish grey mist stretching around the base of the horizon.

'Hell and damnation!' he exploded, peering through his binoculars. 'Bloody pea soup. Thank God we're on our own,' and picked up the captain's intercom. 'I'm afraid we're heading directly into a fog bank, sir. Shall I reduce…'

Able Seaman's Taylor's strident voice coming from the radar room interrupted him.

'Large convoy sighted, dead ahead, sir,' he cried. 'Course green one two oh, speed roughly ten knots. Must be at least fifty ships, strung out in five lines of ten.'

'I heard that, Number One,' said Pendleton. 'How far away are we from Halifax?'

'About two thousand miles, sir,' answered Carter.

'That puts us in mid Atlantic, equidistant from Iceland and Canada. I'm coming up straight away, meanwhile go and check with Taylor and Doyle.'

A few minutes after Pendleton arrived on the bridge. 'Taylor's right about the convoy sir,' Carter said. 'They're heading straight for us.'

'Jesus Christ!' cried Pendleton, heaving himself up onto his chair and placing his binoculars to his eyes. 'At our present speed, we'll be among them in no time. Once inside that blasted fog we might collide with one of them.' Lowering his binoculars he glanced sideways at Carter, and in a calm voice, said, 'Alter course to 120 degrees, Number One. We won't be able to avoid the bloody fog, but we'll miss the convoy. It may mean arriving in Halifax a bit late, but that can't be helped.'

Twenty minutes later *Zimba* was enveloped in vast miasma of bone chilling vapour. In the crow's nest Slinger Wood, a two-badge able seaman had been in fog many times. A sudden feeling of isolation descended upon him. Surrounded by banks of dense, grey mist, he felt as if he were locked in a private world.

The men on the bridge could see nothing past A and B gun turrets. Glancing upwards, Pendleton remarked, 'The bloody stuff is well over mast high, Number One, better sound the siren, just in case we come across a straggler.'

A few minutes later the intermittent moan of the fog siren, added a touch of surrealism to what was already a dank, eerie atmosphere.

However, Pendleton was about to face another serious problem potentially more serious.

CHAPTER NINETEEN

SBA Channon was sitting at his desk in the sick bay, pen poised in hand, trying to compose a letter to Wendy, a buxom barmaid he had met in the Keppel's Head, Portsmouth. The time was a 2115. The shrill sound of the bosun's pipe signalling the completion of night rounds competed with the regular dull sound of the fog siren. Channon was about to continue writing when the phone rang. He reached up and unhooked the receiver from the bulkhead. 'Sick bay, SBA speaking,' he said, sitting back in his chair.

'*It's me, Windy Gale, Doc,*' shouted the leading steward. '*You'd best come quick, the old man says he can't breathe and has a pain in his chest.*'

'Right, I'm on my way,' replied Channon. 'Now calm down,' he added, flinging his pen down, 'and phone the bridge and ask the Officer of the Watch to pipe for the MO to go to the captain's day cabin chop chop. Have you got that?'

'Yeah, yeah,' Gale muttered nervously and hung up.

Channon grabbed a medical valise and left the sick bay. The ship was darkened and after parting the canvas curtains in front of the hatchway he opened the clips and went outside. The density of the fog made moving across a slippery upper deck difficult. Groping his way past the after torpedo tubes and narrowly missing the after lifeboats, he reached the citadel. As he opened the hatchway, an urgent voice cried over the tannoy:

'*Surgeon Lieutenant report to the captain's day cabin right away.*'

Upon hearing the pipe, Channon immediately left his cabin, dashed up a ladder, opened the hatchway and groped his way along the upper deck. By the time he arrived at the captain's day cabin his face and hands were numb with cold.

The professor, wearing a set of wrinkled blue pyjamas was lying down in his bunk. He had one hand over his chest and his face was ashen. It was obvious by his pained expression that he was in considerable discomfort. Gale was standing by the professor's bedside holding a glass of water in both hands. The hammer-like sound of the sea hitting the bulkhead made the cabin shake, forcing Gale to grasp the side of the professor's bunk.

At that moment Doctor Fulford arrived. He immediately felt the professor's pulse and found it full and rapid.

'I have a pain right here, doctor,' muttered the professor, gingerly touching the front of his chest. 'And I can't breathe properly...' His voice trailed away as he sank back into his pillows.

Despite the bouncing motion of the ship, the doctor managed to take the patient's blood pressure and was not surprised to discover it was dangerously high.

'Just try and relax,' said Fulford. Glancing anxiously at Gale he added, 'Get those cushions from the armchairs and settee, put them behind the professor and gently sit him up.'

Gale placed the glass he was holding on a table. He and Channon grabbed the cushions and taking hold of the professor's upper arms, did as Fulford asked.

Opening his medical valise, Fulford took out a small bottle of white tablets. He unscrewed the top and shook two of them into his palm.

'Please open your mouth and swallow these,' he said, 'they're Digitalis, the tablets the heart specialist prescribed for you.'

'Thank you, Doctor,' the professor weakly replied. With the help of a sip of water he managed to swallow them.

'I'm going to give you some oxygen,' said Fulford, reaching down the side of the bunk to where the Dicarbox resuscitation unit was resting. 'It'll help your breathing.'

Feeling the deck swaying uncomfortably, Fulford opened the lid of the box, and removed a small oxygen cylinder and placed it alongside the professor. Connected to the cylinder were an indicator gauge, a length of tubing and a rubber mask with ear attachments. Using a lever he slowly turned on the oxygen and made sure the pressure wasn't too strong, then placed the mask over the professor's nose and mouth.

'Just try and relax and breathe normally, sir,' said Fulford, adjusting the mask. 'And don't worry,' he added, giving his patient a reassuring smile, 'you've had a bad turn, but you're going to be all right.' Leaning against the side of the bunk the doctor opened his medical valise, and went on, 'I'm also going give you an injection of morphia to ease the pain.'

Fulford managed to withdraw a small glass vial from his valise. Using a tiny metal saw he removed the top. Opening a small steel box he took out a 5cc glass syringe and 2inch needle. Swaying slightly, he carefully withdrew the contents of the vial. He then expelled any excess air and using a pair of forceps, changed the needle.

'It's my heart, isn't it, doctor?' the professor murmured, as Fulford injected the morphia into the professor's upper arm.

'I...I'm not sure,' Fulford replied, nervously licking his lips. 'It's too early to tell.'

Without knocking on the door Pendleton came in. His cheeks were red with the cold and a thick muffler was tucked into the top of his duffel coat. The sight of the professor, sitting up in bed, his pallid features half covered with a mask, startled him.

'How is he, Doc?' Pendleton asked, giving Fulford a concerned look. 'What happened?'

'He's had a few pains in his chest, sir,' replied Fulford, trying not to alarm the professor. 'But he's settling down.'

Steadying himself against the roll of the ship, Pendleton managed to walk to the professor's bedside. 'How are you feeling, old boy?' he said sympathetically.

'A bit better,' the professor replied weakly. 'The pain in my chest has gone. But what is that infernal sound?'

'It's a fog siren,' replied Pendleton. 'I'm sorry if it disturbs you, but I'm afraid it's a necessary precaution.'

Taking Fulford by the arm Pendleton led him out of earshot of the professor. 'Just how serious is he?' Pendleton whispered, 'he's not going to...'

Fulford cut him short. 'I don't know, sir, the next twenty-four hours will be critical. Right now it's imperative he gets as much rest as possible, so it would help if you could reduce speed. You know what it is like in those bunks. With each sharp dip and roll of the ship you have to hang on like grim death.'

Pendleton thoughtfully stroked his chin. 'Right, Doc,' he replied. 'But as you know, we're in the middle of a fog bank and speed is essential to get our man to Halifax, but I take your point.'

'How long will it be before we reach Halifax, sir?'

'Three more days,' Pendleton replied. 'But it may take longer.'

As soon as Pendleton left the cabin, Fulford turned and gave the professor a confident smile.

'How is the pain, now sir?' Fulford asked. 'Are you finding it easier to breathe?'

'The pain has eased slightly,' the professor muttered, 'but my breathing is still difficult.'

'I see,' Fulford replied gravely. 'Things should settle down in due course. I'll give you another injection in few hours' time. In the meantime, try and get some sleep.'

The professor turned his head to one side and closed his eyes. Fulford walked away and motioned to Channon follow.

'The next few hours could be crucial,' Fulford said quietly. 'We'll do a four on and four off watch.' Glancing at the wall clock, he whispered, 'It's almost midnight. I'll take the middle and you can relieve me 0400. That'll give you a few hours' sleep before call the hands at 0630.' Fulford glanced warily at the professor, who appeared to be sleeping. 'I'll check his blood pressure, respirations and pulse every half hour. You do the same. In the meantime,' he went on, 'a flask of coffee wouldn't go amiss.'

Leaving the warmth of the professor's cabin, Pendleton returned to the bridge. Visibility was a mere fifty yards. The figures around him appeared ghost-like, swaying silently with each motion of the ship. Pendleton turned to Carter and explained what had happened to the professor. 'And tell any cases reporting sick to see Chief Tolby. Until we reach Halifax, the Doc and SBA Channon will be kept too busy looking after the professor.'

'My God, sir!' exclaimed Carter. 'The old boy's not going to…'

'We don't know,' Pendleton interrupted. 'The Doc thinks if he gets through the next twenty-four hours he might make it. In the meantime, Number One,' he added, adjusting his muffler, 'reduce revolutions two zero, I'm afraid we'll have to do as the Doc suggests, and slow down.'

At 0200 the professor opened his eyes and smiled wearily as Fulford gave him another injection of morphia.

'How are you feeling, old boy?' Fulford quietly asked.

Over his mask, the professor's pale face wrinkled into a faint smile. 'Not too bad, Doctor, not too bad,' he murmured and closed his eyes.

During the next three hours, apart from the constant roll of the ship and the intermittent groan of the fog siren, all was quiet. With his jacket slung over a chair Fulford sat near the professor's bunk. Except for the bedside lamp that was draped with a towel to reduce the glare of the light, the cabin was in darkness. Despite this, the shadowy glow exaggerated the ashen features of the professor's pale, thin, face.

The time was 0345. The professor's blood pressure and pulse still remained dangerously high. And the occasional grimace when he breathed showed he was still in pain. The professor's eyes were closed and his breathing laboured. With a tired sigh, Fulford sat back in his chair, unscrewed the top of his flask and using the small Bakelite cup, poured out the last of the coffee. He hardly noticed the shadowy figure of SBA Channon standing next to him.

'How is he, sur?' whispered Channon, studying the professor's face.

Fulford stood up, stretched his arms and yawned. 'Much the same,' he replied. 'Keep a good watch, the next few hours will be critical.' Picking up his jacket he went on, 'I'll be in my cabin. Don't hesitate to call me if you're worried about anything. Understand?'

'Yes, sur,' Channon replied. 'How much oxygen is left in the cylinder?'

'Enough to last another four hours,' said Fulford. 'Then I'll replace it with the spare bottle.'

'And when that runs out?'

'Let's hope and pray by then he'll be feeling a bit better,' replied Fulford, biting his lip.

An hour later, just as Channon was about to take a sip of tea, he heard the professor's voice. 'The pain's worse!' he cried.

'I...I can hardly breathe!' Both hands were clutching his chest and he was obviously in considerable distress.

'Easy does it, sur,' said Channon, placing a comforting hand on his patient's arm. 'I'll call the doctor, he'll soon fix you up.'

A few minutes later Fulford arrived. He wore a duffel coat over his uniform and his face looked pinched and tired. Approaching the bedside he saw beads of sweat running down the sides of the professor's face.

'Is the pain still in the same place?' Fulford asked, bending close to the professor.

'Yes,' gasped the professor, touching the front of his chest. 'And it hurts when I breathe.'

Using his stethoscope, Fulford listened to the quickening beat of the professor's heart. Doing his best to sound re-assuring, he said, 'Try not to worry, old boy, we'll have you right in no time. I'm going to give you another injection.' A few minutes later, after administering the morphia, Fulford stood back and felt a trickle of cold sweat run down his back.

'Thank you, Doctor,' whispered the professor, his tired eyes staring over his mask. Using a hand, he moved the mask slightly and beckoned Fulford to come near. 'Could you please bring me a piece of writing paper and an envelope,' he muttered wearily. 'I want to dictate a letter to Nadine, just in case I...' He stopped talking and looked away.

Channon overheard the professor's request and left the cabin.

The time was 0600. On the eastern horizon a small hazy sun barely visible through the dense banks of fog, failed to lessen the feeling of isolation felt by everyone.

No sooner had Channon left, than Pendleton came into the cabin. He immediately looked at the professor, who was propped up in bed. The rubber mask had been slipped to one side enabling Fulford to help him to take a few sips of water. Shrouded in the pale light from the bedside lamp, the professor appeared to have aged. His face looked tired and drawn and his shock of white hair an untidy mess.

'How are you feeling?' Pendleton asked, while at the same time glancing furtively at Fulford.

'Not too good, I'm afraid, Captain,' murmured the professor, frowning painfully.

'I see,' replied Pendleton, nervously licking his lips. With a quick glance he motioned Fulford to move away from the bedside.

'How serious is he, Doc?' whispered Pendleton.

'Very serious, I'm afraid, sir,' replied Fulford, shaking his head. 'If he can make it through the day, he may be all right. Otherwise…'

At that moment Channon came in holding a few sheets of writing paper and an envelope. He handed them to Fulford, who looked at Pendleton, and said, 'He wants to dictate a letter to his daughter.'

'Do you think he's well enough to do that?' Pendleton asked, raising his eyebrows.

'No, I don't,' replied Fulford. 'But it could be his final wish, so I can hardly refuse.'

'No, of course not,' Pendleton sighed. 'I'm sure you're doing all you can, Doc. We should be out of this blasted fog in a few hours. Keep me informed,' and left the cabin.

'I'll nip to the galley and bring us some coffee, sur,' said Channon as Fulford sat down at the professor's bedside.

'Good idea,' replied Fulford, resting the writing paper on a book. Taking a fountain pen from his top pocket, he looked at the professor and said, 'Please take your time and don't exert yourself.' After a slight, nervous pause, Fulford continued, 'Now, err… what do want to write, sir?'

Fulford undid one side of the professor's mask. He then picked up a half full glass of water near his bedside and held it while the professor took a few sips. In doing so, Fulford felt a slight constriction in his throat. If the professor were to die, the letter he was about to write for him would be the last communication the old boy would have with his daughter. With a feeling of trepidation, Fulford nervously licked his lips and waited.

The letter, dictated in painful, fits and starts, was short, but heart rendering:

"My Dearest Nadine

By the time you read this letter I will be with your mother. Please try not to mourn me too much. Remember the love your mother and I have had for you. Try to find some happiness in a world plagued with unhappiness and uncertainty. My spirit will always be with you.

God Bless you, my lovely daughter".

The professor took the pen from Fulford and with his hand shaking, managed to sign *Papa*. 'Please seal the envelope,' he muttered weakly, 'and ask the captain if he would be kind enough to deliver it personally should I...' His voice trailed away.

'I understand, sir,' replied Fulford, folding the letter and placing it in an envelope. 'But try not to worry. You're going to get well.'

However, as Fulford sealed the envelope, the constriction in his throat became a hard lump.

CHAPTER TWENTY

During the next twelve hours the professor's blood pressure, heart rate and pulse remained alarmingly high. Fulford and Channon continued to keep a vigilant watch. Channon even missed his rum ration and asked for it to be put in a bottle.

'We can share it later, sur,' he said to Fulford, scratching the stubble on his chin, 'when we reach Halifax.'

Fulford smiled weakly. They were due to reach Canada in two days' time. It was going to be a long forty-eight hours.

The professor's condition spread around the ship like wildfire. However, many ratings on the mess decks reacted with mixed deferment.

'If yer ask me, the silly old sod, should never be here in the first place,' remarked Jumper Collins, accepting his tot from Leading Seaman Dusty Miller, the duty rum bosun. 'Why couldn't the RAF 'ave flown him to Canada?'

'How the 'ell do I know,' replied Dusty. 'All I knows is 'e must be someone really important otherwise 'e wouldn't be 'ere. Now shut up and let me dish out this bleedin' rum.'

In the stokers' mess the news about the professor was greeted with an air of weak condescension.

'Och if the old codger pegs oot,' said Jock Weir, a burly, ginger-headed stoker, 'it'll mean we'll hae to bury him at sea and we'll hae ta slow doon, that'll make us late fer a run ashore in Halifax. And I hear those Canadian lassies love a wee bit of Scottish cock.'

'That's right, Jock,' remarked another stoker, a tall, pale faced Scouser from Knotty Ash. 'I've seen you in the shower and "wee" is the best way to describe your dick.'

In the senior ratings' mess Coxswain, Jack Tolby and the others were well aware of the importance of the situation.

'If the professor dies,' said Jack, before taking a swig of neat rum, 'it'll mean our trip will be a bloody waste of time.'

'And we let that bloody U-boat get away, as well,' rejoined CERA Bill Grundy.

'Well,' added PO Writer Potter, 'at least we'll see a bit of Canada.'

'Oh shut up, Pansy,' said Pony Moore, the chief cook. 'And get yer tot down yer.'

The officers on the bridge tended to leave Pendleton alone with his thoughts. They knew that although the captain couldn't be held responsible for the professor's health problems, their Lords in the Admiralty were hard taskmasters. If the professor were to die, the mission would be deemed a failure and would reflect badly on him.

Hunched up in his chair, Pendleton put his gloved hand in the pocket of his duffel coat and felt the envelope Fulford had given him. No doubt, the Admiralty would inform Nadine if her father passed away so it might be cruel to deliver it. Still, he mused, it would be a way of contacting her...

The muffled voice of OOW, Lieutenant Reed, brought him back to earth.

'Convoy has passed five miles to port, sir,' he said. 'The radar and asdic are clear.'

'Thank you, Frank,' replied Pendleton. 'What's our speed?'

'Twenty-five knots, sir,' said Reed.

'Good, increase revolutions one third,' Pendleton replied.

Throughout the night, Fulford and Channon remained by the professor's bedside. Using the settee, they slept in four-hour shifts, each waking the other with a mug of steaming hot tea.

Shortly before 0600, Channon shook Fulford gently by the shoulder. Fulford opened his bloodshot eyes, yawning while stretching his arms. 'Any change?' he asked sitting up.

'Not really, sur,' replied Channon, handing Fulford his drink. 'He's sleeping soundly. His BP is still the same, although it's due to be checked again at 0600.'

'Thank you,' replied Fulford. After blowing across the top of his mug he took a sip then added, 'I'll do that while you try and get some sleep.'

'I'm all right, sur,' said Channon. 'Gale will be here shortly with our breakfasts. Maybe the old boy'll feel like a bite to eat.'

'Here's hoping you're right,' said Fulford, running his free hand through his untidy hair. 'He hasn't eaten any solids for days now. By the way, what day *is* it?'

'Monday, sur,' answered Channon. 'With a bit of luck we'll be in Halifax tomorrow.'

Shortly after Stand Easy, the fog suddenly cleared. On the bridge, men shielded their eyes as the sun broke through the mist allowing the vastness of the sea to open up before them. Emerging into a bright new world they could finally see the foamy bow waves curling over the fo'c'sle. Even the wind felt slightly warmer.

'At long soddin' last,' Slinger Wood cried out in the crow's nest. 'Now we can bloody well see where we're fuckin' going.'

Slinger wasn't the only one glad to see daylight. Ratings left the cramped mustiness of their mess decks and came topsides.

'Thank gawd fer that,' cried Dusty Miller, stretching his arms upwards then giving his oppo, Big Geordie Roberts, a playful dig in the ribs. 'If I had ter smell you farting anymore, I'd have thrown meself overboard.'

On the bridge, Pendleton glanced warily at his First Lieutenant. 'Better send a signal to C in C Canadian Fleet, Nova Scotia, Number One,' he said scanning the horizon with his binoculars. 'Say…"VIP suffered heart attack. Condition critical.

Request berthing instructions, do not need a pilot, have navigation charts and am familiar with Halifax Road from pre war days. But require ambulance and doctor to meet. ETA 0800. Eastern Summer Time, 26 August". Better request fuel tenders, and ask for fresh meat and vegetables.'

'What about minefields, sir?' enquired Carter. 'They weren't there before the war.'

'Hopefully, the minesweepers will have them well cleared,' Pendleton replied. 'But double the lookouts just in case.'

Just as he finished talking the bridge telephone rang. Lieutenant MacIntyre removed his meerschaum pipe and unhooked the receiver.

'It's the Doc, sir,' he said, nervously, 'he says it's important.'

Fearing the worst Pendleton glanced at Carter and said, 'Better hold that signal, Number One. I might have to amend it.'

Everyone, including both lookouts gave each other an apprehensive glance. They watched as Pendleton leaned across and accepted the receiver from MacIntyre.

Pendleton took a deep breath. 'Yes, Doc,' he said, feeling his heart thump in his chest, 'what is it?'

'A bit of good news, sir,' said Fulford, his voice slightly raised. 'The professor tells me he is feeling a bit better. His blood pressure has dropped and the pain in his chest is lessened. He's even eaten some scrambled eggs and coffee.'

'Thank God for that,' replied Pendleton, raising his voice so everyone could hear him. 'But is he going to be all right?'

'Hard to tell at present, sir, but things are looking much better,' answered Fulford. 'At least we should be able to get him to Halifax alive. I expect the Americans will decide if he's well enough to leave the ship.'

Pendleton's weather-beaten face broke into a huge smile. He shot a relieved glance at Carter who, like MacIntyre and Coburn was standing nearby. 'Thank you, Doc,' said Pendleton. 'I can't tell you how glad I am to hear you say that.' Feeling as though a weight had been lifted from his shoulders, he handed the receiver back to MacIntyre. Turning to Carter, he added, 'Alter that signal, Number One, delete *critical,* and insert *satisfactory.*' Rubbing his gloved hands together, he sat back in his chair and with a satisfied smile, said, 'I don't know about you lot, but I could do with one of Gale's special kye.'

CHAPTER TWENTY-ONE

Just before 0400 next morning, Pendleton came onto the bridge and sat down on his chair. He gave a slight shiver as a bitterly northern wind belted against his face. Directly ahead he could clearly see the twin gun barrels of A and B turret, wet with spray as arcs of greeny-white water cascaded over the fo'c'sle head.

'Good morning, Number One,' he said to Carter, who was OOW. 'What time will we sight land?'

'In about an hour, sir,' Carter replied, stifling a yawn while handing Pendleton a signal. 'It's from Rear Admiral Murray, the C in C North West Atlantic, confirming your request for medical assistance. He suggests you to berth in Pier 21 in Halifax Harbour.' As they spoke the coldness of the air vaporised their breath.

'Thank you,' replied Pendleton. With a strong hint of nostalgia, he went on. 'I remember Pier 21 from my pre days with the Elder Dempster Line. It was used as a passenger terminal then. Thank goodness we don't have to negotiate the Narrows.'

'What are they?' enquired Carter, as the duty messenger arrived holding two mugs of kye. He handed one to Pendleton, accepted the other and took a quick sip.

'It's a narrow channel at the end of the harbour that leads into Bedford Basin,' replied Pendleton. 'That's where the convoys gather before sailing for England and it can be quite crowded. Berthing alongside the pier will make it easier to leave once we've landed the professor.'

Throughout the night Fulford and Channon disturbed the professor only to check his blood pressure and pulse rate. Both remained slightly high, but to Fulford's relief, he felt the danger of a heart attack had passed. Channon lay curled up on the sofa snoring peacefully. Shortly after *Call the hands,* at 0600, Leading Steward Gale appeared carrying two mugs of coffee. His pale features were clean-shaven and as usual his hair was plastered with Brylcreem.

'Thought you two would like a wet,' he said, offering Fulford a mug. 'How's our patient today, sir?' he added, glancing warily at the professor who was slumped back in his pillows sound asleep.

Fulford stood up from the professor's bedside, yawned and stretched his arms. 'All right, so far,' he whispered, accepting the drink. 'Better wake up Channon, it'll soon be time for breakfast.'

Gale walked over to the sofa. 'Wakey, wakey,' he said softly, shaking Channon by the shoulder. 'You can't sleep here, Jack.'

Channon opened his bloodshot eyes, blinked and slowly sat up. 'Cheers, Windy,' he muttered, reaching up and grasping Gale's mug. He then looked across at Fulford and mouthed, 'How is he sur?'

Fulford gave a confident nod, and quietly replied, 'BP is slightly down.'

'That's a good sign, isn't it Doctor,' came the throaty voice of the professor, who was now awake.

'Good morning, Professor,' said Fulford, helping him to sit up. 'You sound quite cheerful. How are you feeling?'

The professor's eyes wrinkled into a smile. 'Much better, thank you,' he replied. 'But I would be grateful for some of that coffee.'

'Here, have some of mine,' said Fulford, offering his mug and holding it while the professor took a few sips.

'Mmm…that's better,' replied the professor, licking his dry lips. He then glanced across at Gale and with a tired smile, said, 'Do you, think I could have some more of those lovely scrambled eggs?'

Shortly before 0700, the dark outline of the Canadian coast appeared on the horizon. The sun, hidden by low-lying cumulonimbus clouds, was almost non-existent, and an icy north wind rattled both cables and rigging.

Pendleton sat on his chair focussing his binoculars on the land. He took a deep breath and allowed himself an all-knowing smile. Perched on a small rocky island at the mouth of Halifax Harbour was the dark shape of Sambro Lighthouse, the oldest in North America. 'The entrance hasn't changed either,' he muttered to nobody in particular. 'It's still narrow and tricky.'

On either side of the harbour, shrouded in early morning mist, stretched the verdant hills of Canada. Without moving his head Pendleton said, 'Pipe hands to harbour stations, Number One, and reduce revolutions one third. Tell Pilot we will be entering the Eastern passage. If memory serves me right there are several buoys to help guide us in.' He then unhooked the bridge phone that connected to his day cabin. Perhaps he was being somewhat cynical, but the sooner he could offload the professor to the Americans the better he would feel.

'Sick bay,' answered Fulford, stifling a yawn.

'Captain, here, Doc,' he replied. 'How is the professor? Do you think he's well enough to be landed?'

'Maybe, sir,' Fulford replied cagily. 'I expect the Americans will want to examine him first.'

'Mmm …I see,' Pendleton replied. 'Keep me informed,' and replaced the receiver.

Pendleton prediction proved correct. Several coloured buoys marked the Channel allowing safe passage for *Zimba* to enter the harbour. Gradually, the busy port of Halifax, dominated by Citadel Hill, hove into view. In 1749 Edward Cornwallis landed here with settlers and built a fortification to protect against the French. Over the next few centuries, Halifax grew steadily and was used extensively for conveying convoys of men and material in both world wars.

'Looks like we're expected, sir,' remarked Lieutenant Foster, peering through his binoculars. 'And there's an ambulance on the jetty.'

'So I see, Pilot,' replied Pendleton, who, like Foster and Carter was studying the activity on Pier 21.

'There's quite a lot of shipping in also, sir,' added Carter, 'and a couple of destroyers. Maybe there's another convoy due.'

'That wouldn't surprise me in the least, Number One,' answered Pendleton. 'Slow ahead, starboard ten.'

'Signal from Admiral Donnington of the Dockyard, sir,' said PO Yeoman Jeffries. 'It reads, "welcome to Canada. Berth aft of the destroyer HMCS Sackville, moored alongside Pier 21. Commander Lewis McCabe USN, myself and Doctor James Petersen, Cardiologist to the US Navy, will come aboard. Provisions and fuel ready for you when docked".'

'Reply, "thank you for your help. Glad to be here".' Glancing cautiously at Carter, Pendleton went on, 'Some welcoming committee, eh Number One? Better tell the Buffer to have the side party ready to receive them.' The side party consisted of the QM, the duty PO and the OOW, Lieutenant Foster. Pendleton and Carter would also be in attendance.

Twenty minutes later *Zimba* was tied up aft of the Canadian destroyer. The gangway was lowered and a tall, distinguished looking American admiral led the way followed by a small, stocky officer with a worried look on his face. Behind them, carrying a shiny black Gladstone bag was an elderly, stout gentleman whose pale features appeared somewhat exaggerated by his dark overcoat and trilby.

'Better warn the Doc to expect visitors,' said Pendleton, glancing at the duty PO, who nodded and quickly left.

Without waiting to be told the QM bent to the tannoy and announced, "Attention on the upper deck, face the starboard".

Walking in single file the three dignitaries reached the top of the brow. As they stepped onboard, they were greeted by the shrill sound of the bosun's pipe. After exchanging salutes Pendleton introduced himself and Carter.

'I am Admiral Harold Donnington,' said the tallest one, 'and this here is Commander Lewis MacCabe who is in charge of the dockyard and this gentleman,' he added nodding towards the elderly civilian, 'is Doctor Petersen, who is a cardiologist attached to the US Navy.'

Pendleton shook their hands then said, 'Perhaps you gentlemen would like to come to the wardroom for a coffee or something stronger?'

'No thank you, Commander,' replied the admiral who spoke with a deep Southern drawl. Glancing at Doctor Petersen, he continued, 'I think the doctor would prefer to see our man. Is that not so, Doc?'

'If it is convenient,' replied the cardiologist. His accent sounded slightly foreign and as he spoke his dark eyes wrinkled into a pleasant smile.

'Of course,' replied Pendleton. 'Our surgeon is with the professor at the moment.'

'How is the patient?' asked Doctor Petersen. 'According to your signal he appears to have improved.'

'Yes he has,' replied Pendleton. 'Our doctor tells me the professor is feeling better.'

'Good,' said the admiral. 'The sooner we get your man ashore the better.'

'Of course,' said Pendleton. 'This way gentlemen.' Looking at Carter, he added, 'I think you and Lieutenant Foster had better remain here in case we have any more visitors, and have the QM pipe the *carry on.*'

Fulford and Channon were standing in quiet conversation when they heard a knock on the cabin door. The professor was sat up in bed, staring enquiringly over his glasses as Pendleton and the three men entered. Suddenly, the cabin appeared slightly overcrowded.

Pendleton quickly introduced Fulford to the American officers and Doctor Petersen. Pendleton explained who the men were and why they were here.

'May I ask how you are, sir?' asked the admiral.

'Much better, thank you,' replied the professor. 'Thankfully the pain has now gone.'

'Mighty fine,' replied the admiral, glancing approvingly at Commander Donnington. 'I'm sure glad to hear it.'

Meanwhile, Fulford quietly explained the professor's condition to Doctor Petersen, and the treatment given.

'The professor's blood pressure and pulse have been almost normal for the past twelve hours,' explained Fulford, 'and he's eaten a good breakfast.'

'Excellent,' replied Doctor Petersen, gently stroking his clean-shaven chin. Smiling benignly at the professor, he added, 'And did you enjoy your breakfast?'

'Yes,' replied the professor, peering over his glasses, 'I enjoyed the scrambled eggs very much, thank you.'

Turning to Fulford the cardiologist went on, 'With your permission, doctor, may I examine him?'

'Of course,' replied Fulford. 'And I'm sure the professor won't mind also.'

Everyone stepped back allowing the cardiologist room to move closer to the professor.

Doctor Petersen unclipped his Gladstone bag and took out a stethoscope and sphygmomanometer. He placed the stethoscope around his neck then felt the professor's pulse while looking at his wristwatch. His fingers were long and delicate like those of a concert pianist. After a minute or so, he gave a satisfactory smile and released the professor's wrist. He then checked the professor's blood pressure and found it slightly above normal. For the next five minutes the doctor, bending close to his patient, carefully moved the end of the stethoscope around, listening to the professor's heart. He then stood up, removed the ends of the stethoscope from his ears, and asked, 'Have you had any shortness of breath?' (Called dyspnoea, a sign that the heart is becoming unequal to its task.)

'Not now, doctor,' the professor replied. 'But I had some pain and difficulty breathing a few days ago, but it's gone now.'

'Mmm...' muttered the doctor, 'that's good.' He then turned down the bedding and examined the lower parts of his legs for swelling (oedema or dropsy, caused by the collection of fluid), and found none. The doctor bent close to the professor and carefully inspected his ears, nose, lips and fingernails looking for evidence of discolouration due to poor blood circulation. With a satisfied expression, the doctor stood up, looked at the professor and said, 'Well my friend, you appear to be making a very good recovery.'

After replacing his instruments in his Gladstone bag, the doctor looked approvingly around, and said, 'I think the professor should be allowed to sit out of bed, and be allowed to move around the cabin.'

Pendleton immediately felt as if a heavy weight had been lifted from his shoulders. Glances of assuagement were immediately exchanged between Fulford and Channon.

'Err...how soon can the professor be transferred ashore?' Admiral McCabe asked Doctor Petersen. 'My people are mighty anxious to have him.'

Doctor Petersen pursed his lips and replied, 'I suggest he remains here for another twenty-four hours. If by then he feels strong enough, he can be transferred ashore to the naval hospital.'

'May I also suggest,' intervened Commander MacCabe, 'that we transfer the professor at night. A couple of German spies with cameras have been caught in the dockyard recently, so we can't take a chance of the professor being spotted. How does that sound?'

'Good idea, Lou,' replied Admiral McCabe. 'Let's say 2145, after dinner.' Glancing warily at Pendleton he went on, 'Could you post an armed guard at the foot of the gangway, just as a precautionary measure you, understand?'

'Of course,' Pendleton hastily replied. 'As you say, sir, we can't be too careful.'

'Right, then,' said the Admiral, taking a deep breath and putting on his cap. 'I'll arrange an ambulance and armed escort to be on the wharf at 2200.' He paused, and gave the professor a confident smile. 'You'll be taken to the naval hospital for further tests, nothing to worry about, just routine, you understand. All being well, you'll be transferred to the scientific centre at Maryland as soon as possible. Now,' the admiral continued, giving Pendleton a meaningful look. 'Perhaps we could take up that offer of something stronger you mentioned earlier.'

An hour later Pendleton escorted the two American officers and Doctor Petersen to the gangway.

'Thank you for your hospitality, Jeremy,' said the admiral, his eyes slightly glazed. 'You Brits certainly know how to live. What say you, Lou?'

'Sure thing, Harry,' added the commander, 'those pink gins tasted almost as good as Kentucky Bourbon.'

'It's just as well we're leaving,' Doctor Petersen added jokingly. 'Many more of those and I'd have to cancel my evening rounds.'

'Not at all, gentlemen,' Pendleton replied, repressing a smile. 'It was a pleasure, and I'd be grateful if you could let myself and our doctor know how the professor is.'

'I'll see to it personally, Commander,' said Admiral Donnington. 'And don't worry, we'll make sure he's all right.'

After shaking hands the Americans saluted the Union Jack. Then, followed by Doctor Petersen, they made their way somewhat unsteadily down the gangway and climbed into a black staff car.

Next evening at 2200, Lieutenant Foster, who was OOD, knocked on Pendleton's day cabin door and entered.

'The ambulance has arrived, Doc,' he said, glancing apprehensively at Fulford. 'Complete with half the American army by the looks of it.'

Tucking his scarf inside his overcoat, the professor felt a lump rise in his throat. He looked at both Fulford and Channon and with tears in his eyes, muttered, 'I...I can't thank you enough for all you've done,' he added as they shook hands. 'Bless you both, I pray you and your crew both get home safely and have a happy life.'

Channon picked up the professor's suitcase and together they made their way up into the citadel. As they stepped out onto the quarterdeck they were met by a bitterly cold wind. High above an orange coloured moon moved imperceptibly between dark clouds bathing the dockyard in a pale, uneven light. Pendleton, Carter and Reed wearing overcoats, waited at the top of the brow.

Peering wistfully over his glasses while shaking Pendleton's hand, the professor said, 'May God protect you and your crew.' With a slight twinkle in his eyes, he added, 'And tell Gale I shall miss his mugs of kye.'

As the ambulance drove away Pendleton remembered the professor's letter to Nadine and hoped he would never have to deliver it.

PART FOUR
THE ATTACK

CHAPTER TWENTY-TWO

'Our orders, Number One,' said Pendleton, holding a signal in his hand, 'are to remain here until a convoy has left the Bedford Basin and passed through the Narrows where it will meet an escort to take it to England.'

The time was shortly after morning Stand Easy. Now that the professor had gone Pendleton could use his day cabin. Carter stood, cap in hand opposite Pendleton who was sat behind his desk.

Sitting forward, Pendleton placed his hands flatly on his desk and went on, 'The first ships of the convoy will pass us this afternoon. The last one should leave around midnight tonight. We will then sail, join the escorts and take up a position behind the convoy. The Canadian destroyer, *Huron,* will be leader. Next day, the convoy will be joined by twenty other merchant ships from America.'

'Mmm...' Carter muttered pensively, 'forty-four ships, eh, that's quite a big one. I see we're to be Tail end Charlie again, sir?'

'Not quite, Number One,' Pendleton said firmly. 'We will leave the convoy in mid Atlantic when warships from England relieve the Canadian and American escorts. We will then sail to Reykjavik, refuel and head for home. You'd better tell Paddy to flash the engine and boiler rooms up. By the sound of things the sooner we leave here the better it will be for all of us.'

Throughout the day, men on the upper deck watched as twenty-four merchant vessels passed through the Narrows. By 2330, the last of them had faded into the darkness.

As the dockyard clock chimed midnight, *Zimba* slipped her moorings and slowly moved from the wharf. With the Sambro lighthouse providing a useful navigation aid, the rear vessels of the convoy were sighted. A bitter, blustery cold wind blew from the north. Partly concealed by angry dark clouds, ghostly rays from a yellow moon turned the sea into sheets of sparkling silver.

Pendleton received a signal from the commodore of the convoy that read, "Welcome to the fray. Good Luck and God's Speed".

'Reply,' said Pendleton with a wry smile, '"Thank you. Glad to be of service. Hope you have a safe crossing".'

The night passed without incident. Half a mile away on *Zimba's* port bow the silhouette of a Canadian sloop, HMCS *Pictou,* could be seen sending up arcs of foamy spray over her fo'c'sle, while all around the masts and funnels of the convoy were silhouetted against the grey sky.

As dawn was breaking, radar operator Able Seaman Chats Harris reported a mass of ships roughly ten miles away.

'That's the Yanks for you,' OOW. Sub Lieutenant Coburn cheerfully remarked. 'Dead on time.' He was about to pick up the captain's intercom when Pendleton appeared.

'What's our course and speed, Colin?'

'One, one two east, sir, fifteen knots,' answered Coburn, 'revolutions two zero.'

'Thank you,' replied Pendleton. He then wiped the lens of his binoculars with a handkerchief before focussing on the convoy. 'And what is our position, Pilot?'

From the small, sheltered chart room at the back of the bridge came the plumy voice of Lieutenant Foster, 'Approaching longitude 52 and latitude 22, sir. Not long to go before we'll be on our own, sir.' Just then the bridge messenger, arrived with a tray of hot drinks and handed them around.

'About a day and a half, I would say,' replied Pendleton accepting a steaming hot mug of tea.

Emerging out of the early morning mist the convoy gradually became clearer. Set against the dark green sea, their superstructure, masts and yardarms stood out against pale sky. Luckily, the relatively calm weather had allowed them to keep good station. By midday, all this changed as twenty American liberty ships, fully loaded with the impedimenta of war, joined the convoy. Signals flashed to and fro between the convoy commodore and the senior American escort ship. Then gradually, as if being carefully moved around a chequer board, the newcomers took up a position five lines abreast of the Canadians. On either side of *Zimba,* an American destroyer took up station. Two more destroyers, sending enormous bow waves in the air, raced down the flanks of the convoy taking positions further afield. While a mile away on *Zimba*'s starboard beam, an aircraft carrier and a cruiser gave added protection to what was now a vast armada.

'Good Lord!' cried Pendleton, watching as the merchant ships manoeuvred into position. 'By the time they've finished, the convoy will be spread over twenty miles.'

'Many of those American ships are packed with troops,' Carter observed. 'Looks as if that second front Stalin is always harping about is about to happen.'

'I don't know about that,' remarked Pendleton, pensively stroking his chin, 'but at one of those boring cocktail parties I attended before we sailed, Admiral Donnington hinted that an invasion somewhere in the Med was on the cards.'

'It'll be just our luck to get back home in time for it,' Carter cynically replied.

'If there is an invasion,' Pendleton added with an ominous sigh, 'I bet many of the poor blighters onboard those ships won't see their homes again.'

On 7 September, the convoy reached mid Atlantic. Pendleton had finished his breakfast and was on the bridge. Standing next to him was the burly figure of Lieutenant MacIntyre, a trail of smoke eddying from the brown-stained drum of his meerschaum pipe. The time was just after 0800.

'Signal flashing from the American carrier, sir,' he said, glancing at Pendleton. 'It says, "Detach from convoy as arranged. Good Luck and thank you for your company".'

'You reply,' said Pendleton, training his binoculars on the carrier, '"Will comply. Safe crossing and Good Luck".' With the binoculars still clamped to his eyes, he rasped, 'Starboard ten. Increase revolution two thirds, steer red one two zero.'

After a full blast on the ship's horn, *Zimba* heeled to starboard. Every rivet and bolt seemed to shake as the ship increased speed. Gradually, the vast armada of merchantmen faded away on the horizon as *Zimba* headed due north.

'Better double the lookouts, Number One,' said Pendleton, easing himself onto his chair, and lighting a cigarette. 'And tell the asdic and radar people to keep their eyes and ears skinned. For the next three days we'll be on our own,' he paused and with a determined glint in his eyes, added, 'and I can assure you, this time we won't turn away if we come across a bloody U-boat.'

However, the next three days passed without incident. The only sightings on the radar turned out to be a heavy shoal of fishes and a humpback whale. Occasional rainsqualls pelted down onto the ship; black clouds raced across a leaden sky, hiding a pale, shadowy sun. Pendleton ordered regular gunnery and fire drills, plus first aid exercises. 'Just to keep everyone on their toes, you understand, Number One,' said Pendleton with a sly smile.'

Early on the morning of 10 September, the rocky coast of Reykjavik with its snow tipped mountains barely visible in the morning mist hove into view. By 0700, *Zimba* was secured alongside a busy, bustling wharf close to where several merchant ships were tied up.

'Not much of a welcome party this time, eh, sir,' Carter remarked to Pendleton. Both officers were leaning over the port guardrail watching as dockyard workers helped sailors to lower the gangway onto the cobble-stoned wharf.

Remembering the two American officers who met them on their outward journey, Pendleton smiled weakly and nodded. 'So I see, Number One,' he replied. 'But I think that person,' he added, indicating towards a portly gentleman wearing a dark overcoat and a bowler hat standing near the foot of the gangway, 'is waiting to come onboard.'

From past experience Pendleton knew that dockyard officials, while organising fuel and stores, also expected to imbibe in as much duty free drinks as possible. With a humorous glint in his eye, Pendleton added, 'Better tell the wardroom petty officer to have plenty of gin at the ready, he'll no doubt add a few pounds to your monthly mess bill.'

'*My* mess bill, sir?' Carter replied indignantly. 'Surely he's your guest?'

With a wry smile Pendleton said, 'Yes, but remember, Number One, you are the wardroom social secretary.'

Zimba remained in Reykjavik for two days during which time canteen leave (leave restricted to within the confines of the NAAFI and dockyard cinema) only was given.

'I wish we could 'ave a run ashore in town,' moaned Able Seaman Geordie Roberts to his oppo, Leading Seaman Dusty Miller. They, like most of *Zimba*'s off duty crew were crowded into the small dockyard canteen. 'I hear the locals are supposed to be very friendly, like.'

'You 'eard what it said on Daily Orders, didn't yer,' replied Dusty Miller, 'local leave is cancelled due to the presence of German spies. If some big mouth got pissed and shot his mouth off about us takin' a professor to Canada, the Jerries would smell a rat, so stop bloody moaning.'

'I bet the officers are ashore 'avin it away with the local beauties,' muttered Able Seaman Jumper Collins, wiping froth from his mouth with the back of his hand.

'Better them than me,' interrupted Mick Channon, who, like the others was trying to enjoy a glass of beer. 'I hear the women in Reykjavik are all poxed up.'

'To be sure,' grimaced Leading Seaman Paddy Doyle, placing his half filled pint glass on the table while staring down the cleavage of the stout barmaid. 'This ale tastes like piss and if they're as ugly as the one that's serving us, they're welcome to 'em.'

The barmaid overheard Paddy's remark. With a contemptuous smile she turned away and "accidentally" knocked Paddy's glass over, spilling beer down the front of his uniform. 'Limeys,' she muttered as she walked away. 'Yer all wind and piss.'

At 0700 on 12 September, *Zimba* left Reykjavik and set sail for Portsmouth. The pale early morning sun and an icy northerly wind failed to dampen the feeling of elation that spread through the crew. Now, they were really on their way home.

'Just think, Swain,' said Dusty Miller, who was closed up in the wheelhouse alongside Jack Tolby. 'In five days' time I'll be in The Keppel's Head, swigging Tetley's bitter.'

'Don't speak too soon,' replied Tolby, giving Dusty a cautious look. 'There's a lot of sea miles to go before we see the Isle of Wight.'

Two days later, ploughing through a high, rolling sea and a force eight gale, *Zimba* passed the Faroe Islands. Continuing south, the snow-capped hills of the Outer Hebrides could be seen on the port bow. They then entered the turbulent waters of the Irish Sea. On 15 September, *Zimba* rounded Lizard Point and entered the English Channel. With the ship roughly eighty miles from Portsmouth, the dark line of the English coast was barely discernable in the early morning haze.

'Better double the lookouts, Number One,' said Pendleton, scanning the horizon with his binoculars. 'It's too damn quiet for my liking.'

'I agree, sir,' Carter cautiously replied. 'The U-boat pens in Brest are less than fifty miles away and...'

Over the intercom the voice of Asdic operator Paddy Doyle abruptly interrupted him. 'Submarine on the surface about five miles away to port,' yelled Doyle. 'It doesn't seem to be moving.'

Straight away, everyone trained their binoculars away to their left. Sure enough, silhouetted against the clear blue sky was the dark cigar shape of a submarine, with its squat conning tower and twin, stubby periscopes.

'She's one of the old type seven A, sir,' Midshipman Porter yelled excitedly. 'Has a crew of forty-six and carries eleven torpedoes and a rapid firing 88mm gun.'

'Thank you, Mid,' replied Pendleton, suitably impressed with the young man's knowledge of the enemy. Turning to Yeoman PO Jeffries, he said, 'Make to C in C Portsmouth, U-boat on surface, give its position and add, intend attacking. Will keep you informed.'

This was the moment Pendleton had been waiting for. He gritted his teeth and focused his binoculars on the U-boat. With a look of determination, he glanced at Carter. 'Sound action stations, Number One, and increase revolutions one third. I think the blighter may be re-charging her batteries. Tell Guns to stand by and alert the Oerlikon crews. Announce over the tannoy that we are about to attack a U-boat. Let's nail the bastard before she dives.'

CHAPTER TWENTY-THREE

Like a greyhound after a hare, *Zimba* sped through the sea sending a massive bow wave curling over her fo'c'sle. Everyone on the bridge had their eyes glued to their binoculars watching as the U-boat became clearer.

'*Why doesn't she dive?*' exploded Pendleton. 'The blighter must have seen us.'

'*She is now, sir,*' yelled Carter, his voice barely audible over the roar of the wind.

'*Bastard!*' Pendleton cried, his voice full of anger and frustration. 'Tell Paddy to give us all he's got. We *must* catch the swine before she goes under. Stand by to fire.'

In the Gun Director Platform, Lieutenant MacIntyre, was sat peering through the rubbery eyepiece of the range finder. Beads of sweat ran down his face as his finger curled around the firing mechanism.

'Target closing, sir,' he shouted down the bridge intercom. 'Range three miles.'

Close by, stood Chief GI Digger Barnes, the range and deflection operator. 'Elevation three hundred, sir,' he cried.

'All guns in a first degree of readiness, sir,' reported Lieutenant Small from the Transmitting Station directly above the GDP.

'A and B guns, *fire!*' retorted Pendleton, trying his best to stay calm.

This was the moment everyone in the ship had been waiting for. Everything onboard seemed to shake. Mess gear, improperly stowed, broke away. Books in the Pay Office became an untidy heap on the deck. Bottles in the sick bay rattled like tin cans in a storm, while men manning the 20mm Oerlikons held on like grim death to anything at hand. In the engine and boiler rooms, men, their faces wet with nervous perspiration, glanced apprehensively at one another and waited. In the gun bays, shells, each weighing fifty pounds, were brought up in hoists. Every shell was then packed with cordite and placed into the gun barrels ready to fire.

In the GDP, Lieutenant MacIntyre took a deep breath and gently squeezed the firing trigger. Seconds later, the ship shuddered violently as four 4.7 projectiles streaked upwards of three miles before descending onto the target.

The first salvo fell short.

By this time the U-boat was less than two miles away.

'Green five,' shouted the Chief GI from the GDP, 'up three degrees.'

'*Fire!*' shouted Pendleton, watching as the sea slowly lapped over the for'd part of the U-Boat's upper deck, 'and that includes the Oerlikons.'

Once again the ship rocked as A and B guns opened up. The cacophony was enjoined by the twin sets of 20mm Oerlikons barking out streams of multicoloured shells. Seconds later, a wall of splashes surrounded the U-boat. This was followed by a series of mighty spurts of white water jettisoning into the air.

As the wall of spray surrounding the submarine subsided, Pendleton pounded the side of his chair. *'Damn and blast, another bloody miss,'* he yelled, angrily. 'Tell guns to fire at will, Number One.'

By this time the submarine was less than a two hundred yards away.

'We're too close, sir,' shouted Carter. 'The main guns can't depress sufficiently to be accurate.'

All eyes became strained on the enemy vessel. There was no sign of her crew, and except for the conning tower and part of her stern, the U-boat was almost submerged.

The submarine was now a mere fifty yards away. For a fleeting second Pendleton felt completely alone. The sound of the sea and the intermittent rattle of the Oerlikons seemed to fade away. Suddenly, Pendleton's mind clicked into gear. Staring at the enemy he could clearly see her pennant number, *U 145,* painted in white on her side. He grabbed hold of the ship's intercom, and trying his best to sound calm, said, 'Captain speaking. I intend to ram the U-boat, hold onto anything you can.' He then glanced at Carter and said, 'Revolutions two thirds, Number One.

Everyone on the bridge, including Pendleton, held their breath and braced themselves. All waited anxiously for the impact they knew would come. Suddenly, there was a grinding *crunch* as *Zimba's* sharp bows sliced into the conning tower. The piercing screech of metal on metal rent the air. *Zimba* shuddered violently. Every nut and bolt screamed out as if in pain. In the engine and boiler rooms a few stokers slid on the slippery metal deck. Ratings manning the guns clung onto railings and stanchions; in the sick bay Channon and the first aid team crumpled onto the deck, but were unhurt. Fulford tried to hold onto the edges of his desk but fell backwards bumping his head on the deck.

With his knuckles white as milk, Pendleton gripped his chair to prevent himself toppling over. Others were not so lucky. Lieutenant Foster fell and hit his head on the base of the barnacle. The two midshipmen collided with Carter but remained on their feet.

'*My God!*' yelled Midshipman Porter, feeling the deck angle upwards. 'The blighter's going to drag us down with her!'

Ignoring Porter's panicky cry, Pendleton reached for the wheelhouse intercom and shouted, 'Slow astern, reduce revolutions two thirds,' adding, 'is anyone hurt down there?'

'No sir,' came the voice of Jack Tolby, glancing warily at Telegraph Operator, Jumper Collins. 'Everyone's OK sir, slow astern it is, sir.'

In the engine room two stokers had slipped over and cut their heads on piping. Another stoker in the boiler room injured his back as he fell against the bulkhead. In the engine room Chief ERA Bill Grundy and Paddy O'Malley saw the arrow on the Telegraph Order Receiver move to *Slow Astern*. Both immediately adjusted the main engine throttle to comply with the order. In a matter of seconds, the two twin 44,000hp propellers went into reverse. *Zimba* gradually moved backwards then slowly regained an even keel. For a few anxious moments the ship rocked dangerously before shuddering to a standstill.

Where the U-boat once lay was now a morass of oily black bubbles. Suddenly, from below the surface of the sea came a dull rumble. A huge explosion that sent a mountain of blackened water surging into the sky quickly followed this. For a few moments it hung in the air like an ugly blanket of death, before slowly subsiding into the sea, leaving behind a mass of debris and human remains floating on the oily waves.

At first nobody spoke. All that could be heard was the vibrations of the ship's engines and the wind whistling in the rigging. All eyes were staring at the spot where forty-six men had died a horrible death.

'What a lousy way to die,' muttered Yeoman Bob Jenkins to nobody in particular.

'It was either them or us, eh, PO,' said Jumper Collins, the port lookout. 'But you can't 'elp but pity the poor bastards.'

Pendleton's rasping voice interrupted their thoughts. 'Report casualties and damage, Number One,' he snapped. 'Better lower a boat and pick up anything that'll prove she's been sunk.'

Pendleton walked onto to the port wing and looked beyond A and B gun turrets to the fo'c'sle. What he saw made him grimace and shake his head. The ship's bows were now buckled into a twisted heap of steel. The fo'c'sle cable deck and windlass lay in ruins and the jackstay had disappeared. Turning to Lieutenant MacIntyre, he muttered, 'My God, Mac, goodness knows how long it'll take to repair this lot.'

Just then Carter arrived. He was out of breath, red-faced and sweating profusely. 'Four stokers with head injuries and a few sailors with minor bruises,' he said, regaining his breath. 'The Doc and the first aid team are attending to them. Other than that, nothing serious.' He paused momentarily before continuing. 'The paint store and for'd magazine are flooded. The Buffer and his damage control party are shoring up the bulkheads. The Asdic dome is a right off and the for'd watertight compartment and cable locker are also badly damaged.'

'What about the engine rooms and boiler rooms?' Pendleton asked, praying no damage had occurred that would prevent the ship moving.

'Paddy tells me he thinks there is some structural damage in the turbine blades due to excess speeds we have been doing,' Carter answered, wiping his brow with a handkerchief. 'He says it'll mean stripping down the engine.'

Pendleton sighed wearily and asked, 'How much speed can we make?'

'Ten knots maximum,' replied Carter. 'But if the weather turns nasty we might have to have a tow.'

'Better send a signal to Portsmouth, report, "U-boat, pennant number 145 rammed and sunk. No survivors". Give the location and ask for an escort.' Glancing warily at the clear blue sky, he added ominously, 'At the moment we're sitting ducks.'

Throughout the morning *Zimba* limped along, rolling awkwardly despite the calmness of the sea. Shortly after noon the welcome sight of a destroyer, HMS *Paladin,* loomed into view. After reducing speed she came some sixty yards to *Zimba*'s port side. Most of both ship's companies came on deck and exchanged cheerful grins and waves. *Paladin*'s captain, a young looking lieutenant commander, shouted, 'Can we help. Will you need a tow?'

'Thank you, but no,' Pendleton replied. Both officers were using loud-hailers and their voices sounded strained and sharp. 'But glad to see you, nevertheless.'

'Will stay close,' replied *Paladin*'s captain. 'Good luck.'

At 1400 the excited voice of lookout Jumper Collins rent the air.

'Aircraft approaching, red two hundred, sir.'

'Christ,' cursed Carter. 'That's all we need, a bloody enemy bomber.'

Heads and binoculars turned skywards.

'No need to panic, Number One,' said Pendleton, his heart beating like an express train. 'It's Liberator, no doubt come to make sure we get home safely. Give the fellow a wave.'

Everyone on the bridge did so, and as the plane came in low they were rewarded by the pilot dipping its wings before rising up and circling high in the sky.

By 1600, the green hills of the Isle of Wight hove into view. Shortly afterwards, with hands fallen in on the upper deck, *Zimba* slowly passed Fort Blockhouse.

Pendleton looked at the duty QM and said, ' Pipe. Attention on the upper deck, face the starboard,' he rasped. He and the other officers moved to the starboard wing ready to salute as they passed a cruiser and several destroyers moored in the harbour.

As the shrill sound of the bosun's pipe echoed around the ship, Pendleton and all on the upper deck were surprised to see and hear many men on the other ships waving and cheering.

'Core blimey, sir,' cried PO Yeoman Jeffries glancing enquiringly at Carter. 'What are they cheering us for?'

'Perhaps it's something to do with us ramming that U-boat,' Carter answered, grinning wildly.

'Signal from C in C, sir,' cried PO Yeoman Jeffries. 'It reads, "Well done. Secure alongside G Berth, Semaphore Towers. Move to Number Six Dry Dock, tomorrow 0900. Welcome home".'

Pendleton quietly murmured, 'Thank you, Yeoman, I only hope the Board of Inquiry will be just as pleased when I explain what happened. Everyone salute, and pipe, "attention on the upper deck, face the port".'

Away to his left Pendleton caught a glimpse of the grey slated roof-tops of the Royal Naval Hospital, Haslar, clearly visible behind HMS *Dolphin*. Suddenly, he remembered Nadine. During the past few days his mind had been so preoccupied with the safety of his ship he hadn't thought of her. Almost unconsciously he placed a reassuring hand over his inside pocket where her father's letter rested. For a fleeting moment he remembered the helpless expression in her sad violet eyes before they parted. The thought of seeing her again sent a mixture of excited anticipation and fear running through him. How would she react when they met, he asked himself? For all he knew she might be involved with someone. After all, she was a very attractive woman, surrounded by young doctors who would certainly ask her out. The thought of her in someone else's arms suddenly made him feel decidedly jealous, a feeling he hadn't experienced for years. But even if he and Nadine were to form some sort of relationship, would the memory of losing his family in the Blitz prove too great a mental barrier for him to relate to her? And with the war still raging, she might think it too much to face the prospect of once again losing someone she had become close to.

Pendleton's uncharacteristic reverie was interrupted by Carter's voice.

'We're coming alongside now, sir,' he said, staring at the glazed expression in his captain's eyes. 'Shall we reduce revolutions?'

'Of course,' Pendleton hastily replied. 'And fall out special sea duty men.'

Half an hour later, *Zimba* was tied alongside Semaphore Wharf.

CHAPTER TWENTY-FOUR

The next morning, with two tugs standing by in case of emergencies, Pendleton managed to manoeuvre his ship into Number Six dry dock.

Shaped like a horseshoe, the dock basin, with its steep, slippery concrete terracing resembled an oblong Roman amphitheatre with one end boarded up. With every turn of a hydraulic screw, seawater was allowed to drain out into the harbour. As the water level fell, dockyard workers using cranes, lowered stout oaken props against both sides of *Zimba*'s outer bulkhead. As the basin emptied the ship gave a shudder. Gradually, the keel settled onto a series of oak beams lining the base of the dock. By this time several more struts were now jammed into place stabilising the ship, making them protrude outwards like the oars of a Viking longboat.

An army of dockyard workers clad in blue overalls now invaded the ship; water, heat and electricity were turned off, emergency power cables for the dockyard use became attached from shore and layers of plywood laid down in passageways to protect the linoleum covered decks. In a matter of hours *Zimba* was transformed from an efficient fighting machine into helpless hulk.

'Better move the crew into barracks and send most of them on ten days' leave, Number One.' Pendleton was at the desk of his day cabin. Carter and Paddy O'Malley were standing in front of him. Paddy's face and white overalls were streaked with black oil. Carter shifted uncomfortably feeling lines of sweat running down his back. The portholes were closed; the dank musty smell of dust and dirt permeated the warm, claustrophobic atmosphere, and the constant sound of hammering had given Pendleton a headache. 'The rest of the officers, including yourself, Number One, can take ten days' leave. I will come in from barracks every day to keep an eye on things.'

'But surely this is a good time for you to take a break, sir,' Carter said. 'With respect, sir, there's very little you can do.'

'He's right, Jeremy,' added Paddy. 'The dockyard engineers said the repairs to the ship would take at least two weeks. Then there's the question of the stress to the turbine blades, not to mention the sea trials afterwards.'

With a tired sigh, Pendleton sat back in his chair and interlaced his fingers over his chest. 'Yes, I know,' he replied. 'But I've a mound of paperwork to catch up with and this is an ideal time to do it.'

However, Pendleton knew Carter and Paddy were right. A break would do him good but holed up in barracks, sipping pink gins wasn't his idea of a rest. Besides, he had some unfinished business to attend to.

He had intended to telephone Nadine the previous day, but delay at connecting the ship-to-shore line had prevented this. This was now remedied. As soon as Carter and Paddy left, he took out his wallet and removed the piece of paper Nadine had given him. He then picked up the receiver and asked to be put through to the Royal Naval Hospital at Haslar. A female voice answered and he asked for extension 145.

'Officers' Medical, just one moment, sir,' replied the voice.

Listening to the recurrent burr of the line he felt his heart rate increase and his mouth go dry.

'Hello, Officers' Medical, leading hand speaking,' came a thick, male voice on the other end of the line.

'Err, my name is Commander Pendleton,' he nervously replied. 'May I speak to Sister Le Brun, please?' With his spare hand shaking slightly, he drew a cigarette from a packet of Players and lit it with a small silver lighter.

'The sister is in with a patient at the moment, sir,' replied the voice. 'I'm LSBA Bamford. Can I be of any use?'

'No, not really,' Pendleton answered nervously licking his lips. 'If she's too busy, please tell her I'll call back later.'

'Oh, just a minute, sir,' interrupted Bamford, 'she's just come in the office.'

In muffled tones, Pendleton heard the LSBA say, 'There's a Commander Pendleton on the line, Sister, he says he can call back if you're too busy.'

'No, no.' Her voice was raised and overtly loud. 'Please, I will speak to him.' There was a faint, crackling noise as Nadine took hold of the receiver. 'Hello, Commander,' she said, 'what a pleasant surprise. How are you?'

Pendleton immediately recognised the same engaging French accent he remembered so well.

'Fine, thank you, Sister,' Pendleton nervously replied. 'We arrived yesterday. If you recall, you asked me to phone when we returned to bring you up to date about your father.'

'Ah yes, I remember,' said Nadine. As she spoke, Bamford, surmising this was a private conversation, discreetly left the room and closed the door. 'Dear Papa,' she went on, as she sat down behind her desk. 'I had a visitor from the War Office. He told me about his heart attack, but he is now recovering well and should be fit to resume his work soon. I can't thank you and your doctor enough.'

'That's good news,' said Pendleton. Suddenly his heart sank, realising the excuse for asking to see her to explain what had happened to her father was gone. Trying his best to disguise his disappointment, he went on, 'Surgeon Lieutenant Fulford will be pleased to hear that.'

After a slight apprehensive pause, Nadine said, 'I heard on the local wireless that your ship was damaged. I hope nobody was hurt.'

'Only a few minor bumps and bruises, nothing serious, I'm glad to say,' Pendleton answered, fully expecting Nadine to thank him again and put down the receiver.

'I think you're being very modest, Commander. The newsreader said your ship had sunk a U-boat, and you had been awarded a medal, the DSO. It sounded very exciting.' She paused and in a slightly nervous voice, added, 'Could we possibly meet and you could tell me all about it?'

Pendleton's heart leapt into the air. 'Why, err…yes,' he stammered, 'that would be fine.'

'*Tres Bien*!' Nadine replied, raising her voice slightly. 'I start a week's night duty on this Sunday, but I'm off duty all Saturday. If you are not busy we could have dinner, yes?'

'Why, y…yes,' Pendleton nervously replied. 'But I'm not too familiar with the restaurants in the area. It's been a long time…'

'I understand perfectly,' Nadine interrupted. 'We could go to The Wild Stag Hotel. It's at the top of Gosport High Street. My friend Iris and her boyfriend often go there.'

'Right,' answered Pendleton, feeling a surge of excitement running down his spine. 'What time do you suggest?'

'Saturday at seven-thirty,' she replied. 'If you catch the Gosport Ferry, I will meet you at the top of the slipway, is that all right?'

Feeling like a schoolboy arranging his first date, Pendleton smiled and said, 'That sounds splendid.'

'In France it is always the man who reserves the table,' she replied with a slight laugh. 'So I hope you don't mind if I arrange one for us, say, eight-thirty.'

Still feeling elated, Pendleton replied, 'I can assure you, Sister, I don't mind at all.'

'I am glad,' Nadine answered. 'And my names is Nadine. And yours is Jeremy, yes?'

'Yes,' Pendleton replied, surprised that she knew his Christian name. 'Until Saturday then.'

'Au revoir, Jeremy,' she said quietly, and hung up.

For a few seconds Pendleton sat holding the receiver, unable to believe what had happened. Today was Thursday. Suddenly, Saturday seemed a long way off.

CHAPTER TWENTY-FIVE

Over the next few days time seemed to stand still. While wading through reports and requests for stores, he would suddenly stop and think about his tryst with Nadine. He would stare out the porthole and remember looking into her beguiling violet eyes before they said goodbye. Even sitting in his cabin listening to stout, grey-haired dockyard officials complain about union problems, and the shortage of materials became an unwanted distraction.

Meanwhile the grating noise of acetylene burners cutting through steel, along with the intermittent racket of riveting continued to echo throughout the ship. To this cacophony, was added dull hammering and the trample of dockyard boots. The unusually warm rays of the September sun poured through the open porthole onto his back making his shirt stick to him like a second skin.

Despite this, Pendleton was able to catch up on the mass of paperwork. This included writing a fitness report on his First Lieutenant. Pendleton found this latter task especially rewarding. After a shaky start, Carter had performed admirably and would one day make a fine commanding officer.

On Friday morning a knock on Pendleton's door admitted the grey-haired figure of Chief Bosun's Mate Bill Conyon.

'Good morning, Chief,' said Pendleton giving the Buffer a cheerful smile. 'How are things progressing?'

The Buffer took off his cap, revealing his usual shock of white tousled hair. 'Mornin' sir,' he said. As he spoke, beads of sweat trickled down the sides of his weather-beaten face. 'All the crew have left for barracks. They've been issued with leave passes and the Chief Stoker has managed to persuade a dozen volunteers who live locally to act as skeleton crew.' He paused, took out an off-white handkerchief and quickly mopped his brow, then continued. 'Before he left the ship, Leading Steward Gale packed your gear and had it sent to the wardroom in barracks. He tells me you're in cabin number twenty-eight.'

'Thank you, Buffer,' replied Pendleton, smiling, 'for all you've done and give my regards to West Kirby.'

'Ta, sir,' said the chief, giving Pendleton a toothy grin. 'That I will. By the way I'm sure you've heard about the invasion of Italy and that the Eyeties have surrendered. It happened on the third of this month while we were at sea. And the Yanks have landed at Salerno. Now we're really giving it to the buggers.'

'Yes, I have,' answered Pendleton. 'The Eighth Army are moving up the east coast and have captured Reggio, Brindisi and Bari. I read about it in some of the old newspapers we received when we arrived. Marshall Badoglio, Italy's Prime Minister, has signed an armistice with the Allies. I also read that the Italian government have halted all ships, trains and vehicles carrying German troops. And the Italian army have overpowered a German garrison on Corsica. Good news, eh, Buffer?'

The Chief gave a rueful grin. 'That means the Eyeties are on our side, don't it sir?'

'That's right,' Pendleton replied. 'And that should please Joe Stalin who's been pressing Churchill for a Second Front.'

The Buffer paused for an instant and added, 'I wonder if we'll be involved when we're sea worthy?'

'We'll just have to wait and see, won't we?' Pendleton dryly replied.

Since Montgomery's victory at El Alamein in July 1942, the tide of war had slowly turned in favour of the Allies. In the Atlantic, the U-boat war was slowly being won. At the same time the Americans had continued their so-called 'island hopping' in the

Pacific. After occupying Guadalcanal later that year and then the Marianas and New Georgia, they were poised to attack Okinawa, a vital stepping-stone towards a proposed invasion of Japan.

Meanwhile the fiercest tank battle of the war so far had been won by Russia at Kursk as the Red Army pushed back the Wehrmacht. And in the Arctic, convoys braved the ice and stormy seas to deliver everything from armaments, aviation fuel and planes to Murmansk and Archangel.

No sooner had the Buffer left than Carter, looking somewhat tired, knocked and came into Pendleton's cabin.

'Yes, what is it, Number One?' Pendleton asked, poised with pen in hand. 'Any problems?'

'Not really, sir,' replied Carter, removing his cap. 'All the officers will leave for barracks at 1400. Is there anything I can do before I go?'

'No thank, you, Number One,' he replied. 'Have a good few days' leave. You and the rest of the men have earned it.'

'With respect, sir,' answered Carter, noticing the dark rings around his captain's eyes, 'you try to do the same.'

Pendleton's thoughts immediately turned to Nadine. 'Thank you, Number One,' he said with a smile. 'I'll do my best.'

After Carter left, he finished signing the rest of the paperwork and placed them in his out tray for Sub Lieutenant Haley to deal with. For the rest of the afternoon he busied himself writing a report to Captain PV McLaughlan, RN, C in C Portsmouth, concerning the ramming of U145, and marked it URGENT.

Now that *Zimba* was in the hands of the dockyard, Pendleton had become a mere onlooker, hoping that the damage caused by ramming the U-boat would soon be repaired. A glance at his wristwatch read 1625. He sat back in his chair, yawned and stretched his arms above his head. The thought of seeing Nadine sent a warm feeling running through him. With an exasperated sigh he ran his fingers through his dark brown wavy hair trying to understand the feelings he had for a woman he hardly knew. After

Zimba had sailed for Canada he had often thought of her, experiencing a deep sense of attraction, hitherto alien to him. Was it her porcelain beauty and captivating violet eyes that had haunted him during those long nights at sea, or was it simply a newfound feeling of sexual attraction? Whatever it was, Pendleton knew he wouldn't rest until he saw her again.

He decided to telephone the motor pool for transport to take him to the wardroom in barracks – perhaps a few pink gins would put things into perspective.

Ten minutes later the tilly took him up Queens Street, a busy road leading from the dockyard, and pulled up outside the Officers' Wardroom. Pendleton thanked the driver, slid the door open and stepped outside. For a few seconds he stopped and stared admiringly at the magnificent red-bricked building looming in front of him.

Built by Sir Henry Pilkington, RE at the turn of the twentieth century, this imposing edifice consisted of two storeys complete with attics. Corniced, multi-fluted chimneys designed in free Baroque rose from a heavy slated roof. The five outer accommodation bay windows, taped to contain bomb splintering, were covered in a multitude of ashlar bands, eaves cornices and architraves. Leaden rainwater pipes with dated heads, descended at each side of the building. A centre block crowned by ionic columned cupolas with ship's finials gave the frontage a distinct nautical appearance. A flight of stone steps led up to a Tuscan entrance over which, delicately carved in stone was the royal coat of arms. Of course, Pendleton had been here before attending dinners and meeting fellow officers. Nevertheless, he was always impressed by its structure, which struck him as being more like a millionaire's mansion than a haven for officers of His Majesty's Navy.

After showing his pay book to the Royal Marine on duty, Pendleton wiped his feet on a large horsehair mat and went inside. Standing behind an oak desk was a tall, clean-shaven man with thinning grey hair and keen brown eyes. He wore a short white jacket and dark trousers.

'Good afternoon, sir,' he said, displaying a row of uneven yellowing teeth. 'My name is Turner, I'm the Hall Porter, and you are, sir?'

Pendleton introduced himself. Turner opened a cupboard and handed Pendleton a heavy iron key.

'Number twenty-eight, sir,' said Turner, giving Pendleton a cheerful smile. 'Several officers from your ship have reported in and have gone on leave.' He paused, raised his bushy white eyebrows and added, 'Oh, yes, I believe there's a suitcase in your room with your gear. Dinner is at seven thirty.'

'Thank you, Turner,' replied Pendleton, accepting the key and putting it in his pocket. Directly ahead a marble columned staircase with an oak panelled balustrade curved gently up to the officers' quarters. Close by, a set of stout, oaken doors led into the main part of the wardroom. Pendleton paused to take in its elaborately carved frieze, its musicians' gallery partially hidden behind a thin wooden screen and elegant marble fireplace. From an arch-braced roof hung four decorative crystal chandeliers. Ornately framed paintings, commemorating famous naval battles, coats of arms of Nelson and his captains at Trafalgar, decorated the wainscot. Leading off from the main room were other rooms, each with ornate fireplaces, Ionic pilasters, marble columns cornices and mirrors. Glancing at the numerous shiny black leather Chesterfields, comfortable armchairs and highly polished tables, Pendleton couldn't help but wonder how many famous naval officers had graced these hallowed halls.

It was lunchtime and the room was full of officers. Most were drinking and talking or sat with their heads hidden behind the latest copy of *The Times*. A hub of conversation echoed quietly around and a haze of tobacco smoke hung in the air like miniature smog.

Pendleton looked around and to his surprise recognised the face of Commander Peter Okey, *Zimba*'s previous captain. He was talking to a tall, dark-haired officer of similar rank. Both held partially filled glasses in their hands. Okey suddenly glanced across and although it was a few years since they had met, he immediately recognised Pendleton. Okey politely excused himself and walked over to Pendleton. As he came nearer, Pendleton stood up and noticed how much Okey had changed since they met two years ago. He had lost weight and dark brown hair was heavily streaked with grey. He walked with a slight stoop and his face looked pale and drawn.

'Jeremy, old boy,' said Okey, as they shook hands. 'Whale Island, 1941 wasn't it?'

His manner was loud but pleasant and he spoke with a slight north-country burr. 'By the way, congratulations on your DSO,' he added, glancing approvingly at the small maroon ribbon edged with blue above Pendleton's breast pocket. 'But tell me, how are things onboard dear old *Zimba*. I hear you had a run in with a U-boat.'

'Yes, Peter,' Pendleton replied. 'She's in dry dock. No serious injuries.'

'Glad to hear it, old boy,' said Okey smiling benignly. 'Do grab a chair and join me. Incidentally, the chap you saw me talking to is Johnny Wilkinson, the captain of your sister ship, *Zetland*, have you met?'

'No, we haven't,' Pendleton replied, looking enquiringly at the officer in question.

Okey beckoned the officer over and introduced him to Pendleton.

'Rumour has it *Zetland* might be sailing for the Med,' said Wilkinson as he shook Pendleton's hand. 'So who knows, perhaps we might meet up. I'd like to stay and have a drink but I have to get back onboard, so please excuse me. Nice to have met you, Jeremy.'

As they watched Wilkinson leave, Pendleton turned to Okey. 'How are you, Peter?' he asked, his voice full of concern. 'I heard you had a touch of pneumonia.'

'More than a touch, old boy,' replied Okey, grabbing a vacant chair. 'I was laid up for a month. I'm now what the medics call

P7R, temporary unfit for sea duty.' He sat forward and lowering his voice, went on, 'By the way, Jeremy, I was terribly sorry to hear about your family. Bloody awful business.'

'Yes, it was, Peter, thank you,' muttered Pendleton, glancing solemnly at the deck. Changing the subject, Pendleton looked up and smiled. 'But tell me,' he went on, 'what are you doing in barracks?'

'I'm on the Admiral planning staff,' Okey replied. Beckoning a steward over he ordered two pink gins.

'Your job sounds very interesting,' Pendleton said, relaxing back in his chair. 'I bet it keeps you busy.'

'Yes, indeed,' Okey replied as the drinks arrived. After signing a chit, he leaned forward, glanced cautiously around and quietly added, 'Between you and me, Jeremy, rumour has it that after Sicily, it'll be Europe itself.'

'Any idea where, or shouldn't I ask?' Pendleton asked cagily.

'Haven't a clue, old boy,' replied Okey. 'But I do know that the Americans on the western flank of Italy and the eighth army in the east have to be kept supplied. And that means regular convoys from here to Italy.'

'Are you trying to tell me something, Peter?' Pendleton asked, giving Okey a searching glance.

'Oh it's only a rumour, you understand,' replied Okey. 'But if it's true, you can bet your bottom dollar we'll need every available ship.'

'That's very interesting, Peter,' Pendleton replied, as he finished his drink. Suddenly he felt tired. It had been a long day, busy day and a few hours' kip before dinner beckoned. He placed his glass on the table and stood up. 'Sorry I can't stay for another,' he added, 'my round next time. It really has been a pleasure seeing you again.'

'And for me,' replied Okey, as they shook hands. With a wistful smile he added, 'Take care of dear old *Zimba* and keep away from stray U-boats.'

'I'll do my best, Peter,' Pendleton replied, and left the room.

Cabin number twenty-six was on the top floor near the end of a long oak panelled corridor. After fumbling with the heavy iron key he opened the door and went inside.

The room consisted of a single bed with its customary blue coverlet embossed with an anchor, a small bedside light, a wardrobe, a small chest of drawers, a writing desk and chair. In one corner close to a window, criss-crossed with white tape, rested a stainless steel washbasin and mirror. A solitary light and lampshade hung from the ceiling, and in one corner attached to the wall, was an electric fire shielded with a wire frame. The walls were decorated in pastel green with fading photographs of past warships and a well-worn blue carpet covered the floor. By the side of the light switch was a notice that read, "bathroom and heads at the end of the corridor".

'Good Heavens,' gasped Pendleton, shaking his head in disbelief, 'I didn't expect the Savoy, but this is more like a cabin in HMS *King Alfred.*'(An officer's training establishment in Hove.) He took off his shoes and jacket and lay down on the bed. However, tired as he was, the thought of seeing Nadine again made sleep difficult.

The first thing Pendleton thought of upon waking up on Saturday morning was Nadine. The time was 0600. Daylight was streaming through the window making small diamond patterns on his coverlet. A knock came at the door and a small, pale-faced, steward wearing a white jacket, came in carrying a tray of steaming hot mugs of tea.

'Mornin', sir,' said the steward. He spoke with a cheerful Cockney accent. 'A lovely morning,' he added placing a mug on Pendleton's bedside table. 'If yer open yer window yer can 'ear the sparrars singin'.'

'No thank you,' yawned Pendleton. 'I'll take your word for it. Thank you for the tea.'

After breakfast he went to the front desk and asked Turner to order a tilly to take him to the dockyard. At that moment, a tall, broad shouldered captain with thick dark-hair greying at each temple approached him.

'Commander Pendleton, I believe,' he said in a sharp, rasping voice. 'I don't think we've met, I'm Captain McLaughlan. Thank you for your report about the ramming incident. Glad to hear you and your crew are all right.'

Captain James McLaughlan, DSO and Bar, had been in the navy for over twenty years. As a Midshipman he had fought at Jutland onboard HMS *Tiger*. He was married and had lost his only son, a sub lieutenant in the army, at Dunkirk. Known as a no nonsense officer, he demanded a high standard of efficiency from his subordinates. Pendleton was aware of this and was pleasantly surprised by the captain's friendly attitude.

'Thank you, sir,' replied Pendleton, as they shook hands. 'As I mentioned in the report it was the only thing I could do, or else the blighter might have gotten away.'

'Yes, quite,' replied the captain, staring directly at Pendleton. 'I see your ship will be laid up for some time.'

Pendleton felt his stomach contract. Despite having sunk the U-boat, he fully expected to face a Court of Enquiry. He needn't have worried. The captain's features wrinkled into a warm smile.

'I had intended sending for you this morning,' said the captain, 'but as we're here, I might as well tell you there's no need to take the matter any further. I consider the behaviour of you and your crew extemporary. Jolly well done.' Still smiling, he added, 'And let me know when *Zimba* will be ready for sea, won't you. I expect we'll have something interesting lined up for you by then.'

'Yes, sir,' replied Pendleton, feeling a flood of relief running through him, 'I'll certainly keep you up to date, and thank you.'

'Thank you and good luck to you, my boy,' said the captain, as they shook hands again.

Turner, the Hall Porter, who had overheard the conversation, grinned approvingly at Pendleton and opened the door for the captain to leave.

During the day Pendleton found it hard to concentrate while holding talks with dockyard officials about the progress of work onboard the ship. His thoughts kept returning to Nadine. He kept glancing at his wristwatch feeling time had suddenly stood still. After being told by a small, rather pompous overweight dockyard engineer that the steel plates for *Zimba's* damaged bow wouldn't be available for another day or two, Pendleton glanced impatiently at his wristwatch and said, 'Sorry to interrupt you, old boy, but I have an urgent appointment ashore.'

'No chance of a quick gin before you leave, Commander?' asked the official, lighting a cigar.

'I'm afraid not,' Pendleton hastily replied. 'There's a tilly waiting for me on the quayside, maybe next time.'

Pendleton arrived at the barrack wardroom at 1600. As he entered, Turner looked up from behind his desk, smiled and said, 'There's a phone message for you, sir, from a Sister Le Brun. I've written it down on a signal pad.'

Oh no, he thought, accepting the note from Turner. Please don't say she's changed her mind. He swallowed nervously. The message read:

"Can't meet you till 2000, something has cropped up. Have rebooked the table for 2100".

'Thank you, Turner,' said Pendleton, breathing a sigh of relief. 'Thank you very much.' After a brief exchange of words with a few officers, he had a cup of tea and a Spam sandwich then went to his cabin. For a while he lay on his bed with his hands clasped behind his neck.

'What on earth does she mean by, "something has cropped up",' he muttered to himself, hoping it was nothing serious. With this still on his mind he closed his eyes and gradually fell asleep. When he woke up it was 1800. In a fit of panic, he leapt off the bed, hurriedly removed his uniform, grabbed his towel and toilet gear and dashed to the bathroom.

CHAPTER TWENTY-SIX

After receiving the unexpected telephone call from Pendleton, Nadine was still in a state of excitement. Feeling her heart racing, she stared out of her office window wondering what on earth had possessed her to suggest meeting him. Of course, deep down she knew the answer; ever since she had slipped that note into his hands and said goodbye that night onboard *Zimba,* she had secretly hoped that one day he would telephone. Her reverie was abruptly interrupted by the sound of the office door opening. She looked up and saw the smiling face of Sister Iris Jasper.

'My goodness!' exclaimed Iris, her hazel eyes wide with surprise. 'You look like a cat that just swallowed the milk. Are you feeling all right, love?'

During the past year Nadine and Iris had become close friends. Iris had told her about her failed marriage to Harold, an accountant, before becoming a nurse. In turn, Nadine had poured her heart out over the death of her fiancé, Pierre.

'No, Iris,' replied Nadine nervously taking out a packet of Players and lighting one. 'I don't think I am.'

'What do you mean?' gasped Iris sitting down on a chair opposite Nadine's desk. 'You're not ill or anything, are you? What's happened?'

'Well,' Nadine replied coyly. 'I've met this man. He's the captain of a destroyer.' Without disclosing any secret details surrounding her father's journey to Canada, she told her friend about Pendleton.

'And where is going to take you?' asked Iris, grinning wildly. 'Do tell…'

'Actually,' Nadine said somewhat shyly, 'it's me who is taking him. I've suggested we have dinner at The Wild Stag, the place you and Larry got to. Jeremy isn't familiar with the restaurants in Portsmouth, so I thought it was a good idea.'

'And so it is,' gushed Iris. With a saucy glint in her hazel eyes, she added, 'You do know it's a residential hotel, don't you? That's where Larry and I...'

'*Ou la la!*' cried Nadine, throwing her head back and laughing. 'I know I'm French, but Jeremy and I hardly know each other.'

'Well don't waste too much time,' replied Iris. 'This bloody war can't go on forever.'

Just then a knock came at the door and a staff nurse came in carrying a tray containing several coloured bottles and small glasses. The intimate expressions on the faces of Nadine and Iris hinted that they had not been discussing medical matters.

'Time for midday medicines, Sister,' she said suppressing a smile.

'And I must away,' said Iris standing up and straightening her white apron. 'Now don't forget,' she added with an impish smile. 'I want to know every little detail.'

Nadine stubbed out her cigarette and walked around her desk. 'Maybe,' she replied tantalisingly, 'maybe.'

The next forty-eight hours seemed like a week. Nadine tried to emerge herself in her work but the thought of seeing Pendleton again kept distracting her. During breakfast on Saturday Iris came and sat next to her.

'Tonight's the night, eh, love?' she whispered gleefully. 'What are you going to wear?'

'I'm not sure,' replied Nadine. 'Would you be an angel and lend me a pair of nylons Larry managed to get you. I've only got those horrible Lyle ones.'

'Of course, love,' replied Iris. 'As a matter of fact I'm meeting Larry this evening also. Anne Patterson is off duty at 1800. She's doing my hair at 1830. I'm sure she'd do yours as well. It'll only take about half an hour.'

'*Tres bien!*' replied Nadine, clasping her hands. After a slight pause, she went on, 'In that case I'd better phone Jeremy and tell him I'll be late. By the way, where is Larry taking you?'

With a mischievous glint in her hazel eyes, Iris replied, 'I'm not sure, but I don't expect I'll be back till the morning.'

'*Mon Dieu!*' replied Nadine, shaking her head in mock indignation. 'Are you sure you're not part French?'

At eleven o'clock, Nadine decided to get some fresh air. The sky was deep blue with hardly a cloud in sight. As she left the mess a warm, early morning breeze caressed her face, relaxing her. Just then, a small black box Ford car drew up at the end of the pathway and out climbed Sister Leila Hansen, the girl from Copenhagen.

'Hello, Leila,' said Nadine. 'Where've you been? As you're on nights I thought you'd be in bed by now.'

'I've just been into Gosport to buy a few things,' replied Leila. 'You're relieving me tomorrow, I believe.'

'Yes, that's right,' said Nadine. Watching Leila lock the car door Nadine suddenly had an idea…

Pendleton left the wardroom at 1915. It was a beautiful September evening with a balmy breeze ruffling the leaves of the ash and elm trees lining Queen Street. Thinking his charcoal grey suit inappropriate and his Harris Tweed jacket too sporty, he had settled on a dark blue double-breasted blazer, white shirt, grey slacks and highly polished black shoes. Before leaving his cabin, he checked his wallet, made sure his tie was neatly knotted and adjusted his dark green cap. He smiled to himself realising that while he had abandoned his doeskin uniform, he was now dressed in a style favoured by naval officers, and would be easily recognised as such. Humming slightly, he slung his canvas gas mask over his shoulder and left the room.

Queen Street was crowded with sailors, hell bent on visiting the fleshpots of Portsmouth. These were joined by others streaming out of the dockyard and diving into the several pubs lining The Hard.

At the bottom of the street, Pendleton crossed over the road, passing several green double-decked buses and tea stalls. Directly ahead was the harbour railway station. The sight of a solitary heavy cruiser and a few destroyers lying at anchor reminded him that most of the fleet were at sea.

Two ferry boats, each the size of a large tug, ran a shuttle service between Gosport and Portsmouth – very handy for the dockyard workers living locally and those sailors who were RA (Rationed Ashore). Because of the blackout the last ferryboat left Gosport at midnight, returning from Portsmouth the next morning at 0630.

Feeling slightly self-conscious, Pendleton handed two pennies to an elderly, grey-haired man sitting behind a counter in a small wooden hut, and was given a ticket. A metal guardrail running down the middle partitioned the covered slipway into two sections. This arrangement allowed those leaving and boarding the ferryboat to keep to the left, thus avoiding any congestion. Pendleton queued up among a crowd of civilians and service personnel.

Everyone watched as the ferryboat, grandiosely named *The Duchess Of York* and billowing black smoke, slowly approached the jetty. Rolling precariously, the vessel squeezed against the large rubber tyres that acted as fenders and spluttered to a halt against the wooden pontoon. A member of the crew threw a heaving line to his opposite number ashore, who quickly secured it over a bollard.

The clinking of chains attached to the guardrails being released onboard the ferry echoed round. A wooden ramp was then rolled into position allowing people to disembark. When the last passenger left, an iron barrier at the base of the slipway was rumbled back enabling the waiting crowd to come onboard the ferryboat.

This was a ritual whose antecedents stretched back to 1843, when the Chancellor of the Exchequer regulated a ferry service between Gosport and Old Portsmouth.

The journey across the harbour took a little over ten minutes. Pendleton managed to find a bench next to a stout lady and a small child. He looked up at the small wooden bridge and saw a ruddy-faced man wearing a battered blue cap, holding the ship's wheel. Puffing away merrily at an old pipe, he calmly navigated the boat in between the warships anchored in the middle of the harbour. Some children, on seeing the ferryboat's sister ship, *Alexandra* passing close by on her way to Portsmouth, shouted and waved excitedly.

Pendleton felt his pulse quicken as the houses of Gosport hove into view. The time was a little after 1945. The *Duchess of York* bumped against a pontoon similar to the one in Portsmouth, and was secured. With his heart racing, he joined the people streaming off the ferryboat and walked up the steep slipway. At the top on the left, was a small wooden ticket kiosk. Behind this was a bus depot with several green double-decker buses parked next to one another.

Directly across the road from where Pendleton stood lay Gosport's main street. This was a busy, bustling thoroughfare crowded with service personnel, traffic, pubs and shops. Pendleton looked around to see if Nadine was there. Sadly, she was nowhere to be seen. A glance at his wristwatch showed him the time was exactly 2000. Feeling somewhat self-conscious, he thrust a hand impatiently into a trouser pocket and with a nervous sigh, gazed across the harbour at the warships lying at anchor.

Suddenly, from behind he heard a female voice cry. 'Bonjour, Jeremy, bonjour. Sorry if I'm late.'

Pendleton turned and saw Nadine leaning against the door of a small black box Ford car.

This was the first time he had seen her in broad daylight. Her complexion and high cheekbones, aided by the application of make-up, was much lighter than he remembered. However, it was those same beguiling violet eyes staring at him under long dark eyelashes that made him catch his breath.

Over a white, open neck blouse she wore a three quarter length fawn jacket. Under this was a pale green pleated skirt with a narrow brown leather belt that matched her shoulder bag. The smart dark leather shoes she wore with medium sized heels enhanced the shape of her slim, nylon-clad legs. A yellow silk headscarf and a single row of lustrous pearls added a touch of elegance to her overall appearance.

'Not at all,' Pendleton replied, recognising the distinct French inflexion in her voice, 'I've only just arrived.' Her grip as he shook her hand encased in a soft brown leather glove, was warm and firm. Glancing behind her at the car, Pendleton raised his eyebrows, smiled and said, 'Don't tell me this is yours?'

Nadine gave a short laugh, 'Not really,' she replied, displaying a row of small, white teeth. 'I borrowed it from Leila Hansen, a friend who's on night duty.' Giving Pendleton a reassuring smile, she added, 'I've driven it before to go shopping in Gosport, so don't look worried.'

'Oh, I'm not worried,' Pendleton hastily replied. 'It's just that it's unusual to see a woman driver.'

'Oh you men,' said Nadine, feigning a disapproving look. 'Women are driving ambulances, staff cars, and before you know it,' she added mockingly, 'they'll even be driving tanks, now stop staring at me and get in.'

Pendleton grinned and climbed into the passenger seat. As soon as he sat down he turned and said, 'My goodness, that perfume you're wearing smells lovely, what is it?'

'Chanel No 5,' replied Nadine, turning the ignition key while giving Pendleton a quick, sideways smile. 'I bought it in Paris before the war.' However, she didn't tell him it was the first time she had worn it since she came to England.

While she spoke, Pendleton looked at her profile and saw how the tip of her slightly curved nose moved slightly when she talked, an engaging trait he hadn't noticed before. He took a deep breath and relaxed back in his seat, and for the first time in months, felt at ease.

CHAPTER TWENTY-SEVEN

The Wild Stag was a large red-bricked hotel situated in a small cul-de-sac at the top of Gosport High Street. After narrowly avoiding a bus, Nadine crunched the gears, and giving Pendleton a quick apologetic smile, parked the car outside the entrance.

'As I told you on the phone, I've booked a table for nine,' said Nadine, switching off the engine and tugging the handbrake. 'That gives us time for a drink.'

'Good,' replied Pendleton, taking a deep breath. 'I think I could do with one.'

Pushing their way through a revolving glass door they were assailed by the peppery aroma of alcohol, mansion polish and tobacco. A dark brown, thickly piled carpet lay on the floor. Just inside the foyer was a mahogany table on which rested a black telephone and a directory. On the left side was reception desk, behind which stood a tall, grey-haired woman wearing a dark dress, busily writing in a ledger. As Pendleton and Nadine entered she looked up, smiled and said, 'Good evening sir, I'm Mrs Pendergast, the proprietor. Do go inside. The lounge is directly ahead of you.'

Nadine gave her a cursory smile and feeling the comfort of Pendleton's hand on her arm, they continued down a well-lit hallway. After passing a side room with a few people standing at a bar, they entered a spacious lounge. Around the oak panelled walls hung pictures of hunting scenes. One of these was an ornately framed reproduction of Sir Edwin Landseer's, *Monarch of the Glen,* beautifully displayed by hooded lighting.

Several couples, some in uniform, occupied the black leather armchairs and tables arranged around the room. A carpet similar to the hotel entrance covered the floor, and from a high, stuccoed ceiling hung a glittering crystal chandelier. Some people were drinking while a waitress wearing a white apron over a dark dress served others. From an open door at the far end of the room, marked "Residential Only", a stairway with a shiny balustrade wound its way to rooms on the upper floor. Another door allowed access to the restaurant from which emanated a strong smell of cooking.

Dominating the room was the huge head of a stag, complete with jagged antlers and piercing, lifelike eyes hanging above a white marbled fireplace.

'My goodness!' exclaimed Nadine, 'what a gorgeous beast. It looks as if it's about to pounce on us.'

'Well,' laughed Pendleton, squeezing Nadine's arm. 'Let's have a drink before it does so.'

They found a table and two vacant armchairs near the restaurant door. Pendleton helped her off with her coat. Close by sat a young army officer and a pretty, dark-haired girl, staring longingly into each other's eyes. Nadine noticed them and gave a quick, nostalgic smile. She then removed her gloves and headscarf allowing her soft chestnut hair to tumble graciously around her shoulders.

'Your hair looks different somehow,' said Pendleton as they sat down. 'It seems longer. Have you let it grow?'

'Not really,' replied Nadine. 'One of the nurses gave me a perm before I left. That's why I had to alter the time of our meeting.'

'Well you can tell her from me she's done a jolly good job,' replied Pendleton.

'Merci monsieur,' replied Nadine bowing her head slightly. 'Flattery will get you everywhere.'

Since meeting Pendleton onboard *Zimba,* Nadine noticed the tinges of grey at the sides of his brown hair had increased. Also, he had dark rings under his pale blue eyes, which bore witness to many hours spent without sleep. Nevertheless, his six feet plus frame, tanned features and broad shoulders gave him the appearance of strength and solidity. She relaxed back in her chair and suddenly realised he was one of the most handsome men she had ever met.

Just then the waitress arrived and in a clear Hampshire accent, said, 'Are you dining straight away or can I get you anything?'

'We've booked a table for nine o'clock,' replied Pendleton. 'But we'd appreciate a drink,' glancing across at Nadine, he added, 'gin and tonic all right?'

'Please,' said Nadine, smiling up at the waitress. 'With plenty of ice, if you would.'

From a side pocket, Pendleton removed a packet of Players. Nadine accepted a cigarette and Pendleton lit both with a small, silver lighter.

'Tell me Jeremy,' she said, turning her head while exhaling a steam of smoke, 'how long have you been going to sea?'

'Before the war I was in the merchant navy for several years,' Pendleton replied. 'I was also in the Royal Naval Reserve, and was called up in 1940,' he paused, and with a tired sigh, quietly added, 'sometimes it feels as if I've been at sea forever.'

'Your friend Commander Okey told me what happened to your family and brother.' She immediately regretted her words and felt her stomach tighten.

Pendleton didn't reply. Instead, he quickly stubbed out his half smoked cigarette in a glass ashtray. Nadine instinctively reached across and covering his hand with hers, said, 'Forgive me Jeremy, I didn't mean to open up old...'

'That's all right,' he replied, feeling her warm fingers squeeze his hand. 'Your father told me about Pierre. It must have been terrible for you.'

'Yes,' sighed Nadine, removing her hand and putting out her cigarette. 'This war has scarred both of us, when in God's name will it end?'

For a few seconds neither spoke. It was as if they were both recovering from being reminded about the pains of the past.

'I really must compliment you on your English,' Pendleton said, as the waitress arrived with the drinks. 'And your father told me your mother taught you to speak Italian.'

'Ah, yes, dear Mama,' Nadine sighed. 'It came in useful before the war if an Italian was admitted to my hospital, but now...' she added as her voice trailed away, 'who knows. Anyway,' she added, taking a deep breath while lifting her glass. 'To Papa and the end of the war,' she paused slightly then with a smile, added, 'and to us.'

Nadine's words "to us" sent a warm feeling running through him. But what exactly did she mean? Was there a hidden message behind her smile or was she merely being kind?

'Cheers,' Pendleton quietly replied. 'I'll drink to that.'

They had another gin and tonic and were about to go into the restaurant when Nadine gave a slight gasp of surprise. 'My goodness,' she cried, 'Iris and her boyfriend have just come in.'

Iris immediately recognised Nadine and gave her a wicked smile. She wore an ankle length fawn coat open to reveal a white blouse and a green pleated flared skirt. Her hands were encased in dark patent leather gloves and her blonde hair, recently washed and set, shone like gold.

Iris's escort was a tall, dark-haired Royal Naval lieutenant. His young, clear-cut features were slightly tanned and the wavy navy stripes on his sleeves indicated he was in the Royal Naval Volunteer Reserve.

Watching them approach, Pendleton's heart sank. The last thing he wanted was company, especially that of a naval officer. He was hoping to have Nadine to himself. Now, he would be forced to make polite conversation to two people he hardly knew.

'Why hello, love,' gushed Iris, doing her best to sound surprised. 'Fancy meeting you here.' Smiling wildly at Pendleton, she added, 'I don't believe we've met. I'm Iris Jasper. Nadine and I work together.'

'Jeremy Pendleton,' he replied standing up and shaking her hand.

'And I'm Larry Henderson,' said the officer. With a boyish grin, he added, 'I'm on one of those destroyers you see can see in the harbour.'

'Nice to meet you, Larry,' replied Pendleton, as they shook hands. 'And I'm the captain of a slightly damaged destroyer now in dry dock.'

'My goodness,' Larry answered, adding a polite 'sir' to his reply, 'I didn't know…'

'Sorry, Larry,' interrupted Iris, giggling like a schoolgirl, 'I really should have told you. Oh, and this lovely lady is Nadine.'

'A pleasure to meet you, Nadine,' replied Larry, shaking her hand. 'I do hope we're not intruding.'

Doing his best to sound hospitable, Pendleton replied, 'Not at all, perhaps you'd care to join us for a drink?'

Sensing that Nadine and Pendleton wanted to be alone, Iris gave Larry's arm a discrete pull. 'Sorry, we can't. We're really in a hurry. Larry has to be back onboard early, haven't you Larry?'

'Oh, err…yes, indeed,' replied Larry. 'Perhaps another time, sir.'

'Of course,' answered Pendleton, feeling a wave of relief run through him. 'Maybe you'd both like to come onboard my ship after the dockyard people have finished.'

'That sounds lovely,' said Iris. 'We'll look forward to that, won't we Larry?'

'Yes indeed,' replied Larry, fidgeting slightly. 'We'll be off then. Nice to have met you, sir,' he added as he and Pendleton shook hands again. 'I look forward to meeting you again.'

'Me also,' said Pendleton, 'and good luck.' Accepting Iris's hand he added, 'A pleasure to have met you.'

With an inward sigh of relief, Jeremy sat down. Together he and Nadine watched as the Iris and Larry walked though the door marked "Residential Only" and disappeared upstairs.

'Now I know why your friend said they were in a hurry,' Pendleton said, giving Nadine a slightly embarrassed look.

Nadine's face broke into an engaging smile. '*Ou la la,*' she said saucily, 'they're both young and who knows what life has in store for them.'

'Yes, I agree,' replied Pendleton. Taking hold of Nadine's hand, he added, 'Perhaps we'd better go into the restaurant. It's nearly 2200, and the last ferry leaves at midnight.'

The restaurant was smaller than the lounge. Several couples, some in uniform, sat at tables covered with pristine white tablecloths. Thick blackout curtains were drawn across two bay windows and a chandelier, similar to the one in the lounge bathed the room in a clear, even light. A small, stout waitress wearing a white cap, and a matching apron over a dark skirt, showed them to a corner table. After consulting a leather-bound menu, they agreed on chicken, followed by pork chops and vegetables.

'And if you have it, perhaps a bottle of red wine, please,' Pendleton added handing the menu to the waitress.

'I'm afraid we've only got French wine, sir,' replied the waitress writing their order on a small pad. 'Will that be all right?'

Looking approvingly at Nadine, he grinned and said, 'That will do perfectly.'

They spoke very little during the main course. Half an hour later, having enjoyed the meal Pendleton poured the last of the wine into their glasses.

'How long will your ship be in dry dock?' Nadine asked taking a sip of wine, 'or is that what is called classified information?'

'Yes, it is,' replied Pendleton, feeling the wine warm his insides. 'Actually I'm not sure,' he added lowering his voice. 'It all depends on the efficiency of the dockyard. But without disclosing details, I expect to be at sea in about two weeks' time. Sorry I can't be more precise.'

'Perhaps it is just as well,' replied Nadine, toying with her glass. 'As I start a week's night duty tomorrow.'

Pendleton looked across and for a fleeting moment thought he saw a glimpse of concern in Nadine's eyes. Suddenly, he wanted to reach across and touch her. Instead, he took out a packet of Players and offered her a cigarette and lit it. It was a small gesture but it broke the nervous tension he felt had arisen between them.

At that moment the waitress arrived carrying the coffee cups and saucers.

'We close in half an hour, sir,' she said, placing them on the table. 'It's the blackout you see.'

'Thank you,' replied Pendleton. 'Perhaps we could have the bill, then?'

Acting "mother", Nadine poured milk into the cups then said, 'Do you take sugar?'

'Yes, thank you,' he replied, pushing his cup and saucer towards her, 'two spoonfuls if there's enough for both of us.'

Asking him about the sugar was a simple question, but one that made her aware how little she knew about him. Watching Pendleton stir his cup she suddenly wanted to know where he was born, what his parents were like, what schools he went to, what hobbies he had and the girls he knew. These, and a myriad of other question flooded her mind as she drank her coffee.

After finishing his drink Pendleton glanced at his wristwatch, and said, 'It's after eleven. I believe the last ferryboat leaves at midnight.'

'I know,' replied Nadine. 'Just think,' she added with a sly smile, 'if you became stranded you'd have to stay here overnight.'

'My goodness,' said Pendleton, giving her a mocking laugh. 'I couldn't do that, I haven't got my pyjamas with me!'

A balmy warm breeze fanned their faces as they opened the door of the hotel and stepped outside. Everything seemed quiet. The only sign of life was a passing cyclist, his blue headlight dimmed and dipped. High above in a cloudless sky, a full moon, surrounded by a myriad of twinkling stars, cast its yellow glow on the rooftops of the houses.

'Isn't it a lovely evening, Jeremy,' muttered Nadine taking a deep breath. 'What a pity it's so late, we could have left the car and had a pleasant stroll to the ferry terminus.'

'Then you would have had to walk back to collect it,' replied Jeremy. 'And you might have got lost in the blackout.'

Putting on her headscarf, Nadine smiled and looked up at him. In doing so Pendleton noticed how the reflection of the stars in her eyes made them shine. 'But,' she replied, 'I'm sure the walk would have been worth it.'

Neither of them spoke as Nadine drove down Gosport High Street. After a grating gear change, the car came to a halt near the ferry terminus. The scene that met them differed dramatically from the bustling activity they had witnessed earlier. Across where Nadine had parked the car, rested two double-decked buses, their dark outlines silhouetted against the night sky. The soft chugging of the ferryboat coming alongside the jetty intruded into the quietness of the night. A few sailors and civilians could be seen lining up outside the ticket booth before disappearing down the darkened slipway. A small crowd of passengers emerged from the boat, some hurrying to catch what was probably their last bus home.

Nadine applied the handbrake then turned and saw Pendleton looking at her. The expression in his eyes was one of longing, so different from the sadness she had seen when they first met. For a few seconds neither spoke. Then, Nadine reached across and took hold of his hand.

'Thank you for a lovely evening, Jeremy,' she said, feeling his fingers entwine around hers. 'I really enjoyed myself.'

'So did I,' Pendleton replied, returning her gaze. 'It's a pity it has to end so soon.'

'Yes, it is,' Nadine quietly answered. 'Incidentally,' she added, gently squeezing his hand, 'I finish nights next Saturday, so if you're not too busy, we could meet on Sunday – say seven thirty, here, same place.'

'That sounds splendid,' replied Pendleton, feeling his heart suddenly lurch, he added, 'I'll look forward to it.'

'Me also,' Nadine said. 'And if for any reason you can't make it you can call me at the mess any morning after ten.'

Instinctively, their arms went around each other, and as they kissed, time seemed to stand still. The cramped conditions inside the car made their embrace more intimate. Pendleton felt the softness of her body against his and smelt the intoxicating aroma of her perfume. Nadine was conscious of the warm, hardness of his lips and the eagerness of his grasping arms around her shoulders. Seconds later they broke away, slightly out of breath and feeling their hearts pounding like an express train.

'Quickly, Jeremy,' said Nadine, glancing at her wristwatch. 'You'd better hurry. The ferryboat leaves in five minutes,' with a coy smile she added, 'and remember, you haven't brought any pyjamas.'

A quick kiss made him want to remain in his seat. Instead he opened the car, climbed out and after a parting smile, hurried away. Nadine watched as he reached the small, wooden kiosk, fumbled in his pocket and bought a ticket. He then turned and gave her a final wave before hurrying down the slipway.

CHAPTER TWENTY-EIGHT

The following morning, Pendleton held a meeting in his day cabin with Mr Harold Barnes, a senior dockyard official and Paddy O'Malley. The time was just after 1000. The atmosphere was warm and muggy. The closed portholes partially diminished the constant hammering and grating noise of riveting. In sharp contrast to the pristine whiteness of Barnes's overalls, those worn by Paddy were dirty grey and oil-stained. The two men were sat in armchairs smoking cigarettes. Pendleton was behind his desk listening intently to what they had to say.

'The for'd watertight compartments have now been repaired,' said Barnes a tall, sallow-faced official with thin greying hair. 'But the engineer tells me the bulkhead in the paint store will take a few more days before it's ready for use.'

'And what about the turbine blades, Paddy?' Pendleton asked, sitting back and crossing his hands over his chest. 'What state of readiness are they?'

'The Chief ERA and his team have been working day and night, so they have,' Paddy replied. 'But the spares have only just arrived, so it'll be at least a week before they're in commission.'

'As you know,' said Pendleton, furrowing his brow, 'I have to inform Captain McLaughlan about the ship's progress.' He paused and then slowly stood up. Placing both hands flat down on his desk, he looked at them and with an exasperated sigh, continued, 'And judging by what you've told me it'll be another seven days before we can undergo basin tests, and after that it'll be sea trials. That brings us almost to the end of the month.' He paused, smiled weakly and added, 'Thank you, gentlemen, I'd like a progress report every day.'

Despite being surrounded by a mountain of paperwork, Pendleton's thoughts kept turning to Nadine. In the middle of writing a report, he would suddenly stop and imagine her curled up in bed sound asleep after a busy night on the ward. He would have been surprised to know that he too was constantly on Nadine's mind, wishing the week would pass quickly so they could be together once more.

The thought of having to wait almost a week before hearing Nadine's voice again was suddenly too much. On Thursday morning shortly after 1100, Pendleton picked up the receiver and asked to be put through to the sisters' quarter in Haslar. A female voice answered. Pendleton identified himself and asked to speak to Nadine. A few minutes later she came on the line.

'Bonjour Jeremy,' she said, slightly out of breath, 'it's lovely to hear your voice. How are you?'

Nadine's voice with that familiar French inflexion sent a surge of excitement running through him.

'Fine, thank you, Nadine,' he replied. 'I hope I'm not disturbing you.'

'Not at all,' she replied. 'I don't go to bed until midday. Is everything all right for Sunday?'

'Yes, everything's fine.' Feeling his mouth suddenly go dry, he added, 'I hope you don't mind me saying so, but I'm really looking forward to seeing you again.'

Pendleton's deep, resonant voice sent a shiver down her spine. 'I don't mind at all,' she quickly replied. 'It is the same for me.'

'Good,' said Pendleton. 'Then I'd better leave you to get your beauty sleep, not that you need it, you're so…'

She quickly interrupted him, 'Thank you, Jeremy,' she said smiling. 'I'll see you on Sunday. Au revoir,' and put the receiver down.

That evening, Pendleton was sat in the barrack wardroom mess reading a copy of *The Times*. According to the headlines, Stalin had dissolved the Comintern (The International Communist Organisation), in an effort to appease the Allies. Another, smaller headline stated that clothes rationing had saved the country six hundred million pounds.

'Does it mention anything about convoy losses in the Mediterranean, Jeremy?'

Pendleton looked up and saw the slightly stooped, six-foot frame of Commander Okey smiling down at him.

'Good evening, Peter,' said Pendleton, folding his newspaper. 'Nice to see you again, had a good leave?'

'Yes, thank you,' replied Okey. Catching the eye of a steward he ordered two pink gins.

'I thought we'd cleared the Med of U-boats,' Pendleton said, giving Okey a searching look. 'What have you heard?'

'Three merchant ships have been sunk off the coast of Libya,' Okey sombrely replied. 'The Boche still have U-boat bases in Sardinia and the Luftwaffe remain a danger from Greece and northern Italy.'

'What about losses to our ships?'

'The *Orion* and *Newfoundland* were slightly damaged but they're all right,' replied Okey as the drinks arrived. 'But the U-boat threat in the area is far from over.'

'I see,' said Pendleton, finishing his drink. 'If I remember, I owe you a round.'

'Splendid idea,' Okey replied with a smile.

An hour later, feeling relaxed and tired, Pendleton said a cheerful goodnight to Okey and left the mess.

Pendleton woke up on Sunday morning to the sound of the wind rattling his cabin window. He leapt out of bed, tore open the curtains and saw a canopy of dark, low lying, angry cumulonimbus clouds. As he showered and shaved the distant rumble of thunder echoed around the room.

After breakfast his usual tilly took him to Number Six dry dock. The time was just after 0900. Shrouded in early morning mist, *Zimba* looked forlorn and deserted. The rattle of riveting echoing from within the ship told Pendleton work was in progress. The only signs of human life was the occasional appearance of a dockyard worker and a security guard wearing a greatcoat and side arm, huddled in a makeshift shelter near the top of the brow.

Another meeting with Paddy, Mr Barnes and Chief ERA Bill Grundy confirmed that work on the ship was almost completed.

'The blades for the turbines have only just arrived, Jeremy,' reported Paddy, shifting his bulky frame uncomfortably in his chair. 'Bloody unions, but I expect they'll be in place in the next forty-eight hours.'

'And the damage to the bows have been repaired and new plates are being riveted in position,' said Bamford, puffing heavily on his cigar. 'In my opinion, Commander,' he added waving away a cloud of smoke. 'You could have basin trials, say, on Wednesday.'

'Good,' Pendleton replied. 'Everyone should be back from leave by then. I'll speak to the Admiral Superintendent of the Dockyard and arrange it.'

By 1600 the weather continued to deteriorate further. Rain had begun to fall and the wind increased in volume, bending branches and scattering leaves.

'Bloody change from last week, eh, sir?' the driver remarked as he drove Pendleton to the barrack wardroom mess. 'Not much good for a trip to Southsea for the missus and kids.'

'Quite so,' came Pendleton's disquiet reply. 'Please pick me up here at 1845 and take me to the harbour station.'

At 1730, he had a quick cup of tea, took a shower and changed into civilian clothes. Under his naval Burberry he wore his usual double-breasted dark jacket, a white shirt and naval tie, grey trousers and black shoes. Making sure his dark green, flat cap was on straight he left his cabin.

The tilly was waiting outside on the road near the entrance to the mess. Pulling up the collar of his raincoat, Pendleton slid open the door and climbed inside.

'Gawd 'elp the sailors on a night like this, eh, sir,' the driver said laughingly as he switched on the engine. 'I 'opes you've brought your umbrella.'

'As a matter of fact, I haven't,' said Pendleton, feeling rather stupid. 'Maybe it'll ease off.'

'Pigs might fly, sir,' grinned the driver as he drove off.

CHAPTER TWENTY- NINE

Because of the unusual high winds the journey across Portsmouth harbour took longer than the normal ten minutes. Everyone took shelter below in the small rooms, grasping the end of their seats or each other to avoid falling over. The whine of the wind echoed around as waves bounced against the hull of the boat. It was no mean feat of seamanship by the pipe-smoking captain to avoid the warships riding at anchor.

After a second attempt, the ferryboat was finally secured alongside Gosport jetty. Pendleton left the room and joined the wet and bedraggled passengers leaving the boat. In doing so he heard the rain battering against the slipway's corrugated covering and wished he had brought his umbrella.

Pendleton reached the top of the slipway and immediately recognised the black box Ford lying by the kerbside. Nadine saw him and smiled, then opened the passenger door. The same yellow silk headscarf she had worn before was tied neatly around her neck. Under her service Burberry she had chosen to wear a dark green floral, button down dress, matching high-heeled shoes and a pair of nylons, borrowed once again from Iris. A small golden Star of David suspended on a delicate silver chain had replaced the row of pearls.

Pendleton climbed inside the car and was immediately cocooned by the sensual aroma of Chanel No 5. No sooner had he sat down, than Nadine reached across and kissed him.

'Your face feels like ice,' she said, touching his cheek with her gloved hand.

'Then you'd better kiss me again and make it melt,' replied Pendleton.

'Later,' Nadine replied, smiling while sitting back in her seat. 'I don't know about you, but I'm starving.'

'I see you managed to borrow the car again,' said Pendleton, stating the obvious. 'What did you tell your friend?'

'Nothing,' Nadine replied as she switched on the ignition. 'Leila's in bed with a cold.'

'Well, if this weather doesn't improve,' said Pendleton, hearing the rain clatter against the roof of the car, 'we'll all probably catch pneumonia.'

As he spoke, a loud clap of thunder echoed all around the ferry terminus. This was quickly followed a flash of lightning that momentarily lit up the insides of the car. An even stronger deluge of rain began to pour down.

Nadine drove slowly up Gosport's Main Street painfully aware that despite the use of the windscreen wipers, visibility was reduced to a mere fifty yards. The sound of the rain hitting the car competed with the steady splutter of the car's engine, and the swish of the tyres sending arcs of water streaming over the bonnet. Pendleton glanced across and noticed the intensity in Nadine's eyes as she peered through the windscreen.

'Are you sure you're all right?' he asked, his voice full of concern. 'Would you like me to drive?'

Without moving her head, Nadine replied. 'Thank you, I'm fine,' adding laconically, 'we have storms in France as well as England, you know.'

They arrived outside the hotel at 2000. As they left the car a jagged bolt of lightning lighted up the front of the hotel. By the time they arrived into the warmth of the foyer, their Burberrys were saturated with rainwater.

'*Mon Dieu,*' cried Nadine looking down at her legs. 'My nylons are soaking wet and my headscarf is ruined.'

At that moment a tall, portly man wearing a black raincoat and trilby, entered the foyer. With him was a small woman clad in an oversize yellow Macintosh. The blue beret she wore was saturated and looked more like a pancake, and her round, pale face was wet with rainwater. Both were out of breath and breathing heavily. For a few seconds they stood panting while using their hands to wipe water off their coats.

'Beastly weather, what?' grunted the man, removing his hat to display a shock of white hair. 'I've just heard on the local wireless station that the Gosport ferry has been cancelled till further notice. Isn't that right, Cora?' he added, giving the woman a questioning look.

'Yes, Henry,' said Cora, taking off her beret. 'And it looks like it's on for the night.'

'Indeed,' said Pendleton, frowning as he helped Nadine to shrug off her Burberry.

The proprietor, Mrs Pendergast, arrived.

'Good evening,' she said, 'what an awful night. May I take your wet things and hang them up in the cloakroom. The fire in the lounge will soon dry you out.'

Not wishing to become too friendly, Pendleton nodded casually to Henry and said, 'Please excuse us, we'll no doubt see you later.'

'Of course, old boy,' he replied. Turning and giving Cora an all-knowing smile, he added, 'We remember what it's like to be young, don't we dear?'

'Speak for yourself, Henry,' Cora answered curtly. 'Now take me inside and buy me a large gin and tonic.'

As they entered the lounge the warmth from the log fire crackling in the grate, caressed their faces. Above the marble mantelpiece the same steely eyes of the deer stared menacingly at them. Outside the rain rattled against the bay windows, around which the blackout curtains were drawn. However, as each clap of thunder resounded around the room, the lights flickered eerily.

'My goodness,' remarked Pendleton, as the chandelier swayed slightly. 'It's like a scene from a Bela Lugosi film.'

'Bela who?' asked Nadine, giving Pendleton an enquiring look.

'Never mind,' replied Pendleton, gently squeezing her hand. 'Let's sit down on those two vacant armchairs and order a drink.'

The same waitress that had served them the previous Saturday arrived.

'Nice to see you again, sir,' she said, holding a pad and pencil. 'May I get you a drink? Gin and tonics, if I remember correctly.'

'Thank you,' replied Pendleton, smiling, 'that'll be fine.'

Taking out a packet of Senior Service cigarettes he gave one to Nadine then lit them both.

'Now,' said Pendleton, sitting back and exhaling a steam of tobacco smoke. 'How the blazes am I going to get back to Portsmouth?'

'I could always drive you around the harbour,' replied Nadine. 'I've never driven that way before, but I'm sure I could manage it.'

'In this weather?' retorted Pendleton, shaking his head, 'not a chance. If you had an accident I'd never forgive myself.'

'What will you do?' asked Nadine.

'Let's worry about that later, shall we,' replied Pendleton, as the drinks arrived. 'Who knows, perhaps the weather will lift.'

But it didn't.

With the exception of young army lieutenant and an attractive, blonde WAAF, they had the restaurant to themselves. By the time they had finished their meal of poached haddock, the wind had increased its velocity and the rain became heavier.

Pendleton ordered coffee.

'It's almost 2200,' he said, glancing at his wristwatch. 'It looks like I'm here for the night,' he added, looking somewhat apprehensive.

My God, Nadine thought, staring across at him. He reminds me of a little boy who knows he is going to be late for school. Suddenly, she had the urge to reach across and touch his face and comfort him. For a fleeting second she imagined him lying upstairs in a double bed, staring up at the ceiling smoking a cigarette, listening to the elements beating against his window, while she lay in her narrow bed in the hospital, wishing she were with him.

Pendleton finished his coffee and with a gesture of finality, stubbed out his cigarette.

'I suppose I'd better see if they've got a room for a stranded sailor,' he said trying to force a smile. 'If the weather gets any worse, you might find yourself stranded also.'

Nadine reached across and placed her hand over his. 'Then perhaps I'd better stay here as well...just in case. After all I'm not on duty till 1200 tomorrow.'

For a few seconds neither of them spoke. The implications of her words made Pendleton's heart rate increase. He looked across at Nadine and noticed the slight blush on her cheeks. He reached over and gently placed his hand over hers and was about to speak, when the waitress arrived.

'Hope you enjoyed your meal, sir,' she said placing the bill on the table. Just then, a gust of wind and rain rattled the windows. 'Looks like this is on for the duration, don't it sir?'

'Yes it does,' replied Pendleton, quickly withdrawing his hand from Nadine's. He glanced at the bill, took out his wallet and gave the waitress a pound note. 'That should cover everything,' he said. 'And keep the change.'

'Thank you, sir,' said the waitress, who, after a quick nod of appreciation, moved away to the army officer and his girlfriend.

'I expect they'll give us a couple of single rooms,' Pendleton said, feeling his mouth go dry.

'Jeremy, darling,' said Nadine staring longingly into his eyes. 'I don't think we need two single rooms, do you?'

'Are you sure, I mean...?' He muttered nervously.

'You must think I'm some sort of loose woman,' Nadine replied, suddenly feeling embarrassed. 'Because believe me, I'm not.'

'The thought never entered my head,' Pendleton answered, trying not to show his embarrassment. 'But they may ask for a marriage licence. And besides,' he gave a tentative pause, 'it's been a long time since I...'

'And me, Cheri,' Nadine said, squeezing his hand. 'And don't worry about the licence, I don't think they bother, but if you'd rather we had separate rooms, I'll understand.'

Nadine's usage of the word 'Cheri' sent a warm feeling running through him. It was the first time she had referred to him as such, and it served to increase the intimacy of their situation.

'No, no,' Pendleton stuttered. 'It's just is so sudden. I didn't expect...' His voice trailed away.

'Neither did I,' replied Nadine, releasing his hand. 'And anyway,' she added, glancing furtively at the windows, 'we can always blame it on the weather, can't we?'

'That's a poor excuse and we both know it,' said Pendleton, standing up and smiling nervously.

'Yes, you're right,' replied Nadine. She stood up and picked up her shoulder bag. Seeing the hesitant express on his face, she added, 'Do you want me to come with you while you book the room?'

'Err...no,' replied Pendleton somewhat sheepishly, 'I'll see to it.'

They left the restaurant and entered the lounge, which was empty except for the army officer, his girl, Henry and Cora. All four were sitting in armchairs close to the log fire. Not wishing to be too conspicuous, Nadine and Pendleton found two chairs in a far corner. Pendleton gave her a cigarette, lit it then left the room.

CHAPTER THIRTY

Mrs Pendergast came in from a side door as Pendleton entered the hall.

'Good evening sir, this beastly weather,' she said, her blue eyes crinkling into an understanding smile. 'I take it you want a room?'

'Ahem…yes please,' Pendleton replied after clearing his throat. 'Just for the night.'

Adopting a business-like manner, Mrs Pendergast said, 'A basic double is thirty shillings, one with a bathroom en-suite is two and six extra and that includes breakfast.'

'We'll take the en-suite, please,' said Pendleton, hurriedly groping for his wallet. 'Shall I pay now?'

'Thank you,' replied Mrs Pendergast as Pendleton handed her two crumpled pound notes. 'Now if you'll just sign the register, everything will be hunky-dory.'

Pendleton accepted the pen and after an uneasy glance at the woman, signed *J Pendleton, Portsmouth.*

Mrs Pendergast smiled benignly, turned and unhooked a key from the board.

'Number five,' she said. 'Second on the left upstairs. Do you want a call in the morning?'

'Thank you,' said Pendleton. 'Six o'clock, if you don't mind.'

'Fine,' she replied. 'I'll ring your bedside telephone.'

Pendleton thanked her again. He turned around and met Henry and Cora coming out of the cloakroom.

'Staying the night, I see,' boomed Henry, his heavy jowls a deep crimson colour. 'Can't say I blame you, old boy, lovely girl, eh what.'

'Don't be coarse, Henry,' said Cora, pushing him towards the door. 'And give me the car keys, you're not in any fit state to drive.'

After collecting his and Nadine's Burberrys from the cloakroom, Pendleton returned to the lounge.

'All done,' he said, showing her the key. 'We'll be given a call at zero six hundred.'

Nadine stood up, picked up her gloves and placed her bag over her shoulder. Suddenly she felt nervous. The last person she had slept with was Pierre and that was over two years ago. The feeling she had for him then was now a warm memory, one she would always cherish. But as they climbed the stairs, Nadine knew she was falling in love again.

Pendleton also felt guilty. Since meeting Nadine thoughts about the death of Martha and Harold had not been so painful. It was as if Nadine acted as an emotional buffer between him and the trauma of the past. He was secretly ashamed to admit it, but when he was with Nadine, memories of Martha and his son did not seem so acute. Perhaps it was time to make a new start. But what with the war and the prospect of him going to sea very soon, could this be possible? These thoughts were still running around his head as they arrived outside room number five.

Feeling his hands shake, he placed the key in the lock, turned it and pushed the door open.

The curtains were drawn and the room was in darkness. The wind and rain rattling against the window and the intermittent crash of thunder lit up the room, increasing their nervous tension.

Nadine switched on the light. The room was quite large with a dressing table and chair, a wardrobe with frontal mirror and two brown, leather armchairs. Pale green wallpaper with a multitude of small, coloured flowers decorated the wall, and under the window sill the heat from a small gas fire helped to warm the damp atmosphere. The floor was covered with a multi-patterned carpet and in one corner was a round highly polished table and a brown Bakelite wireless. A cream coloured lampshade hung from the ceiling and an open door led into a bathroom. However, it was the king size bed, covered in a bright pink quilt that occupied their gaze.

'Well, the room's certainly big enough,' remarked Pendleton, taking in the two bedside tables, and solitary black telephone.

'The bed or the room,' replied Nadine, trying to disguise her nerves with flippancy.

'Err…quite,' replied Pendleton.

Nadine came close and placed both arms around Pendleton's neck. Her violet eyes, now on fire, stared passionately into his.

'Commander Pendleton,' she said, mockingly. 'If you don't kiss me I shall scream.'

Pendleton didn't need a second invitation. He immediately dropped their Burberrys on the floor. As he pulled her against him he felt her body tremble. Nadine's lips were soft pliant and warm. In turn she felt the hardness of him pressing against her. To this was added the slight prickly roughness of his upper lip and the warmth of his nasal breathing. When they parted each could feel the blood pounding though their heads. For what seemed like an eternity they stood holding one another so close, wondering if either could hear the other's heartbeat. Even fully clothed, Pendleton was only too aware of the softness of her stomach and breasts. Feeling his penis stiffen, he moved slightly away from her. However, she held onto him, aware of his arousal. Nadine slowly ran her hands down his back and over his buttocks, feeling the hardness of his thighs pressing against hers.

Once again Pendleton moved away from her in an effort to hide the embarrassment of his erection.

'Please, Cheri,' she murmured softly. 'We cannot stand her all night. Switch off the main light but keep the bedside lights on while I go into the bathroom.'

'All right, but don't be long,' he muttered as he cupped her face her in his hands and kissed her.

'I won't, Cheri,' Nadine replied, reaching up and gently touching his face. 'So why don't you turn off the electric fire and the main light while I'm away.'

With a gentle smile, she broke away from him, picked up her shoulder bag and went into the bathroom. With mounting nervousness, Pendleton did as she asked. Except for the yellow glow cast by the bedside lights and the thin white line under the bathroom door, the room was now in darkness. The faint sound of running water echoed from within the bathroom as he quickly undressed. Modesty forced him to keep his service issue underpants on. The rest of his clothes he placed over the nearest armchair. He then threw back the pink eiderdown and climbed into bed and lit a cigarette.

Suddenly, the bathroom door opened and Nadine stood, silhouetted against the light, wearing only a knee-length, black slip. In one hand she carried a crumpled mass of stockings and underwear, while the other held her handbag.

Pendleton watched as Nadine walked across the room and placed her clothing next to his. As she did so, the silky material of her slip wrinkled tantalisingly against the contours of her slender body sending a sensual thrill of excitement running through him.

'My God, Nadine!' he gasped inhaling the intoxicating aroma of Chanel No 5. 'You look absolutely stunning.'

'Merci boucoup, monsieur,' she coyly replied, noticing the small mass of dark curly hairs on his chest. 'And so do you.'

Pendleton peeled back the eiderdown and blankets and watched as Nadine slid into bed. She knew he was watching and allowed her slip to rise tantalisingly up her body displaying her nakedness.

'Now,' she said, feeling his firm, muscular legs and thighs next to hers. 'Please let me take off take those horrible under shorts and put your arms around me.'

With his heart thumping, Pendleton stubbed out his cigarette and felt the softness of her hand drag down his shorts. In doing so he gave a guttural gasp as she brushed against the stiffness of his penis. 'Oh Nadine, darling,' he muttered almost incoherently, 'I want you so.'

'And I you, Cheri,' she gasped, pressing her body against his. 'For God's sake make love to me, please...'

In an instant all their inhibitions faded into oblivion. They lay facing one another, she, aware of the warm shaft of his penis pressing against the softness of her stomach, and he, fighting against the slow volcanic eruption building inside him. With undue haste Pendleton pulled down the straps of Nadine's slip and cupped her breast, feeling her nipple harden under his eager fingers. Her short animal cry gave way to a passionate gasp. With her slip now around her waist, her legs parted as his fingers entered the warm wetness of her body. She gave a throaty cry and rolled over dragging him on top of her. Wrapping her legs around his waist she cried, 'Now, cheri, now...'

As he entered her, their mutual sensations of lust and love became lost in a world of intense passion. Nature, and years of celibacy suddenly caught up with them as they climaxed together. For what seemed like an eternity, they lay breathless holding one another, their eyes closed, listening to each other's hearts pounding like an express train.

Finally, bathed in each other's sweat, Nadine opened her eyes and murmured, 'Oh Jeremy, that was so wonderful, I could cry.'

Pendleton's head rested in the nook of her neck. He glanced up and with a heavy sigh, replied, 'Yes, I know exactly what you mean, but everything happened so quickly, I...I'm sorry.'

'Do not worry,' she answered, turning slightly and kissing his forehead. 'Remember we have plenty of time.'

Throughout the night they made love again and again until totally exhausted, they finally fell asleep, cocooned in each other's arms.

The ringing of the telephone woke Pendleton up. Nadine's warm naked body lay curled up against his back. One of her arms was draped over his waist, her fingers curled and still, the other tucked by her side. Pendleton carefully reached over and picked up the receiver.

'Hello,' he whispered.

'Your six o'clock call, sir,' said Mrs Pendergast. 'I hope you slept well.'

Pendleton thanked her and put the receiver down. At that moment he felt Nadine stir.

'What time is it, Cheri,' she whimpered, allowing her hand to descend onto his stomach. The gentle touch of her fingers on his pubic hair immediately aroused him.

'Six, darling,' replied Pendleton, turning around and pulling her gently against his nakedness.

'Then,' she said as her warm hand gently caressed his testicles. 'Kiss me again…'

An hour later, having showered and dressed they left the hotel. The storm had abated but a cold westerly wind and dark clouds promised more rain.

'What a difference a day makes,' sighed Nadine glancing across at Pendleton as she drove down Gosport High Street.

Pendleton reached over and gave her hand a quick squeeze. 'Any regrets?' he replied as they arrived at the ferry terminus.

'Don't be silly, Cheri,' she answered, applying the handbrake. 'I've never felt so alive in years.' Feeling tears welling up in her eyes, she added softly, 'I can't wait to see you again, whenever that'll be.'

Nadine's words made him feel as if he were being mentally and physically reborn.

'I expect we'll be at sea next week,' he replied. 'I'll call you when we get back.' He paused, swallowed hard and feeling his throat suddenly go dry, went on, 'I...I think I'm falling in...'

Nadine quickly placed her hand over his mouth. 'Don't say anything, Cheri,' she cried. 'Not now, not until we're both sure.'

'Yes, darling,' he replied feeling his face redden. 'You're right.' Glancing anxiously at his watch he said, 'I think I'd better go or I'll miss the boat.'

After a final kiss Pendleton left the car. Uttering a small prayer for his safe return, Nadine watched as he joined the queue of sailors and civilians at the ticket kiosk and disappeared down the slipway.

PART FIVE
THE RAID

Bari Harbour: 2nd December 1943

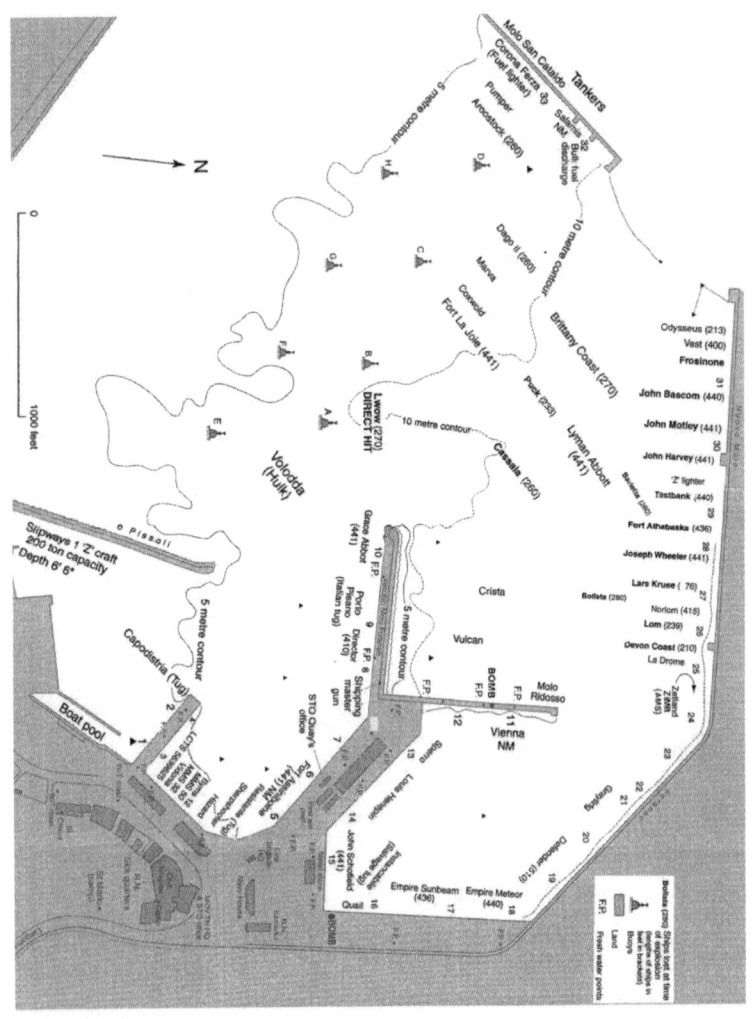

CHAPTER THIRTY-ONE

The date was Monday 29 September.

Pendleton was sat at his desk reading dockyard reports and provision requests. In front of him stood the First Lieutenant.

'Leading Cook Wilson and Able Seaman Miller are sick on shore, sir,' Carter reported. 'Also, three ratings have come back adrift and will be seen by you at defaulters at 1300. Otherwise, everyone else is onboard. I trust you had a good leave, sir?'

'Very pleasant indeed,' Pendleton answered, relaxing back in his chair. 'Do have a seat and a cigarette,' he added, passing an open packet of Players across his desk.

Normally, when Carter reported to Pendleton he was kept standing. 'Thank you, sir,' he replied, somewhat puzzled by Pendleton's sudden burst of hospitality.

'Now,' said Pendleton, leaning forward and placing both hands palm down on his desk. 'As you know, the ship has a new jackstay and bows. The magazine, paint shop, cable locker and the dome are repaired, and Paddy tells me the turbine blades are in place. Therefore,' he added with a satisfied smile, 'I have arranged for basin tests to take place on Wednesday at 0900. Better make sure this is on Daily Orders.'

'And sea trials after that, sir?' Carter asked, leaning across and flicking ash into an ashtray.

'All being well,' replied Pendleton, pursing his lips. 'Maybe Friday or Saturday,' he added. 'That'll be all, Number One, now please be good enough to ask Gale to come in.'

Carter stood up, left the cabin and closed the door. Outside he met the lanky figure of Leading Steward Gale, who was talking to PO Steward Knocker White.

'The captain wants to see you, Gale,' said Carter. 'He seems in an unusual happy mood today. Must be because we'll be sailing soon.'

'Beggin' yer pardon, sir, no it ain't,' replied Gale, giving Knocker a sly wink, 'Bagsy Baker, one of our stokers saw him getting out of a car across in Gosport. And wot's more, the party driving it was the same one wot came onboard when we took that professor to Canada. And,' he paused, 'Bagsy saw them kissin' so 'e did.'

'*Really,*' Carter replied, raising his eyebrows in surprise. 'No wonder the old devil's smiling.'

The word about Pendleton's liaison with Nadine soon spread around the ship.

At rum issue, Gale announced it to all and sundry. His salacious remarks could easily be heard in the nearby seaman and stokers' messes.

'The randy bugger,' remarked Steward Jock Thompson, before downing his tot in one gulp. 'Who'd 'ave thought it, eh?'

'And from what I 'ear,' came the voice of Leading Seaman Dusty Miller, 'she's from France, and you know what they're like. I wouldn't mind giving her one.'

'Bugger off,' yelled Podge Peters, a tall, pale-faced stoker from Doncaster, 'she'd suck you in and blow you out in bubbles.'

'Bollocks to the lot of yer,' said Mick Channon. 'Remember he lost his missus and kid in the Blitz, so good luck to him, that's what I say.'

The senior ratings heard the news with understanding borne out of experience.

'I don't blame him,' remarked Danny Wilson, the Chief Stoker, pouring out his glass of neat rum. 'He's still only young and this bloody war won't last forever.'

'I'll drink to that, and to both of them,' added Jack Tolby, savouring his tot. 'And may Liverpool win the league when this fuckin' war is over.'

'Pigs might fly,' PO Steward Knocker White replied dismissively. 'And don't forget you owe me sippers for that ham sarnie I got you from the wardroom.'

In the wardroom the officers reacted with equanimity.

'Anyway,' growled Lieutenant MacIntyre, trying to catch the eye of the steward. 'It's about time he got off the ship and enjoyed himself. All work and no play makes Jack a dull boy. Now, where's me pink gin?'

'I hope he brings her onboard,' said Lieutenant Reed. 'I believe she's a nurse,' he added, looking at Surgeon Lieutenant Fulford. 'Maybe she could give you a few tips, Doc.'

'Any help would be more than welcome,' grinned Fulford, mockingly bowing his head.

Wednesday 1 October dawned dull, overcast with a stiff north-westerly wind blowing downriver. The time was just after 0900.

Everyone on *Zimba*'s bridge stared intently at Pendleton waiting for him to give the order to open the valves on the dockyard gates.

'Ready when you are, Captain,' shouted Mr Bamford, the senior dockyard official leaning over the port wing. In one hand, Mr Barnes held a walkie-talkie. He would use this to communicate with the dockyard engineers waiting to turn on a series of hydraulic keys, very much like those used by men on turnpike canals.

Zimba would leave the basin bow first. A quick glance by Pendleton confirmed the fo'c'sle party were closed up ready to accept the tow from *Growler,* the tug that would take them to Fountain Lake Jetty.

Pendleton gave a nodded signal towards Mr Barnes, who, after nervously clearing his throat, spoke into his machine.

Like an angry tide race, seawater poured in from the open vents, picking up the oddments of wood and debris, which, after two weeks, had accumulated on the bottom. On the side of the dock basin, men wearing yellow waders and holding long-handled hooks waited to collect the props as they floated free.

Pendleton, Lieutenants Small and Foster leant over the port wing. Digger Barnes, the Chief GI along with PO Yeoman Bob Jeffries watched the proceedings from the starboard side. 'Won't be long, now, sir,' said Lieutenant Sam Small, taking a deep breath. 'The water is almost past the anchor.'

Pendleton didn't reply. He was more concerned hoping there wasn't any leakage following the repairs.

Higher and higher came the water, dense and dark green, swirling around the ship's side. One by one the props floated off and were retrieved. Then, as the last one was removed, everyone felt the ship give a sudden, sharp tremor. As if being jostled by an unseen hand, the deck rocked awkwardly before settling on an even keel.

'My God,' sighed Pendleton, 'that feels good. What say you, Guns?'

Lieutenant Small was about to answer when the intercom rang. This was the call Pendleton had been anxiously waiting for.

'To be sure,' came the dulcet tones of Paddy O'Malley, 'she's as dry as the Sahara Desert, so she is, and ready to sail anywhere you like.'

'Thank you, Paddy,' replied Pendleton, 'that's just what I wanted to hear.'

No sooner had he spoke than the dock gates opened and the towlines passed to *Growler*. Shortly afterwards, *Zimba* began to move forward.

'I'll feel a lot better when we're under our own steam, Number One,' remarked Pendleton, who along with Carter was leaning over the port wings.

'Not long to go now, sir,' Carter replied, ensuring the fender parties were protecting *Zimba*'s paintwork. 'Once we've passed through those two docks, we'll be alongside Fountain Lake Jetty.'

And so it proved. By midday *Zimba* was secured alongside her new berth.

'Thank God for that, Number One,' Pendleton said to Carter as *hands to dinner,* was piped. 'Now we can get back to normal routine. We'll be going to sea on Friday morning to test the turbine blades. I'm sure Captain (D) in Semaphore Towers will have his beady eyes on us, so I want the ship looking spic and span.'

'Any news where we'll be going after that?' asked Carter.

Pendleton shook his head. 'I really don't know,' he cautiously replied. 'It could be anywhere.'

'I'll bet you a pink gin it'll be the Atlantic again,' replied Carter with a sly smile.

Pendleton shrugged his shoulders and grinned. 'You're on,' he replied, 'and you can make it a large one.'

That evening Pendleton telephoned Nadine.

'Oh, Cheri, it's lovely to hear you,' she cried, her voice full of emotion. 'When can we see each other again?'

'I'm not sure, darling,' replied Pendleton, nervously biting his lip. 'I'll be having an important meeting on Sunday morning with a senior planning officer. By then things should be clearer.'

'You sound as if you're expecting a mutiny,' laughed Nadine. 'Is everything all right?'

'Yes,' said Pendleton. 'It's only a slight technical problem. I'll call you on Sunday night, around eight.'

'Make it nine, Cheri,' she replied. 'I don't come off duty till eight.'

'I miss you, darling,' said Pendleton, feeling his heart thumping in his chest. 'If I don't see you soon, I think I'll go mad.'

'I know exactly what you mean, Cheri,' Nadine replied. 'Till Sunday then,' and put the receiver down.

Shortly after 0800 on Friday 3 October, *Zimba* left Portsmouth harbour and nosed her way into the Solent. Pale rays from the sun cast a dull shadow on the grey waters and a fine drizzle filtered down from the dark, cirrocumulus clouds.

Directly ahead lay the rolling hills of the Isle of Wight, shrouded in dank mist. Away to starboard, the slanted rooftops of the naval hospital, Haslar, were barely discernible in the early morning light.

'Starboard ten, Number One, increase revolutions one third,' snapped Pendleton as *Zimba* passed Fort Blockhouse. 'And fall out special sea duty men.'

'Starboard ten, sir, revolutions increased one third,' repeated Jack Tolby below in the wheelhouse.

The sharp buzzing of the engine room intercom echoed around the bridge. Pendleton reached across and unhooked the handset.

'Captain here, what is it?'

'To be sure, Jeremy,' came the voice of Paddy. 'When do you intend opening her up?'

'Not long now,' he replied. 'After we've passed the Isle of Wight and have a clear run into the Channel. How are the turbines sounding?'

'So far so good,' Paddy said, glancing cautiously at Chief ERA Bill Grundy. 'I'll soon let yer know if anything happens, so I will.'

The ship gradually heeled to starboard and increased speed. A few miles to starboard stretched the leafy coastline of Hampshire with the hangars of HMS *Daedalus,* a naval air base, visible a mile or so inland.

'Anything on the radar?' Pendleton asked Sub Lieutenant Coburn, as he surveyed the horizon with his binoculars.

'A small convoy and escort approaching from the south, sir,' replied Coburn. 'It's roughly ten miles away. And a much bigger one coming down Channel some eight miles to the north.'

'Aircraft approaching, red four oh, sir,' yelled Jumper Collins from the crow's nest.

Everyone on the bridge trained his binoculars high in the air to the left.

'Sound the alarm!' shouted Pendleton. 'It's a Junkers 88!'

Gradually the plane's twin engines, grey fuselage and distinctive black cross on either wing became clear. All eyes watched as the bomber descended almost to sea level.

'The bugger's too low for the main guns to traverse,' yelled Lieutenant Small.

'All Oerlikons, fire at will!' shouted Pendleton down the intercom. 'Port Twenty.'

Almost immediately, *Zimba* heeled over to the left. At the same time the 20mm Oerlikons opened up, sending lines of coloured shells streaking towards the enemy plane. Ignoring *Zimba*'s deadly fusillade, the fighter approached the ship almost at mast height.

'Starboard ten, full speed!' cried Pendleton.

In a matter of seconds the Junkers had disappeared into the low-lying clouds. But not before it had released a stick of six black bombs hurtling towards *Zimba*.

'Port five,' ordered Pendleton.

Masts and yardarms angled in the sky as *Zimba* turned sharply to her left. Instinctively, everyone on the bridge ducked as a series of watery explosions erupted all around. Shock waves from the detonations bounced against the ship's side causing her to rock like cork. Then suddenly, except for the hissing of the sea and the throb of the engines, all was silent.

'Check for casualties and damage, Number one,' said Pendleton, steadying himself against his chair. 'That was too close for comfort.'

The engine room intercom sounded. Pendleton answered.

'Just thought you'd want to know Jeremy,' said Paddy. 'The turbines came through just fine. How are things up top?'

'Still in one piece, thank God,' replied Pendleton. 'Anyone hurt down there?'

'Just a few bumps and bruises,' answered Paddy stoically. 'To be sure, my stokers are a hardy bunch.'

At that moment Carter arrived, his handsome features covered in perspiration. 'Two of the gun's crews have bomb splinters and one of the cooks has scaled his arm, sir,' he said. 'The Doc says they're not serious and is dealing with them. One of the Carley floats is smashed to pieces and the port whaler is badly damaged.'

'What about the places that were repaired after we rammed the U-boat?'

'The Buffer tells me they're dry as a bone, sir,' Carter replied cheerfully.

'Well, Number One,' said Pendleton with a satisfied sigh. 'It could have been a lot worse. Secure from action stations and let's return to harbour.'

CHAPTER THIRTY-TWO

Captain McLaughlan looked up from his desk as an attractive, Third Officer Wren opened his office door allowing Pendleton to enter. The time was a little after 1000 on Sunday 5 October.

'Ah, Jeremy, nice to see you again,' he said rising and shaking Pendleton's hand. 'Take off your greatcoat and have a seat. I'll be with you as soon as I've signed these blasted papers, and smoke if you want to.'

Pendleton removed his cap and coat then sat down opposite the captain's desk. He lit a cigarette, crossed his legs and looked around. The room was quite large and simply furnished. Thick blackout curtains hung in long rounded folds either side of a wide bay window, criss-crossed with tape. A shiny green metal filing cabinet rested in one corner close to a glass drinks cabinet. Most of the oak panelled walls were lined with leather bound books, box files and photographs of warships old and new. The captain's desk was cluttered with papers and bulky, cream coloured folders. A strong smell of tobacco hung in the air and an old briar pipe lay smouldering in a glass ashtray. Near at hand were two telephones, one black the other red. Behind the desk a large coloured map of the world filled most of the wall. Close by was a framed photograph of King George V1 and Queen Elizabeth. Strip neon lit the room rescuing it from the dullness of the morning sky, and a dark blue carpet with small gold anchors covered the floor. It was, Pendleton thought as he took a deep drag of his cigarette, neat and efficient, reflecting the personality of the man sitting opposite him.

Captain McLaughlan placed his fountain pen on his leather bound blotting pad, picked up his pipe and after a few puffs, succeeded in producing a cloud of swirling grey smoke.

'Well now,' he said, removing his pipe and waving a hand to clear the air. 'How did the sea trials go? What shape is *Zimba* in?'

With an air of satisfaction, Pendleton replied, 'The ship performed very well, sir. Turbines excellent and no problems with the repairs.'

'Splendid, I take it then *Zimba* is fully fit for sea duty?' The captain's voice was sharp and brisk.

'Yes, sir,' answered Pendleton, 'perfectly fit.'

'Then you will replenish ammunition and provisions and sail this Wednesday at 0800. The next morning at approximately 0600, you will rendezvous with a fast convoy coming from the Med fifty miles off Lands End, latitude 50 degrees, longitude ten degrees. The cruiser, *Belfast,* and three destroyers will be escorting the convoy. Most of the thirty ships will contain wood and food, but others will be filled with ballast.' He paused for an instant and took a few puffs of his pipe, emitting another deluge of pungent smelling smoke. 'When you reach the Mersey Estuary, ten merchant ships will detach and sail into Liverpool. The remaining twenty will be escorted to Glasgow. Here, *Zimba* will wait at Greenock and be joined by the sloop, *Jaunty,* and escort a convoy of five merchantmen carrying coal to Bristol. In all it should take about ten days, providing the Luftwaffe or the U-boats don't interfere with you. Any questions?'

'No, sir,' replied Pendleton, stubbing out his cigarette. 'Everything's quite clear?'

'Splendid,' said the captain, opening a drawer and taking out a buff-coloured envelope marked TOP SECRET. 'It's all in here,' he added, handing the envelope to Pendleton. Rising up he extended his hand, smiled and said, 'Good luck, my boy. I'll no doubt send for you when you return.'

As soon as Pendleton returned to the ship he sent for Carter, Paddy and Sam Small.

'Sailing on Wednesday, eh?' said Paddy, furrowing his brow. 'To be sure, that doesn't give us much time, does it Jeremy?'

'Not really,' replied Pendleton. 'But I'll be sending urgent signals requesting fuel lighters tomorrow at 0700. I'll be consulting with John Hailey to see what extra provisions we will need. How about you, Guns?' he went on, glancing expectantly at Sam. 'I take it you'll manage to ammunition us by then?'

'Of course, sir,' replied Sam, smiling. 'My gunnery department won't let you down.'

'I never doubted it for a moment,' said Pendleton, with a sly grin. 'And by the way, tell the other officers what's happening. Put it on Daily Orders but don't tell the crew where we're going. I'll do that when we're at sea.'

As arranged, after rounds at 2100 Pendleton telephoned Nadine from his cabin and got through quite quickly.

'Hello, darling,' said Nadine, her voice trembling slightly. 'I was expecting you to call. How is everything with your ship?'

'The ship's fine,' she heard him sigh.

'Then what's the matter, Cheri,' she said. 'You sound worried.'

'I'll tell you when I see you tomorrow,' Pendleton replied. 'I'm sorry, darling, but I can't say any more over the phone, careless talk and all that.'

'Of course,' Nadine answered, her voice was quiet and stilted. 'I understand.' She paused for a few seconds, then went on, 'Leila has loaned me the car again. Seven thirty tomorrow. I can't wait to see you, Cheri.'

That night Pendleton lay awake thinking about Nadine. Already, in his mind he was missing her. However, remembering the thousands of women who had husbands and boyfriends overseas, many of whom would never return, made him feel guilty. After all, a ten-day parting was nothing to what they had to endure. Eventually, he fell asleep wishing the night would quickly end.

The next three days onboard *Zimba* were hectic. Every member of the crew was engaged in storing ship or loading ammunition.

At 1600 on Tuesday, Carter knocked on Pendleton's cabin door and went inside.

'Everything loaded and secure, sir,' he said with an air of satisfaction.

'Thank you, Number One,' Pendleton replied, sitting back in his chair. 'Paddy has already told me all the tanks are full. We'll slip at 1145 tomorrow. Hands fall in for leaving harbour at 1130. And by the way,' he added with a wide smile. 'You owe me a large pink gin.'

Pendleton left the ship at 1830. Dusk was falling and the blackout curtains on shops and houses were draw across windows. An insipid yellow moon flitted in between clusters of grey clouds and the brown overcoat he wore over his dark blue jacket and fawn trousers, failed to keep out the biting northerly wind.

This time Nadine had abandoned the box Ford and was waiting near the top of the gangway. The blue headscarf she wore matched her ankle length coat and as she hurried towards him, her black, high-heeled shoes rattled against the cobbled-stoned pavement.

'Oh, Cheri,' she said, her violet eyes lighting up. 'I've missed you so. It seems like an age…'

'Yes, darling, I know exactly what you mean,' Pendleton replied, squeezing her hand. Despite the presence of passers-by he kissed her passionately on the lips. The wolf whistle this brought forth was ignored as they broke away and walked to the car.

'Now tell me, Cheri,' said Nadine glancing apprehensively at Pendleton as she started the car. 'What was so secret you couldn't tell me over the phone?'

Staring directly ahead, Pendleton tersely replied, 'We're sailing on Wednesday.'

She immediately stalled the car.

'For how long,' she asked, crashing the gears before re-starting the engine.

'Roughly ten days,' Pendleton replied, as she drove off.

'*Mon Dieu,* ten days, is that all?' she cried. 'I thought you were going to say you were going away for an age.'

'It will seem like an age to me, darling,' Pendleton remarked as they arrived outside the hotel.

Mrs Pendergast was standing behind her desk and greeted them with a welcoming smile.

'I take it you'll be staying overnight, sir?' she asked Pendleton, noticing they were holding hands.

'Err...yes, we will,' Pendleton replied, quickly disengaging his hand from Nadine. Booking a room for the night was still an embarrassing business and he felt his face redden.

'And I take it you'll both be dining?' she asked, smiling benignly at Nadine. 'The roast chicken is especially good tonight.'

'Sounds delicious,' replied Nadine, glancing up at Pendleton, 'doesn't it Jeremy?'

'Yes indeed,' Pendleton answered, nervously licking his lips.

'Splendid,' replied Mrs Pendergast. 'I'll book a table in the restaurant for eight thirty. Is that suitable?'

'Yes, that'll be fine, thank you,' said Pendleton as he signed the register, 'and a call in the morning at six o'clock.'

'Room number five,' said Mrs Pendergast, 'and payment in advance as usual.' With a faint, all-knowing smile playing around her thin lips, she handed Pendleton the key and added, 'I take it you know where it is?'

Pendleton didn't reply. He merely nodded slightly, took out his wallet and paid for the room.

As they entered the lounge, Nadine took off her headscarf. Under her coat she wore a white blouse with a ruffled collar, and a black skirt that showed off her slim figure. She shook her head allowing her shiny chestnut hair to tumble around her shoulders.

Pendleton bent close and whispered in her ear, 'You look absolutely ravishing. Maybe we should forget about dinner.'

'A good idea, Cheri,' Nadine replied coquettishly, giving Pendleton's hand a gentle squeeze, 'but I suppose we must eat something to keep up our strength.'

After a few gin and tonics they adjourned to the restaurant. The roast chicken was cooked to perfection, but with each mouthful, they felt their excitement rise.

'Do you want a dessert, darling?' asked Pendleton, refilling Nadine's glass with white wine.

'Not really, Cheri,' replied Nadine, feeling her cheeks burning, 'shall we…'

Pendleton looked across at Nadine, nodded and said, 'Yes, darling, let's go.'

Pendleton paid the bill, and with their arms around one another, they left the restaurant and walked arm in arm upstairs and entered their room.

At first they made love with such passion that neither wanted to end. Pendleton was a tender, emotional lover whose only concern was giving Nadine total sexual and emotional fulfilment. After a pulsating mutual climax, they lay in each other's arms, naked and breathless with contentment beyond their dreams.

Sometime later, Pendleton reached across in the dark to his bedside table for a packet of Players, lit two and gave one to Nadine.

'You know, Cheri,' muttered Nadine, lying back and taking a deep drag of her cigarette. 'Where were you born, you know you've never told me.'

'Actually darling,' Pendleton replied, giving Nadine a quick kiss of the forehead, 'I was born in Penzance. That's a large fishing port almost at the tip of Cornwall.'

'It sounds delightful. Cheri,' Nadine replied, gently stroking the fine hairs on his stomach. 'Were you happy there?'

'Oh yes,' said Pendleton. 'My father was an accountant and my mother taught at the local primary school.' He paused for an instant, moved his head and exhaled a stream of smoke into the darkness. 'David, my younger brother and I passed a scholarship and went to the Grammar School. Penzance is a picturesque place facing the sea with fine scenery and fresh air. It was an idyllic place to grow up in.'

'Maybe one day you could take me there,' Nadine muttered, cuddling closer to him.

'Perhaps I will, one day,' he replied flicking ash into an ashtray.

Early next morning they left the hotel. Rain drizzled down from a dark sky, as the stars were about to deliver their last flickering light.

'Call me as soon as you get back, Cheri,' Nadine said as she drove down Gosport's deserted main street. 'I'll be counting the hours and days.' She stopped the car at its usual place. She turned and feeling her throat suddenly contract, looked into Pendleton's eyes and said, 'You do realise I'm very much in love with you, don't you?'

Her words sent a shiver of delight running through him. He gently touched her face and felt warm tears running down her cheek. 'I fell in love with you,' he quietly replied, 'when I came back from Canada. At first I wasn't sure, but darling, I am now.'

'Oh, Jeremy,' she pleaded. 'No matter what happens, tell me we will always belong together, please tell me…'

'Remember, darling,' he said holding her close. 'Wherever I am, you will always be with me, and one day we will be together for good. I promise.'

After a farewell kiss, he opened the door and left.

CHAPTER THIRTY-THREE

Shortly after 0600 on Wednesday morning *Zimba* slipped her moorings and slowly pulled away from the jetty. Banks of low lying dark clouds promised rain and a fierce northerly wind rattled the ship's rigging. Ratings fallen in on the fo'c'sle and quarterdeck wore black oilskins, and chinstraps prevented caps being blown overboard.

On the bridge Pendleton bent over the voice pipe.

'Port ten, slow ahead,' he said calmly.

From below in the wheelhouse came the distinctive voice of Chief Coxswain Tolby. 'Port ten, sir,' and then, 'ten o' port wheel on, sir.'

'Midships.'

'Midships… Wheels amidships, sir.'

'Steady.'

'Steady…Course south, ten eighty west, sir.'

'Steady as she goes.'

Close by, four destroyers rolled gently in line ahead secured to a buoy. Not far away towered an aircraft carrier. Pendleton watched as the tiny Gosport ferry chugged under the bows of its curved, overhanging fight deck, remembering his trysts with Nadine.

"Attention on the upper deck, face the port", came the pipe.

Pendleton and Carter stood to attention and saluted as *Zimba* cruised past under the eagle eyes of the C in C, watching from Semaphore Towers.

The *carry on* quickly followed this.

Zimba increased speed and sailed into the Solent.

'Starboard fifteen, Number One,' ordered Pendleton, looking at the compass repeater. 'Anything on the radar?'

'No, sir,' replied Carter, 'nothing as yet.'

As *Zimba* gradually heeled over to starboard the brown-stoned buildings of Haslar could be seen on the Hampshire coastline. Raising his binoculars Pendleton stared longingly at them knowing it would seem like an eternity until he held Nadine in his arms again.

During the night the wind increased to gale force. The ship, darkened and alone, plunged through the high, rolling sea. All hatchways, scuttles and anything moveable were secured. Nevertheless, despite these stringent precautions, seawater found its way into mess decks and passageways.

In the wheelhouse, duty telegraphist Able Seaman Geordie Roberts turned to Leading Seaman Dusty Miller, who was on the wheel and said, 'I wish to fuck we were in the Meddy. I'm bloody sick of the pissing Atlantic.'

'Ah stop fuckin' moanin' will yer,' replied Miller, who was concentrating on keeping the ship on a steady course. 'You 'eard the old man. We might even get a run ashore in Greenock. I hear the Scottish lassies love it.'

'And you a happily married man,' said Roberts, shaking his head in mock disgust. 'I hopes you catch the boat up, so I do.'

Lieutenant Foster was sharing the morning watch with Midshipman Percy Stockforth-Johnson. Both lookouts were closed up and nearby stood the duty signalman and bridge messenger. Even though they wore duffel coats, Balaclavas, woollen scarves and sweaters, the bitter wind still managed to penetrate their clothing.

Shortly after 0630, Foster checked his chart and informed Pendleton the ship had reached its rendezvous point. In the east, a glimmer of pale blue light lay across the horizon. Yellow rays from an amber moon dappled the inky black sea with speckles of gold.

Pendleton came onto the bridge in time to hear radar operator Leading Seaman Taylor's voice on the intercom. 'Convoy approaching, due south roughly five miles away,' he cried. 'About thirty of them I'd say, sir.'

'Well, at least they're on time,' said Pendleton giving Foster a friendly glance.

Half an hour later Jumper Collins in the crow's nest, reported, 'Large convoy dead ahead, sir, two destroyers in the van.'

Sure enough, three lines of merchant ships, their masts and superstructures could be seen silhouetted against the dawn sky. The convoy was spread out in a rectangle covering some twenty miles. In the van was light cruiser, its curved, foamy white bow wave a sharp contrast to the blackness of the sea. On either side of the convoy a destroyer provided a protective screen.

'Cruiser flashing a signal, sir,' shouted PO Yeoman Jeffries, 'it reads, "welcome to the party. Please take up position one mile, rear of convoy. Will be turning fifty degrees to port at 0730".'

Reply, said Pendleton, '"Good to see you. Will comply". Increase revolutions two zero, port ten.'

Zimba turned left and bounded forward and took station as ordered.

A series of flashing signals between the commodore of the convoy, whose ship was in the centre of the middle column, ordered the small armada to slowly turn to port. An hour later, with Land's End a distant smudge on the horizon, they entered St George's Channel, a fifty miles stretch of sea waterway separating the tip of Southern Ireland, and into the Irish Sea. Shortly after this the heavens opened up and torrents of rain fell, peppering the sea with miniature explosions. Intermittent rolls of thunder echoed around like gunfire and jagged flashes of forked lightning lit up the sky.

'What time are we due at the mouth of the Mersey estuary, Pilot?' Pendleton shouted to Foster, his voice barely audible over the howling wind.

Wiping his face with the back of his gloved hand, Foster cried, 'Against this sea and at this speed, about 0700 tomorrow, sir.'

'Will we have time for a run ashore Liverpool, sir?' quipped PO Yeoman Jeffries, giving Pendleton a hopeful look.

'Sorry to disappoint you, Yeoman,' replied Pendleton as lines of rainwater dripped from his cap. 'But as I announced over the tannoy, some of the convoy will leave and go into the port. We then escort the rest to the Clyde. So you can forget about a night out in Lime Street.'

The Yeoman's disgruntled reply was lost in the wind.

During the night the storm abated. Shortly after 0600 the dark outline of the Isle of Man appeared on the ship's port quarter. An hour later the convoy reached the Bar Lighthouse near the mouth of the River Mersey. Away to starboard, the rugged coastline of North Wales was barely discernable in the morning mist. And on the left, across the estuary, the flat terrain of Lancashire disappeared in the distance.

'Signal from the Commodore, sir,' said PO Jeffries. '"Convoy reduce speed to five knots. Ten ships to leave for designated berths in Liverpool at 0900. On completion, remainder of convoy and escorts to proceed at full speed to Clyde. I will remain in Liverpool".'

'Reduce revolutions, slow ahead,' ordered Pendleton, noticing the other escorts slowing down. Like everyone else on the bridge, Pendleton watched, as one by one, each merchant ship slowly turned and headed towards Liverpool, receiving farewell signals from those ships remaining.

'Better do the same, Yeoman,' said Pendleton. 'Say, "Good luck and give our regards to Lime Street".'

Before the last merchant ship disappeared, the remaining twenty ships gathered speed and continued northwards. Once again the weather deteriorated. Entering the Northern Channel, a stretch of narrow seaway between the coast of Ireland and western

261

Scotland, the convoy was buffeted by heavy seas and a howling gale.

On Sunday 14 October, the convoy entered the relatively calm waters of the Firth of Clyde. On the port beam loomed the snow-capped hills of the Isle of Arran. A few miles ahead lay the Isle of Bute, its rugged peaks rising up from under layers of dark, foreboding clouds.

'Signal from C in C Clyde, sir,' said PO Jeffries. 'It says, "Convoy to proceed independently to docks as prearranged. *Belfast* and escorts to refuel at Greenock, then sail for Scapa Flow. *Zimba* to anchor off Tail of the Bank at 1400. Five coaling barges and sloop Jaunty will join from Victoria Harbour, Greenock at 1600. Sail for Bristol when convenient".'

'Well, Number One,' Pendleton said, giving Carter a salutary glance. 'Now we know exactly what we're to do.' For a fleeting moment he thought of Nadine. With a bit of luck and good weather, in five days they would be with each other. 'How about a nice warm mug of kye, Number One,' he said, rubbing his hands together, 'before I freeze to death.'

Facing Helensburgh, and surrounded by the snowy hills of Kilcreggan, The Tail of the Bank is a wide, natural anchorage near Greenock. In peacetime it is the haven of the Home Fleet. But as *Zimba's* two-ton, bronze anchor splashed into the water, Pendleton noticed a paucity of warships only too aware they were fully occupied elsewhere.

Shortly after 1600, HMS *Jaunty,* a small, "J" Class sloop, was sighted leaving Greenock. Behind the sloop, five squat barges followed in line ahead. The barges, painted black, were low in the water, indicative of their heavy load. Each vessel had a tall, black funnel situated aft of the bridge from which rose a thin plume of smoke. As the small flotilla approached, some of the crew came on deck and gave *Zimba* a cheerful wave.

'My God,' muttered Pendleton, 'They're no bigger than tugs, I don't suppose they can do more than ten knots at best.'

'Now that's what I call a quiet number, sir,' replied Carter. 'Chugging along without a care in the world.'

'Better weigh anchor, Number One,' said Pendleton. 'The sooner we leave here the quicker we'll be back in Portsmouth.' Turning to PO Jeffries, he went on. 'Make to *Jaunty,* "follow behind me". Then, signal the lead barge, "Nice to see you. Take position behind *Jaunty*. What is your maximum speed?"' Aldis lamp flashes from the lead barge soon followed.

"Twelve knots at best", came the reply.

'At that speed how long will it take us to reach Bristol, Pilot?' Pendleton asked, thoughtfully stroking his chin.

Using a pair of dividers, Lieutenant Foster retreated to the back of the bridge and bent over his chart. 'Four days, sir,' replied Foster. 'We should reach the mouth of the Avon on at approximately 0800 on Friday.'

'I see,' pondered Pendleton. 'Then it'll be another two days before we arrive in Portsmouth.'

'All being well, sir,' Carter added, glancing dubiously up at the clusters of grey clouds racing across the sky. 'Providing we have a spell of reasonable weather.'

Two hours later the small group of vessels reached the mouth of the Firth of Clyde, then turned to port into the North Channel. The next day saw the small flotilla enter the North Sea.

'Who would have thought one of the fastest warships in the navy would be playing nursemaid to a few miserable coalers,' remarked Carter, using the compass repeater to check the distance between *Zimba* and *Jaunty*. 'Makes you wonder, doesn't it sir?'

'Remember, Number One,' Pendleton replied cautiously, 'it takes all kinds to help win a war. That coal they are carrying will be used to smelt steel and iron.'

'I expect you're…' Suddenly a voice from the lookout in the crow's nest interrupted him.

'Unidentified aircraft approaching red two hundred, sir.'

Everyone immediately focussed his binoculars away to the left.

'Sound action stations,' retorted Pendleton. 'Here's hoping it's one of…'

'Looks like a bloody Focke Wulf, sir,' shouted Midshipman Porter. 'And it's beginning to circle.'

'The bastard's preparing to dive on us,' muttered PO Yeoman Jeffries. Like the others, he was hurriedly donning his anti-flash gear and steel helmet. 'Do you think he'll attack, sir?' he said, nervously licking his lips.

'I wouldn't be at all surprised,' Pendleton said gravely. 'Those barges can't manoeuvre very well and as such they're sitting ducks.'

'The pilot of the bomber must be laughing his head off,' muttered Carter.

'Then let's give him something to laugh about,' Pendleton snapped. 'Tell Guns to open fire.'

'But the sod's out of range, sir,' replied Carter.

'I know that,' retorted Pendleton. 'But it'll tell him we mean business. Signal *Jaunty* to do the same.'

Within seconds, *Zimba*'s 4.7 guns angled upwards and opened fire. To the cacophony was added the continual *rat-tat-rat* of the 20mm Oerlikons. Almost immediately the grey sky became a mosaic of woolly blobs of black smoke.

'He's losing altitude, sir,' yelled Midshipman Porter, pointing upwards. 'The blighter is diving towards us.'

'No he's not, Mid,' shouted Carter, his voice barely audible over the gunfire. 'The sod's making for the barges.'

Everyone watched apprehensively as the enemy plane, oblivious to the deadly curtain of gunfire, swooped downwards towards the leading barge. Suddenly, a stick of five black objects fell from the bomb bay doors. At the same time the bomber's port wing burst into flames as a shell from one of the ships hit home. For a fleeting second the plane seemed to hang in the air. It then exploded into a ball of red and yellow flames, before disintegrating into pieces of jagged debris and splashing into the sea.

However, the Focke Wulf's bomb aimer had done his job. A series of huge, ear-splitting explosions rippled along the barge. Immediately the small vessel was engulfed in clouds of swirling black smoke and crimson flames. Another detonation followed this. In seconds, the small vessel rolled over and disappeared under the sea, leaving behind a whirlpool of oil and an ugly film of black dust.

'Jesus Christ!' muttered Carter, who like Pendleton and the others stared dumbfounded at bits of bodies and pieces of wood. 'The poor sods…'

'Cease fire, and send a signal to C in C Clyde, repeated to Admiralty,' Pendleton said quietly. 'Give the position of the attack and tell them what happened,' adding sardonically, 'What price coal, now, eh, Number One.'

Carter didn't reply. With furrowed brow he took a deep breath and turned away.

Friday, 20 October, dawned wet and windy. The pallid sun, peaking through dense grey clouds cast an eerie glow on the gunmetal sea. But in the distance the mountains of South Wales provided a welcome sight. Later that day the depleted flotilla passed Cardiff and sailed into the Avon estuary. After a brief "thank you, and good luck" signal to the escorts, the barges headed downriver to Bristol Docks.

No sooner had the last barge disappeared than *Zimba* increased speed and sailed into the choppy waters of the Bristol Channel. On the bridge, Pendleton listened to the constant whine of the ship's turbines knowing each revolution brought him closer to Nadine. The thought made him feel light-headed with anticipation.

The journey down the English Channel was uneventful. Shortly after 0700 next morning, with *Jaunty* close behind *Zimba,* both ships sailed into Portsmouth Harbour. *Jaunty* detached and berthed further down alongside Fountain Lake Jetty. *Zimba* moored alongside Gunners Wharf, close to Semaphore Towers.

'Ring off main engines, Number One,' said Pendleton. Stretching his arms above his head, he smiled and added, 'It certainly feels good to be back in Portsmouth, doesn't it?'

'Indeed, sir,' replied Carter. Noticing his captain's jovial mood, he went on, 'Leave to the first and second part of port watch and to those who are RA, sir?'

'Yes, Number One,' said Pendleton. 'I expect those who live local will want to get ashore as quickly as possible. Who's Officer of the Day?'

'Lieutenant Small, sir,' replied Carter. 'I hear his girlfriend is coming up from Plymouth to see him tomorrow.'

'Good for him,' said Pendleton, with a wry smile he added ominously, 'They should make the most of what time they have as you never know what lies ahead of us.'

At that moment PO Yeoman Jeffries arrived. 'Signal from C in C planning, sir, it says, "Good to see you back. My compliments and please report to me at 1200 today".'

Pendleton gave Carter a rueful glance and muttered, 'Captain McLaughlan said he would send for me. I bet he's got something special lined up for us. Oh, and I expect we'll have a visit from a few of those dockyard officials wanting an early morning snifter.'

Leading Steward Gail was waiting in Pendleton's cabin holding a mug of hot tea. As Pendleton entered, *Mail is ready for collection,* was piped over the tannoy.

'Thank you, Gail,' said Pendleton smiling while accepting the drink. 'That's just what I need.'

A knock came at the door and in came Sub Lieutenant Hailey. 'I have your official mail, sir,' he said, placing a small bundle of brown envelopes on Pendleton's desk. 'And, err…there is this one sir.' He paused and handed Pendleton a small white envelope. On the top right hand corner was a blue, two-penny stamp with the head of King George V1. 'It's obviously a private letter, sir. It smells rather…'

'Yes, yes,' Pendleton replied impatiently. 'Give it to me.'

The corners of Pendleton's mouth broke into a smile as he recognised the faint aroma of Nadine's Chanel No 5, and Nadine's small, neat handwriting. Glancing apprehensively at Hailey and Gale, he stood up and said, 'Thank you, that will be all.'

No sooner had they left his cabin than he placed his mug on the desk and tore open the envelope. But as he read its contents, he felt the blood drain from his face.

"Jeremy Mon Amour,

By the time you read this letter I will have left Haslar. Two days after you sailed, the matron sent for me and said a sister who spoke Italian was urgently needed abroad to join an army medical unit. She ordered me to pack my uniform and ensure I had plenty of tropical clothing. She also told me I would be taken to HMS Daedalus and flown in a Dakota to somewhere abroad, but couldn't tell me where. But my guess is it will be either Sicily or Italy. When I know exactly where I am being sent, I shall write to you. By the way, my father is very well and hopes to return to England when his work is completed. He sends his best wishes to you and your crew.

Oh, Cheri, my heart is aching. The thought of not seeing you is tearing me apart. I love you so. You will be in my heart forever. I have to close now as my transport to Lee-on-Solent is due any minute.

May God bless you and keep you safe.

Yours, until we meet again, Nadine".

Pendleton quickly reread the letter. In doing so, an empty, sickening feeling slowly crept over him. He felt his legs weaken and slumped into his chair. 'Why, God, why?' he inwardly cried, clutching the letter, 'why couldn't you have found someone else?' But received no answer.

CHAPTER THIRTY-FOUR

Captain MacLaughlan was sat behind his desk puffing gently on his briar pipe. Lying open in front of him was a file marked TOP SECRET. The haze of pale blue tobacco smoke hovering above his head added to the warm, muggy atmosphere. Rays of sunlight from a bay window shone down highlighting the wrinkles on his stern features and exaggerating the greyness of his dark brown hair.

'Commander Pendleton to see you, sir,' came a female voice from his desk intercom. 'Shall I tell him to wait?'

'No, Janet,' the captain replied, closing the file. 'Please send him in.' He removed his pipe and placed it lovingly in a large, brass ashtray, half full of used matches and grains of dark tobacco.

Pendleton opened the door and came in.

'Ah, Jeremy,' enthused the captain, using a hand to disperse a cloud of tobacco smoke. 'Nice to see you again, old boy.' He stood up and extended his hand.

The news of Nadine's sudden departure still hung heavy on Pendleton's mind. He felt slightly depressed and was in no mood for the captain's cheerful reception.

'Good morning, sir,' Pendleton quietly replied.

'Do take a seat and help yourself to a cigarette,' said the captain, indicating to a silver box lying next to a small stack of buff-coloured folders.

Pendleton removed his cap and sat down. He took a cigarette out of the box and using his small silver lighter, lit it.

For a few seconds the captain furrowed his brow, then spoke. 'I'll come straight to the point,' he said, staring hard at Pendleton. 'I'm sure you're aware that the Eighth Army is advancing up the eastern side of Italy while the Americans are doing the same on the western littoral. The rugged terrain of the Apennines is making progress difficult and the weather is against them. Mark Clark's men have met with stiff resistance at Salerno and the British are in difficulties north of the Volturo River. The British and Americans are in urgent need of supplies and the only way to get them there is by convoy.' He paused, picked up his pipe and took a few puffs causing a minor cloud of smoke to gather around his head.

'And I take it, sir,' said Pendleton dryly, 'that's where *Zimba* comes in?'

'Yes, indeed,' replied the captain, leaning back in his chair and removing his pipe. 'On Friday, 1 November, a fast convoy of twenty ships code named, KM22, will sail from Glasgow for Malta. The convoy will have an escort of three destroyers and the cruiser, *Cleopatra.*' He paused momentarily allowing his words to sink in. '*Zimba, Zetland* and *Bicester* will leave Portsmouth on Wednesday, 30 October at 0600 and rendezvous with the convoy after it has passed through the St George's Channel two days later at approximately 0800. Lieutenant Commander Wilkinson in *Zetland* will be Captain (D).'

MacLaughlan stopped talking, picked up his pipe and took another puff, then went on. 'When the convoy is twenty miles off Land's End they will be joined by two destroyers, the carrier *Victorious,* the cruiser *Nigeria* and the Royal Fleet Auxiliary vessel, *Wave Ruler.* Admiral Sir A L St G Lyster has his flag in *Victorious.*

'Mmm…the same admiral who commanded the Force Z during Operation Pedestal?' muttered Pendleton. 'It must be a very important convoy to have him in charge.'

'It is,' the captain added stiffly. 'Any questions?'

'You said this was a fast convoy, sir,' replied Pendleton. 'I take it the destroyers will refuel at Gib?'

'Yes,' said the captain. 'Fuel lighters will be waiting for the destroyers. Now,' he went on, 'upon arrival at Malta, *Zimba* and

Bicester will leave the main convoy and escort another convoy, code-named KM32, coming from Oran to Bari. Bari is a port on the west coast of Italy just north of Brindisi. You are due to arrive there on 30 November. *Cleopatra* will accompany you, then she will return to Malta. Clear so far?'

'Yes, sir,' Pendleton replied, leaning forward and flicking ash into an ashtray. 'Quite clear.'

'Good,' said the captain. '*Zetland* will detach from convoy KM22 at Malta and escort a separate convoy of twenty ships, code-named KM51, also to Bari, arriving on 2 December. *Victorious* and her escort group will accompany this convoy to Bari then return to Malta. Every merchant ship in the convoys will contain ammunition, bombs and aviation fuel and oil.' The captain stopped talking and gave a deep sigh, shook his head then continued, 'Where we get such brave men to man these potential death traps never ceases to amaze me.'

'I take it secrecy is of paramount importance?' Pendleton asked, reaching across and stubbing out his cigarette.

'Of course, but all officers can be informed. Now, old boy,' grunted the captain, his watery blue eyes glancing out of the window. 'The sun's over the yardarm, how about a pink gin?'

Later that day in his cabin Pendleton told Carter what was happening.

'As discretely as possible, Number One,' said Pendleton. 'Tell the officers. I'll speak to Paddy myself. Five days leave can be given to each of the watches and night leave will expire at 2359 on the Tuesday prior to sailing.'

That evening several of *Zimba*'s ship's company were in the Keppel's Head, a pub on The Hard. They were joined by a few ratings from *Zetland* and *Bicester*. The names on their cap tallies simply read HM SHIPS, a security measure to prevent any enemy spies from knowing what ships were in harbour. However, many of them knew each other either from basic training or having served previously on various ships.

'My guess, Geordie, is that we're bound fer the Meddy,' quipped Leading Steward Gale.

'What makes yer think that, lovely lad?' asked Big Geordie Roberts, *Zimba*'s Telegraphist.

'This afternoon, the old man told me to check his tropical uniforms,' replied Gale, taking a swig of beer. 'And when I asked him why we'd be needin' 'em, he chocked me off real gruff-like. "Just do as I say", he said. He's been like a bear with a sore head since we arrived from Scotland, so 'e as.'

'I think yer right,' chipped in a small, dark-haired rating from *Zetland.* 'I'm the Navigating Officer's runner, and I overhead the Jimmy telling him to make sure he had the charts fer thc Tyrrhenian Sea, wherever that is.'

'It's in the Meddy,' interrupted Bungy Williams, a tall, red-faced three-badge seaman off *Bicester,* 'on the east coast of Italy. That's where the Eighth Army are fighting. It was on the wireless.'

'What about you, Doc,' said Gale, draining his glass and staring at Mick Channon. 'Has your boss said anything to you?'

'Funny you should ask,' replied Channon. 'He did suggest I checked to see if we needed anything as we might be sailing soon.'

'If yer ask me,' said Bungy Williams. 'I think we're going to Malta.'

'What makes yer think that?' asked Channon, placing the empty glass on the bar.

'Our NAAFI manager's wife works as a steward for the C in C, in barracks,' replied Bungy. 'And that's wot she 'eard someone say.'

'Bloody great!' exclaimed Channon, excitedly rubbing his hands together. 'A run ashore down the Gut is just what the doctor ordered. Now,' he added, staring expectantly at the others. 'Whose round is it?'

The change in Pendleton's demeanour hadn't gone unnoticed by the officers.

271

'I'm sure it was something in the letter he received when we returned to port,' said Sub Lieutenant John Hailey. The time was 1400. Hailey and some of the officers were in the wardroom having coffee. 'It was a personal letter and smelt faintly of perfume.' Hadley's remark was addressed to Carter and Lieutenant Reed.

'Mmm...interesting,' muttered Reed, taking a sip of coffee. 'I wonder if it was bad news.'

'Well, something's eating him,' said Carter. 'He even gave the Buffer a bollocking in front of the men for something or other, and that's not like him.'

Paddy O'Malley came into the wardroom. Earlier that day he had reported to Pendleton in his day cabin. As Paddy entered, he noticed Pendleton was sitting staring blankly out the open porthole. His face was pale and drawn, and he looked tired.

'What's the matter, Jeremy?' said Paddy, taking off his grimy, oil-stained cap. 'I hear you bawled the Buffer out. What's wrong, are you crossed in love, or something?'

Pendleton didn't reply. With a hand he indicated Paddy to sit down. He then explained the details of the convoy.

With a tired sigh, Pendleton went on, 'It looks like a long haul, Paddy. I suppose we should be thankful we're not going to the Atlantic.'

Paddy leaned forward, pursed his lips and with an all-knowing expression on his face, said, 'Jeremy, I know something else is bothering you. Now tell me exactly what it is.'

Next to Pendleton, Paddy was the oldest man on the ship. Both of them had served in the merchant navy before the war and as such, Pendleton felt he could confide in him. By now, it was common knowledge he was seeing Nadine, the stoker who saw Pendleton with her in Gosport made sure of that.

'It's Nadine,' said Pendleton, turning around and frowning. 'She's been sent abroad. I was unable to see her before she left. She sent me a letter...' His voice trailed away.

'Och, don't worry, Jeremy,' he said, soothingly. 'To be sure you'll meet up again. This bloody war can't last forever. But you've got to pull yersell together. Remember, lots of men and women are in the same situation, and you've got a ship to run, talking of which,' he paused and with a faint smile playing around his lips, added, 'we're fully topped up with fuel and ready for sea.'

Now, standing in the wardroom, Paddy glared at PO Steward Knocker White and grunted, 'Coffee, coffee, or I'll have yer keel-hauled.'

'Maybe you can shed some light on the captain,' said Lieutenant Sam Small. 'Is he sick or something?'

'You could say that,' replied Paddy, as Knocker handed him a cup of coffee. He then told them what the problem was.

'Once we set sail on Wednesday,' replied Lieutenant Small, 'he'll be all right. After all, those of us who are married or with girlfriends feel the same.'

'I know,' replied Paddy ruefully, 'but they haven't already lost a wife, a son and a brother in the war.'

CHAPTER THIRTY-FIVE

Dawn was breaking as the small flotilla sailed in line ahead out of Portsmouth Harbour into the Solent. A stiff westerly wind whipped the sea into angry white topped waves, while high above a fading, amber moon flitted between clusters of dark, foreboding clouds.

'We always seem to be tail-end-Charlie,' muttered Percy Stockforth-Johnson to his fellow midshipman, Harry Porter. Both young men were on the bridge. Close by stood Pendleton, Carter and Sub Lieutenant Coburn. Next to them was PO Yeoman Jeffries and Able Seaman Jumper Collins, the bridge messenger. All wore duffle coats, mufflers and caps. Some stamped their feet and blew into their hands. Directly ahead *Bicester* cut through the sea leaving behind a bubbly, white frothy wake.

'That's because we're junior ship, stupid,' replied Porter. 'Now shut up and keep your eyes on *Bicester*'s stern.

While he was on the bridge, Pendleton managed to put Nadine out of his thoughts. However, the few times he retreated to his cabin he found sleep hard to come by. Every time he closed his eyes he saw the beautiful, oval face of Nadine smiling at him. When he finally slept he was almost glad to be woken up by someone calling him on his voice-pipe.

One such message came informing Pendleton convoy KM22 from Glasgow had been sighted. The time was 0600 and dawn was gently breaking. Still fully clothed, Pendleton heaved himself off his bunk and donned his duffle coat. It had been three days since they left Portsmouth and he had hardly slept. As he arrived on the bridge a gust of wind ripped against his face. He blinked a few times to accustom his eyes to the gloom. A dull, blue light from the navigator's chart room situated in a small cubicle behind the bridge, cast a shadowy glow over those on duty.

'How far away are they, Number One?' Pendleton asked, tucking a scarf around his neck. 'And what course are they on?'

'Ten miles on our starboard beam, sir,' Carter replied, 'steering one, one five.'

Just after 0900, the convoy came into view. An hour or so later, two lines of ten merchant ships appeared out of the morning mist. The cruiser *Cleopatra,* a huge bow wave billowing over its long, pointed fo'c'sle led the way. A destroyer, with its green and black camouflage barely visible against the dull morning sky, ploughed through the sea away to port. Two more destroyers drew up in the rear. There quickly followed a series of flashing signals from *Cleopatra* ordering *Zimba* to take a position on the convoy's starboard beam. *Zetland* and *Bicester* took station a mile away on either side of the convoy.

'By the time we meet up with *Victorious,* Number One,' said Pendleton, peering through his binoculars at *Cleopatra,* 'there'll be thirteen ships in all to protect the convoy.'

With a wry smile, Carter, replied, 'Unlucky number for some, eh, sir'

'I hope not,' Pendleton answered warily, lowering his binoculars. Glancing apprehensively up at the dark grey clouds scampering across the sky, he added, 'Better double the lookouts, Number One. In a few hours we'll be we'll within range of enemy bombers from France.'

Pendleton's concern was well justified. Shortly after Stand Easy, Able Seaman Jumper Collins in the crow's nest sighted an unidentified aircraft approaching on the port bow.

'Roughly ten thousand feet, sir,' he shouted. Straining his eyes through his binoculars, he added, 'It looks like an ME109.'

'Sound action stations,' Pendleton snapped.

Carter and the others immediately clamped binoculars to their eyes and peered upwards into the grey sky.

'There she is,' cried Midshipman Porter, pointing upward to his left, 'and the blighter's starting to dive.'

'All guns ready,' came the brisk voice of Lieutenant MacIntyre, from the Gun Director platform above the bridge.

'Fire at will,' shouted Pendleton.

Immediately, *Zimba*'s 20mm Oerlikons and those from the escorts let loose a tirade of tracer bullets Anti-aircraft weaponry onboard *Cleopatra,* plus the armament in the other destroyers belted out a massive fusillade. The noise was deafening. Almost at once the grey sky was pockmarked with bursts of black smoke.

'Christ almighty!' shouted Yeoman PO Jeffries, 'the bastard's coming straight for us!'

The ME109 came at *Zimba* almost at sea level, tiny flames flickering from each wing. Suddenly the sharp, metallic sound of bullets hitting the bridge made everyone duck as the yellow nosed fighter zoomed over the ship.

As the plane disappeared over the horizon PO Yeoman Jeffries, cried, 'Bloody hell that was too close fer comfort!'

At first, nobody noticed Midshipman Porter slumped against the port bulkhead. Suddenly he began to slide onto the deck, blood oozing through his anti-flash gear on the left side of his young face.

'Quickly, someone call the Doc!' cried Midshipman Stockforth-Johnson, attempting vainly to catch his friend. *'Porter's been hit!'*

Stockforth-Johnson gently lowered his friend onto the deck. He removed Porter's steel helmet and ant-flash gear, only to reveal a huge area of matted hair and blood.

'Harry! Harry!!' Stockforth-Johnson yelled, cradling his friend in his arms. *'Speak to me old boy, open your eyes.'*

Leading Seaman Dusty Miller bent close to Stockforth-Johnson and placed a shell dressing over Porter's wound. By this time, Pendleton, Lieutenant Small, PO Jeffries and the two lookouts were staring grimly down at Porter's ashen, bloodstained face.

Surgeon Lieutenant Fulford and SBA Channon arrived.

'Get back everyone,' Channon shouted. 'And let the doctor see to him.'

Kneeling down, Fulford felt for a pulse in Foster's neck and wrist. With a sombre expression in his eyes, he looked up at Channon and slowly shook his head.

PO Yeoman Jeffries and the lookouts swapped painful glances. Stockforth-Johnson, visibly shaken, slowly and gently, lowered Porter's head onto the deck. Sub Lieutenant Coburn, his face grey with shock, simply turned away.

Pendleton, who was standing next close to Channon, placed a comforting hand on Stockforth-Johnson's shoulder. He then glanced around at the others, and said, 'It's no use, the poor boy's gone.'

For a few seconds everyone was too shaken to speak.

'Signal from *Cleopatra,* sir,' shouted PO Yeoman Jeffries, '"report damage and casualties".'

'Reply: "No damage. One officer dead",' Pendleton gravely replied.

'Jesus Christ, a year ago he was at Grammar School, and now...' murmured Carter as Channon covered Porter with a blanket.

Midshipman Porter was buried the next day. At 0800 all officers that could be spared along with those ratings off duty, stood bareheaded on the quarterdeck. The engines paused; Pendleton read out the simple burial service. As the ship's bell was rung, Lieutenant Small, Sub Lieutenant Coburn, Lieutenant MacIntyre and Midshipman Stockforth-Johnson, all grim-faced, raised a stretcher containing Porter's body, secured in a weighted hammock and covered with a white ensign. They then tipped it onto the guardrail and watched as it splashed into the clear blue sea.

Midshipman Porter was *Zimba's* first fatality. Everyone wondered if it would be her last.

Victorious and the cruiser *Nigeria* plus covering force were sighted the next day. A signal from the carrier informed *Cleopatra* they would remain some twenty miles away, ready to come to the convoy's assistance if necessary. This message was relayed to the close escort group. During the next four days the convoy zigzagged and headed into the Atlantic in order to avoid the U-boats patrolling the Bay of Biscay. On 10 November, the huge armada turned ninety degrees to port and headed for Gibraltar.

'Mail will close at 2000,' came a voice over *Zimba*'s tannoy.

'Better make the most of it,' Pendleton overheard Lieutenant Reed say to Carter. 'After we reach Gib, it may be the last time we'll be able to write home till we get to Bari.'

'And receive any mail,' replied Carter, who, like Pendleton was watching the movements of the escorts ahead of *Zimba*.

Carter's remark sent a message of hope running through Pendleton. With a bit of luck there could be a letter from Nadine waiting for him at Gibraltar.

On the evening of 12 November, Europa Point, the southernmost tip of Gibraltar, hove into view. Darkness had fallen and after passing Cape Spartel, the massive, jutting jaw of the Rock could be seen silhouetted against the night sky. A few miles away on the port bow the lights of Algeciras on the Spanish coast, twinkled like diamonds.

'I bet there's a few Jerry spies over there watching our every move, eh, Swain?' said Able Seaman Geordie Roberts. Roberts and Chief Coxswain Jack Tolby were closed up in the wheelhouse as the escort group entered the Straits of Gibraltar.

The busy port of Algeciras was a haven for enemy agents, who, in Franco's neutral Spain, reported to Germany the movements of Allied shipping and their escorts.

'Wouldn't surprise me in the least,' the coxswain muttered dismissively. 'Now pipe down and keep yer hand on the telegraph, I expect we'll be stopping when we enter the harbour.'

Under the protective guns of Gibraltar, the harbour was crowded with cruisers, destroyers and smaller craft, plus several merchant vessels. Some lay at anchor; others were alongside wharfs and jetties en transit for Alexandria, Malta or Sicily.

Shrouded in darkness, the main body of the convoy sailed quietly into the vastness of the Mediterranean. Meanwhile, the destroyer escorts stopped allowing lighters to come alongside to refuel each vessel and swap mail-bags. This was done quickly and expediently, after which each escort caught up with the convoy. *Victorious* and her covering group followed on two hours later and took up station ten miles away on the convoy's port beam.

'Pity we couldn't have had a run ashore in Gib,' muttered Able Seaman Jumper Collins, the bridge messenger, to PO Yeoman Jeffries. 'I hear it becomes a sort of Boom Town at night. Bars, gorgeous, dark-haired dancing girls, and the ale's supposed to be all right, as well.'

'Don't kid yersell, Jumper,' replied Jeffries, his binoculars clamped to his eyes anticipating a signal from *Cleopatra*. 'Those dark-haired beauties you mentioned, bugger off back to Spain at midnight after they've spent all yer cash.'

'What about a bit of "how's yer father"?' Jumper salaciously replied while making an obscene gesture by bending his elbow.

'No bloody chance,' said the PO, lowering his binoculars. 'Now keep yer eyes skinned, the buzz is there's U-boats about.'

At 1200 the eagerly awaited pipe, *Mail is ready for collection,* came over the tannoy. Pendleton had just left the bridge and was sitting in his cabin, writing up the ship's log. After knocking on the door, Sub Lieutenant Hailey came in holding a solitary white envelope.

'A letter for you, sir,' he said, handing it to Pendleton. 'Nothing else of importance.'

Hailey smiled as he saws his captain's eyes lighted up.

'Thank you, John,' said Pendleton, almost snatching the letter from Hailey. 'That'll be all.' Recognising Nadine's small, neat handwriting he felt his heart thump against his ribs.

'Yes, sir,' replied Hailey. 'Good news, I hope, sir.' Then feeling slightly embarrassed, hurriedly turned and left.

Pendleton ripped open the envelope. As he read its contents, he hardly noticed his hand shaking. Her address was simply Sister N. LeBrun, c/o RFPO Army Mediterranean. The letter read:

"Mon Amour, Jeremy,

Let me begin by saying how much I miss and love you. I lie awake each night thinking of you, and praying for the day we can be together again.

I am now settled in my new post. I cannot tell you exactly where, but I am attached to a small naval sick quarters. However, if you remember Iris's boyfriend, the naval officer you met in the Wild Stag, and substitute the first letter of his name for the second letter of the alphabet, that should give you a strong clue as to where I am".

Pendleton paused and thought. Suddenly, he cried out, 'I remember! It's Larry, Larry something or other!' He picked up a pencil and on his blotting pad wrote the name down. Then, after deleting the letter, L, he added B and couldn't believe his eyes. 'Barry! Of course, Bari!' he gasped. 'She's been sent to Bari! The port we're taking the convoy we picked up at Malta!'

With his heart racing like an express train, Pendleton read the rest of the letter.

"Do not worry about me. We hear the sound of gunfire in the distance but the place where I am is safe. Many of the patients are Italian, so my use of their language is vital. I must close now as the mail leaves shortly.

You are constantly in my thoughts and I do so love and miss you,

Yours forever,

Nadine".

Pendleton reread the letter again then sighed with relief. *'Bari!'* he cried out loud. 'She's at Bari, and with a bit of luck, we'll be there in ten days.'

CHAPTER THIRTY-SIX

'You can't beat the dear old Meddy, eh, Digger?' sighed Chief Bosun's Mate Bill Conyon. He and the Chief GI were on the quarterdeck, standing by the guardrail smoking a cigarette. Both were bareheaded and as it was still officially winter, they, like the ship's company wore blue trousers and d white shirts, (Number 4 uniforms). Before them stretched the vast, sparkling blueness of the Mediterranean Sea.

The convoy had left Gibraltar three days ago and except for the occasional radar contact and the odd Focke-Wulf spotter plane, all had been quiet. A warm, spicy breeze blew fanned their faces and an eye smarting sun beat down from a clear blue sky. Directly ahead the frothy wake from two lines ships disturbed the stillness of the sea. Nearby the cruiser *Cleopatra,* camouflaged in dark green and black, dipped graciously in and out of the sea. Close by, destroyers, bounding about like greyhounds, maintained a protective screen.

'You're right, there, Bill,' replied Digger, watching a stream of tobacco smoke dissipate in the air. 'That water looks as clear as glass. Those fishes you can see look good enough to eat. I've known it to get pretty rough this time of year, but so far we've been pretty lucky.'

'Enjoyin' the cruise, Buffer?' quipped Leading Seaman Nutty Slack, grinning as he walked passed them holding a bucket of dirty water which he threw over the side.

'Bugger off, you young whippersnapper,' grunted the Buffer, his white hair flaying in the breeze. 'Or I'll throw you over the side.'

At that moment the pipe, "asdic contact bearing red four oh. Hands to action stations", came over the tannoy.

'I knew it were too good to last,' grunted the Buffer, quickly flicking his dog-end into the sea.

Once again, the familiar "pinging" echoed from the tannoy as men dashed to the respective stations. *Zimba* immediately heeled to port, gathered speed and headed away to the left into the open sea. *Zetland*, *Bicester* and another destroyer, HMS *Tumult* soon followed.

'Contact three hundred yards away, red two, two five,' yelled Radar Operator Leading Seaman Paddy Doyle, his voice resounding around the bridge.

'Increase revolutions one third, three degrees to port, Number One,' Pendleton ordered. 'Stand by depth charges, tell Sub Lieutenant Coburn to set them for 150 and 200 feet.'

On the quarterdeck a team of ratings, using special spanners, opened an aperture on each depth charge and set the various levels as ordered. When launched, seawater flowed into the apertures. A hydrostatic mechanism then caused the depth charge to explode.

Zetland, Tumult and *Bicester* also joined the attack. In a matter of minutes all three ships fired twin sets of depth charges aimed at the contact area.

After a slight pause, a series of massive explosions sent mountains of white water thundering into the air. *Zimba*'s deck shook violently. For what seemed like an eternity, pillars of seawater hung in the air before settling into the sea, leaving behind whirlpools of angry waves and blankets of fizzy mist.

'A definite oil slick a hundred yards away to port,' cried the port lookout, 'and bits of debris, sir.'

'By Jove he's right,' said Pendleton, peering through his binoculars. 'What do you think Number One, is the blighter bluffing, or what?'

At that moment, a small part of a U-boat's dark, round bows broke the surface. For a few seconds it lay still before disappearing under the waves in ever widening ripples of black, shiny oil. Then, from beneath the sea came a dull rumbling. More oil together with black smoke followed this. Suddenly the sea was strewn with bits of wood, debris and gruesome body parts.

'I don't think so, sir,' replied Carter, giving Pendleton a searching, sideways glance. 'But it's a bloody awful way to die.'

Pendleton was about to reply when a sharp detonation from the far side of the convoy interrupted him.

'Looks like a U-boat has got one of the convoy,' shouted Yeoman PO Jeffries. 'There's a column of smoke rising from one of the freighters.'

In the distance the sound of more depth charges exploding in the sea could be heard as the ships of the covering escort attacked the U-boat.

'Signal to *Zetland,* Yeoman, "As you have noticed, one U-boat sunk. No survivors".'

A few minutes later the reply came. "Yes, well done. Have informed *Victorious.* Will lower a boat and collect evidence. But which of the three of us sunk her?"

Two days later, on 15 November, the convoy was roughly two hundred miles off the coast of Tunisia. A lazy offshore breeze made very little impression of the white ensigns flying from the quarterdecks of the warships. High above, clusters of cotton wool clouds seemed to hang in a sky, whose dazzling blueness was reflected in the clear, calm water.

The time was just after 0800. On the bridge Yeoman PO Jeffries turned to OOW Lieutenant MacIntyre, and said, '*Cleopatra*'s flashing, sir. Signal reads, "The freighter, *City of Lincoln* has engine trouble and cannot make good headway. Have ordered her to leave the convoy and sail to Bizerte. *Zimba* to accompany, then wait at Bizerte for further orders. *Bicester* to meet and escort convoy KM32 to Bari. Effective immediately".'

'Bloody hell, sir!' exploded Jeffries, handing the signal to Lieutenant MacIntyre 'The captain won't like this, I can tell you.'

'Well, my 'andsome,' replied MacIntyre giving Jeffries a frosty glare. 'You'd best take it to him and find out 'addn't you?'

With a shake of his head, Jeffries hurried below and knocked on Pendleton's cabin door. Pendleton was sat at his desk writing. He looked up as Jeffries entered. For a few seconds, Jeffries stood with a sullen expression, holding the signal.

'Well, don't just stand there, man,' said Pendleton. 'What is it?'

Without replying, Jeffries handed him the sheet of paper.

As Pendleton read the signal he felt his heart give a sudden lurch.

'What the hell!' he gasped, staring at the signal. If *Zimba* was detached from the convoy, it would prevent him meeting Nadine. The thought of this made him want to cry out in anger. Instead, he glared at Jeffries. '*Damn and blast, Yeoman!*' retorted Pendleton. 'Tell the Officer of the Watch I'll be up straight away. This is what comes of being junior ship.' He grabbed his cap and hurried onto the bridge.

'Reply to *Cleopatra*,' Pendleton snapped angrily. '"Message received and understood". Now, where's that damn freighter?'

'She's roughly five miles on our starboard quarter, sir,' replied Carter.

'*Not roughly, man,*' barked Pendleton. 'I want to know exactly how far away the beggar is.'

Feeling his face redden, Foster bent down over the Pelorus. 'Exactly, five and half miles, sir,' he replied.

'Speed?'

'Five knots, sir.'

'Thank you,' grunted Pendleton. 'Set a course to join her, Pilot. And Number One,' he went on, frowning at Carter, 'you'd better tell the ship's company our change of plans.'

'Bloody great, Nutty,' grinned Bridge messenger, Jumper Collins to Leading Signalman Slack. 'A run ashore down the Gut at last.'

'I suggest you pipe down,' interrupted Pendleton, giving Collins a withering stare, 'or you'll find yourself on duty if and when we get there.'

Ten minutes later *Zimba* had changed course. Soon the ship was a hundred yards away on the *City of Lincoln*'s port side. Like the rest of the merchant ships her Plimsoll line was barely visible above the water. Several members of the freighter's crew had come on deck and gave *Zimba* a welcome wave. Her captain, his black beard visible under a white cap, could be seen on the ship's starboard wing.

'Slow ahead,' said Pendleton. He then grabbed a loud-hailer and moved to the port wing. 'Can I be of any assistance? Do you want a tow?' he yelled.

Also using a loud-hailer, the captain replied, 'No thank you. Can make about five to eight knots only, nice to have you for company. Come aboard in Bizerte for a drink.'

Pendleton was about to reply, when the excited voice of Yeoman PO Jeffries interrupted him. 'Another signal from *Cleopatra,* sir, it says, "*Bicester* reports a case in urgent need of hospitalisation. *Bicester* will now escort freighter into Bizerte. *Zimba* to resume escort duty as planned".'

Pendleton's face broke into a wide smile. 'Thank you for the offer,' he yelled through the hailer. 'But another destroyer will be taking our place. Good luck.' He turned to Carter, and with a twinkle in his eyes, said, 'Come on Number One let's rejoin the convoy.'

Shortly after 0700 on 20 November, the southern shores of Malta hove into view. The sky was a cloudless blue and the sea covered under a steamy haze. One by one, the twenty merchant ships of convoy KM22 slowly edged their way passed the breakwater into Grand Harbour. Away to port the imposing, crenulated walled fortress of Fort St Angelo swept majestically downwards onto a bed of grey rocks. A mile or so on the opposite side another edifice, Fort St Elmo, bristling with guns, guarded Valetta and the harbour entrance.

PO Yeoman Jeffries gave Pendleton a sorrowful look and said, 'Pity we couldn't have a run ashore, eh, sir?'

'I'm afraid not, Yeoman,' replied Pendleton. '*Cleopatra* and ourselves have to wait for the convoy coming from Oran. It should be here pretty soon.'

They didn't have long to wait.

Half an hour later Telegraphist Roberts came onto the bridge. 'Wireless signal from *Victorious,* sir, it reads, "Your convoy, KM32 approaching twenty miles to port. *Zimba* and *Cleopatra* detach as ordered and proceed to Bari. *Zetland* to remain and meet convoy KM51 in two days' time".'

Roberts shot an envious glance at Jeffries and said, 'Lucky buggers, the lads off the *Zetland* will all be down the Gut baggin' off.'

'Thank you, Roberts,' snapped Pendleton, doing his best to suppress a smile. 'Reply, "Signal received and understood. Thank you for your company. Good Luck and God's Speed".'

'Signal from *Cleopatra,* sir,' shouted PO Yeoman Jeffries. '"Follow and take station two cables in my rear".' (This is roughly half a land mile.)

Pendleton turned to Carter and ordered, 'Port ten, Number One. Increase revolutions one third.'

An hour later Jumper Collins in the crow's nest reported nine merchant ships accompanied by a solitary sloop, three miles away on the port beam. After careful scrutiny, he added, 'There's five tankers and four cargo ships, sir.'

Cleopatra also saw the convoy and with *Zimba* following, turned to meet them.

'They're a mixed bag sir,' remarked Midshipman Stockforth-Johnson. 'There's ships from France, Poland and Holland. And they're all low in the water.'

'Tanks, guns and aviation fuel do tend to weigh heavily,' Carter sarcastically replied.

'Signal flashing from the lead merchantman, the *John Harvey,* sir, it reads, "Sure glad to see you both. You are most welcome".'

'She's an American, I believe,' muttered Pendleton, using his binoculars to observe the Stars and Stripes flying from the merchantman's yardarm.

'Oh, splendid, sir,' gushed Stockforth-Johnson. 'Perhaps they'll invite us onboard for some ice cream.'

'Do something useful, Mid,' groaned Carter while shaking his head, 'such as taking a fix. The sun should be high enough by now.'

'The convoy will be entering the Strait of Ortranto this evening, sir,' replied Foster. (This is a fifteen miles stretch of water separating the southern heel of Italy and the coast of Albania.)

'Thank you, Pilot,' Pendleton replied giving Foster a satisfactory smile. 'That means we should soon be turning to port and reach Bari in four days. Now,' he added, enthusiastically rubbing his hands together, 'how about some kye?'

CHAPTER THIRTY-SEVEN

During the next forty-eight hours the convoy made good progress through the Adriatic Sea. On 22 November, shortly after 0700, the coastline of Bari, shrouded in the early morning mist, appeared two miles away on the port beam. The night before in Pendleton's sea cabin, Carter and Navigating Officer, Lieutenant Foster, had studied a map showing the topography of the port, including the harbour.

'According to what I've read,' said Foster, 'the Romans founded Bari in the third century BC. As they were prone to do, they built roads into the Italian hinterland, and it seems we're still using the same route to supply our troops.'

'Thank you for the history lesson, Pilot,' said Pendleton. 'The harbour certainly looks pretty big. See how it's shaped like a horseshoe with a jetty poking out from its middle,' he added, tapping his forefinger at the map. 'It almost divides the harbour in two. The information on the map says the mole on the right side is called the Molo San Cataldo, apparently, that's where the tankers discharge their cargo.'

'Where will we tie up, then, sir?' Carter asked.

'The signal I received this morning from the port authority informed me *Zimba* will tie up at number 25 berth. As you can see that's on the outer mole called Nuovo Molo, on the left as we enter the harbour.'

'The town is just outside the harbour, sir,' remarked Carter. He then gave Pendleton an appreciative glance before adding, 'and I see there's a sick quarters and hospital on the far side near the harbour wall.'

'Yes, thank you Number One,' replied Pendleton, raising his eyebrows and smiling. 'I've already noticed that.'

Carter and Foster grinned and swapped all-knowing glances, while Pendleton continued studying the map. 'Number 25 berth is quite a long way from the hospital and administrative building,' said Carter. 'Looks like the doc and you will have a long walk if we need anything.'

'The exercise will do us good,' replied Pendleton with a grin.

Everyone on the bridge watched as the walls of the harbour, hitherto shrouded in early morning mist, slowly became clear. The ends of each of the two moles that formed the entrance were about half a mile apart. Behind the town, the dark, undulating hills of the Apulian plains stretched away in the distance. A stiff cold easterly wind that had replaced the warmer westerlies attacked their faces and dark low-lying clouds, racing across the sky heralded the oncoming of rain.

The convoy slowed down and waited while the workhorses of the Royal Navy, the minesweepers, were kept busy clearing mines from the harbour entrance. The date was Saturday, 1 December. Two hours later, greeted by hordes of squawking seagulls, the convoy entered the port.

'There seems to be plenty of ships already here, sir,' remarked Carter, surveying the harbour with his binoculars. 'There's three minesweepers, two destroyers and four MTBs tied up at the far end of the harbour, not to mention several merchant ships unloading on the quaysides.'

'Yes, you're right, Number One,' Pendleton replied wryly. 'It's going to be a rather crowded when convoy KM51 arrives.'

Using his binoculars, Pendleton noticed the many cranes and Bedford trucks, off-loading a mass of military impedimenta onto the wharfs. He strained his eyes searching the buildings on the far side of the harbour, wondering which one was the hospital. The thought that before the day was out Nadine might be in his arms sent a surge of excitement running through him.

The strident voice of Yeoman PO Jeffries interrupted his reverie. 'Signal from *Cleopatra,* sir,' "Boom opened. Tankers to enter first, followed by freighters, secure as ordered. *Cleopatra* and other escorts will put to sea and return to Malta. Good Luck".'

'Thank you, PO,' said Pendleton, 'reply, "signal received and understood, sorry to see you leave. Thank you and Good Luck to you".'

By 1300, the nine ships had cleared the boom and were safely in the harbour. Two Italian tankers, the *Corona Ferza* and *Salamis,* who were not part of the convoy, were lined up on the Molo San Catalado, discharging their fuel.

Due to the congestion in the inner harbour convoy KM32 had to tie up on Nuovo Molo. The Dutch tanker *Odysseus* was the first to enter the harbour and berthed at the end of the mole. Next came the SS *Vest,* a naval coal ship. The Italian tanker *Frosinone* and the USS *John Harvey,* the ship that Major Williams described as carrying "vital cargo", came next. Five other merchantmen sailed in, the last of these securing alongside the MV *Devon Coast,* a small coastal tanker that was not part of the convoy.

No sooner had the ships tied up alongside the quay, than several cranes moved into position. Using bulging black metal nets and, aided by a team of industrious Italian workers, their precious cargo was lowered onto the quayside. These were then transferred into sheds flanking the dockside to be transported northwards by rail or truck.

'My goodness, sir,' Foster remarked to Pendleton, as *Zimba* came alongside berth number 25. 'They certainly are a busy lot. Just to think, not long ago the Italians were fighting us. Now they seem to be breaking their backs to help us win the war.'

Pendleton ignored the young man's comment. Having received a message from Carter on the fo'c'sle, telling him the ship was secure, he rasped, 'Stop all engines. Fallout special sea duty men.'

At that moment, the slightly built figure of Surgeon Lieutenant Fulford came onto the bridge. His pale features broke into a smile.

'Good afternoon, sir,' he said pleasantly. 'With your permission, I'd like to visit the hospital to check on the medical facilities.'

'Splendid idea, Doc,' retorted Pendleton, 'I've received a signal asking me to report to a Major Williams, the port commandant, so I'll come with you.'

'Shall we say, half an hour, sir?' replied the doctor, a sly smile playing around his mouth.

'Make it twenty minutes,' said Pendleton. Glancing at Carter, he went on, 'There's nothing I can do here at the moment, is there Number One?'

'No, sir,' answered Carter. 'The fuel lighter will be here in half an hour, but Paddy can deal with that.'

Just after 1430, Fulford preceded by Pendleton, went ashore. Both wore their best doeskin uniforms. After being at sea for a long time the cobble-stoned surface of the quayside felt uncomfortable and unnatural. Pendleton gazed expectantly across the harbour. Somewhere in one of the buildings Nadine was blissfully unaware he was so close.

'The port is much bigger than I imagined,' Pendleton remarked as they walked along the quayside. 'Look at those floodlights rigged around the quayside. They must work through the night.'

'I'm sure they do, sir,' Fulford replied. 'It's almost as if they are trying to make up for fighting against us.'

With a feeling of disquiet, Pendleton looked around the harbour again and added, 'You know, Doc, those ships of the convoy we brought in are too close together for my liking.'

'I agree, sir,' Fulford answered. 'There's also several merchant ships tied to buoys in the middle of the harbour, not to mention those minesweepers and a destroyer moored alongside that long jetty poking out from the centre of the wharf.' (The minesweepers were the MMS50, and 32. The destroyer was HMS *Vienna.*)

Continuing along the outer mole, Pendleton saw stacks of bombs, shell cases, petrol cans and boxes marked, "small arms", lying idle on the dockside.

'I must say, Doc,' said Pendleton warily. 'Security seems rather lax, don't you think?'

'Indeed it is,' replied Fulford. 'One can only assume they are waiting to be loaded onto lorries and shipped up north.'

Returning the salutes of several ratings and army personnel, they passed a destroyer (HMS *Quale),* moored alongside the quayside. Nearby was a large wooden hut marked "Naval Stores".

After passing the naval barracks, and an official looking edifice called "Navy House" they came to a large red-bricked building with a flat-roof close to the harbour wall. From a tall flagpole on the roof fluttered a flag showing the Geneva cross. Above the arched entrance, was a large, wooden sign, painted in red on a white background that read 98th British Base Hospital. Close by was a smaller, white-painted building with a similar sign marked Naval Sick Quarters. Waiting nearby were half a dozen army ambulances, camouflaged in dull, green and brown. About fifty yards away was a railway cutting and rolling stock.

Pendleton held his breath as a couple of nurses with their blue cloaks wrapped firmly around them, came out of the hospital entrance. One or two stopped and started talking to a group of ambulance drivers who were standing about smoking cigarettes. Pendleton quickly realised none of the nurses were Nadine.

'I take it you want to come inside, sir?' asked Fulford.

Pendleton only half heard him. He was too engrossed in wondering in which of rooms in the hospital Nadine might be working.

Pendleton gave a nervous cough and replied, 'Err, yes. Of course I'll come with you.'

CHAPTER THIRTY-EIGHT

The poignant smell of antiseptic and polish met them as they opened the door and went inside the hospital. On their left, a thick set, heavily tanned army sergeant sat behind a trellis table. He was busy writing something into a ledger. He looked up, saw them and immediately stood up.

'Can I 'elp yer sir?' he asked, in North Country accent.

'Yes,' replied Fulford. 'I'm looking for the medical officer in charge.'

'That would be Major Cranworth, sir,' replied the sergeant. 'You can find 'im down the corridor you see facing you. It's the second door on the left.'

While the sergeant was speaking Pendleton glanced around. The floor was tiled in black and white and neon lighting was secured to a low, white ceiling. Directly opposite them a long, corridor dissected the place in two. Three nurses emerged from a door, their starched uniforms rustling as they walked passed. One caught Pendleton's eye, and for a fleeting moment he was tempted to ask her if she knew Nadine. However, the voice of the sergeant interrupted him.

'And you, sir, do you wish to see the major also?' he asked.

'Err...no, Sergeant,' Pendleton replied. 'Can you tell me where I can find a Sister Le Brun?'

The sergeant's walnut features broke into a wide grin. 'Oh yes, sir,' he said. 'Sister Le Brun is in charge of the naval sick quarters. That's the white building next to this one.'

'Thank you,' said Pendleton. Suddenly his mouth felt dry. He glanced at Fulford and running his tongue nervously along his lips, went on, 'My appointment with the port commander isn't till 1600. I'll meet you here then.'

'Very good, sir,' answered Fulford, 'and, err…give Sister Le Brun my best wishes,' he added with a smile.

'Thank you, Doc,' replied Pendleton. 'I'll do that.'

Pendleton turned and left. The naval sick quarters were smaller than the main hospital. He opened the door, went inside and walked down a corridor passing two nurses on the way.

Then, through an office door window he saw Nadine. She was sitting behind a desk writing in a book. She wore a white, long-sleeved button down uniform and her wide cap, concealed most of her chestnut hair. A small watch hung from her left breast pocket above which a tag indicated her name and rank The porcelain features he remembered so well were slightly tanned, making her look even more beautiful than he remembered.

For a few seconds Pendleton stood staring at her, so excited he could hardly move.

Then, as if she felt someone staring at her, she looked up.

'*Mon Dieu!*' she cried, wide-eyed, while dropping her pen. *'Jeremy, is it really you?'*

Transfixed by those beguiling violet eyes he had seen so often in his dreams, Pendleton opened the door and went inside. 'Yes darling,' he said. 'It really is me.'

At that moment a nurse arrived holding two brown files and placed them on Nadine's desk.

'Two fresh cases have just arrived, Sister,' she said, glancing first at Pendleton then at Nadine. 'They're in ward two, shrapnel wounds.'

'Thank you, nurse,' replied Nadine, still staring at Pendleton. 'I'll be there in just a minute.'

With a faint smile playing around her mouth, the nurse glanced at both of them, turned and left, closing the door behind her.

Nadine immediately left her desk and fell into Pendleton's arms. Their kiss was so hard they both could feel the other's teeth pushing against their lips. The pungent smell of carbolic that had replaced the sensual aroma of Nadine's Chanel No 5, smelt like heaven. Through the thin material of her uniform, Pendleton could feel the softness of her body crushing against him; the body he had lain awake at night thinking about, wondering when, or if, he would ever touch it again. She in turn held him close, feeling the buttons of his uniform pressing against her. Thank you, God, she said to herself, for bringing him back to me.

'Oh, darling,' Pendleton gasped as they broke away. 'I can't tell you how much I've missed you. When I read your letter telling me you had been sent abroad, I was beside myself with worry.'

With tears running down her cheeks, Nadine reached up and touched Pendleton's face and murmured, 'I've thought about you night and day, Cheri.' With her eyes shining with excitement, she added, 'But when did you arrive and,' she paused, and after wiping away a tear with the back of her hand, asked, 'how long are you here for?'

'I'll know the answer to that after I've see the port commander,' Pendleton replied. Glancing at the wall clock, he went on, 'and that's in ten minutes' time. When can we meet?'

'Damn and blast,' Nadine forcibly replied. 'I'm on duty tonight. What about tomorrow night, can you get away?'

'I expect so,' said Pendleton, gently kissing her forehead. 'After rounds, say 2115.'

'Wonderful,' said Nadine, unable to contain her excitement. 'Where are you tied up?'

'On the far side of the harbour at number 25 berth,' replied Pendleton. 'Do you think you can find it?'

Nadine gave him a hug and said, 'Don't worry, mon amour, I'll find it. Now give me another kiss and leave. I've missed you so and can't wait till tomorrow.'

Major Peter Williams, RASC was standing behind his desk quietly smoking and staring out of the office window. He was a tall, thirty-year-old man, with dark brown hair whose well-tailored khaki uniform fitted his bulky frame almost too perfectly. Before the war he had worked for The Mersey Docks and Harbour Board. Now, as Port Commandant, he was responsible for the docking of the many convoys that came and went from Bari.

The major's office was sparsely furnished. The floor was covered with a dark brown, threadbare carpet. In one corner was a bulky, green metal filing cabinet. Then came a small table on which rested a Bakelite wireless, a kettle, a teapot and a few cups and saucers, one of which was chipped. A collapsible wooden chair lay opposite a trellis desk covered with a green baize cloth. In each corner of the desk rested wooden IN and OUT trays containing buff-coloured folders and papers. A black telephone lay close to a glass ashtray half full of dog-ends, and from a low, concrete ceiling hung a yellow lampshade. On the whitewashed wall behind the desk was a framed photograph of the Royal family.

'When that convoy from Malta arrives the day after tomorrow, the harbour will be so crowded you won't be able to berth a tug.' These disturbing remarks were addressed to a small, ruddy-faced sergeant, standing opposite his desk.

'Yer right there, sir,' the sergeant replied warily. 'There won't even room for a seagull to piss in, if yerl excuse me French.'

'Err...quite,' said the officer, turning around and sitting at his desk. 'That'll be all, Sergeant, thank you.'

The sergeant left the room as Pendleton appeared in the doorway. The major's pale blue eyes wrinkled into a welcoming smile. 'Ah, do come in,' he said, standing up. 'You must be *Zimba*'s commanding officer.' This was more of a statement than a question. 'Peter Williams, do sit down,' he added, offering his hand.

'Yes,' replied Pendleton, introducing himself as they shook hands. 'You wanted to see me?'

'That's right,' replied the major. 'But first, can I offer you some tea?'

'No thanks,' Pendleton replied, anxious to know what the major wanted.

'Right then,' the major said, stubbing his cigarette out as he sat down. 'I'll come straight to the point. I'm afraid your stay in Bari will be brief.'

The major's words suddenly filled Pendleton with alarm. 'What do mean, *brief*?' he asked, quickly sitting forward.

'There is a convoy due to leave Brindisi on the 4 December for Malta, then on to England,' said the major taking out a packet of Players, giving one to Pendleton, and lighting them both. 'Unfortunately, one of her escort destroyers has developed engine trouble.'

'I see,' interrupted Pendleton, knowing full well what was coming next. 'And *Zimba* has to take its place?'

'I'm afraid so,' the major said. 'The order came straight from the Admiral St Lyset in *Victorious.*'

'It's rather short notice, isn't it?' Pendleton replied, taking a deep drag of his cigarette. 'When do I sail?'

'0600 on 3 December,' the major replied. Ignoring the frown on Pendleton's brow, he went on, 'You are to refuel and take on stores and ammunition today and tomorrow. I'm sorry, commander, but there it is...'

'I understand, major,' Pendleton said, flicking ash into the ashtray. 'I don't suppose the convoy we brought in today will stay here long. Most of them seem loaded below their Plimsoll Lines.'

'Yes, they are,' replied the major, 'every ship is packed to the hilt with ammunition, aviation fuel and the likes. All, that is, except one.'

A curious expression spread across Pendleton's face. 'And which one is that?' Pendleton asked, leaning forward and stubbing his cigarette out.

'The *John Harvey,*' said the major, glancing down at an open file on his desk. 'She's American. It states on the manifest that she is carrying "special stores", whatever they may be...'

'Yes, it does sound rather odd,' Pendleton replied cautiously. Accepting another cigarette from the major and lighting it, he went on. 'May I ask a question unrelated to the order?'

'Of course,' replied the major, 'do so by all means.'

'As you know, another convoy is due to arrive in two days,' Pendleton said. 'Surely the harbour will be dangerously overcrowded. And I've noticed floodlights around the quayside. If you work at night, what if there's an air raid?'

'Let me assure you that won't happen, old boy,' the major said, giving Pendleton a wry smile. 'Yesterday in Algiers, Air Vice Marshall Conningham gave a press conference and stated that in his opinion, the Germans have lost the air war in southern Italy. He also said, and I quote, "I would consider it an insult if one enemy plane came over Bari".'

Pendleton gave the major a searching look. 'That's sheer nonsense,' he cried, sitting forward. 'How on earth could he say such a thing? I heard that Naples has been attacked four times in the last month.'

'Well,' replied the major, nonchalantly shrugging his shoulders. 'That's what Conningham said, so who are we to question his so-called expert opinion?'

Pendleton sighed wearily. 'Expert opinion indeed,' he replied, angrily stubbing out his cigarette. 'Thank you Major,' he added standing up and extending his hand. 'I'd better get back and tell my crew their stay in Bari is to be cut short.'

Shaking the major's hand Pendleton felt his heart sink, wondering what he was going to say to Nadine.

'Sailing in three days' time, eh, sir?' said Carter, rubbing the back of his neck with a hand. 'Shall I put it on Daily Orders, or is that too risky?'

Pendleton returned onboard *Zimba* and immediately sent for his First Lieutenant. The time was 1730 and dusk was about to suddenly change to night.

'You might as well, Number One,' said Pendleton dryly. 'But from what I've seen ashore, security in the port is almost nonexistent. It wouldn't surprise me if the locals knew we were sailing before we did.'

The next morning ship's company greeted the news with alacrity.

'With a bit of luck we'll be home fer Christmas,' said Leading Steward Gale. He and several others were grouped around the main notice board in the passageway, reading Daily Orders.

'And a run ashore down the Gut,' cried Able Seaman Knocker White, giving Windy a friendly nudge in the ribs.

'You married men are all alike. All knackers and no ackers,' Mick Channon remarked churlishly. 'But don't worry. If anyone else catches the boat up, I've got some nice long needles to stick down the eye of your welt!'

In the senior ratings' mess, PO Potter and a few others were about to climb into their hammocks. The time was 2200 and *pipe down* had just sounded.

'It'll be just our luck to get torpedoed on the way home,' muttered PO Writer Potter, as he levered himself into his hammock.

'Fuckin' Jobe's comforter, Pansy,' muttered Chief Coxswain Jack Tolby, from under the bedclothes in the next hammock. 'Now pipe down and let me get some kip.'

Pendleton found sleep difficult. The thought that in less than twenty-four hours, Nadine would be in his arms, kept him tossing and turning all night. Every time he closed his eyes he saw her beautiful eyes smiling at him. She was still in his dreams when Gale woke him up at 0530.

'What's the weather like?' yawned Pendleton, sitting up and stretching his arms.

'It's pretty clear, sir,' said Windy, giving Pendleton his usual cheery smile as he handed him a mug of tea. 'But there's a cold wind blowing down the harbour.'

After breakfast, Carter reported that the fuel lighter was alongside. He and Pendleton were in the captain's day cabin. *Stand Easy* had just been piped.

'Paddy and his stokers are seeing to it, sir,' said Carter, 'and John Hailey tells me a stores barge is due at midday.'

'What about ammunition?' asked Pendleton, indicating Carter to take a seat.

'Guns tells me it is arriving at 1400, sir,' replied Carter, accepting a cigarette and a light from Pendleton. 'He and the Chief GI are preparing hoists to take the shells onboard.'

Pendleton sat back in his chair, took a deep puff of his cigarette, and said, 'Thank you, Number One.' With a tired sigh he exhaled a steady stream of smoke, and added, 'A pity we couldn't stay here a little longer, the crew could do with a rest.'

With a solemn shake of his head, Carter replied, 'Couldn't we all, sir,' then left.

CHAPTER THIRTY-NINE

Glancing at his wristwatch, Pendleton gave a frustrated sigh. The time was 1600. The five hours he had to wait until meeting Nadine were going to seem like an eternity.

Shortly after *Hands to dinner* was piped, Carter came into his cabin and reported the ship fully stored and ammunitioned. His heavily tanned features broke into a wide grin. 'The weather forecast for the day after tomorrow is good, sir,' he said, 'so we should make good time to Brindisi.'

'Thank you, Number One,' replied Pendleton. Trying to sound casual, he added, 'and by the way, I'll be going ashore tonight after rounds.'

'An official call, sir?' Carter asked, trying his best to disguise a smile.

'Ahem,' Pendleton replied, nervously clearing his throat, 'you could say that Number One, and I'm, err...expecting a guest.'

In the wardroom PO Steward Knocker White overheard Carter telling a few of the officers that Pendleton was going ashore.

'I bet he's meeting that gorgeous nurse he met in Pompey,' said Lieutenant Small. 'The doc told us she's been sent here.'

'Good luck to him,' chimed Paddy, 'to be sure he's earned a little relaxation.'

'Is that what it's called now,' sniggered Hailey, taking a sip of his Horse's Neck.

'Oh shut up, John,' interrupted MacIntyre, holding up his empty glass. 'And I do believe it's your round.'

'I'll be leaving the ship about 2100,' Pendleton said to Gale. 'So please lay out my number one uniform.' The time was 1930.

Pendleton was sitting in his cabin. He had just finished dinner and was sipping a coffee.

'Very good, sir,' replied Gale, who, like most of the ship's company, knew where he was going. 'Shall I attach yer medals?'

'Don't be stupid, Gale,' grinned Pendleton. 'I'm not going on divisions.'

'No, sir,' replied Gale, biting his lip to stop himself laughing.

"Clean up mess decks and flats for rounds" came the pipe at 2000. "Men under punishment muster outside the coxswain's office."

Half an hour later Pendleton heard the piercing sound of the bosun's call. This was accompanied by the thumping of feet as the duty PO, QM and OOD passed outside his cabin. The noise gradually faded away as they made their way around the ship.

After ensuring his tie was straight, Pendleton left his cabin. As he made his way to the quarterdeck he felt his pulse quicken and his heart pound against his ribs.

The sight that met Pendleton as he arrived onto the quarterdeck startled him.

'Good Lord!' he exclaimed, looking around as Lieutenant Small approached him. 'The place is lit up like Piccadilly Circus.'

High above a full moon flitted between clusters of grey clouds. On the wharfs, unloading was taking place and the pale yellow floodlights lit up the harbour. Every light in the town was shining brightly. The lights from every merchant and warship added to the clarity of the scene, turning night into day.

'Yes, sir,' replied Small, nervously shifting his feet. 'I only hope a Jerry spotter plane doesn't come over. He'll have a field day.'

'Quite so,' said Pendleton, shaking his head.

Just then, the gruff voice of duty PO Bob Jenkins attracted Pendleton's attention.

'There's a vehicle coming along the wharf, sir,' he cried. 'It looks like a Yankee jeep.'

Pendleton felt his stomach contract. He watched as the jeep stopped at the bottom of the gangway. The small side door opened and out stepped Nadine. A dark blue cape covered most of her white uniform. She looked up at the ship, smiled and gave a short wave.

'Err…I think your guest has arrived, Jeremy.'

Pendleton turned and saw Paddy O'Malley. Nearby stood Lieutenants Foster, Small Reed and MacIntyre. Also several ratings stood on the far side of the quarterdeck doing their best to look inconspicuous.

'Thank you, Paddy,' replied Pendleton, feeling his face redden. 'The word certainly gets around, doesn't it? Kindly tell this lot,' he added glancing over his shoulder, 'to carry on.'

As Pendleton hurried down the gangway he could feel a dozen pairs of eyes staring at him. However, when he saw Nadine all thoughts of those onboard watching him left his mind. Pendleton's first reaction was to throw his arms around her, but protocol forbid this.

'It's a far cry from your friend's old Box Ford,' remarked Pendleton, looking at the jeep. 'Where did you get it?'

'Courtesy of our American friends,' replied Nadine gazing longingly at him. 'Oh Jeremy, I can't tell you how much I've waited for this moment.'

'Me too,' said Pendleton standing close to her and staring into those beguiling violet eyes he had pictured so often. 'You look absolutely marvellous.' As he spoke the sensual aroma of Chanel No 5 wafted delicately under his nose increasing the already cadence of his heartbeat.

'Oh Jeremy, mon amour,' Nadine replied, reaching out and touching his arm. 'I've missed you so.' She paused and glanced up at the ship. 'But do you think you could take me onboard. I do so want to thank everyone for looking after Papa.'

Pendleton looked up and saw Lieutenants Foster and Small standing at the top of the gangway. With a reluctant sigh, he said, 'I suppose we could go to the wardroom for a quick drink, but only for a short while. Besides, there's something I have to tell you.'

'What is that, Cheri?' Nadine asked, giving Pendleton a puzzled look.

'I'll tell you later, darling,' he said, as they moved away from the jeep. 'Incidentally,' he said taking her arm and helping her up the gangway. 'How can the ship contact me if I'm needed?'

'The hospital number is 177 and my cabin is extension 16,' Nadine replied. 'I'll write it down for you.'

The officers and the duty PO saluted as Nadine and Pendleton stepped over the brow onto the deck. As they did so, Paddy, Carter, Reed and Sam Small came forward. Pendleton noticed they were wearing their best uniforms and inwardly smiled.

'Quite a welcoming party, eh, Number One?' remarked Pendleton looking around.

'Yes, sir,' replied Carter somewhat sheepishly. 'We heard you…'

Pendleton cut him short and said, 'I'm sure you did, Number One, I'm sure you did.'

Even though Nadine had briefly met Carter before the ship sailed for Canada, Pendleton introduced her to him and the officers.

'Perhaps we should adjourn to the wardroom,' said Paddy, rubbing his hands together. 'To be sure it's getting a might chilly.'

While the group made their way into the citadel, Leading Seaman Dusty Miller turned to his oppo, Able Seaman Geordie Roberts, and salaciously muttered, 'The dirty lucky bugger. I bet he gives her one before the night's out.'

'I 'opes he does, lovely boy,' replied Roberts, digging Dusty in the ribs. 'She's a right smasher. If 'e don't I'll volunteer to do the job.'

'You and a dozen others,' chimed in Able Seaman Jumper Collins.

'Pack it in you lot,' shouted Jenkins, the duty PO. 'You sound like a shower of sex starved virgins.'

'But we are, PO,' sighed Leading Seaman Paddy Doyle.

'Then yer know what to do,' said Jenkins, motioning his hand up and down. 'Now get below.'

With Pendleton leading, Nadine and the officers arrived in the wardroom where PO Steward Knocker White greeted them. He wore a pristine short white jacket complete with shiny brass buttons. Standing behind him were the rest of the ship's officers, all of whom concentrated their attention on Nadine.

'Good evening, ma'am,' said PO White, ignoring the officers. 'Can I take your cape and get you something to drink?'

'Thank you,' Nadine replied, removing her blue cape and handing it him. 'I'd like a pink gin, please.' With a dazzling smile, she looked at the officers and said, 'Good evening gentlemen. How lovely to see you, especially you, Doctor,' she added offering her hand to Fulford.

'A pleasure to meet you again, Sister,' replied Fulford, shaking her hand. 'I trust your father is well?'

'Yes, he's fully recovered,' said Nadine. 'I can't thank you and your assistant, for all the help you gave him.'

'I'm very pleased to hear it,' Fulford replied graciously. 'I'll pass on your thanks to SBA Channon.'

The drinks arrived and Pendleton stood back allowing the officers to surround her.

'Are there many nurses ashore in the hospital?' asked Sub Lieutenant Coburn.

'Yes,' Nadine replied, finishing her drink. 'About half a dozen.'

'Splendid,' chimed in Lieutenant Foster. 'What a pity we're...'

'Thank you Pilot,' interrupted Pendleton, glaring angrily at Foster. 'Perhaps you could oblige Sister Le Brun with a re-fill?'

'Err...of course, sir,' said Foster, feeling slightly embarrassed, 'right away.'

Half an hour later Pendleton caught Nadine's eye, frowned and gave a discrete sideways movement of his head.

'Mon Dieu!' exclaimed Nadine, glancing alarmingly at her wristwatch. 'Is that the time? I have to be on duty early tomorrow, so gentlemen,' she added, giving each officer another dazzling smile, 'I'm afraid I'll have to leave you. It's been a pleasure meeting you.'

PO White appeared and helped Nadine on with cape. She smiled and thanked him. Feeling tears welling up in her eyes, she looked around and said, 'Thank you, gentlemen. Goodbye, good luck and God bless you all.' With Pendleton and Carter in close attendance, she quickly turned and left the wardroom. When they arrived at the top of the gangway, Nadine took out a notebook from her bag and wrote down her telephone details. She tore out the page and handed it to Pendleton.

'I can be reached at this number if required, Number One,' he said, passing the note to Carter.

'Very good, sir,' said Carter doing his best not to smile, 'but I hope that won't be necessary.' Giving Nadine a smart salute, he added, 'Goodnight, Sister, it was a pleasure seeing you again.'

With Pendleton holding Nadine's arm, they made their way down the gangway onto the wharf, and climbed into the jeep.

The drive around the harbour to the nurses' quarters only took a few minutes. On the way they passed the naval barracks and several buildings Pendleton had seen earlier. Each one had its lights on. A cold breeze blew in from the sea and high above a mass of twinkling stars dotted the heavens. From a cloudless sky the moon's incandescent glow, aided by the harbour floodlights bathed the area in a clear white light. Cranes lowering huge nets of stores from ships lined the wharfs while an army of workers transferred them onto trains in the side cutting. As usual, the noise was deafening. Was Bari *really* safe from air attack Pendleton asked himself as the jeep slowed down? He looked around and was suddenly overcome by a deep-seated sense of foreboding.

CHAPTER FORTY

Nadine stopped the jeep outside the nurses' quarters. Lights from the hospital windows lit up the surrounding area. Before leaving the jeep, Nadine turned, and with her eyes shining, looked up at Pendleton and whispered, 'Jeremy. Cheri, please kiss me.'

Pendleton didn't need any encouragement. 'I thought this moment would never come,' sighed Pendleton.

With their arms clasped around one another they left the jeep and went inside and walked down a short, well-lit corridor. They stopped outside a door and untwined themselves. Nadine opened her bag, fumbled nervously then produced a large iron key and unlocked the door. They went inside and she switched on the light. The fragrant aroma of body powder, make-up and Chanel No 5 permeated the air as they entered.

The room was quite large and pleasantly furnished. A single bed complete with a yellow eiderdown, side table and shaded light occupied centre stage. From a low ceiling painted white, hung a pink lampshade and a plain brown carpet covered most of the floor. In one corner rested an oak dressing table and mirror. Close by was an unlit gas fire. An open door led into a bathroom tiled in white. Next to this was a black leather settee and armchair above which was a small window that afforded a panoramic view of many ships in the harbour, including *Zimba*.

No sooner had the light come on than their arms flew around one another. Their kiss was long and passionate leaving them breathless. Pendleton reached up and with his hand shaking slightly, undid the top button of Nadine's cape.

'Don't you think I'd better draw the curtains first, Cheri,' whispered Nadine, feeling his hardness pressing against her through his trousers.

'I suppose you must,' muttered Pendleton, as he opened his jacket.

With pent up desire they watched as each hurriedly removed their clothing. In a matter of minutes Pendleton's jacket, gas mask and cap was a wrinkled mound on the floor. After hastily removing his shirt, Nadine burst into laughter as Pendleton, hopping on one foot, almost fell over taking off his trousers. She took off her cape and cap, undid her hair allowing it to tumble around her shoulders. Then, with her violet eyes on fire, she stood tantalisingly in her white, silk panties and brassier. She then sat down on a chair and slowly undid each of the buttons on her suspender belt and peeled off her black stockings. When she was naked she stood up and stared excitingly at the bulge in Pendleton's shorts. With a wicked smile, she said, 'Mon amour, if you don't take me to bed I'll scream the roof tops off!'

Their lovemaking was long and passionate. With each orgasm, Nadine dug her fingers into Pendleton's back and cried out. Finally, bathed in warm perspiration they lay in each other's arms and fell asleep.

An hour later Pendleton woke up. He was lying on his side with Nadine's warm naked body curled into his back. She had one arm around his waist, resting on his stomach. The other arm was tucked somewhere beneath her. For a while, Pendleton lay listening to Nadine's steady breathing and feeling her firm breasts pressing into him. Trying not to disturb her, he reached across and picked up a packet of Players off the bedside table. His efforts were in vain. Nadine opened her eyes, blinked a few times and with a faint smile playing around her lips, snuggled closer into him.

'Light one for me, Cheri,' she said in a hoarse whisper. Looking up at him, she yawned and added, 'What time is it?'

'Ten past two,' Pendleton murmured, taking out two cigarettes and lighting them both. 'What time are you on duty tomorrow?'

'Zero eight hundred,' said Nadine, sitting up slightly and accepting the cigarette. In doing so she pulled away from him, displaying the cherry red nipples he had recently kissed and caressed. 'And I come off duty at nineteen hundred. Will you be able to get away?'

'I think so, darling,' Pendleton pensively replied. Realising the ship would be under sailing orders, he hastily added, 'You could come aboard and we could have dinner in my cabin. Say 2030, if that's all right?'

'That sounds lovely,' replied Nadine. With a curious note in her voice, she went on, 'By the way, Cheri, what was it you were going to tell me?'

This was the moment Pendleton was dreading. For a few minutes he didn't speak. He took a deep drag of his cigarette, pushed himself up and sat against the headboard. Taking a deep breath, he replied, 'We're sailing the day after tomorrow at 0600.'

The expression in Pendleton's eyes suddenly filled her with alarm.

With her cigarette poised expectantly in her hand, she gasped, *'Jeremy, you are coming back, aren't you?'*

Pendleton felt his mouth go dry. He nervously ran his tongue along his dry lips and said, 'No, darling. We're going to Brindisi, after which we sail for Malta and then...back to England.'

'Mon Dieu, No!' she cried sitting bolt upright. 'Surely not! You've only just arrived here. Why?'

Pendleton stubbed out his cigarette and slowly shook his head. 'It's orders, I'm afraid, darling,' he replied putting his arm around her and pulling her close. With a feeling of dejection, he went on, 'And there's nothing we can do about it.'

Fighting back tears, she put her cigarette in the ashtray. 'Oh, Jeremy,' she cried. 'This bloody war...'

The sudden ringing of the telephone startled them. Both gave one another anxious looks.

'Better answer it, darling,' said Pendleton, reluctantly unwinding his arms from around her. 'It may be for me.'

Nadine reached across and lifted up the receiver.

'Sister Le Brun,' she said, trying to control her voice. After a few seconds, she looked at Pendleton and added, 'Yes, he's here. One moment.' Holding her hand over the mouthpiece, she whispered, 'It's your ship, Cheri,' and handed him the receiver.

Pendleton sat forward and took the receiver. 'Yes,' he simply said. After listening for a minute or so, he replied, 'Thank you Number One. You did the right thing. I'll return to the ship immediately,' and handed the receiver to Nadine. 'That was my First Lieutenant,' he said throwing back the bedclothes. 'German E-boats are laying mines outside the harbour. Our MTBs are investigating and my ship has gone to action stations.'

'Of course, you'll have to leave, Cheri,' Nadine replied, leaving the bed and gathering her underwear. 'Hurry and I'll drive you back.'

Ten minutes later they were in the jeep driving around the harbour. Flashes of gunfire lighted up the sky beyond the harbour entrance, followed by the occasional *thud* of an explosion.

When the jeep was a hundred yards from *Zimba*, Pendleton asked her to stop the car. 'Just so we can…'

With a tearful expression in her eyes, Nadine replied, 'Yes, Cheri, I understand.'

Nadine did as he asked. On the left side of the wharf dockyard workers were too busy unloading a cargo vessel to pay attention to them.

With a feeling only lovers have experienced at such moments, they looked into each other's eyes. Uttering a painful sob, Nadine flung her arms around him. 'Oh, mon amour, I love you so,' she cried.

Feeling his throat contract, Pendleton murmured, 'and I you, darling,' as they kissed.

After a tearful glance, Nadine started the car. Both of them found it hard to speak. When the jeep arrived near the bottom of the gangway, Pendleton reached across and gently touched her face.

'Until tomorrow, my love,' she said, reaching up and placing her hand over his. 'I'll meet you here at 2000.'

'Goodnight, darling, I'm missing you already,' Pendleton replied reaching across and squeezing her hand. He then climbed out of the jeep, glanced up at the ship and walked up the gangway.

Unlike the merchant ships tied up alongside the wharf, *Zimba* was cloaked in darkness. Only the dim, blue light on the QM's desk was visible near the top of the gangway. Carter saluted as Pendleton stepped onboard. Pendleton returned the salute then turned and watched as the jeep disappeared along the quayside.

CHAPTER FORTY-ONE

Flying at 20,000 feet (6,100 metres), Luftwaffe Lieutenant Werner Hahn peered down from the cockpit of his Messerschmitt Me 210 reconnaissance plane. The date was 2 December, the time, 1045. Below, lay the medieval port of Bari with at least twenty merchant ships secured along its wharfs. In the distance, the Mediterranean Sea stretched away towards the horizon like a dazzling blue carpet.

Suddenly, Werner couldn't believe his eyes. Looking like tiny white specks he saw the wakes of a large convoy. Even at that altitude he knew the ships were heading for Bari harbour.

Werner was twenty-three and had taken part in Hitler's Blitzkreig of Poland and the Low countries. Although not a card-carrying member of the Nazi party, he supported the Führer's rehabilitation of Germany following the humiliation of the Versailles Treaty. Like his colleagues, he was only too aware that Bari was the main port supplying the Allies with much needed aviation fuel ammunition, tanks and bombs.

'Mein Gott!' he exclaimed to himself. 'There must be over twenty merchant ships down there. The harbour will soon be full. Surely they must know how exposed they are.' Shaking his head in disbelief he banked his plane hard left and set a course for the German air base in northern Italy.

Shortly before 1100, Pendleton, Carter and Lieutenant Foster were standing on *Zimba*'s bridge watching *Zetland* and three minesweepers, *Mullet, Hazard* and MMS50, shepherding convoy KM51 into the harbour. Close by stood PO Yeoman Jeffries, and Able Seaman Jenkins. A bright yellow sun promised another warm day, and the brilliant blueness of the sky was reflected in the calm waters of the harbour. Suddenly the attention of the group was disturbed by the faint, throbbing of an aircraft high in the sky. All eyes, shaded by hands, turned upwards. The plane was so high its white contrails could barely be seen.

'I'll be one of ours,' Carter casually remarked, squinting against the sun's glare. 'Probably an American from one of their bases in Sicily.'

'Mm...' Pendleton murmured doubtfully, 'maybe...'

As the sound of the plane's engine gradually faded away, Pendleton and the others watched as the convoy of twenty merchantmen entered the harbour and berth on the Nuovo Molo. *Empire Meteor* and her sister ship, *Empire Sunbeam* came in first and tied up alongside berths 17 and 18. The American tanker *John Biscom* followed on and managed to squeeze in next to the *John Motely*.

Turning to Carter, Pendleton sarcastically remarked, 'If they get any closer they'll be able to spit at one another.'

'You're right there, sir,' replied Carter, watching as the cargo vessel *Fort Athabaska* berthed between the British tanker SS *Testbank* and the tanker, USS *Joseph Wheeler.* Sandwiched between these two was the American cargo ship, *John Harvey* that had arrived earlier with convoy KM232. Further down the mole came the Norwegian cargo vessel, *Norlom* and the Danish tanker *Lars Kruse* and *Lom.* By this time the Nuovo Molo was so crowded the remaining eleven ships had to anchor or tie up to a buoy in mid harbour. Among these were the American tanker *Fort Le Joie,* the Polish tankers SS *Lwow* and SS *Puck* plus two Italian oilers *Barletta* and *Cassala.*

The time was 1400. As *Zetland* berthed next to *Zimba,* the pipe "attention on the upper deck, face the port", was called. The *carry on* followed this. *Zetland* was now about ten yards on *Zimba*'s port side. Like the merchant ships, *Zimba* and *Zetland* were moored stern to on Nuovo Molo. A few of *Zetland's* officers were on the bridge. Pendleton gave her captain, Commander John Wilkinson a friendly wave. He leant over the starboard wing and shouted, 'Come over for a quick drink, Jeremy. I hear you're leaving us.'

'Thank you, Johnny,' yelled Pendleton. 'I'll be over right away.'

A few minutes later Pendleton left the bridge and walked along starboard side of the ship towards the quarterdeck. On the way he passed the duty watch, their blue overalls tucked inside rubber sea boots, hosing down the upper deck. Other ratings were busily working on the two twin 20mm Oerlikon guns or polishing brass work.

'A fine afternoon, sir,' remarked OOD Lieutenant MacIntyre, hurriedly placing his meerschaum pipe by his side and saluting.

'Yes, Jim,' Pendleton replied, returning MacIntyre's salute. 'I'm just going across to *Zetland*. I should be back before 1600.'

'Captain leaving the ship,' shouted duty PO Jenkins. He, MacIntyre and a few ratings working on the quarterdeck immediately stood to attention. Pendleton saluted and walked down the gangway onto the cobbled quayside.

The OOD, a tall, fair-haired sub lieutenant and the duty petty officer met Pendleton onboard *Zetland*. Returning their salutes, Pendleton introduced himself.

'This way, sir,' said the sub lieutenant, 'the captain is expecting you.'

The captain's day cabin was situated in the same place as in *Zimba*.

'Come,' grunted Commander Wilkinson, after the sub lieutenant had knocked and opened the door.

Like Pendleton, John Wilkinson was an RNVR officer. He was a tall, wiry, thirty something with a shock of dark hair, going slightly grey. Before the war he had been a barrister with a law firm in London. He and Hilda his wife and three-year-old son lived in Hamble, Hampshire. Wilkinson was called up in 1941 and was slightly senior to Pendleton. *Zetland* was his second command, the first being a sloop.

The cabin was almost a replica of the one in *Zimba* with floral coloured furnishings and a dark blue carpet. Upon seeing Pendleton he immediately stood up.

'Jeremy, how nice to see you again,' he said as they shook hands. 'Thank you for coming.' As he spoke his dark brown eyes wrinkled into a grin. 'Do sit down,' he paused then went on, 'let me see, the last time we met was in the wardroom in Pompey barracks, wasn't it?'

'I do believe so, Johnny,' Pendleton replied, sitting down in one of the two armchairs. 'If you remember, you hinted that we might meet up in the Med, and here we are.'

'Indeed,' said Wilkinson, reaching across his desk and pressing a red button. 'But what's all this about you going home?'

Before Pendleton had time to answer the pantry door opened and in came a small, pale-faced steward wearing a short white coat.

'Two large Horse's Necks, please Rogers,' said Wilkinson, 'and don't spare the brandy.'

A few minutes later the drinks arrived. Pendleton sat back in his armchair and told Wilkinson about his meeting with Major Williams.

'So Air Vice Marshal Conningham thinks Bari is safe from air attack, eh?' said Wilkinson, finishing his drink. 'I can't say I share his optimism. As you know, Naples has been bombed four times in the last month and the ground defences in Bari are far from adequate. This, plus the fact that there are no RAF fighters based here make the whole area very vulnerable. Anyway, old boy,' he went on, before taking a deep gulp of his drink, 'if there is an air raid, you'll be out of it on your way to Malta.'

'Yes, we will,' sighed Pendleton, thinking about Nadine. As he finished his drink he was suddenly overcome by a deep-seated sense of foreboding.

CHAPTER FORTY-TWO

For the rest of the day Pendleton did his best to take his mind off Nadine by catching up with a mound of paperwork. At various times he was tempted to telephone her, but realising she was on duty, changed his mind. No sooner had *'Secure'* been piped at 1600, than Gale came in from the pantry holding a mug of steaming hot tea.

'Thought you'd like a drink, sir,' Gale said, placing the mug on a nearby table.

'Thank you,' said Pendleton. Doing his best to sound casual, he added, 'and by the away I'll be having dinner in my day cabin with a guest tonight. What's on the menu?'

'Roast chicken, sir,' Gale replied. With a slight grin, he added, 'May I ask who your guest is, sir?'

'Mind your own damn business,' Pendleton hotly replied. 'But make sure there's a decent bottle of French wine at hand.'

'Of course, sir,' Gale answered doing his best not to smile. 'I'll speak to Knocker err...the wardroom PO.'

Two hours later, "cooks to the galley, hands to supper. Men under punishment muster outside the coxswain's office", came over the tannoy. Shortly afterwards Pendleton decided to have a shower and change into his number one uniform. Just after 1900, he left his cabin and made his way along the main corridor towards the quarterdeck. On the way he passed a queue of ratings outside the NAAFI buying nutty, (naval parlance for sweets and chocolate) and cigarettes. All of them snapped to attention as he went by. Pendleton acknowledged them with a smile and carried on.

One rating, a small, portly able seaman, dug his oppo in the ribs and said, 'He seems pretty cheerful, maybe he's on a promise.'

'With the ship under sailing orders, that's more than any of us are,' his mate sullenly replied.

Stepping onto the quarterdeck Pendleton was met by Lieutenant Small who was OOD. Nearby stood the rangy figure of Chief Coxswain Jack Tonby and Able Seaman Roberts, the duty QM.

'Lovely evening, sir, a full moon and not a cloud in the sky,' Small remarked as he saluted.

'Yes it is, Guns,' Pendleton replied. Returning the salute, he added, 'I'm expecting a guest around 2000. If I'm not here send the QM for me.'

'Very good, sir,' Small answered, doing his best to disguise a sly grin.

The raid started shortly after 1915.

Jack Tolby was talking to Able Seaman Roberts. Suddenly, he stopped and looked up at the sky. 'Hey, Robbie!' he cried. 'Do you 'ear what I 'ear? That sounds like bloody airplanes coming from somewhere to the north!'

Pendleton, Small and Tolby also heard the drone of aircraft and immediately turned their heads skywards. Gradually the sound became clearer and louder. Suddenly the black outlines of two planes, flying at approximately 10,000 feet became visible. Just then, a huge crescent-shaped shower of silver tinfoil appeared, fluttering wildly in the darkness.

'*Great Scott!*' exploded Pendleton, 'they're JU 88 pathfinders and they're dropping Chaff. Sound action stations Number One. I think we're about to be attacked!'

The Germans called Chaff, "Duppel". It consisted of aluminium strips impregnated with glass fibres and was used to jam radar reception.

Onboard *Zetland,* the jangling sound of their alarm bells joined in with that coming from *Zimba.* The clatter of boots echoed around both ships. In a matter of minutes everyone was closed up at their respective stations.

In *Zimba's* sick bay, Channon was about to make a pot of tea. Fulford was sitting at the desk writing up a medical card. Both gave each other cautious looks as the alarm bell rang out.

'Better forget the tea, Channon,' Fulford said cautiously, 'and check on the first aid parties, we may need them.'

In order to obtain a clearer view of the harbour Carter and Pendleton dashed to the bridge. Lieutenant Foster, Chief GI Digger Barnes and Seaman PO Bob Jenkins joined them. Suddenly several small white parachutes descended from the plane's undercarriages and burst into a flickering yellow glow. In a matter of seconds the harbour and the town were illuminated in clear, red and green lights.

'I don't know why the bastards need flares,' shouted the Chief GI. 'As it is, the place is lit up like Trafalgar Square on New Year's Eve.'

With a furrowed brow, Pendleton turned to Carter. 'This looks like the air raid a certain high ranking officer said was impossible,' he said gravely.

'And the lights of the town are making things even more easier for the beggars,' added Carter. 'Every ship in the harbour must stand out like sore thumbs.'

A few seconds later, the dull drone of JU88s could be heard directly overhead. Looking like big black spiders, they broke formation and came in at heights varying from 4,000 to 6,000 feet.

'*Jesus Christ, sir!*' yelled Jenkins, '*there's about fifty of them. You can see the bloody crosses on their fuselages and wings!*'

At that moment, the undulating wail of the air raid siren echoed around the harbour.

Then came the piercing scream of falling bombs.

'*Take cover!*' someone yelled. Everyone on *Zimba*'s bridge instinctively flung himself on the deck. Seconds later the *crash* and *crump* of bombs exploding nearby, shook the ship.

'Tell Guns to open fire at will, Number One,' shouted Pendleton, as everyone staggered to their feet.

Seconds later, the barrage from *Zimba*'s heavy guns began firing. All at once the air was filled with smoke and the acrid smell of cordite. Beady arcs of red, white and green tracers from the Oerlikons streaked into the night sky. The noise was deafening as *Zetland*'s guns and those from the merchant ships joined in the barrage. Flashes of gunfire from the solitary shore battery added to the cacophony. In a matter of seconds the darkness was dotted with masses of yellow puffs of smoke and shells bursting.

The tankers, *Corona Ferza* and *Salamis* on the Molo San Cataldo were the first to be hit. Both vessels were suddenly engulfed in a huge ball of flame. Jagged pieces of metal and debris soared up into the air. Burning oil began to spew from the gaping holes in both tankers. The harbour water appeared to be on fire as flames threatened to engulf other vessels anchored nearby. Men, some with their clothes burning, dived overboard, their screams deadened by the roar of bombs bursting all around.

The Polish coastal tanker, SS *Lwow,* anchored in the middle of the harbour was the next victim. A stick of bombs exploded along her upper deck. The ship quickly became a raging hulk. A blinding flash immediately followed. With a sickening crunch of metal she slowly sank, leaving her bows poking defiantly out of the water. None of her crew of twenty could possibly have survived.

Not too far away, lying at anchor lay the USS *Fort Le Joie,* and the SS *Puck.* Both vessels suffered direct hits and disappeared under mountainous of clouds of yellow flames and billowing black smoke.

With horror etched in his eyes, Pendleton watched the carnage unfold.

'Great god in heaven,' he muttered, shielding his eyes from the glare of the fires. 'Those poor men are being burnt to cinders and there's very little we can do about it except pray.'

Below the waterline in the engine and boiler rooms, stokers clung onto anything at hand. Bathed in sweat they waited, gripped with fear, listening as the shock waves thudded against the ship's hull.

Not knowing how long the action would take, the cooks in the galley were busy making corned beef sandwiches and brewing urns of tea.

In the sick bay, Fulford, Channon and his first aid team sat, nervously smoking cigarettes.

The gun's crew manning the 20mm Oerlikons were so busy firing they didn't have time to ponder their fate. Suddenly, Leading Seaman Nobby Clarke, peering through the port gun sight caught a glimpse of a JU88 as it flashed past.

'If this carries on much longer,' he yelled as he opened fire, 'the fuckin' barrel will melt.'

'Ah, pipe down,' yelled ammunition feeder Able Seaman Bagsy Baker. 'Anyway yer missed the bugger. He's going after the ships in the harbour.'

At that moment a massive white flash almost blinded them as the Italian vessels, MV *Barletta,* and SS *Cassala,* anchored in mid harbour blew up.

'Jesus Christ!' exclaimed Nobby Clarke. 'Much more of this and we'll all fuckin' melt.'

Meanwhile, from *Zimba*'s bridge Pendleton and the others watched with baited breath as several the JU88s, ignoring the barrage put up by the DEMs (Defensively Equipped Merchant Ships) came in very low.

'They're making for the two big cargo ships on the far side on the mole,' yelled Lofty Day, the port look out.

Lofty was right. A few seconds later the *Empire Sunbeam* and her sister ship, *Empire Meteor,* became engulfed in walls of white water as a sticks of bombs erupted near their hulls. Both vessels became a mass of swirling smoke as fires broke out on their decks. Many of the crew jumped overboard in an effort to avoid being incinerated.

By this time most of the harbour water was ablaze with burning oil. Despite this, Pendleton ordered both sea boats to be lowered.

'See if they can rescue some of those men,' he yelled, leaning over the bridge, his face streaked with sweat.

Jack Tonby the Chief Coxswain and the Chief Bosun's Mate Bill Conyon, both experienced men, had pre-empted the order. The whalers were lying outboard and were fully manned. The order, "Slip", was given and both vessels hit the water simultaneously. Ignoring the flames, *Zetland's* sea boats and several MTBs were already picking up survivors.

Despite the barrage put up by the merchant ships, the JU88s continued to swoop down, dropping their deadly cargo. The night sky was criss-crossed by lines of coloured tracers and littered with exploding shells. The sickly smell of cordite and smoke hung in the air like an invisible shroud. The noise was so loud that those on *Zimba*'s bridge couldn't hear themselves think.

'There's more of them coming in from the south,' yelled Lofty Day from the port wing. 'Another fifty, I'd say.'

One by one, the JU88s in the second wave peeled off and joined their fellow attackers. Suddenly the sky resembled a horde of black bees buzzing around, diving at will onto their victims.

Meanwhile, *Zimba*'s two whalers along with those belonging to *Zetland,* braved the flames flickering on the water and managed to rescue several men. The oil covering them failed to hide the large, white blisters on their faces and backs. When the whalers were full, both coxswains ordered their crews to pull back to *Zimba.* Standing on the port side of the well deck, Chief Bosun's Mate Conyon ordered the guardrails to be taken down and scrambling nets placed over the side.

'Look lively you lot,' he shouted, as strong hands helped the injured onto the deck. 'And get those men inboard.'

Fulford and Channon, aided by the medical team treated the worst of the casualties where they lay. Those with burns received shots of morphia. Many of the blisters had burst and were treated with sulphonamide powder. Soon, the three bunks in the sick bay were full. The rest were laid down in the passageway, covered with blankets and given a hot drink.

'If we receive any more,' said Fulford, glancing warily at Channon, 'we'll have to use one of the mess decks.'

Just then another explosion rocked the ship.

'Bloody hell!' barked Channon, who had fallen against a bulkhead. 'I think we've been hit.'

Luckily it was a near miss and the ship, after swaying awkwardly, settled own.

Meanwhile, those on the *Zimba*'s bridge instinctively ducked as a stick of bombs straddled the *Devon Coast.* Sheets of scarlet flames erupted along its deck and jets of flaming fuel spurted high in the air. More explosions followed this as several merchantmen, anchored in the harbour sustained direct hits. An enormous blast of hot air hit the men manning *Zimba*'s guns. Luckily, their anti-flash clothing prevented any serious burns.

Further along the outer mole the Norwegian cargo ships *Lars Kruse* and *Lom,* lying at the end of the mole, were attacked. Both vessels became shrouded in walls of water. Ripples of explosions along their decks quickly followed. Seconds later, the ships blew up sending palls of smoke and flames jettisoning in the air.

The scene unfolding before Pendleton's bloodshot eyes was one of utter devastation. Sporadic detonations continued to erupt from many of the ships that were on fire. A layer of thick black smoke from the blazing ships was beginning to roll over the harbour like an ugly tidal wave.

Then came the moment that would live in Pendleton's mind forever. From among the low flying attackers, a JU88 made a low approach along the far side of the harbour near the hospital. Suddenly, a stick of bombs hit the nurses' quarters. In a split second, a wall of flames and smoke rose in the air like an ugly grey mushroom. Remembering Nadine would have been off duty at 1900 and in her room, Pendleton was immediately overcome by grief and became unaware of the deafening din and devastation around him. Visions of Nadine's mutilated body flashed before his eyes. Like a wounded animal, he clutched the side of the bridge and cried out, *'No! No! Please God, no!'*

'Are you all right, sir?' shouted Carter, who, despite the noise, overheard Pendleton's desperate cries. However, the look of pain he could see in his captain's eyes told him otherwise. 'Are you injured, sir?' he hastily added.

'No,' replied Pendleton, his throaty voice barely audible. 'I...I'm all right,' he paused and steadied himself against the starboard wing. With a painful sigh, he frowned and looked at Carter. 'The nurses' quarters have been hit. The building is...is completely gone.'

Realising the implication of Pendleton's words, Carter said, 'But sir, she might not have been there.'

'She was,' Pendleton replied, still clutching the side of the bridge. 'I know she was...' The rest of what he said was lost in the noise of the battle.

Lieutenants Foster and Small who were standing close to Carter overheard Pendleton. Both men looked gravely at one another and then turned away.

'Great Scott!' gasped Carter, putting a consoling hand on Pendleton's arm. *'Surely this bloody lot can't get any worse.'*

But worse was yet to come.

CHAPTER FORTY-THREE

For a few seconds Pendleton stood and stared ahead of him, seemingly oblivious to his surroundings. Just then, a tremendous explosion some distance along the outer mole brought him to his senses. Once again *Zimba* rocked and strained at her moorings as a shock wave reverberated against her hull.

'It's the *Joseph Wheeler*, sir,' yelled the port lookout. 'Looks like she's taken a direct hit.'

Shielding his eyes against the heat, each man looked away to their right. A torrent of fire suddenly swept through the hull of the stricken vessel. This was followed by a blinding coruscation of orange and yellow flames. In an instant, forty-one of her crew were incinerated. Moored close to *John Wheeler*'s port side the British cargo vessel, *Fort Athabaska* blew up as more deadly missiles struck home. Within seconds the both vessels became a deadly inferno.

The night continued to be lit up by shell bursts and coloured tracer bullets bending high into the sky. The noise was deafening as explosions continued to rent the air.

With a conscious effort, Pendleton forced himself to regain his composure. *'There's more of the blighters diving on the other ships on the mole,'* he yelled frantically. *'Better take cover.'*

Heeding Pendleton's advice, everyone cowered down against the sides of the bridge and listened as all hell continued to break loose.

Near the end of the outer mole the Norwegian cargo ship *Vest* was straddled by a stick of bombs and burst into flames. Her captain immediately ordered the ship to be abandoned. Seconds later the vessel in the next berth, the Dutch cargo ship SS *Odysseus*, disappeared under billowing clouds of black smoke, killing many of the crews. The fire spread to the SS *Frosinone*, an Italian oil tanker. A series of massive flaming geysers shot into the air, spraying everyone and everything with burning fluid. Tied up next to the Italian was the American liberty ship, *John Bascom*. The stick of bombs straddling her upper deck ignited her cargo of high-test gasoline. With a sickly sounding *whoosh*, the ship blew up, scorching to death most of her crew.

However, the Germans were not getting everything their own way. As a group of JU88s swarmed down on the outer mole, one burst into flames. Like a circus acrobat, the plane turned a few somersaults before crashing into the harbour. It was a hollow victory considering the carnage the enemy was inflicting, not only on the merchant ships but also the inhabitants of the town.

On and on came the enemy planes, their black crosses clearly visible on their dark green fuselages and wings. Four JU88s swooped down on the three merchantmen that so far had remained intact on the Nuovo Molo. These were the SS *John Motely*, packed with tons of ammunition, and the British coastal tanker SS *Testbank*. Berthed between the two ships lay the USS *John Harvey*, carrying a cargo that would be responsible for one of the greatest disasters of World War Two.

Just before the attack, Surgeon Lieutenant Fulford came onto the bridge. His face was streaked with sweat and his normally pale blue eyes red rimmed.

'I thought you should know, sir,' he said, looking at Pendleton, while catching his breath, 'that one of the survivors we picked up has died. I've had him covered up on a stretcher and placed on quarterdeck.'

'Thank you, Doc,' Pendleton replied, his voice barely audible over the constant sound of *Zimba*'s guns. 'Keep me…'

'*The John Motley has taken a direct hit!*' shouted one of the lookouts. '*The whole bloody ship is a mass of flames. She must have been carrying ammo, the poor bastards...*'

Almost immediately, another ear-splitting detonation filled the air as the SS *Testbank* blew up. The shock waves sent Pendleton and Fulford stumbling backwards onto the deck. Lieutenant Foster and Lieutenant Small, PO Yeoman Jeffries and the lookouts, ended up on in a startled heap. Dazed but not seriously hurt, everyone managed to stagger to their feet.

Then came the biggest explosion of the night. A searing, bright yellow flash coupled with what sounded like a terrific clap of thunder, erupted from the *John Harvey*. A swirling mushroom of red, green and yellow smoke rose into the night dwarfing explosions from the other ships.

'*Good God in heaven!*' gasped Pendleton. Squinting while shielding his eyes he stared at the blazing mass unfolding before him. 'All her crew must have been burnt to death. It's like watching a volcano erupt!'

By 2000, the raid was suddenly over. Other than a full moon, the sky was empty. The enemy bombers had suddenly disappeared northwards, no doubt proud of the carnage they had inflicted on an unsuspecting foe. Explosions of varying intensity continued to resound around the harbour, mingling with the ear-piercing jangle of ambulances and fire engines. The acrid odour of cordite filled the air, invading nostrils and throats. All that was left were rows of blazing ships and the water burning with a lethal mixture of oil, petrol and aviation fuel.

'My God!' muttered Pendleton staring at the carnage laid out before him. 'It looks like a scene from *Dante's Inferno.*'

However, the enemy left behind a death-dealing legacy.

'What's that in the air?' cried Carter, wrinkling his nose. 'It smells like garlic or something.'

'I dunno what it is, sir,' shouted PO Yeoman Jeffries, blinking furiously, 'but it don't 'arf hurt me eyes.'

Fulford suddenly frowned. Then staring warily at Pendleton, he said, 'That's mustard gas, sir. It's coming from that yellow cloud you can see hovering above the *John Harvey.*'

'*Mustard gas!*' Pendleton cried, somewhat perplexed. 'Are you sure, Doc?'

'Yes, sir,' Fulford quickly replied, 'I did a lot of work on gases at university.'

'I've heard it can be extremely dangerous,' said Pendleton, 'is that right?'

'If the gas is inhaled it can burn the lungs and cause death,' Fulford replied gravely. 'It can also result in severe blistering of the skin and eye infections.'

'What about our gas masks?' Pendleton asked. 'Will they give us much protection?'

'Not much good, I'm afraid,' Fulford replied. 'If the gas got caught inside it could burn their faces. But the anti-flash clothing might help.'

Turning to Carter, Pendleton shouted, 'Make a pipe, Number One. Tell the men there's mustard gas in the air. Stress they are to keep on their anti-flash clothing and make sure their overalls are buttoned up and tucked inside their socks.'

'Mustard gas, eh, sir,' Carter remarked, pulling his anti-flash hood closer to his eyes. 'Just to think, we took that professor over to Canada to work on the stuff. Now it could kill us instead of the Germans.'

The irony of the situation wasn't lost on Pendleton. With a heavy heart he realised Nadine could very well be a victim of her father's expertise.

CHAPTER FORTY-FOUR

During the next three hours, whalers from the two destroyers together with MTB boats, continued to pick up men out of the burning water. Channon was in one of the whalers, helping to pull the injured inboard. All of the men were covered in black, greasy oil. Many were simply exhausted and clambered onboard desperate to avoid being burnt to death. Others had developed blisters on their face and body caused by the scorching effect of the mustard gas. There was very little Channon could do except administer morphia to the seriously hurt.

'*It's me back! It feels on fire! For God's sake help me!*' one man cried, as he was helped, naked to the waist, into the whaler. His eyes, staring wildly from a face streaked with oil, stared pleadingly at Channon. As the injured man was laid down in the boat, Channon saw several huge red blisters covering most of his back.

'Easy does it me old mate,' Channon said, inserting the small needle of a monoject ampoule of morphia into the man's upper arm. 'We'll get yer fixed up when we get you onboard.'

The man turned his head and with a desperate look in his eyes, slumped back onto the freeboard. By the time the whaler arrived alongside *Zimba* he was dead.

Shortly after 2300, Fulford came onto the bridge. His pale face was wet with perspiration and he was out of breath. 'We've rescued about fifty men, sir,' he managed to say. 'The sick bay's full with the seriously injured and I've put the others in the main passageway and canteen flat. They've been given a hot drink and blankets. Channon and the first aid lads are doing the best they can.'

'How many dead?' Pendleton asked gravely.

'Seven, so far, sir,' Fulford replied. 'They've been taken onto the quayside on stretchers and covered up. The ambulances should be here any minute to take them and the injured away,' he paused, cleared his throat then added, 'may I suggest before we sail the ship and all compartments are hosed down to clear away any remnants of the gas.'

'A good idea, Doc,' said Pendleton. 'Did you hear that Number One?' he added nodding at Carter who was standing close by.

'Yes, sir,' Carter answered. 'I'll speak to the Buffer.'

Paddy, looking remarkably calm arrived. His normally pristine white overall were stained with oil and he had removed his anti-flash gear. 'We're all ready for sea, Jeremy,' he said, wiping his hands on a piece of cotton waste. 'I take it we'll still be leaving at 0600?'

'Of course,' snapped Pendleton, 'unless I hear otherwise. Why do you ask?'

'I thought the harbour might be too blocked with wreckage,' Paddy replied, rubbing the stubble on his chin. 'It could be tricky.'

Pendleton furrowed his brow and replied, 'Yes, I know, but we'll make it.'

By 0100 the ambulances had taken away the injured and dead. The process of hosing down the ship began. *Zetland* followed suit and shortly after 0300 both ships had completed the job.

On the bridge Pendleton turned to Carter. With a weary sigh, he said, 'Hands will not be required to fall in for leaving harbour, Number One. The duty part of the watch only will be needed at 0530.'

'Very good, sir,' replied Carter. Noticing Pendleton's haggard appearance and bloodshot eyes, he went on, 'May I suggest you get some sleep. Lieutenant Small and myself will share the middle watch.'

'Err ...all right,' murmured Pendleton. 'I'll be in my sea cabin. Call me if you need me.' Before turning to leave, he stared across the harbour. Even without his binoculars he could see the ruins of the nurses' quarters, smouldering against the night sky. Suddenly he felt nauseous and held onto the side of his chair.

'Are you all right, sir?' Carter enquired, well aware of what Pendleton was going through. 'Shall I send for the Doc?'

Pendleton took a deep breath. 'No, no,' he quickly replied. 'I'm quite well, thank you.' He then turned and left the bridge. As he walked down the steel ladder leading to his cabin, the dull throbbing of the ship's engines reminded him that in a few hours he would be leaving behind the place where the woman he loved had perished. By the time he reached his cabin his heart was pounding and he was bathed in sweat.

Pendleton's sea cabin was directly below the bridge. It was quite small and devoid of creature comforts consisting mainly of a small, wooden table and chair resting close to a narrow bunk. Above the bunk was a shaded lamp and voice pipe. The deck was covered with a well-worn carpet. Ventilation was provided by a series of adjustable vents in the pipes along the deck head. An electric fire, screwed to the bulkhead and protected by wire mesh, provided heating.

The solitary strip of pale, yellow neon lighting exaggerated Pendleton's unshaven appearance. He took off his cap and tore off his anti-flash gear and with an exhausted sigh, slumped onto the chair. The thought of never seeing Nadine again weighed heavily on his mind, filling him with a sadness and nausea. 'Why God, why,' he muttered, holding his head in his hands. 'Why?'

For a while he lay staring at the deck head unable to grasp the fact that Nadine was gone. Suddenly, a knock on his cabin door interrupted his reverie.

'Come,' his muttered, removing his hands and looking up.

The door opened and in stepped Carter. 'There's someone to see you, sir,' he said. As Carter spoke his sweat streaked face broke into a wide smile. He stepped aside and there stood Nadine. He closed the door and left.

The expression on Pendleton's face changed from abject sorrow to incredulity. For a second he couldn't believe his eyes. The woman he thought to be dead was standing before him, larger than life!

'*Nadine, darling, is it really you?*' he cried, bounding from his chair and reaching out for her. '*I saw your quarters in flames. I was sure you must have been...*'

'*No, Cheri,*' she gasped, feeling his arms around her. 'When we heard the air raid siren, instead of going off duty, myself and the other nurses remained in the hospital. That saved our lives. But I had to come and see if you were safe.'

'Thank God you're all right,' Pendleton replied, pressing her close. 'I was at my wits' end...'

Nadine's white uniform was stained with spots of blood and her beautiful tanned features smudged with oil. Looking up at Pendleton's face, she noticed dark rims under his bloodshot eyes. For what seemed like an age they held each other in a tight embrace, unable to speak. Pendleton could feel the blood pounding in his head. She, in turn, felt her heart beating a cadence in against her ribs. Finally, with her tired, violet eyes brimming with tears, she looked at him and said, 'A doctor in the hospital thought there was mustard gas in the air. Was he right?'

Pendleton hesitated before replying. 'Yes, darling,' he quietly replied. 'Apparently an American ship, the *John Harvey* had it onboard and took a direct hit.'

A look of deep concern came into her eyes. 'So the terrible burns on the men, women and children in the hospital,' she said, gripping his arm, 'are due to the mustard gas? The hospital is completely full. At first the doctors weren't sure how to treat them. All they could do was use morphia to quell the pain, but many have died. The doctor in charge has sent an urgent telegram to Allied headquarters in Algiers asking for help.' She paused and released his arm. 'What would Papa think if he saw such suffering,' she added solemnly. 'To think it was he who helped...'

'This is not the time for recriminations,' interrupted Pendleton, placing a finger across her lips. 'The Americans would have found someone else to do your father's research. It's no use blaming him.'

With a pitiful sigh, Nadine replied, 'Maybe you're right.'

'Darling, I love you so much,' Pendleton said, holding Nadine close, 'and one day I want you to be mine forever. Will you wait for me?'

'As long as it takes, Cheri,' replied Nadine, her eyes still wet with tears. 'And if that's a proposal, then I accept with all my heart.'

They kissed long and hard, knowing they must soon part.

A knock on the door brought them back to reality.

'Signal from Port Officer, sir,' came the voice of Carter. 'It reads, "Proceed 0600 as ordered. Boom will be raised at 0500. Good Luck and God's Speed".'

'Thank you, Number One,' replied Pendleton. 'I'll be along shortly.'

'And I must go, Jeremy,' said Nadine, staring forlornly into Pendleton's eyes. 'I'll be wanted at the hospital. I have the jeep on the quayside.'

Releasing his arms from around Nadine's waist, he took a deep breath and said, 'Yes, my love. I suppose you must leave.'

'But before we go,' Nadine replied, reaching up and gently touching the bristles on his face, 'please kiss me again.'

They did so with such passion, only lovers in such circumstances could experience.

The time was almost 0430.

Only the vibrations of the engines and boilers, flashed up ready for sea disturbed the silence as they walked along the main passageway onto the quarterdeck.

'*Mon Dieu!*' cried Nadine, looking across the harbour. 'The water is still on fire. Those poor men…'

'I'm sure most have them have been rescued,' Pendleton replied reassuringly.

Meanwhile, the emergency jangling of army ambulances could be heard coming from the mole as fire fighters continued to launch jets of water onto the flames of burning ships.

Waiting on the quarterdeck was the tall figure of Lieutenant Small. Close by stood PO Jenkins and Able Seaman Lofty Day.

Small saluted Pendleton, then looking at Nadine, said, 'I'm glad to see you're all right ma'am. A pity to meet again in such circumstances.'

'Yes, it is, thank you,' muttered Nadine smiling weakly.

Pendleton and Nadine walked slowly to the top of the gangway. Lieutenant Small nodded to the other two and they moved away allowing Pendleton and Nadine a few moments of privacy.

For a few seconds the two lovers stood and looked into each other's eyes, unable to speak. With her voice trembling with emotion, Nadine whispered, 'I'd better go now, mon amour. Remember I will love you forever.'

Feeling his throat contract, Pendleton replied, 'And I you, darling. Come, I'll walk you to the jeep.'

'No, no, Cheri,' she cried. 'I'll leave now before I make a fool of myself.'

She turned quickly and hurried down the gangway, and without looking back climbed into the jeep and switched on the ignition and drove off.

With a heavy heart Pendleton watched as the jeep disappeared along the wharf, wondering if or when they would meet again.

At exactly 0600, *Zimba* slipped her moorings and moved slowly away from the outer mole. Flames from patches of oil and fuel flickered amongst the early morning mist rising from the harbour. Palls of black smoke from ships still burning became silhouetted against dawn's pale grey sky. Hunks of twisted metal, parts of bridges and fo'c'sles protruded ominously out of the water, while dotted around the harbour, masts and yardarms marked the spot where other vessels lay.

'Christ almighty, sir!' exclaimed PO Yeoman Jeffreys, who was on the bridge next to Carter and Pendleton. 'It looks like a ship's bloody graveyard, so it does.'

'Yes, "bloody" is the correct word,' Carter muttered, shaking his head in disbelief. 'It's a disaster that never should have happened. I wonder who's to blame? What do you think, sir?' he added, giving Pendleton a searching look.

Pendleton frowned, and stared thoughtfully at the remnants of what were once two proud convoys. 'Overconfidence, ignorance and sheer bloody stupidity,' he replied laconically. 'Now, let's set a course for Brindisi.'

Ten months later on a sunny September afternoon, Nadine and Pendleton were married in St Luke's Church, Haslar. They looked the epitome of happiness: she in a shimmering white gown and veil, he resplendent in his best doeskin uniform, his dress sword shining in the sun. Sisters Leila Hansen, Anne Patterson and Iris Jasper also in white, were bridesmaids. Lieutenant Carter was best man and a frail looking Professor Goldberg gave the bride away. Lined on either side of the gravelled path were members of nursing staff, and most of *Zimba*'s crew, in uniform. An archway of glittering swords held aloft by the ship's officers provided a guard of honour.

Emerging from the church they were met by a flurry of white confetti, made from tiny pieces of newspaper. Blushing with happiness, Nadine smiled warmly and threw her bouquet of red roses to the crowd. A squeal of delight rose from the portly figure of Matron O'Hara as she reached up and caught the flowers.

'There's hope for you, yet, Matron,' shouted one of the nurses jokingly.

'A week's honeymoon in your home in Penzance can't come quick enough, darling,' muttered Nadine as she clutched Pendleton's arm.

A shiny, brown Bentley complete with white wedding ribbons rested on the road at the end of the gravelled pathway. The driver stood with the door open. Nadine immediately recognised him as the same one who met her when she arrived at Portsmouth. He was dressed in the same blue suit and cap and wore a grin as wide as the Solent.

'It's Mr Lloyd, isn't it?' she cried, laughing with delight. 'I recognised the cap!'

Lloyd gave her a generous smile and added, 'But do you remember I said you could get married in St Luke's Church.'

'Yes, I do,' she replied as Pendleton helped her into the car. 'And I'm so glad I took your advice...'

EPILOGUE

The air raid on Bari on 2 December in 1943 sank 28 ships and killed over 2,000 military, merchant seamen and civilian personnel. Severe mustard gas burns caused most of these casualties. It was not known until shortly after the first bombs exploded that the *John Harvey* had a cargo of 2,000 M47A1 mustard gas bombs each weighing 60-70lbs, plus 505 tons of ammunition. Several of *John Harvey*'s officers, including her Master, Captain Knowles, who was killed, knew the ship carried mustard gas bombs. This must have been listed in the ship's manifest. Three copies, including the original of this important document were never found. The Naval Officer in Command of Bari, Captain Campbell, RN, had not been informed of the *John Harvey*'s deadly cargo. Had he known, he could have insisted the ship anchor outside the harbour and allowed to enter later, thus saving many lives.

At first the Allied High Command tried to conceal the disaster but there were too many witnesses to do this effectively. The Americans therefore issued a statement emphasising that the US had no intention of using chemical weapons except in retaliation. However, General Dwight D Eisenhower, the Allied Supreme Commander and Winston Churchill ordered all documents to be purged, listing mustard gas burns as "burns due to enemy action".

Records were declassified in 1957 but details of casualties remained obscure. In 1986, the British government finally admitted liability. Survivors of the raid who suffered chronic effects of mustard gas poisoning had their pension payments amended. The attempt to cover up one of the Second World War's worst disasters had failed.